Tommy's Forever

Rubie Ann Graves

PublishAmerica
Baltimore

First printing

ISBN: 1-60441-436-7
PUBLISHED BY PUBLISHAMERICA, LLLP
www.publishamerica.com
Baltimore

Printed in the United States of America

Tommy's Forever

Rubie Ann Graves

Dedicated to Bill R

Special thanks to David J,
Who reminded me that every moment you are not
doing anything is wasted on doing nothing.

And Jenn B
For closing the door

The First Day of High School

It was almost the beginning of grade nine, high school. I had great expectations that things were going to change. Things were going to get better. With the hopes of new friends and new dreams, I felt in my heart things just had to change. In some sort of funny way, my life as I knew it almost depended on something becoming very different, something better.

The last few months of grade eight I had found myself in quite some trouble. I was caught for a break and enter into our local town hall, had broken my ankle while being someplace I should not have been, gotten caught trying to buy pills for a girl at school, we even stole my friends mother's car once and ran it in the ditch, and a few other things I would rather not mention. I was in desperate need of a change and some new friends and I knew it.

My parents were at their wits' end at what to do with me. They knew that the grounding me time after time was not working, and the older I got, the less influence they had over what they were able to control. After all, I had learned the hard way that taking care of me was the most important thing and I felt like I had been doing that for years, although lately I had not been doing a very good job of it.

Lizzie is my best friend. I have known her for as long as I can remember, in fact I never remember a time without her. She knows me most of the time better than I know myself. She is the one who picks me up and dusts me off when I fall or encourages me to do my best when I doubt that I could do anything at all. She listens to me laugh and she listens to me cry. She helps me grow through my fears and dries off the tears when they fall. Lizzie and I could be whoever we wanted to be together and no one ever asked why. I could bounce ideas into her brain and she would help me sort out the insanity. I did not need to explain things to her because she already knew what I was thinking or feeling before I said the words aloud. She accepted me for who I was, even the ugly parts.

Our parents had always been friends, and therefore so were we, third cousins, in fact. We lived our entire lives within a few blocks from each other, started kindergarten together, and most likely took our first few steps together since we were born almost exactly a month apart. When we were kids we used to even pretend we were twins.

My other best friend, Kayla, was older than Lizzie and me. Her family had moved into our small town quite a few years ago. Kayla was not a native to the farming community that we had grew up in but quickly became part of our group.

The group consisted of all the youth in our small town that had a population of about six hundred people. Most of us from the group were born here or lived here the majority of our lives but we accepted anyone that came along. We were kind of all like brothers and sisters although some of us got along better than others. Our ages varied about fifteen years from the youngest member to the eldest, but for the most part we all got along quite well. We had no choice really because if you did not hang out with everyone you had no one and so we all tried as hard as we could to get along and help each other when we could despite whatever came our way.

We all had seasonal jobs working on the farms during the summer, and the money was good for young adults our age. We all had worked seasonally since we had been barely twelve or thirteen years old. We were no strangers to hard work. It was the consensual idea that if you worked hard you got to play hard, too. Playing hard usually always meant a good party.

Friday and Saturday nights were the biggest parties of the week, but we usually went out every night. After we got home from work we would get ready to go "out town," which meant dropping in at a house or barn party to see what trouble we could find. We would eat a bit for supper, usually a couple pieces of dry bread or some French fries. We would get in Kayla's car and go see if we could get someone to get us beer for the night. Finding someone to buy Kayla and me beer usually was not a problem because we would bribe them with something or another like a beer or two for the trouble. Most of the time our friends would oblige us for a favor owed to them for repayment sometime down the road, but they hardly ever asked for one back.

The parties were always the same, though. The music was too loud to talk, and after a few beers it seemed better that way. A handful of the regulars were always in attendance. When Kayla first started taking me to parties it was fun, but after a few the novelties wore off.

We would start drinking at the party and she would disappear for a while, wherever it was she went. I would sit with the others, mostly boys and continue to socialize. Occasionally a new boy would come around that would interest me but it would only last a while, and I was back to my newly developed social skills. I had discovered that if I was drunk or stoned enough I did not feel so alone or afraid and even the boring things seemed more fun that way.

I enjoyed feeling pain free so much that I would drink myself to intoxication every time I got started. Sometimes I would even black out and only remember parts of what happen. One time I got so drunk I thought Kayla had backed the car up in reverse all the way home.

For a short time a man sixteen years older had taken an interest in me. I was not sexually interested in him, although I did like the attention. I led him to believe that I might have considered any offer that came along, but I really did not. Having his attention gave me someone to talk to while my friend had disappeared to fulfill her own agenda. On one occasion we were kissing and touching, and I vomited all over him. I was embarrassed but thought he had gotten what he deserved. I eventually showed my disinterest in him by making it well known I was dating someone my own age, but really it was just someone from our group that rescued me when I asked. That is what our group would do for each other.

Thursday, Friday, Saturday and Sunday nights we would do it all again. We always did the same things and always ended up in the same places with the same group of people. We were creatures of habit.

The summer was over and had brought forth changes in us all. I had matured inside a person or so I thought and was maturing into young woman trying to find my place in the world. I was not yet ready to go back to school and follow someone else's rules; I still wanted to have fun. I did not want summer to end.

I had been carefree all summer with very little parental guidance.

The harvest had been a long season this year, and I was late to start classes in the fall. Most of the other students had already returned to school about two weeks ago but just as harvest was finishing up I became very sick with tonsillitis, and I took and additional week off school to get well. For me getting very sick was par for the course, working outside when the cold rainy weather hit. I did not mind the late start, though, because the teachers had not assigned much of a workload yet. I could catch up on the homework from the other students' notes, or that is what Kayla suggested I do. She knew all the tricks of high school, as this was her third year.

It was finally the first day I attended class. My anxiety ran high, and I sought comfort in familiar things, my friends. I did not know my way around. I did not know where my classes were. I did not know which of my friends I had classes with. I did not even know where we were to go to eat lunch. All I knew for sure is that I was here for the first day and did not like it much. Kayla and Lizzie said they would help me find my way to the first couple of classes but after that I was going to be on my own.

Once I had gotten started it really was not as bad as I thought it would be. On the way to school, Lizzie and I compared schedules, and we had a few classes together. Kayla and I had the same lunch period so that was good but Lizzie had a later lunch period than we did. I did not like that much, but she did not care.

Kayla was in grade eleven; therefore, I had no actual classes with her, but Lizzie said that some of our other friends from public school had some classes with us too. They both assured me everything would be fine as soon as I got the hang of where I was going. Lizzie assured me it was not going to be as hard as it seemed the first day of school, but I doubted that. She had gotten it over with already.

I muddled through the first few periods of classes. It did not take me long to figure out what I liked and disliked. The classes were short periods and if you were not that crazy about the subject at least you did not have to sit long and listen to one teacher lecture half the day like public school. I liked that part.

If you hurried through the hallway you could go outside for a smoke with your friends between classes. Kayla said it was much easier to meet in the bathroom on the second floor to smoke if all your classes were already upstairs. She said if we were caught we would be suspended but the girls did it all the time. I was not sure if I wanted to take that risk; after all, I was going to try to turn a new leaf this year and hoped that trouble did not call my name from anywhere including the upstairs lavatory.

As soon as I walked into geography class I noticed him sitting at the table ahead of me with Sandy, a girl that was a friend of my cousin Shelly's.

"Who is that?" I asked my girlfriend, Bobbi, whom I had known from public school. She had saved me a seat beside her since the very first day classes began.

"I don't know," she said, as she shrugged her shoulders. She was not paying much attention to who I was talking about.

I threw a crumpled up paper to the table ahead of me to where Lizzie sat with a note asking the same question with an arrow pointing toward the table beside her. She opened the note and shrugged her shoulders without turning around. I knew she meant she did not know either.

I wondered if staying out of school this long had been a good idea after all. Now I had to play the catch-up game as to who was who, and I really wanted to know more about him. I wondered if because he was sitting with Sandy there was something go on between them and she was his girlfriend. I did not know Sandy well enough to ask her, so I thought I might ask Shelly when I saw her next. She would know for sure and she would tell me.

My only chance to find out anything about him was to do my own investigating. He had already stirred my interest, now I wanted to see what I could find out.

I sat behind him and waited to hear him say something in class or for the teacher to call his name but I had no luck. I watched for him in the hallway during class changes in hopes we might have more classes together but we did not. I watched for him outside in the common smoking area to see who his friends were and it seemed as if he might be in grade eleven because the other boys he was with were and so was Sandy. I knew a few of them from around town and from Kayla.

I wondered if Kayla would know who he was or had any classes with him, as she was in grade eleven too. If he was in grade eleven then that is why he would be sitting with Sandy in geography class. I knew that Kayla knew some of his friends because I had seen her talking to them several times in the hallways but I was not sure if I was ready to ask Kayla for help in my investigation just yet. I would wait.

A few weeks had passed since I had started class, and I was all caught up on the work I had missed. Things were going well at school for the time being but the novelty was wearing thin and it was not as great as I thought it would be. The best thing about high school so far was that you got a cooked meal for lunch, could smoke at school without getting into trouble, and I had all the classes with my friends. Lizzie and Kayla were right this was not as bad as I had once thought after I had gotten the hang of it.

The Dance

"Are you going to the dance tonight?" Bobbi asked, while we were sitting in class before the afternoon bell rang.

I must not have heard what she had said the first time because I was staring out the window watching the first winter snowfall. I wondered how every little snowflake could really be different from the next, and no two the same. How did they know that? Each time I try to catch a flake that falls from the sky in my hand it melts so quickly that the next one I am lucky enough to catch looks exactly the same. I was lost in the amazement of how the snow fell onto the ground covering everything in a blanket of white and knowing all life would die and return in the spring or so we hoped.

Every year upon the first snowfall I would wonder what we would do if when the snow melted nothing came back to life. I tried to find the trust in nature that it would make the promise to return to life once it was gone but I was never really sure until I saw the sun again in the spring. Winter always seemed so long, and I hated the accumulation of the snow. I think we all did.

"Did you say something?" I turned to her. I had barely caught her voice overtop of all the other noise he room.

"Are you going to the dance on Thursday, or is that tonight?" She looked frustrated. I was not sure why.

"Oh, I don't know. Are you?"

I had not thought about the dance much. It was the first high school dance of the year, and I did not have a date. I had plenty of other things to think about like watching the snowfall and wondering about spring that preoccupying my time with things like a date for the dance seemed rather silly.

"I want to go, but I don't have a date. Do you?" she asked.

"Have a date or want to go?"

"Both?"

"No, I don't have a date, don't really want one either. You know all the jazz is really a pain in the ass, but I kind of want to go. If you are going we could meet at the dance."

"Sure," she accepted the roundabout invitation to accompany me to the dance; that way neither one of us would have to go alone.

I did want a date, and I was envious of my friends who had steady boyfriends. It was a cover up of my own feelings to pretend I would rather go to the dance alone. I wanted to be like the other girls that got flowers, telephone calls, walked to class, held hands with their boyfriends and had lots to talk about every morning while we waited for the bus. I did not like the other parts that came with the attachment though, the crying, the disappointment, and the break-ups. It always came eventually. It seemed like avoiding any kind of relationship was in my best interest anyway because I was working hard at making better choices for myself and staying out of trouble. Sometimes it seemed that boys and trouble came hand in hand for a young girl my age.

The school day passed and was rather uneventful. I watched for the boy from geography class as I usually did but did not see him. I wondered if he came to school today. I wondered what other classes he had. I wondered where his homeroom was. I wondered if Kayla knows him. I wondered if he would be at the dance and if he did would he have a date?

As the afternoon rolled on into the night, and I began to get ready for the dance, I was not sure if I still wanted to go. I wanted to call Bobbi and tell her I was not feeling well or make up some other kind of excuse to get out of it. If I did that for sure she would be upset with me for standing her up so I had better not do that to a friend. Kayla and Lizzie would be upset also even though I think they had dates waiting for them there we had all already made plans to go together. I wondered what the night would bring with my first high school dance. I was feeling as anxious as I did on the first day of school.

The phone rang as I was just about to walk out the door.

"Hello," I answered.

"Hey." It was Kayla. "Did you get it?"

"Yeah."

"When are you coming down?"

"Was just on my way."

"Okay, see ya in a bit."

"Okay." I hung up the phone.

I knew she was asking about the homemade wine we had stolen from the basement of my house that my father had made last winter. We thought stealing it was a good idea because it was cheaper than buying stuff to drink and we knew it had quite a kick to it. We also knew that if we had a few glasses each before we left we would be in better shape to attend any kind of party if we could stand the taste of it. Although this was a dance, Kayla assured Lizzie and me we would have a good time. We both trusted her judgment on that one because she had been to several before.

Kayla was going to drive us to the dance in her mom's car and since her parents were not home so we could all gather at her house to drink and finish getting ready. I was already ready to go, but the other girls always took longer than I did. I did not mind because I could drink more wine while I waited for them and relax before we set off.

We hid what wine we did not drink in the trunk of the car for later. When we wanted more we could go out to the car and refill our bodies with the poison that we thought was helping us feel good. None of us wanted to take the risk of trying to sneak the wine in into the school, because if we were caught we would have to leave the dance and would have been suspended from school. I thought it would give Bobbi and me an excuse to leave the dance when we needed to escape for another drink. It was a rather developed plan, or so I thought.

I had walked across the school parking lot with my girls, Lizzie and Kayla. They desperately wanted to see what was happening inside as soon as we arrived but I just hoped we had found Bobbi soon because I was going to meet her there. We greeted everyone we knew and were on our way to see who was with whom and who had already arrived.

Everyone inside the school was restless. The night had just begun with all the possibilities in our heads of what might happen for each of us. After all the high school dance was where all the romance was to happen or so I thought but I did not know for sure because this was my first one. We had heard stories from Kayla about the magic that happens between a teenage boy and girl as soon as the lights went out and the slow songs began. I was not sure if I wanted to wait around for either one of those things to happen. After all, Bobbi and I were dates, so that is where I thought the wine would come in handy.

As soon as Kayla disappeared, Lizzie and I headed for the rest rooms. Lizzie was one of those girls who liked to spend lots of time in front of the mirror to make sure every hair was in place and her make up was perfect. I was not so particular, and I did not wear makeup much. I was not sure if I was one of those natural born beauties or not but only on special occasions did I apply myself to looking perfect. I did not figure a high school dance was one of those times but I followed along for something to do.

I was leaning against the sink facing the opposite direction of the mirror and was reading the notes that were written on the bathroom walls when Bobbi walked in.

"I knew I would find you guys in here," she greeted us in an unusual way.

"Yeah, she has to make sure she is perfect," I commented toward Lizzie.

"Well, it is too late for that," Bobbi remarked back.

I nodded in agreement as Bobbi and I laughed, but Lizzie could not see the humor in that statement or the snickers from either of us.

"Let's go." Lizzie sighed as she turned and walked out the door. It was obvious she was frustrated at both of us for making jokes about her appearance and not at all amused by our laughter.

Lizzie soon found her date waiting for her and Bobbi, and I thought it was a better idea to go back outside to hang out in the parking lot and have some wine to engage in our own fun while we watched the other students come and go and poke fun at them. After all, the parking lot was the best place to catch up on the good gossip. We knew we would meet up with Kayla and Lizzie sooner or later and Bobbi had a few other friends she was still waiting for to arrive.

"Here, take these," she said, as she handed me a couple capsules that she had just pulled out from inside her pocket. "They will keep you awake."

I took them from her and swished them down with another drink from the bottom of the wine bottle. "Thanks," I said as I handed her the rest of the bottle to take the pills she still had in her hand. "Ready to go back in?" I asked, as soon as she took the last drink.

"I am now."

I had found myself separated from my girls and was sitting on the bench alone in the gym waiting for someone to come along and chat about whatever events had arisen in the last few hours. The DJ had put on yet another slow song and everyone seemed to be enjoying it but me. From the bleachers where I sat I could see that my recent ex boyfriend had just asked some girl to dance and it appeared as if she said yes because he was leading her by the hand to the middle of the dance floor. I was not in the mood to sit here and watch this episode of what seemed like the daytime drama affair as he looked directly toward me when he took her in his arms. If I was not mistaken, that seemed intentional. I was not going to wait around to watch any more of that game show because I did not care much about what the prize was.

I had seen Kayla a few minutes before and she appeared as if she was having lots of fun with her beau, and I supposed I would see her dancing slow soon, too. It was hard to remember if he was the one she had come to meet at the dance or she had switched partners already. I did like the gossip but I had a hard time keeping track. It seemed at times the only memory I had was the one in the moment.

I had not seen Lizzie in a while, and I think Bobbi went to pee. I could not be sure though, it was hard to keep track of everyone coming and going all the time. The only thing I knew for sure was I wanted be anywhere else but sitting alone on the bench alone. Only losers did that.

My head was fuzzy and my stomach felt like it was doing flips on a roller coaster that was starting to swirl. The feeling of the wine was wearing thin and Bobbi was right I was awake but I wanted to go home. I knew the other girls would not want to leave because the night was only half over but I had been watching everyone else engage in romance for the last few hours and was becoming rather unoccupied with it all.

I saw the boy from geography class as I was climbing down from the top of the benches as he was walking into the gym. I did not want to look suspicious but I was trying to look for the girl he might have been at the dance with. I had not heard any gossip that concerned him or so I had thought since I still was not sure of his name. I did not want to look up and stare aimlessly at him or anyone that might be with him. I was much to cool to go over and desperately start a conversation but I wanted to talk to him.

Please, please, please, God, let someone come and find me right now! I was stuck in the moment of not wanting to be the only loser without a date, and now not wanting to be alone as the ex was making it clear he had a new lustful interest in mind.

I wanted to go home but I knew my friends would stay until the end of the dance. I wanted Bobbi to hurry up and come back but she had been gone a while already so I assumed she must have gotten side tracked some place. Maybe she had found the friends she was waiting for while we were in the parking lot. I thought about going to find comfort in her friendship and it would give me something to do.

I could feel the burn of someone looking at me but I tried to ignore it. I was afraid to look up to see who it was. My heart hoped it was he, but my nerves of steel had worn off long ago, as it had been a while since I had been in the parking lot for the poison in the trunk.

Before I knew what I was doing, I was standing in front of him and smiling. "Wanna dance?"

"Sure." He smiled back. He looked a bit confused for a moment.

I felt like I was an alien within my own body. What the hell was I doing? Did I just ask him to dance? Did he just say yes? Where did that nerve come from? What was I doing? *Thank you, God, for sending him so quickly to my rescue, but I am not sure this is the rescue I wanted.* I needed a moment to clearly think because it was now that I had wanted to take asking him to dance back.

Just as soon as he agreed he took my hand and led me onto the dance floor walking directly in the center of everyone else that was dancing. He stopped as to motion to begin to dance but I did not want to be that close to the newly formed couple of which I would have rather avoided. I knew he would not know that but I did.

"Over there more, please," I begged, as I pulled him by the hand toward the back door that was open to let in the fresh air. "It is a bit cooler over here."

It seemed just as he began to draw me closer toward him the song had played the last few notes and was over. We had not had anytime at all to get close to each other. I was sure this was God's joke on me but I thought it was a good one because it at least changed the focus on feeling the uncomfortable sting being on the bench alone.

"Looks like we were too late." He smiled.

"Yeah, I guess we were." Being a few notes too late seemed to be the constant story of my life for one reason or another.

"Next time?"

"Sure," I agreed. I hoped there would be a next time to attempt to dance with him, but I was feeling queasy inside. I was not sure where the courage came to ask him to dance in the first place but now at least he knew I was alive. If that was all that happened out of this episode, it was worth the effort, even if I was scared at first. I had gotten one moment of his life and for now I was feeling like that had been enough.

I was not sure where the boy had gone ahead of me after he had let go of my hand but I surely needed a smoke in the café. I really just wanted to sit down for a while. I needed a few quiet moments to figure out in my head what just happened and reclaim my mind back from the alien that had swooped in and stolen it in the gym. I was not sure if I was maturing now into an adult because all I felt like was a high school girl with a fluttering heart and a spinning head.

"Where are all your friends?" It was Jamie. It was truly odd to see him alone. He was a senior in high school, and one of the most handsome, charismatic, charming boys in school, and he knew it. The girls flocked around him like flies and the high school boys befriended him too because that is where the girls were.

I had seen him around a few times hanging out with the group from town and had seen him talking with Kayla at school. I was not really friends with him, but at least I knew his name.

Before I answered the question, I heard Jamie greet someone by saying, "Hey, Tommy!" and slapping him on the back hard enough that the leather of his jacket clapped under Jamie's hands.

I looked up and to my surprise there he was. I could feel my skin getting hot on my cheeks, and I tried hard not to smile. My heart began to pound so hard that I could feel it in my neck. My head started to spin, and I could not tell if I was happy to see him or just wanted to scurry away like a little tiny grey mouse. I was glad that he had come back to where I was, but now was feeling much to shy to even look up at him. In an instant the answered prayers had turned into what I was sure to mess up somehow if left to my own best thinking.

Please, please, please, God, send someone else my way so I can make an escape to get out of here. I had not had enough time to figure it all out yet. I was hoping I had not made a complete fool of myself by asking him to dance in the first place because he disappeared so quickly after the song was over. As I tried to scan the room with my eyes, I helplessly searched for my girls to rescue me again from the most awkward situation I had gotten myself into yet this school year.

"Want to dance?" I heard Jamie say. I looked at him to accept his invitation, until I saw Kayla had been standing beside me. He was talking to her. I did not know how long she had been standing there because I had been lost in my own prison of apprehension for what felt like an eternity. God had again sent someone to the rescue and taken her away before I noticed she was there. I swear God was in heaven playing these games with my life simply for His own amusement and laughing at me being bound in shackles of anxiety as I was officially a teenager with a crush.

I looked at Kayla and begged her with our non-verbal friend language not to go. She would surely know what I meant given that she was one of my best friends.

"Sure." She smiled when she looked at me and then left with Jamie.

I felt like a chicken without feathers, a dog without a bone, a flower without petals, a baby without a bottle, a bear without a cave. It seemed as if I had a big flashing sign on my head that was blinking above my head in bright lights, "HELP ME!" I wanted to disappear and fade into the orange brick wall I was leaning against. I just wanted to get out of there alive, because I swear, my heart would explode or my body would spontaneously combust from the heat that had gathered behind my cheeks.

"Looks like it is just you and me here now." He smiled.

"Yeah, I guess we are." I tried to be casual and avoid all eye contact. I reached toward the ashtray and put out the smoke I had been hanging on to for distraction.

I thought back to my original prayer and remembered that this was not the kind of wanting to get out of there I had in mind when I asked God for help. It was even better even though I was terrified of it.

"Want to try again?" he asked. I knew he meant to dance.

"Sure." I was trying to be nonchalant and not show any childish emotion.

Tommy led me into the gym by the hand. I was sure he could feel me sweating bullets though the pores of my skin. He turned to put his hands around my waist when he found the perfect spot in the darkest corner of the gym to hold me close before we swayed to the slow song that was broadcasted over the speakers. I draped my arms over his shoulders and could feel his body close to mine. His breath on my neck was warm and tender. His hair smelled of cigarette smoke as it flowed over his shoulder and onto the skin of my arms. I could feel his skin was soft when he touched me. I wondered if he could feel my body shaking. I was in heaven or the closest to it I had been in a long time. Maybe God was not amusing himself with my crush after all. Maybe He was helping me out with it. This was not so bad after all.

Every note of the song echoed between my ears as I closed my eyes and held him close to me. I did not want to let go. I did not care what the DJ played next as long as it was another slow song. This was my first chance and for all I knew it could be my only chance to be close to him. I was standing on the highest clouds in the sky and Tommy was standing right there with me. I wanted us to stay here forever. I hope it did not start to rain or we would for surely both fall off the cloud I was standing on.

"Do you want to go for a walk?" he asked, since the song was over, and he was still holding my hand tightly.

"Sure." I had no idea of where he would take me but I knew right then I would follow him to the end of the earth and back as long as he did not let go.

I hoped that he had not noticed that my hands were still sweating. I wondered if it was from the wine, the pills, or just being close to him that was causing all the pins and needles in my head. I wondered how he was feeling, what was he thinking, where was he going to take me? At that moment I could not make any comprehensible thought other than the fact that I did not want to go home anymore.

We walked out of the gym still holding hands toward the exit doors. I was nervous and was not sure if I wanted anyone to see me with him just yet. I knew my friends would start asking me questions that I did not have the answers to. I did not know what to say or how to explain myself just yet. I needed time to process was happening and the excitement I was feeling. My insides were smiling so loudly I was sure everyone could see a ray of sunshine beaming from my heart instead of the flashing red light that had been on my head earlier.

He led me into a stairwell where the telephone booth was. I knew we were not going upstairs, but I was not sure why we were there.

"Need to make a phone call?" he asked.

"No." I shook my head.

"Well, at least it is quieter in here," he said as he sat down on the first few steps.

I sat down beside him. "Sure is," I agreed.

As we sat down he was still holding my hand. I did not know what to say or do to cover my excitement. He had been talking about something that I could not comprehend. I was trying my hardest to listen to him but the noise in my own head was much louder than anything he was saying.

"I saw you in geography class the other day. Sandy, the girl I was sitting with, said you were her friend's cousin."

"Oh, yeah, I am. Isn't she in grade twelve?" I wondered why she was in our grade nine geography class.

"I think she is. We both thought we would take that class as an easy credit," he explained. "I am in grade eleven. Sandy and I ride the bus together."

It was all starting to make sense to me now as I was finding out more about him. If he was in grade eleven and I in grade nine; he must be a few years older than I was. I wondered if he would want to be seen with a grade nine girl, and I imagined the gossip that would be spread about us before the dance was about to end. I was not sure who had already seen us together but right then I did not care. The more we continued to talk the easier it was to put all of the pieces together that I had been wondering all along about him.

The conversation was coming to a lull, and I could not think of anything to say. I wondered if he was getting tired of being with me yet and if he had changed his mind about wanting to be alone with me. I wondered how I would break this up and make some kind of excuse to take the pressure off him to get out of here.

I straightened my back and stretched out my arms for a moment. "These stairs are hard on the butt." I began to stand up.

"Yeah, they are," he said, as he stood up and stepped toward the phone. He picked up the receiver and handed it to me. "It's for you."

I smiled at him as I stepped closer to take the phone. He pulled the receiver around behind him so that I had to reach to grab it. We were in very close bodily contact and he must have thought that was a perfect time to steal a kiss.

His lips were soft as they touched me. I closed my eyes because I wanted this moment to last forever as I kissed him back. I still was not sure what was happening because it was all going too quickly, but I was not about to say no to this. I wanted to be an active participant in this kiss because it was much too sweet to spit out.

At first, I thought that it was going to be one of those short kisses between strangers but I was wrong. He seemed to be taking every teenage boy opportunity to get all that he could from this chance of good fortune. I did not want to mistake him as acting like any boy who wanted as much physical attention from a girl as he could, but he was moving into rubbing his tongue against mine very quickly. My mind was racing and my heart was throbbing as I was trying to decide if I liked his kisses or not. Since I could not pull myself away from his magnetism, I guess I did.

I heard the door of the stairwell swing open with a squeak. I pushed him away as quickly as I could but it was too late, we were caught. I was embarrassed but I did not know who the other student was that had just pushed on the door.

"There is a teacher coming," the girl said, as she looked at Tommy as if she knew him.

"Thanks." H nodded toward her. "Let's go." He seized my hand and escorted me toward the door.

As soon as we stepped around the corner, a teacher was walking toward where we had just left. I was trying hard not to smile and look guilty of anything but wondered if I had been successful at trying to hide my emotional state. I felt like I had just gotten caught with my hand in the cookie jar.

"Where were you?" the teacher demanded to know.

"I had to call home for a ride," Tommy explained.

"Oh." The teacher walked past us but looked as if he knew Tommy was not being exactly truthful.

"Good one." I nudged him with my elbow.

I had lost track of time while we were in our secret world, and I had no idea how long we had been there. Some of the students were already leaving the school through the front doors and we could see a few others still standing around in the café. I wondered where my girls were. I did not hear any music playing so I figured the last song had already been played.

Tommy let go of my hand just before we got close to the doors to join our friends.

"I got to go in here." I smiled, then motioned toward the bathroom.

I kept walking into the café. It was the first place I would look for my friends before I tried looking for them outside. We had not developed a plan to meet if we had been separated from each other because that was something that came up unexpectedly. Being with Tommy was something that I had only dreamed of. I did not think it was going to actually come true.

Lizzie, Kayla, Bobbi, Jamie and a few others I did not know were all sitting on the benches smoking and chatting up a storm when I quietly came up behind them. I wanted to blend in as quickly as I could because I was not sure what I might say when they asked me where I had been. Where had I been? Nirvana was about all I could think of as an excuse but I doubted they would understand.

I returned to the reality once again from which I had been lost. Being lost from the real world with Tommy felt like it was a good thing. I had decided then that I did in fact like his kisses. I hoped that I would get more of them. I wonder if I would.

"Hey, there you are," Bobbi greeted me. "I was wondering if you needed a ride home."

"Nah, I can catch a ride with Kayla," I said, as I pulled my smokes out of my pocket and began to take one out.

"Where ya been?" Kayla asked as she wrinkled her eyebrows like my mother would.

I was not sure what to say and was hoping I would not have to answer the question. I fumbled with the lighter for as long as I could and pretended I could not get it to work. I leaned over and asked Jamie for a light.

Just as he was flicking the flint I leaned over to put the leaves in the flame. Tommy had just returned from the bathroom and stood on the other side of Jamie. Neither Tommy nor I made any kind of motion to give any clue that we had been together.

Jamie leaned over and whispered in my ear so that no one else could hear, "I bet I know." I pulled my smoke out of the flame and smiled at him. I did not say a thing. It was going to have to be up to everyone else to figure it out. I did not want Tommy and me to be the newest gossip of the school dance or at least not until the fog cleared out of my head and had a chance to sort it all out.

"Are we ready to go?" Lizzie asked. It looked like she was just coming from the gym.

"Yeah," Kayla said. She stood up and began to walk out of the café ahead of everyone else.

"I'll catch up in a minute. I am going to wait with Bobbi until she finds her ride," I advised them, as they were already walking away.

Bobbi shook her head at me. She knew I was lying because I had been standing beside her when she was talking to her friends about meeting them at the car after the last song was over, but she did not give me away.

Tommy took me by the hand again and led me out of the café and out the front doors of the school. He turned to stand in front of me while he took both of my hands in his. I gazed into the bluest eyes I had ever seen. Peering into the wide-open widow of his soul he leaned toward me and kissed me softly on the lips while we stood under the star lights of the parking lot.

His mouth tasted sweeter than it did before, like candy, his lips were soft like silk and his hair was still flowing over his shoulders and blowing gently in the wind like a stallion standing on the open mountaintop. My heart was pounding so loudly I was sure he could hear it when he hugged and kissed me goodnight. With the softest kiss and the warmest hug I had ever known he smiled sweetly.

"I hope to see you tomorrow." He turned and walked away before our friends noticed us beside the car. I stood in all glory while I watched him run a few steps to catch up to Jamie and the other boys he must have come to the dance with.

I opened the door of the car and pushed Lizzie on the shoulder. "Get over." I sat down beside her in the seat and smiled to myself.

"Thank you," I whispered to God under my breath.

"Were you dancing with Tommy?" Kayla inquired.

"Yeah, I guess, if that is his name." I still smiled quietly inside. "He asked me to dance after you and Jamie left, so I said yes."

"I didn't know you liked him. He is a friend of Jamie's," she informed me, but I already knew that much.

"Oh," I replied, "I don't really know him. He just asked me to dance," although that part was not completely all true. He asked me to dance after I had asked him in the gym. I remember for a moment how it had started it in the first place. In the end I guess the alien that invaded my head had led me in the right direction when I made a spilt decision that ended up turning out much better than I could have ever hoped for.

"Oh, I couldn't tell that from the kiss!" she giggled, as she signaled the car onto the highway toward home.

Lizzie began talking about the fun she had, telling us gossip she heard while she was at the dance with her new boyfriend and a few other girls she had met.

"Did you guys hear about…" her voice faded into the rhythm of the song on the radio. My thoughts drifted back to the first kiss by the phone booth.

My thoughts twisted and toiled around ideas of things that were still unknown to me about him. Did he feel like I felt? Was he thinking about me? Did he want to tell his friends about kissing me? Did he like kissing me? Did he like holding me close while we were dancing? Had he noticed me before tonight? Did he want to talk to me again? Kiss me again? Should I tell my friends? Would they laugh at me? Could they help me get to know him? Did they know him? Did they like him? Does he like me?

"We're home," Kayla advised us as we approached Lizzie's driveway, but we could already see that for ourselves. We all lived on the same block. Lizzie lived just two houses down from me in one direction, and Kayla lived three doors down in the other.

"What?" I asked, as I snapped back into reality like a sling shot.

"We're home. Did you want me to drop you off at your house?" Kayla asked.

"Yes," Lizzie said, "I am tired."

"Ummm, no, I can walk from there," I muttered.

"Okay," she said as she stopped in front of Lizzie's place, and we both got out of the car together before she drove away. "See you tomorrow."

As we watched the taillights of the car as she drove away Lizzie asked, "Are you okay? You were kind of quiet on the way home."

"I am just getting a headache from the wine," I complained, but that was only half the truth.

"Me too, and I am very tired. I am going in. Night." Lizzie let the door close on its own behind her when after she went into the house.

I stood outside until I saw her bedroom light click on. I wanted to see if she would make it to the bed before she passed out. I could see her shadow in the window as I took another smoke from my pocket. I thought I would walk around the block first before I went home. I needed to clear my head, and the fresh air would do me good.

The night air hit my lungs like daggers that had been thrown hard enough to kill a dragon. Winter was certainly here, and making itself comfortable as it was not going to go away for a while. A picture formed in my brain. I could see Old Man Winter and what I thought he looked like. I thought of an old man that has no love in his heart and scares all the children away that are asking for candy on Halloween. I bet old man winter is more miserable than a mutt that has been in a cage too long and full of rueful ideas. I bet he enjoys making people miserable, because this cold is sure to prove that.

I was standing again at Lizzie's window. The light was off now, and I did not know if I had been standing there all that time or had walked around the block. My thoughts were a blur, and I knew I was not thinking clearly. The cigarette butt burnt my throat as I took the last drag. I must have walked around the block at least once because my feet were getting cold. It was below zero degrees outside, and it was snowing again. I was sure I could sleep now.

The Day After

I saw him again the next morning at school in the common area just before class started. He was standing with his friends. I pretended not to notice him and as he quickly glanced toward me then looked away. I think he was pretending not to notice me, too.

Kayla, Lizzie, Bobbi, and I walked outside and stood in our own group instead of joining the boys whose company we had enjoyed last night. I was not sure why we would join the boys today anyway, that was not our usual habit. Today I wanted to change it up a bit for reasons of my own but I was sure my friends would not empathize with my motive. I was not sure if I would want to tell them anyway. The night had seemed to pass so quickly that I was not sure how I was feeling about the entire encounter last night. I wondered if it was just the magic of the kiss, the wine and pills or if I wanted something more.

His hair looked very good today, shining in the sun against his brown leather jacket. I smiled at him from across the paved area. I knew he was watching me from the distance. Neither one of us wanted to make it obvious we had shared a brief emotional bond for a few short moments under the stars last night. I guess it was still somewhat of a secret.

My friends were still talking of the dance last night so I am sure they did not notice my attention had drifted away from the conversation for a second but they would be used to that. The girls were talking about things I was not listening to. In my mind I was back at the dance last night too but I was remembering what it had felt like to have his breath on my skin, his lips on my lips and his hair falling over my skin while I held him close as we danced to someone singing about a stairway to heaven.

The bell rang, and classes were to start, and I was going to be late for class again. I hurried to homeroom, then looked at my calendar to see when I had geography next, in hopes of seeing him soon. To my disappointment it was not today.

The day had passed, and I was not as successful as I had hoped earlier that morning in seeing him. I had not seen Tommy all day. It was when I was at my locker gathering my homework for the weekend and was about to walk to the bus alone. I heard a voice that I did not recognize.

"Hey, wait up!" the voice called in my direction.

When I turned around to familiarize myself with the calling, it was Tommy. My heart skipped a beat, my palms got sweaty, and I could feel my face get hot again. I had waited to see him all day and now that I had the chance I did not know if I wanted to stop and wait for him or run away.

"Are you going on the bus, or did Kayla drive the car today?" he asked.

"The bus," was all I could muster out. How did he know I sometimes rode with Kayla?

"Can I walk with you? I think your bus is close to mine."

"Sure, I guess." *I guess, I guess,* my words echoed in my head. *Of course you can walk with me. I want you to walk with me. I would love you to walk with me,* is what I should have said, but *I guess* is all that came out. I would hate to show too much enthusiasm this early in the game even if that was how I felt. How did he know where my bus was?

"Geography Monday, huh?" he started the conversation.

"Oh, is it? Are you going to class?"

"I thought I might skip it," he replied.

"Oh, yeah, me too; that class is a bore," I lied just to agree with him.

We walked and he talked until we arrived at his bus stop. Another goodbye was right around the corner but I did not want to say it to him. I wanted him to kiss me again. My thoughts raced how to give him a clue that I was interested in more than walking to the bus. I did not know how. I felt like I did not know anything except that I liked being close to him. I did not have to question my feelings now I knew that one for sure.

Kayla came running up behind from behind and pushed me out of her way, as she gave me a friendly swat on the head with a magazine she was carrying.

"I thought you were going to wait for me at the lockers?" She sounded a bit upset, then looked at Tommy. "But that is okay. I was late getting out of class. Hi, Tommy," she said without breathing. "Have you seen Jamie today?" She interrupted any conversation I was having with him but had once again saved me from saying an uncomfortable goodbye.

In the same instant as they were talking about our mutual friend Jamie, I became sidetracked into another conversation with Lizzie, who had joined our trio right behind Kayla.

"Stand with me at the bus," Lizzie said, but it was more of a demand than a request. She tugged on my sleeve, so I really had no choice in the matter.

I smiled at Tommy as I left him standing talking with Kayla as I walked away with Lizzie. I wanted to say goodbye to him, but the circumstance of time forced me in another direction. This was not how I wanted my day to end but what else could I do? A girlfriend' demand is a girlfriend' demand even if it got in the way of my personal agenda.

Kayla joined Lizzie and me while we were waiting for the bus to arrive. "What were you doing walking with Tommy?" she asked.

"Oh, nothing really. He was in the hall when I was waiting for you guys at the lockers, so when I saw him we started walking together," I explained, but I was not sure why I felt I had to justify my actions to her.

"That is funny. His locker is upstairs," she advised, then started to say something about Jamie, but I must have forgotten to pay attention.

It was a short bus ride home. My thoughts ran wild as I thought of Tommy. If his locker upstairs why was he at mine downstairs? Was it an accident he saw me or it intentional? Did he know where my locker was? Does he like me? Has he asked his friends about me? Where does he live? Will I see him on Monday when we return to school? Do my friends know how I feel about him? Will he skip geography class? What did he talk to Kayla about? Will I kiss him again? I had a million questions with him on my mind and a warm fuzzy feeling in my heart. I tried not to mirror my emotions on my face, as I looked out the window into the sun.

It was the weekend and we all looked forward to that. This time though I did not. I could not wait to get back to school on Monday to see him again. I knew it was going to be a rather long weekend waiting to say Hello to him, or at least hoping to get that chance. I was not very good in relationships with those that had the other chromosomes. It seemed they were from another dimension and they spoke a language I did not understand.

After school we all arrived at our gathering place out in front of the community store. We would gather with all of our friends who lived in the rural town because some of them did not go to school anymore. We would congregate and speak of the day's events and gain some kind of perspective that would make sense as we began to try put the pieces together to the bigger picture of this thing we called life. Us younger teens in the group would look toward the elders for advice. They always seemed to know better than we did about what life would bring because they had a few more years of experience at living it. I wanted my peers' thoughts on love, but I did not know how to ask.

Lizzie might know since she had been dating Luke for a few months now but had a crush on someone else. Kayla had been flirting around with a few boys at school but it was nothing serious and did not seem to be like love at all. She had been talking favourably about Jamie so I wondered if he would be her next boyfriend.

The conversations with our friends was running thin, and I decided it was to too cold to stay outside. On my way home I became lost in my own thoughts of how life was supposed to work. I wondered about love.

There are many different kinds of love I knew that for sure but I wondered about that forever kind of feeling. How does that start? What is the difference between love and obsession? How does your heart make the decision to invest itself without fear? How do you take that step within yourself between a simple kiss and a dedicated commitment to want to be with someone? What is the real difference between loving a person forever and loving a pet? How does your heart feel? How do you know if the other person feels the same? How do they act? How do you trust them if they tell you they do? How do you trust yourself to be honest and true? How do you say it out loud? What do you think about? Is there really such a thing as love at first sight? How do you know?

I searched for answers inside myself as I walked home in the cold. I zipped up my coat as far as it would go as the wind blew across my neck and down my shirt. I sure hated this cold, and I was wishing I had worn a scarf.

"Someone phoned for you while you were out," my mother said when I walked into the warmth of the house. "They didn't say who they were, but it was a boy," she continued.

"What did he say?" I anxiously inquired.

"He just asked for you, and that was it."

"Did he say he would call back?" My mind ran in circles again. A boy?

"I told him you were outside and would be back around nine p.m."

I looked at the clock to see what time it was, quarter to nine. I hoped whoever it was would call back soon. I hoped it was Tommy, yet I was not sure how it could be since he did not have my phone number.

"Thanks. I am going to study in my room." I escaped that situation before she started asking questions I was not equipped to answer. I could not answer because I did have any. In my heart I hoped, wished, dreamed she would have said it was Tommy.

I opened my text and looked at the pictures of the digestive system in my biology book. My eyes were seeing the words on the pages but my ears were listening for the phone to ring. My heart was back at the high school dance when he was embracing my hand. I remembered his blue eyes and his candy kisses. In my heart I knew there was a connection between us. I could feel it with the deepest corner in my soul. I knew this flicker in my heart would somehow grow into something beautiful or I hoped it would.

Who Is in the Car?

I had awaked with my head still in my books and the bright sun shining through the window. I must have fallen asleep while I was studying last night because I was still lying backwards on the bed. I wondered why my sister had not come home and woken me up.

Rose, my sister, was five years older than I. She was well past the age that she needed parental supervision, and is engaged to be married soon. She had been dating him for a few years and would often stay at his place overnight. She had a job in a factory working midnight shift so I did not see her much anymore. I did miss her company but I understood she was all grown up and had a life of her own now.

Rose was more of an authority figure to me and often had to give me parental guidance when my parents where not around. I could talk to her about my personal feelings and she would give me advice but her view of things was always different than my own. I am sure she knew lots about love, as she was about to be married, yet I am not sure she would like the kind of boy that Tommy was. She would tell me what she really thought about everything whether I liked it or not. I was not sure if I should ask her just yet, but I did wish she were around so that if I wanted to I could.

I called Kayla on the phone, but her mother said she was already out and about somewhere. I called Lizzie too, but her brother did not know where she was. I imagined they were already out in our usual spot or hanging out at someone's place. I knew I could find them if I tried but would to wait until after I showered and had breakfast.

"Your friend called back," Mom said, as I was getting the cereal out of the cupboard.

"Oh, did Kayla or Lizzie already call?" I wondered what time it was as I looked at the clock on the wall. I had been asleep longer than I had thought. It was Saturday morning, and today time was of no issue.

"No, that boy, the one that called last night. He called back, but when I looked in you were already asleep, so I did not wake you up," she said, as she wiped up the drops of milk I had spilt on the cupboard when I was fixing my breakfast.

"Did he say who it was?"

"No, but I suggested he try to call again this morning. He sounded very nice."

It was strange that mother thought a prospective boyfriend sounded nice. After the last one I dated she would think anyone was nice. She did not like Jesse much. In fact she did not like him at all. If she knew all the things we had done together she would certainly have had reason not to like him.

"Do you have plans for today?" she asked, but the ringing of her saying he sounded nice was the last thing I heard.

"I said, do you have plans for today? I wondered if you wanted to go shopping with me this afternoon." She paused, then offered, "We could get you some new clothes."

I ignored her offer for a moment as I thought about what it was that I wanted to do today. I was not sure where my friends were and what everyone else was up to. If I had nothing better to do, going shopping was okay, but any other option was better than that. I really did not like to go shopping and even more I hated shopping for new clothes. I hated pushy sales people, and the sales women in stores that told you something looked good even when it did not. Besides, my mother was always trying to get me to get new clothes that looked nice, but my personal style was a bit different from that. Mother would prefer skirts and turtlenecks, and I would rather choose jeans and a low-cut sweater.

"I don't know." I shrugged. "I'll think about it."

I ate the rest of my cereal in front of the TV while I watched the Saturday morning Bugs Bunny cartoons. I laughed a few times at that silly coyote tying to catch that roadrunner. Did he ever give up? If I learned anything from that coyote it was to try to try again. He must have real good self-esteem, because if I had failed at something that many times in a row I would surely have given up a long time ago. It was funny to see him fall off a cliff for the one thousandth time and watch the rocks fall on top of him like they always did. There was one thing about Saturday morning cartoons you always finished watching the show feeling much better than the coyote.

I had decided not to go with Mom shopping today. I wanted to go find my friends instead. Mom went shopping almost every weekend, so it was always an option to go with her again next weekend. She might be disappointed, but she would understand.

I zipped my coat up and yelled toward the kitchen as I walked out the door, "Be back later." The door slammed tightly behind me as the wind from outside whisked it from my fingertips.

While I walked down the road I wondered where my friends were. Checking the hangout spot on the main road was my best option, and it was not as far to walk as the other places I guessed they might be. I hoped when I found them I could convince them to go inside where it was warm. It was snowing again, and I was already cold. I had wished I had gone shopping with my mother instead of coming outside. I wondered if she had left for town yet, because if I did not find my friends then I thought I would go with her for the afternoon after all.

I leaned against the wall of the front of the old church where we hung out. I tried to duck behind the wall to stay warm as I lit a smoke and watched the cars on the highway go by. The girls were not around yet, so I decided to wait for a while to see if anyone would show up. I wondered where they might be but I was not ambitious enough to walk much farther to look for them.

A car pulled up in front of the steps that I did not recognize. I could not see through the window until he rolled it down that it was Jamie. He had someone with him in the passengers' side of the car but I could not see who from where I was standing.

"What are you doing out here standing in the snow?" he yelled toward me, as he rolled down his window.

The gesture when he rolled down his window was an obvious invitation to go closer to the car and have whatever conversation might arise. I assumed it would end up to be a conversation about Kayla. I walked toward the car trying to see who was in the other side but I was not close enough to tell for sure.

"Hey, what's up? What are you doing around here?" I asked.

"Just going for a cruise," he said, as he looked at his passenger. "We didn't have much else to do today but just hang around the house, and we wanted to get out. You know, we were tired of playing video games, and it is not cold enough out for the pond to freeze to play hockey yet," he said, then started to get out of the car. "I need to go into the store and get some smokes. I'll be right back." He walked across the street toward the store in the other direction.

I leaned over to see who was in the other side of the car. I wanted to be sociable after all most of the kids from school were all friends since we all spent our entire lives within a few miles of one another. Growing up in a small community had its benefits and disadvantages.

33

The number one benefit was that everyone knew everyone else or someone that did. There were never very many new comers to this rural area because the same people lived here forever. There seldom were ever any strangers. This was home and it was safe. Nothing bad usually ever happened around here and nothing good usually happened either. Life was always the same.

The disadvantage was that everyone knew everyone or someone who did therefore, nothing was ever a secret. Some people had nothing else to live for except gossip or so it seemed. You gossiped about someone or the gossip was about you. Either way, everyone knew everything about each other or so we thought.

I was sure I would know the person in the other side of the car but was surprised when I recognized who it actually was. It was Tommy.

"Hi," I greeted him, at the same time as I realized who it was. "What's up?"

"Just cruisin' with Jamie, you know; I had nothing better to do." He had a gleam in his eyes that I had not seen in a boy before. "You?"

The sun was shining through the window onto his golden brown hair and faded skin, his leather jacket was tarnished and had tiny cracks around the collar, and his shirt was undone to the second button. The heater was on in the car and the air was warm coming through the window. I leaned in closer toward the warmth as I looked at him and smiled. I was delighted to see him.

"Ah, I just came out for a smoke, you know, was thinking about going shopping with my Mom." With my Mom, my voice echoed in my head. Where did that come from? I did not want to look like a loser, having not met up with the girls yet and walking around in the freezing cold by myself. That would seem worse than going out town with my Mom for my image of being like the cool kids around.

"Jump in; you look cold." He pointed to the driver's seat of the car and leaned over to open the door.

When I opened my mouth to say something, I was sure the million little white butterflies would take to the air, the kind you see in the summertime in the open fields or in the garden. I was not sure they would make it past the lump in my throat where my heart was now sitting.

"Sure." I climbed in behind the steering wheel.

"I tried to call you last night, but you were out," he said while he looked straight into my eyes with a grin on his face.

"Oh," I barely opened my mouth to speak because I did not want the insects that were still in my stomach to come out all over him.

"Kayla gave me your number yesterday while we were waiting for the bus. She said you wouldn't mind if I called you."

"I didn't mind," I mumbled.

Jamie opened the car door and attempted to get in, "Mind what?" He paused. "Get over." He pushed me across the seat.

"Damn, it is cold out there. What are you doing out here anyway? Wanna smoke?" he reached across my lap and offered one to Tommy.

"Where is everybody today? Where is Kayla?"

"Did you come here to see her?" I wanted to see if my hypothesis was correct.

"No, we came here to see you." He smiled and put his arm over my shoulder to hand Tommy the lighter for the smoke he had just given him. He leaned in close into me, and I could feel the warmth of his body against mine. It might be cold outside, but it sure was getting hot in the car.

It was difficult to tell what Jamie might have been thinking. He played the flirting game with all the girls. The more I got to know him the more I realized that he made us all feel special in some way or another. We all liked him for that. On the other hand he may be covering up with lusty desires for any girl who would say yes to his advances although I knew it was a silly game with me.

"Didn't we, Tommy?"

Tommy did not say anything. He just smiled and lit the smoke as he rolled down the window and exhaled.

"And I thought it was just because you guys had nothing better to do than play video games." I thought for a second. I wanted to play Jamie's game, too. "But I am glad to see you both." I slid my hand onto Jamie's knee over his tight faded blue jeans. I pushed myself closer to him as I reached deeply into the pocket of my coat to get my own smokes out. I opened the pack and took another one, even though I did not want it.

"Can I have a light?"

"We heard there was a party here tonight." He put the car in gear. "You know, around the corner from here." He turned the car onto the side street. He pointed out the window toward a house of boys that were friends of Kayla's brother. "Are you going?" he asked.

I had forgotten about the party. I recalled someone had mentioned it last week while we were standing in front of the old church. Lizzie I think, because she said she was not going to go to the party because she had to babysit or something. She said she did not mind missing the party as she was not much into drinking anyway. I must not have been paying attention when they were talking about it.

"Oh, yeah, I think there is." I looked at Tommy. "Are you going?"

He nodded his head to say yes because he was hauling off the smoke. Jamie turned the car around another corner and drove up the street. He pointed to my house. "She lives there," he told Tommy.

Tommy nodded again. "How do you know?" He was starting to sound a bit frustrated at Jamie's game playing.

"He gave Kayla and me a ride home last week from school. He and Kayla have got something going on, or he is trying to." I nudged Jamie in the ribs while he drove the car past my house.

"Wanna come with us to get some beer?"

"Let's kidnap her." Tommy leaned ahead to flick ashes in the astray. He touched my leg as he did.

"Okay," Jamie answered immediately, as if I had no choice in the matter. He then turned up the stereo in the car so loud it was impossible hear each other talk. He threw his cigarette butt out the window and pulled a joint he already had rolled out of his pocket. He dug in his pocket for a lighter. The car swerved, crossing the yellow line, which was hard to see from the mixture of the salt and snow reflecting in the sun through the window.

I handed him my lighter. "Take this one before you kill us all. I don't want to die with you two freaks."

"Ha, damn, girl, if you did you would die with two that were no better. I would." Jamie took the lighter, touching my hand before lighting the joint.

"Me too," Tommy agreed.

Jamie turned the car into the beer store parking lot. There was a familiar car already ahead of us. We simultaneously all looked into the driver's side window as soon as we pulled in alongside of it.

Kayla waved from the other vehicle then rolled down her window when she recognized us. Lizzie was in the other side. "Hey," she greeted us all and looked quite surprised. She smiled and shook her head. "What kind of motley crew is that?" She meant the duo with which I was currently keeping company.

Jamie got out of the car and walked over to her window. "Will I see you there? At the party tonight, I mean?" he asked her as if she was the only one in the car.

I leaned over to Tommy and whispered, "And I thought he was here to see me, huh? I knew he really wanted to see her." I made a small gesture toward his back, which was turned toward Tommy and me.

"I guess if he came here to see her you're stuck with me. Too bad, isn't it?" he rolled his eyes a bit. I was not sure if that was a question to seek information on my feelings or an attempted statement of sarcasm.

All of the sudden the bigger picture became clearer now. The pieces of the puzzle were starting to fall into place for me. Jamie was at the dance with Tommy when he asked Kayla to dance which left us standing alone. Kayla gave Tommy my phone number at school yesterday, and Jamie brought him here today. Is bringing him to the party tonight and showing him where I lived a conspiracy that has my name on the agenda?

I was trying to think of a question I could ask that would help me get closer to any indication as what he was throwing out to let me know how he felt. I had not prayed for this situation, but even I could see God's sense of humour this time. I smiled and said, "Thanks," under my breath to God for thinking of me. He could not be serious when he planned this one out ahead of time. For Kayla and Jamie to be the cupid messengers in setting up any kind of love game, that was amusing. The THC must be going to my head because something of that sort just could not be true.

"Isn't it?" he asked again.

"Ah, no, I don't think that would be a bad thing." I was I could see a little white butterfly sitting on top of his head as I made the first attempt at showing a bit of my private emotions.

Jamie turned around and brushed off the top of Tommy's head through the open window. "Look, it is starting to snow." He walked off into the store.

"Do you want a ride home with me? If those guys are going to the party we will see them later tonight. We can go get ready together. I already got the beer for us!" Kayla yelled through the open glass between the cars.

I put my hand on Tommy's thigh and smiled, "Let me out." I asked with an undertone of demand. "I'll see you tonight, and tell Jamie thanks for the ride."

He appeared disappointed for a moment but then opened the door and slowly stood up. He left barely enough room for me to squeeze out of the car around him. I wondered if this was a deliberate way of telling me he did not want me to go or the THC was going to his head, too. Since he did not move out of my way to let me out so I assumed it was a pleasant gesture to quietly say that he did not want me to go with Kayla.

"See ya," he said as he leaned closer to me when I brushed past him.

The Party

Kayla had left for the party without me. I must have fallen asleep again while I was getting ready at home. It was later than I had intended to arrive but I would tell them I was fashionably late. I am constantly making up excuses for my promptness anyway so no one would be surprised by it. As I walked down the street toward the festivities, I wondered if Jamie and Tommy were already at the party too. I hoped they were. I wondered who else would be there.

I walked up the steps and heard someone say, "Come in," before I got to the door. We were all one big happy family anyway, so I would have walked in without knocking. While I took my shoes off and unzipped my coat my eyes scanned the room quickly to see who had arrived. When I stepped into the room where everyone was, Kenny, an old friend of our group, was sitting by the end of the table. He stood up and greeted me with a hug. "Sit here," as he pushed the rest of the people that were also sitting on the bench over.

Kayla uncapped a beer and set it in front of me. "This was waiting for you."

I smiled in gratitude at her. A beer was just what I need to calm my nerves.

I was not sure why I was nervous this time. I had seen Jamie sitting beside the empty spot where Kayla had just sat down, but I did not see Tommy. He must have changed his mind and not come to the party after all. I was disappointed.

I looked again around the room to take a good look at all the company. Everybody from our town was there and a few others I was surprised to see. Jackson, Kayla's brother and Jesse were sitting in the far corner playing some kind of card game where the loser had to drink a shot of whisky. It appeared as if they had been playing the game for a while because they were both well on the way to being intoxicated.

Aaron had some rolling papers in front of him and was about to roll a joint. From the smell of the room when I arrived it was not the first one that had been passed around.

"Wanna help?" He threw the papers toward me.

"Okay," willing to at least be doing something that would occupy my time for a while.

Steve was over in the corner going through CDs to find something to put on the stereo because someone was complaining about his previous choice. I thought it was a good one for the party.

"Looks like those guys have been here a while," I laughed as I pointed over to the guys in the corner trying to play cards.

"Yeah, they have been here all day." Aaron said, but he never looked up because he already knew whom I was talking about.

Jamie and Kayla were writing some kind of notes on a paper passing it back and forth. It was some kind of private flirting game they were playing but did not care to share it with the rest of us. Maybe they were too embarrassed to. Jamie was most likely trying to get her to have sex with him but I was not sure Kayla was interested in taking the flirting quite that far.

Jesse looked up from the game he was playing with Jackson and realized I had arrived. He attempted to stand up but tripped over Jackson's feet, then stumbled toward the floor. We all started laughing at him.

"Nice one," some else yelled just before Jesse staggered out the door to go outside.

"Ah, he is not that drunk," Jackson said as he slurred his words. "I lost the game."

We started in a game of cards together at the table as we passed the joints we had rolled around.

Jesse walked back through the door and sat down beside me before he asked, "You guys didn't wait for me?"

Aaron passed the joint to him. I leaned over toward him and asked if he wanted to help me play cards, to which he agreed. Secretly, or so we thought, it was just an excuse for him to sit next to me for a while without making it look too obvious that we longed for something more.

Sitting that close to Jesse brought back fond memories of what we had shared together. Despite the fact that I could not share the same love which he had stated he had for me when we spent all our time together about a year ago. The beer and THC were leading me to believe it was a good idea to try again although the rest of me knew it most likely was not.

I had not seen him in a few months nor had I even thought about him much but being near him reminded me of a comfort that I was longing for. I was lonely. As I watched Kayla flirt with Jamie. I wanted that too. Although my heart had been preoccupied with someone else for a while this familiar feeling felt good, it felt safe. I knew Jesse well, and I knew what I could expect from him.

Jesse tilted his body toward me as he kissed me on the check. "Miss me?" He knew from the look in my eyes that I did.

"No," I said as I put my hand in the pocket of his shirt. "Got a light?" He knew that I was just using the lighter as a reason to touch him. I knew that the flirting would only last a while and we would be right back where we had left off. I also knew that my subtle advancement tactics would not be rejected. It was easy for anyone to see he had missed me as much as I had missed him maybe even more.

"Wanna take a walk? I need to go to the store," he asked, as he winked his big brown eye toward me.

Looking into his eyes reminded me of everything that we had shared. It was last summer when I first got to know Jesse. He started to come around town because he was friends with Jackson. For a while he was Kayla's boyfriend, but I did not know much about him then. Actually I did not know him at all, and I certainly did not know he was her boyfriend.

One hot summer night Lizzie, Abby, who was Kayla's youngest sister, and I were playing around the baseball diamond with a soccer ball when Jackson and his friend joined us in the game. One thing led to another and soon the soccer game became much more physical than what we had been playing and somehow it ended up in becoming some kind of tackle touch tag. One thing led to another, and I found myself kissing Jackson's friend in the quiet, dark corner of the ball park as we looked up at the stars.

It was not until the next day when I heard Kayla talking about her boyfriend that I had realized it was the same boy that I had enjoyed company with. I wondered if she would understand my mistake and that I would never have kissed him if I had known who he was. I thought she probably wouldn't so I thought it best not to say anything at all. That scenario only worked for a while, and then she had reported that he had broken up with her because he liked someone else. I knew it was me, but I could not ever tell her that. Secretly that was the best feeling I ever had. Someone was more interested in me than Kayla or Lizzie. Both of my friends were physically more mature than I was and all of the boys saw me as more of a friend than a romantic

40

interest. I was just one of the guys where most of them were concerned. For the first time in my life someone had picked me first. I liked that but I did not want anything to upset my best friend.

It was shortly after that I became Jesse's girlfriend at the expense of losing my friend. It created a big issue between Kayla and me, but after a while things got better. I was not sure if she accepted the fact Jesse and I were dating or ignored it, but all was well again after a few weeks within the group. Jesse and I spent lots of time together talking and hanging out, and in some strange way he kept me out of trouble for a while.

He was a few years older than I and had more experience at things that I did not. Our relationship had several firsts for us but the biggest thing he did for me was gave me someone to talk to when I got in trouble with my parents, the law, and when I wanted to run away from home. Things at home sometimes got crazy because of situations that were beyond my control and sometimes I just wanted an escape toward something almost normal. Jesse could provide that for me even if it was only for a few hours at a time.

In search for attention somehow Jesse and I found each other. He had a different kind of home life than I did. His mother was a single parent and the only father figure he knew would be whoever his mom was dating at the time. He was also looking for affection in any way he could get it. He found that with me, and I had lots of time on my hands with little guidance along the way.

I would sleep outside in a tent in the summer because I did not want to go into the house where all the arguing and fighting happened as it was usually like a war zone. I would rather be alone than be in the middle of all that dysfunction. He would come to the tent late at night when no one was around and we would talk or sit by the camp fire. We would tell each other about our lives, our dreams, our troubles, and whatever else we could think of. We spent a lot of time together secretly that not even my friends knew about. I could understand why he thought it was love. I was just too young to know.

"What are you thinking?" he asked as he nudged me in the ribs.

"What?" I asked him. My mind had drifted away thinking about what we had shared.

"What were you thinking? I asked you if you wanted to go for a walk?" he repeated himself.

Before I could answer the question the front door swung open and Tommy walked through the frame. "Damn, it is cold out there. It is an awful long walk from here to the store." Then he threw Jamie a pack of smokes. "Next time, you're going." He sat down.

My heart hit the floor as his eyes met mine from across the room. I tried to move away from Jesse as quickly as I could to cover up my mistake of sitting so close, but it was too late. I slid closer to Aaron, but with either way I was squirming to get out from behind the table. I was trapped.

Aaron pushed me back closer toward Jesse and motioned, "Get over. There is no more room over here. A second ago you had more than enough room where you were." Aaron had not looked up, and therefore, did not see the dynamics of what had just taken place. He certainly was no help to save me.

"Just wondered if you needed any more help rolling those joints?" I need to make up some kind of an excuse and fast. It was hard enough that I had embarrassed myself, but the entire room did not need to see it.

Jesse did not see the correlation between Tommy entering the room and my attempt at changing the seating arrangements because he put his arm over my shoulder and began to play with my hair. I put my head down as far as I could so I did not have to make eye contact with Tommy again. Jesse figured that was an invitation and was trying to feel my skin under the neck of my shirt. This was not what I wanted at this moment even if I did consider it a good idea a few minutes ago. What was I going to do now?

Tommy picked up the bottle that was sitting close to Jackson and tipped the whisky back as he chugged a drink. I closed my eyes with guilt. I may be the only one in the room other than him that knew he was masking his emotions with the bottle. I was sorry but I could not say it. I looked toward anyone for help to get me out of this situation I had put myself in because I just wanted to slide under the table and disappear.

"God, if I ever needed you before it is right now. Please, please, please, help me out of this one," I pleaded under my breath.

"Are we going for that walk?" Jesse said as reached across where I was sitting and picked up another joint. He stood up and tugged at my coat. "I know you want to come outside with me for a bit and sit in the car." His gestures were obvious enough that everyone could see and hear that there was no denying that before Tommy had walked in I would have gone with him anywhere.

"The car?" That got Kayla's attention. She had been oblivious to the situation as she was engaged in conversation with Jamie. "Give me a ride to the store?"

Kayla did not seem to understand, but how could she? I wanted to make excuses not to leave with Jesse because I knew what that would lead to. That situation would dismiss all my further chances with Tommy. At this point I knew one thing for sure, walking out of here with someone else would for surely mean it was over before it started. Since I had already fallen into the relationship hole with Jesse it was not my first choice to do it again. I was trying to think as quickly as I could to get myself out of this one but I did not know how.

"You guys go, and I will come out later when you get back," I stuttered. How could I cover this one up?

"Come with us," Kayla begged as she got up to get her coat. I knew she would not leave with Jesse alone.

"She can't leave right now. We are in the middle of this card game." Aaron insisted I stay. It seemed he was noticing my uncomfortable mess, thank God.

"I'll go too, then." Jamie stood up too, and they walked out together.

Whew, I had been saved for now. I was not sure if I should thank God this time or Aaron.

Aaron tilted his head and looked through my soul and whispered quietly, "You fucked that one up, didn't you?" He pushed me over toward the end of the bench. "Let me out."

I stood up and went over to stretch out on the beanbag chair beside Jackson who was still sitting in the corner drinking the bottle. It was not clear if he was even sober enough to know if Jesse had stopped playing the card game or if he thought that he was still losing. He was drinking as if he was. I wanted to sit beside Tommy who was also sitting near Jackson. I did not know how to repair the damage I had already done. I was not sure if I even could.

At the same moment I sat down, Tommy stood up and walked toward the door. He went outside again, despite that fact it was freezing out.

I was dumbfounded at my actions. I was not sure if I had done something wrong toward Tommy or not. I justified my actions to myself and thought I did nothing wrong, after all, he only kissed me. I was interested in him but it was not as if we were going out together or anything. In fact I was not sure until the last few minutes that he might even have had any feelings for me at all. Nevertheless, I knew that what Tommy had witnessed between Jesse and me was not what I wanted him to perceive. I was sorry in my own quiet heart, which now could be scrapped up off the floor. I knew I had let myself down. I was sorry to Tommy and sorry to myself.

Kayla, Jamie, Jesse, and Tommy came walking back into the party together. I was not sure what exactly had taken place outside or if they had even made it to the store. Time passed so quickly, I must have gotten lost in my thoughts again. I looked up. Aaron was sitting in a different chair and Jackson was now sitting at the table trying to shuffle the cards.

"Wanna play strip poker?" He looked around with a sly grin at everyone in the room.

Someone had changed the tunes again. Kayla laughed aloud and threw a beer cap at her brother. "No!" Since she was his sister that was an expected answer, and since she did it for us, the rest of us girls did not have to answer his question.

Jesse slandered over and sat down on the beanbag chair beside me. This was looking worse and worse for me all the time. I just wanted to go home. I wanted to get myself out of here. I had wasted time not getting away while he was gone and now I had to start all over again and plan to make the grand escape.

Jesse rolled over and straddled me while I sat on the chair underneath him.

"Wanna bite?" he asked as if he was trying to seduce me sexually. He put a red Smartie in his mouth and leaned toward me and then he waited for me to respond.

We had played this game together several times before. We had played with marshmallows, candies, chocolate bars, apples, gum, or whatever we had to share. In the relationship that Jesse and I shared, everything had a sexual undertone.

He liked to pretend he was the stud in the crowd that he was getting all the action. It was the male hierarchy and pecking order thing, which was something we girls could not understand. It appeared the guy that was getting the most sex was sitting at the top of the throne and those males who were not were all placed underneath him. As long as Jesse allowed everyone think he was having sex with me he was in good standing. It did not seem to matter if we actually were or not, he let everyone believe we were. Unfortunately, that did nothing for my positive reputation because they all believed him. I was too young at the time to even understand the tales the boys told each other to make themselves feel good until it was already too late.

I wondered now if he knew about the feelings I had for Tommy and was putting on a show for him too. I wondered if Jamie or Kayla said something toward that situation while they were in the car or if they were all too drunk to really care. Maybe I would get lucky and no one would remember this in the morning because they would all have a big, drunken blackout. I hoped at least Tommy would but I doubted it.

I took the candy from Jesse with my teeth. I am not sure why. I did not have the strength to push him off. His touch and attention along with the familiar comfort of his kisses felt good. I knew that whatever choices I was making were bad ones but it was already too late. I might as well enjoy the options that I am being presented with rather than wait for those I have not. If I have messed it up already, I suppose I have nothing else to lose and it was better than feeling sorry for myself.

Jesse fed me red Smarties one by one by holding them each in his teeth from where I would take them into my mouth. Before I let the chocolate melt he would enter his tongue into mouth and crush the Smartie. Therefore the chocolate would melt between both our taste buds. We could experience the same taste of the same Smartie at the same time. I particularly liked this game when we played with strawberries or marshmallows but I suppose the corner store did not carry either of those this time of year. Smarties were the next best thing.

The game of candy kisses was very simple. We only had one way to win with no rules. The first one who closed their eyes lost. The loser had to do anything the winner desired them to do. Nothing was out of bounds to ask of the other person. As the loser you could not say no. That was not an option. You had to comply. That was the fun part of the game. We had to trust that the demand would be fair and kind and something we both liked.

If we both closed our eyes at the same time we would call a tie and start over again.

We could touch each other wherever or however you wanted, kissed passionately or get as affectionate as you wanted. The object was to win the game however you could.

I took the bait and put my tongue in his mouth, and I crushed the candy. We tasted it together. Then I closed my eyes. For a moment he was the only other person in the world and all that mattered was the way we were kissing right then. I wanted to stay in this moment forever. I could die here now and everything would be just fine. For a moment I had forgotten everything else but him.

"You win," I said as I opened my eyes. I would have done anything he asked me to. I was vulnerable and completely under his control. He knew it.

"Come out to the car with me right now," was his request. "We'll play again to see who wins next time." He held up the extra large box and gave it a shake. He pulled me up by the hand from the chair and led me toward the door. I followed him like a puppy in the rain.

Tommy was sitting in the corner with Kayla, Jamie, and Jack Daniels. He put the bottle to his mouth and looked toward me. He appeared to be having some kind of funny conversation with them and a few other friends because they were all laughing at something I could not hear. I wondered if Tommy even cared that I was leaving the room anyway. Until he poured the rest of the bottle into his mouth as I walked out of the room behind Jesse.

I changed my mind. I did not want to play this game any longer. I let go of Jesse's hand. He turned around to look at me to see what was wrong, but my eyes had already hit the floor. He lifted up my chin and looked into the core of my soul.

"I win." He took my hand again and led me out the door.

The air astounded me as soon as I stepped outside. It was cold. Jesse started the car as soon as we got in it and turned the heat fan on high. He turned the radio on so low I could hardly hear it. He handed me the box without saying a word. It was my turn to hold the Smartie. We played the game again.

This time he held his tongue on top of the Smartie and let the heat incubate it inside our mouths to melt it slowly. He lifted my shirt and touched my breasts with his cold hands. I did not want him to stop. I wanted to feel the cold winter air on my skin, even for a moment. I closed my eyes again. He closed his eyes also and circled his tongue in my mouth. Slowly he put my shirt back down and twisted his body away from mine.

"I win." I pushed him away from me. "Anything I want, you cannot say no."

"Yes," he agreed, then paused. "No, I think I won." He realized I was trying to cheat to win the game.

"Okay, what do you want?"

He reached over, turned the radio off, and turned on the interior light in the car. I looked into his brown eyes as he said, "Tell me you are sorry for breaking my heart."

"I am sorry," although I am not sure I was.

"I know you were young. I should not have walked you through some of those experiences, but I loved you. I know you could not love me back in the same way then because you did not know how. I know things were different for you than they were for me, and you see why I had to let you go. I knew that was what was best for you. You deserve better than I am, and someday I am sure you will find it."

"Why are you saying this now?"

"Because I have not seen you in a long time, and I realized how different our lives were then. I told myself that the next time I saw you I wanted to tell you that things are changing for us, and I am not sure that I will see you much anymore. I wanted you to know how I felt. I will always love you."

"I will always love you."

"No, you won't. You don't need to say that just to make me feel better. You are different than I am, and you do not know how to love me in the same way."

"Well, maybe not in the same way, but I love you."

"I know you loved me as much as you could. As much as you knew how."

"But why did I break your heart?"

"I guess you didn't. It was the fact that I had to let you go that did, but I knew it was for the best."

"For the best? It did not feel like that to me."

"I know, and I am sorry, but it was the best for you. Letting you go was the hardest thing I have ever done, but it was the best for you. I hope someday you understand that."

"I will never understand how letting something you love go is the best for anyone. That sounds silly to me."

"I know."

I gave him the box again. "It is your turn."

"I don't want to play anymore." He opened the door and got out of the car. He stood there for a moment until he finally asked, "Are you coming back in the house?"

"In a minute," I said, and he closed the door.

The other chromosome had gotten the best of me again. It was like I was in the Garden of Eden, except this time, it was Adam that handed the apple to Eve. Once she took it, he took it back, then would leave her standing there to be devoured by temptation alone.

I lit another smoke and went back in the house. I scanned the room and everything was the same as when we left. Jesse went back over and sat by Jackson and Tommy, who where still sitting in the corner with Kayla and Jamie. Aaron was still rolling joints. The stereo was on ten and everybody else was playing cards. I sat down beside Kayla and elbowed her in the arm.

"Let me see your notes."

Kayla handed me another beer from the cooler, and I opened it.

47

The Make Up

I had not talked to Tommy in almost two weeks. It was clearly understandable why he was upset at me. He would not look at me in the halls, he skipped geography and he rode home with Jamie instead of on the bus. He went to the parking lot to socialize before school instead of the common area. I did not see him anywhere and it seemed that he was avoiding me at all costs.

I was sorry for the way I behaved and if I could have a chance to tell him I thought I could make it all okay again, or at least I hoped I could. He disliked me now and he had every reason to. I had been a victim of a temptation that I could not overcome. I knew my chances with Tommy were over but I wanted have a chance to say I was sorry I treated him badly even if nothing would ever develop into a relationship I still wanted to at least be friends. It seemed I would never get the chance as long as he kept avoiding me. I wanted to find a way to talk to him.

I walked up stairs to his locker after the bell rang at the end of the day. He was standing by his locker with a girl. I did not know who she was, and I wondered if he was now investigating her as a possible new friend. It sounded like they were talking about some work they needed to do for some kind of class assignment but I wondered if it was just an excuse to get her attention, boys are like that. I heard a locker door bang shut and the combination lock click closed. Tears began to well up in my eyes because I still wanted to be some sort of his pleasurable pastime.

Please, please, please, God, give me the strength to do what is right. To apologize for what I have done. I at least want the opportunity to say I'm sorry even if I don't get another chance with him.

I opened my eyes at the same time as he walked around the corner. My books fell to the floor because he had collided into me, an unfortunate surprise. He would not have known I was standing there listening to him talking with her, whoever she was.

"Are you okay?" he asked. He bent down and started to help me pick up the books.

Here was my chance. God had answered that prayer; now the rest was up to me. The tears were starting to rotate behind my eyes. I blinked quickly a few times to wash them away.

"Yeah." I fumbled with some papers on the floor and touched his hand. I looked up into his eyes.

"I am sorry about the party. I never meant for that to happen." I started to pick up the papers again as I looked toward the floor. God gave me too much strength, because now I did not know what to say.

"As long as you had a good time." He handed me a book without looking up.

"I just wanted to say I am sorry, and I hope you call me again if you still have the number. Thanks." I piled the last pieces of paper inside the red, three-ring binder.

He stood up and smiled before he turned and said, "Sure," before he quickly walked away.

I went to the bus alone today. I hung my head low as I walked slowly down the hall staring at the dirty dusty rose carpet. That did not go as well as I had hoped it would. I dreamed that he would say everything would be okay again. That he would remember the dance, the stars in the parking lot, the moon falling over us, the kiss. It was my desire that I could intelligently say something that would remind him he had once liked me. I remembered what we shared and wondered if he actually had any feelings for me in the first place. I could have just made the story up in my head to raise my self-esteem because I was lonely or missed Jesse. Maybe he did not ever like me at all.

I do not remember the bus ride home much as my thoughts were lost in the distance even far from myself. It felt the insanity inside my head as I tried to think of anything else but him. I wanted him to call me again. I wanted to talk to him again. I wanted him to know me as a different person not the bad person that he thought I was. I wanted him to give me a second chance at a fresh start. I swear if he did that I would surely not blow it this time.

I sat down in front of the TV with a bowl of popcorn. I pushed the buttons on the remote until I found something interesting to watch. The Bugs Bunny Roadrunner show was on. I laughed a bit while I ate the buttered snack. This time I felt like the coyote, having fallen so many times but I could not get back up. In my heart I felt like the Roadrunner, always running away from things one way or another.

The phone never rang as I sat with my comfort food as I asked myself, "Was what I did really all that wrong?" I kept reminding myself that it was if I ever wanted to be with Tommy. I had wanted to send the message to him that I was interested, but I had done the exact opposite. How could I be so stupid?

I wish I had thought more clearly before I acted even like a stranger to myself that night of the party. I guess it did not matter how much I tried to forget it I could not erase my actions and therefore I must just get on with life and do my best for next time. A lesson learned. Now I could just forget it and come to terms with the idea that I had lost what I wanted before I even got it. That must be God's way of saying that I did not deserve it in the first place, and I had better let it go. Period.

I needed to do something other than sit by the phone and wait for it to ring. I did not think Tommy would call anyway. Keeping me here waiting for him was antagonizing and putting me in unnecessary torture. I thought I would go for a walk. I hoped I did not see my friends while I was outside. I did not want to have to explain why I had been so aloof on the bus ride home from school. I doubted they even noticed.

As I walked I continued to fixate on Tommy. I wanted to have a chance to explain to him the things he did not know about Jesse and me. I wanted to tell Tommy that I was not Jesse's girlfriend or did not want to be. I wanted to tell him about the relationship I had experience with Jesse and how much he had helped me a few years ago when things were so terrible. I wanted him to know that things about me that he had probably not heard from his buddies yet. Things they could not know.

I smiled as I thought of my childhood friend again but I did wish I could take what happened at the party back. I wished Tommy had not seen that. Maybe I was in love with Jesse at one time and did not know it or maybe I was still too young to understand what brings people together in love. I hoped that he was doing well since I had not seen him since the party. I spoke the words aloud as if I was sure God or the angles would send my words to him in the wind, through the stars, with the sunrise, from my heart to his. *God, please send Jesse my love and all my wishes that he is doing well and receiving everything he needs to keep him safe and as happy as he can be. Now that we don't carry each other anymore, I hope he is strong enough to carry himself.* I knew that God would know what my simple words meant, and I knew Jesse would, too.

The snow had fallen on the trees and everything reminded me of a postcard. Winter had several disadvantages but the beauty of the fresh fallen snow and the way the air bit the back of your throat when you swallowed was comparable to nothing. I loved being outside in the winter, as long as it was not too cold. I was reminded that all would be new again soon, and I had to find the faith that love would be the same.

I walked about an hour before my feet got cold, and I returned home. The fresh air done me good and cleared my head a bit. My obsession had disappeared, and now I could focus on something more productive, like homework or something.

"I'll get it," I yelled, because the phone was ringing as soon as I opened the door and stepped into the house.

"Hello?" I asked more than greeted anyone who was on the other end of the line.

"Hello, is Emily there?" the voice asked.

"This is." I was not sure who it was. I knew that whoever was on the line I had not ever talked to before because I did not recognize his voice. "Who is this?"

"It's Tommy. You said I could call," his voice sounded shaky and shy as if he was nervous.

"Yeah, I am glad you did." Now I had the chance to talk to him I did not know what I was going to say. My heart skipped a few beats, the lump in my throat came back instantly, and I suddenly became hot. It was funny how he had the exact effect on me every time I was taken off guard by his actions. I was starting to see a pattern.

My shoes were dripping snow on the floor, and my scarf was still wrapped around my neck. I did not want to take the phone away from my ear for one second to miss the sound of his voice or my opportunity to finally talk to him after all the anticipation.

"I was just thinking about you." I wondered why I would be so honest so soon with my thoughts. I might as well just throw myself out on a platter and let him cut me up with a sharp jagged knife.

"I was just thinking about you too," he said.

"Oh, that is good. What about?" I wanted to somehow take the pressure off me, but I do not know if that was intentional or natural instinct to want to run away again.

"I was just wondering how your boyfriend was." He sounded disappointed.

"Boyfriend? You mean Jesse?"

"The jerk from the party." He elaborated.

"No, he is not my boyfriend." Now was my chance to explain, but all of the sudden that did not seem as important as I thought it was. The only thing I could think of was to tell him how I felt about him, not hurt him any more with my behaving badly. The past relationships I had did not need to be any part of what I was trying to put together now.

"Well, it sure did look like it." Tommy was sounding upset.

"Yes, I know it must have, and I am sorry. I was not expecting him to be there or for that to happen. If I had known he was going to be there I would not have shown up. It really was not what it looked like." I lied. I still would have gone.

"You were pretty drunk. How did you feel the next day?" I said with a giggle. I wanted desperately to change the subject. I had him on the phone now; I did not want to waste our time talking about something that might again be misleading. I only wanted to convey my interest in him, not hash out the mistake with Jesse. After all, I could not take my actions back but I could try to make things better now between us.

"Sick with a hangover," he laughed, "and you?"

"About the same," I agreed.

I hoped this would be the beginning of a new start, and all I really wanted was his attention and affection. Now that I had it, I did not know what to do with it.

"It was nice to talk to you today. I wish we could have walked to the bus, but I rode to school with Jamie. He was waiting for me in the parking lot. We went to town after school today to buy him a stereo for his new car," he explained.

"Oh, I see." I did not know what else to say. I did not want to talk about Jamie or his car, but my brain went blank.

"Are you going to school tomorrow?" he asked.

"Yeah, are you?" I did not want to talk about school or our friends but any conversation would do as long as we were talking. I was really sweating now in my outdoor clothes. I wanted to take them off; I was really getting hot.

"Yeah, can I meet you outside for a smoke in the morning?"

"Sure."

"Okay, it's getting late. I had better let you go. I'll see you tomorrow," he said.

"Okay, bye." I hung up the phone.

As I lay myself down to sleep I could hear his words repeatedly in my head, "Can I meet you outside for a smoke in the morning?" I smiled. I wondered if this meant that he really had been avoiding me for the past few weeks because he believed that Jesse was my boyfriend. I wondered if he had forgiven me for making the mistake at the party, was glad I went to his locker today, wanted to be with me, or cared if our friends saw us together. Again I heard his voice in my head, "Can I meet you outside in the morning for a smoke?" I could not wait to see him.

As I fell asleep with a smile on my face and in my heart as I thanked God again for giving me the strength today to go to his locker today. I could see how the phone call tonight was a direct result those actions. I wished I had not wasted so much time and gone right after the party. Yet I knew I needed to give myself time to comprehend what was going on inside of me, and I am sure he needed time, too.

Want a Ride?

The sun shone so brightly in the morning that I could hardly see the car that was honking in my driveway as I looked out the window. The noise of the horn did not register in my brain because I was still asleep. I rolled over to look at the clock. I had slept in by an hour. It must have been Kayla to pick me up for school. She must have been able to get the car. I jumped up out of bed, threw my housecoat over my pajamas, and ran to the door. It was not Kayla's car, and I did not know who it was.

I saw the passenger side door open, and someone got out and yelled from the lane, "Want a ride?"

I watched him in amazement as his breath froze coming out of his lungs. It looked like cigarette smoke. It was Tommy and Jamie driving Jamie's new car.

"Ummm," I stood at the door in amazement and shock. It was one thing for Kayla or Lizzie to see me in my housecoat but not Tommy and Jamie. My face turned red in embarrassment. "Can ya give me half hour to get ready?" I smiled and waved as if to invite them in the house to wait. I knew if they came in we would all be late for school because a half hour would never be enough time for me to do all that I needed to do to prepare myself for the day. I did not want to get them in trouble with the school for being late, but on the other hand I doubted they would care.

"Yeah," Tommy answered before he even asked Jamie if he would mind, "we can wait." He leaned in the car and said something to Jamie that I could not hear from the doorway where I stood. I could barely see Jamie's face because of the sunshine but I think he smiled toward Tommy and then said something toward his direction. Tommy closed the door of the car as he got out and Jamie backed out of the driveway. Tommy walked toward the house.

"Gee, it's cold out this morning," he said, as I held the door open for him to come in. "I thought you'd be ready by now. We thought you might want a ride to school with us today. He smiled and pointed at the pink fuzzy housecoat I was wearing, "Nice."

I smiled back at him. "I was running a bit late. I had a bit of trouble getting to sleep last night," I said, as I was thinking about the phone call we had shared and the last waking thoughts I had were of him. "Would you like something to drink while I take a shower?"

"Sure," he answered. He sat down and lit a smoke. He looked around then added, "You alone?"

"Yeah, everyone is at work already."

He nodded in acknowledgment as I walked away in a hurry. I needed to get out of this housecoat.

I could not believe he was here sitting in my kitchen waiting for me to get ready for school. I tried to hurry, but my dexterity was off because I was no nervous having him here. I wondered where Jamie went and when he would be back. I wondered if they cared if we would be late for school. I turned the radio just before I got in the shower in hopes it would ease the silence as he waited and possibly calm my nerves.

"Where did Jamie go?" I asked Tommy, as I dried my hair with a towel and looked at the clock. Classes start in ten minutes, and I knew for sure we would be late.

"I don't know, but I am sure he will be back soon," he said, as he watched every move I made while I slung my long, brown hair down and began to run a comb through it.

"We'll be late. You guys should have just gone without me." I tried to make conversation. Everyone knew that Jamie and Tommy did not give much effort or consideration to anything about school. School was a social gathering for them, not a function of higher education. They did not care if they were late, and I was surprised they were actually going to attend school at all today, since it was Friday before Christmas holidays and all.

Tommy stood up and looked out the window on the door. "Looks like he is here now. I think he has someone with him." He strained his eyes as he was trying to look into the blinding sun. I walked over behind him to brush the ice off the window as I looked over his shoulder.

"I think it's Kayla."

I could feel the heat from his body I was standing so close to him. I could feel his energy radiating from being near me. If I could imagine his aura; it would be bright orange like the sunrise surrounded with blue, like his cool, calm exterior.

"Yeah, I think it is," he said, as he turned around to face me. Instantly I transformed into another world where we were all made of Jell-O. I wanted to kiss him again right there on the spot. I stepped back a small step and sneaked a quick look into his eyes. I wanted to crawl inside myself for a moment to catch my breath. I was not as ready to be this close to him as I had thought I was. I had been this close to boys I crushed on before but I did not recall having feelings quite like this. I could not even describe it to myself.

"Guess I better get my coat," I muttered, as I quickly backed away from him.

"They'll wait," he said. He put his hands around my waist. I knew they could see us from the car. I did not know what was happening just then because I got an instant rush of adrenaline to my head as he pulled me closer to him. He looked directly into my blue eyes and then dropped his hands, "Yeah, maybe you better."

"We're going to be late," Kayla said, as Tommy and I got into the back of the car.

"I slept in," she added.

"Yeah, me too." I looked at Tommy and smiled. "Without the ride to school I do not think I would have made the bus."

"Me either," Kayla agreed. "Ma has the car today, so we would not have had a ride." She lit a smoke just as Jamie just put one out.

Jamie turned up the radio so loud that we could not hear each other talk even if we wanted to. That was the usual anyway, life was always a party with him and since it was so early in the morning. I doubted anyone had anything sensible to say. I had way too much going on in my head to want to say anything out loud, and I was sure the butterflies would come out of my mouth and land on someone's unsuspecting head again. Kayla would understand, but I did not think the boys would.

I was excited inside. With a start to the day like I was having nothing could bring me down. I was as happy as I could have ever imagined. I was not sure what falling in love was, but I think I was tripping over it or into it or whatever someone does. I did not know. I did not want to ask any questions about it either because I liked how I felt exactly in that moment in the back of the car with Tommy. I closed my eyes for a second and quickly said thanks to God, with the trust of a child, because I knew that everything was about to get better. I reminded myself how mystical love really is and wished this moment would last forever.

Jamie drove straight past the school with all of us in the car. I did not notice until we were well on our way to some place else. Kayla was fumbling with something in the glove box as Jamie continued to drive as if he had some destination in mind. It seemed that the rest of us had been kept out of the loop about it. Tommy and I sat silently in the back of the car as I looked out the window and wondered where exactly we were going. Nobody made any kind of motion to disagree with Jamie. In that instant he had made the choice for all of us. We all had a silent pact in agreement that we were not going to school. If they had not come and give us a ride we would have both missed the bus anyway. I was already planning excuses in my head to make skipping out on school today totally acceptable. Since it was the last day before Christmas holidays, and the only thing we would miss would be uneventful assemblies and stale candy canes, spending the day with Tommy or any part of it would be the best Christmas present I could have asked for.

We drove in silence of conversation for what seemed like eternity until Jamie turned the stereo down. I could smell from the back of the car that he had just lit a joint. I assumed that is what Kayla had been fumbling around with a few minutes ago.

"Ere," he attempted to say, as he handed it into the backseat toward us. I had to slide over into the center of the seat closer to Tommy to reach it. I did not really want to partake in smoking this today. I was feeling good enough naturally to want to influence it with any kind of artificial stimulation that might hinder the things was I was really feeling. On the other hand, I did not want the people to think I was a stiff either. I wanted them to be glad they picked us up today so maybe they would have a good time and do it again. I took a couple small tokes off the joint and passed it on to Tommy.

"Where are we going?" I leaned closer to the back of the seat where Jamie was sitting and blew the smoke out his open window.

"For a ride," he advised me, as he took the half-smoked joint from Kayla.

We spent most of the morning aimlessly driving around in the car with nothing else to do but continue to smoke a few more joints and listen to the tunes that Jamie turned back up. Eventually we ended up at the mall where we did some shopping in the music store before we sat at the tables to grab a drink and watch the mall rats waltz by.

I watched the people scurry about catching up on the last minute shopping and wondered of all the children's happy faces on Christmas morning. To all those parents who were trying to beat the rush so Santa could bring all the right toys I bet it was worth every moment of pushing people out of the way, getting run over by shopping carts, reaching for the last toy on the top self, then standing in line only to pay for over prices. Then wait and cross your fingers on Christmas morning and hope the child's eyes lit up with amazement when they saw the gift that was wrapped inside the perfect box. I bet it was worth in then. I wondered if I would ever have children. I looked toward Tommy smiled.

I remembered the time in my life when I was a little girl and believed in Santa Clause. I loved Santa Clause because for at least one day of the year I always received what I wanted. Most of all I wanted my family to be together and happy for one day.

We would wake up early Christmas morning and see all the presents under the tree. Gift by gift my sister and I would open our presents with suspense increasing with each one. Every year Santa tucked the best one of all way in the back so it was the last one on the list to open. We would play with all of our new toys while my mother would make the best dinner of all year with turkey, potatoes, vegetables, and wonderful deserts. Last year she forgot to put the bottom crust in her cherry pie, she was so caught up in all the excitement. I am not sure why, but it was funny.

Our dinner guests would arrive one by one or two by two, and soon our house would be full of happy people and laughter. Christmas day was a day that we were all together, and nothing else mattered but the good food and the company we kept. I wished it could be like that all year long, with everyone only thinking of the blessing we had received the past year and kindness in our hearts. It was perfect.

I turned and looked toward Tommy, who was standing in line at the concession booth getting a pop. I doubted I would spend this Christmas with him this year, but I wondered if there would be any in the future. I smiled to myself and hoped that there would. I began to think about what gift I might buy for him or what he would enjoy to make him happy. I wondered what he wanted. I did not know him that well yet, but in a year from now I might. I wondered if I would buy him just the perfect gift for all to see just how I cared for him.

"Want a drink?" Tommy asked as he sat down beside me.

"Sure." He handed me the pop. My mouth was dry from the last joint we smoked in the car. I was now wishing I would have stood in line with him and gotten a pop for myself. The drink was refreshing. The pop was a good idea.

"Where did those two disappear?" he asked. I knew he meant Jamie and Kayla.

"I think they went back into the music store. Jamie wanted to get something he had seen in there a while ago or maybe they went to the bank to get some money, and then were going back into the music store." I was fumbling over the words because I did not know where they had gone for sure. I remember they said something in mentioning heading in the opposite direction but I was not really paying attention, as usual. It was when I was watching Tommy standing in the line to get the drink.

I did not want to be so consumed with Tommy, but my feelings were taking over the rest of me, and I did not know how to control them. I thought that as long as the feelings were good ones I wanted to let them flow through me as a river runs deep as long as I was not a babbling brook. I wondered if putting my trust and giving my heart to Tommy was a good idea or if I would just end up getting hurt. Seeing as it was Christmas time this seemed like a sign from God.

"You two look good together," Kayla mentioned, as she came walking back with Jamie.

I smiled and then looked in the other direction. I hoped Tommy thought so too, but he did not acknowledge she had said anything.

"Yeah, they do, from a distance." Jamie smiled. He was walking up behind her on the right side.

"You guys getting ready to go?" Tommy asked, a few seconds later. He took the pop can from my hands then took another drink. "We have been waiting here a while." Nevertheless, I wondered if he really minded or if he enjoyed sitting here with me. I did not mind at all how long they had taken. I wished they had taken all day.

Tommy stood up and stretched his back out straight. "Let's go." Then he turned around to look at me; he put his hand on my shoulder and asked, "Coming?"

"Yeah." I stood up beside him. He had barely given me enough room to stand up without rubbing against him again. It sure did not seem like he minded the wait then. I was trying to read his body language, but I could not tell for sure. He was stoned.

I walked out to the car beside Kayla while Jamie and Tommy walked ahead. We pretended to look at the purses and girl stuff but she really wanted to talk about Tommy. We knew they would not join us to look at girl stuff because they were much to cool for that.

"What is going on with you two?" I was not sure if she was excited or surprised. "You are looking pretty comfy together, like two peas in a pod."

"We were just waiting for you guys to get back. He was not saying much," thank God, but I only added that comment in my head.

"Well, he seemed to be enjoying it, and so did you." She had made a correct observation. I hoped.

"Yeah, he seems all right." I smiled, but she knew what I meant.

"Hurry up!" Jamie yelled across the mall to us.

Kayla dropped the purse she was looking at and winked at me. "We had better get going." She had found out all the information she wanted to know.

"Damn, it is cold out here," Tommy advised me when we got in the back of the car and sat down on the leather seats.

"Sure is," but I was thinking in my head, *like I do not already know.*

"Sit close, and it will be warmer. It takes a while for this heater to warm up," informed Jamie as he started the car.

Tommy slid over to my side of the car and put his arm around my shoulder. He looked toward me and smirked. "This should make it warmer."

"In a hurry," Kayla added.

I put my hand on the inside of Tommy's leg and moved it inward. "And this should speed things up a bit."

Then I started laughing because Tommy twitched a bit. "But I think we will be all right." I took his arm off my shoulder and put it down between us. I wanted all the flirting he had to offer, but I also wanted to enjoy the chase.

We drove back home with the new CD playing on the stereo. Nobody said a word, and I think it was better that way. I could enjoy my own thoughts and Tommy sitting next to me. He did not move over when the car warmed up, and it was a forty-minute drive home. I was glad.

As soon as I got home I went in and lay down on the bed. My ears were ringing from the music being so loud. I wondered what Tommy was thinking and if I would see him again over the holidays. I was not old enough to drive a car yet but he was. I wondered if he had his permit. I knew for sure Jamie did. Maybe Jamie would come down to see Kayla and he could bring Tommy with him again. I doubted that idea, it was a silly one.

Going Steady

Christmas came and went, and I did not see or hear much from Tommy. I called him to wish him Merry Christmas but he was not home. I asked his mom to give him the message. I hoped she did. I wondered if he knew I had called because he had not called me back. I had been busy with my friends and not around home that much so maybe he did and someone forgot to tell me about it. My sister might have taken the call, but she worked midnight shift at a factory, and I did not see her much anymore. Nonetheless I was anxious to get back to school on Monday after the holidays to see him. I thought I would surely be able to tell then, or I could ask him about the call.

The phone rang just as I was getting ready for bed. I wondered who would call this late at night, it was almost ten. I hoped my father would not get upset at me because he did not allow calls much after nine from my friends unless it was important. He said that anyone that needed to talk to me could call at a decent hour and respect the working people's need to get up early in the morning. Since he left for work at four in the morning all of my friends knew when they had to call.

"It's for you," Mom yelled from the kitchen.

"Hello?"

"Hey, what's up?" It was Tommy. I was glad to hear from him.

"Just getting ready for bed. You?"

"Just came from my friend's. He lives up the road beside the store." He paused. It sounded like he was taking a drag off a cigarette. "I have been spending lots of time there since he is on holiday from work."

"Ah." That explained it. "I have been busy, too," and hoping that he would call. I did not say that part.

"How was your Christmas?" he asked.

"Okay, I guess. Yours?"

"Good."

"What did you get?" The conversation went on from there for about another hour. I wondered if he was thinking about me all this time, too.

"I'll see you tomorrow at school?" I asked.

"Yeah, come and have a smoke with me?" I was not sure if that was an invitation or a demand.

"Yeah, we'll see."

"Good night."

"Good night."

I fell asleep with a warm heart and nice thoughts of him. I was looking forward to seeing him in the morning.

It was that Monday and every other Monday after that that we spent together in the smoking pit. We were going steady now, and I was happy. He was happy, too.

I do not recall the exact thing he said when he asked me to be his girlfriend, and I am not sure he really ever did. It just seemed that we fit together so well, after our new beginning, that it was automatically assumed that we were a pair. We started hanging out together when we could at school, and I suppose he just never had to ask.

I remembered the first time he said he loved me. It was over the phone one night after we had seen each other at school. I told him I loved him too and it was rockets and fireworks from there on in.

We had gotten in trouble from the teachers at school a few times when I was sitting on the stage in the café and he was standing too close. He was trying to or succeeding at looking down my shirt. I always wore low cut shirts to school to tease him because I knew he liked that. Tommy told them to go to hell or something like that and he got in more trouble. He did not care.

He was late for homeroom every day because he carried my books to class in the morning after we met in the smoke pit. My homeroom was at the other end of the school from his which was on the second floor. Sometimes he would just skip homeroom so it would appear he was absent from school; then he could skip any other class during the day he wanted because his name would be on the attendance list. He would skip his fourth period class a lot to have lunch in the café with Bobbi and me.

He sat between Bobbi and me in the back of geography class. Those of us that sat at the back had gotten a bunch of carbon copy sheets from the office so only one person had to take notes and we could all get copies. We were supposed to take turns every day being the one that actually wrote the notes.

I always wrote more than everyone else because I took Tommy's turn, too. If I did not do the writing we could hardly read the notes when he took his turn, because his handwriting was so messy, and he did not press hard enough to make all the carbon paper work. I think he wrote sloppy on purpose, but he denied he did it that way. We all had the same answers on the test, too. We all cheated, but the teacher never caught on, or at least did not bust us for it if he did.

He met me at my locker every day after class but sometimes he was late, and I would have to wait for him. It was not often that I would go to his locker because it was all the way upstairs. We would walk to the bus together. Every now and again we would take the long way around the school to spend more time together. We would hold hands when we walked. He kissed me every day before we got on the bus. We were a pair and everyone knew it.

"Did you hear the cops were here today? They had the drug dogs with them. Sniffing out people's lockers for stuff. They think someone is selling drugs at school," Bobbi announced, while we were standing in the smoking area.

"They were?"

"Yeah, and they were at Tommy's locker. He is in the back office with the principal right now."

I looked at my watch, and it was almost noon. I tried to look into the office from where I was standing, but it was too far. I could not see. I could see through the windows in the front of the school that the K-9 police unit was parked in the front. She was right.

"Holly shit." I did not know what to say. "Is he busted for anything?"

"I don't know." She was looking around to see if she could see anything I had missed.

Just as the conversation had gotten started, over the PA system of the entire school I heard my name being called to go to the office. I closed my eyes for a second and took a deep breath. This could not be a positive situation for any of us. I did not know if Tommy was selling drugs at school or not but I hoped for his sake he had not.

"Come in and sit down," the vice principal directed me, as he pointed at the empty chair in front of his desk. He was dressed in a dark-gray suit with white running shoes on. We called him God when we saw him walk around the school because we thought that is who he thought he was. Just like God, the vice principal had the power to change life as you knew it. I felt like my fate was in his hands. I was scared for me and for Tommy.

"We've got Tommy in the next room. We think he has been selling pills around here. They are in the shape of pink hearts. Have you seen them?" He stared directly into my eyes from the standing position as I sat in the chair directly beneath him. He had authority over me, and we both knew it. Even the seating arrangement I was in told me I was the lesser one in this conversation.

I had seen them. In fact I had taken some a couple of times. I did not get them from Tommy—well, I was supposing now not directly.

"No," I lied. I stared right back into his eyes. "I have not seen them around."

"I know you and Tommy are together all the time, and I know you know. He is in the other office, and we have already asked him questions. I told him to wait a bit, and I'm letting him sit there a while to think about it. He will never know you are here, and he will never know you have told me anything. What do you know?"

I smiled at him for a second. "He is in there right now?"

"Yes." I wondered what Tommy must have been thinking. I knew he would not tell them anything. I wondered if they found anything in his locker. I also knew they would not tell me if they did. I did not even know he was selling pills.

"Nothing." I shook my head at God and then stood up and walked out.

He did not have anything on me. He could not keep me here any longer. I was not about to tell him anything about Tommy. In fact, I did not know anything about what he was talking about anyway. I was not surprised to hear it but Tommy would have never passed on any pills to me or put in my any situation that would cause me harm. He wanted to keep me out of trouble not get me into it. Tommy knew I could find all the trouble I wanted without his help, and he knew that my getting in trouble would certainly be the end of my parents' letting me even accept his phone calls every day, let alone date him. Neither one of us wanted that.

I went back out into the smoke pit and told Bobbi what happened. I wondered if they had taken Tommy out the front doors yet in front of everybody else in the school that was watching. If they cuffed him he would want to walk right out front so everyone could see. He would get a kick out of that. Everyone would talk about that for months around here.

The cop car was out front all afternoon, and I imagined Tommy was with them. They searched his locker and threw all his books in the hallway. They were looking for drugs or anything else he was not supposed to have in there.

They did not find anything. If he had anything to hide it was not in there. Tommy just smiled at them as he strode off as if nothing had happened.

It seemed after that incident things got crazy at school. I am not sure what happened inside of me but my old character defects of getting into trouble hit me hard. I wanted to be a good student but sometimes things just happen that I had to respond to. Before I knew it there I was, right back to the person inside myself that I was trying to change the most despite my best efforts.

He held my hand and ran with me through the school the night after I got into a fistfight with a girl after classes. I was not sure what exactly the fight was about, something that had started in grade-nine math classes. It might have been because someone hit her with a hot penny. We would heat them up with lighters and throw them at each other and she thought it was I. For whatever reason I could not back down from that; after all, I had the same point to prove as anyone else. I would not be pushed around no matter what.

"Don't answer the phone when they call you after school; you will get suspended," he told me just before we got on the bus.

He was right; I was suspended for four days for fighting. I was grounded and in big trouble with my mom and dad.

Tommy rode the bus to school then skipped homeroom so he could walk to my house for the day. I did not live that far from the school. We would spend the day together watching TV, playing cards, or he would watch me do some homework. Sometimes we spent part of the day kissing for a while but nothing ever happed that serious between us then. The nicest thing about Tommy was that he never pressured me to have sex with him. Although being alone together all day at my house seemed like it may have been a good idea it just did not seem right to me. Besides my sister was home in the day time so we couldn't.

He would walk back to school just in time to catch the bus again to go home. They caught him the last day I was suspended and gave him a week's worth of detentions. He said it was worth it because he had like spending time together. I wondered why they waited until the last day to catch him. They should have known where he might have been going, since God, the vice principal never claimed to miss anything that went on at school.

The school called his mom but he said she did not care. Because of his detentions he could not walk me to the bus for a week, so I would stand and watch him through the window while he wrote me love letters while I waited for him to come and kiss me goodbye.

The next time I was suspended from school was later in the spring for smoking pot in the pit. The vice principal came out when Kayla, her friend, and I had just finished three joints.

"You are officially busted," he said, then he escorted us into the office and put us in different rooms. I already knew what that was all about since I had been there before. I tried to lie about it, but he was watching us through the library window.

After that, I tried to forge a note to skip school on a long weekend in May to party with my friends and got caught at that, too. I had to write an essay on honesty and have my mom sign it before I could go back to school. I thought that was a joke, but I wrote it anyway, and she signed it.

That was the last straw my parents could handle, and they said they were going to send me away to live in a group home or something. I did not believe them because they had told me that before when I had been dating Jesse. They tried to keep me from seeing him, but the funny thing was, he was the one telling me I had better smarten up because he did not want me to have to leave, so I started minding the rules for a while so I could remain Jesse's girlfriend.

I had always wondered where "away" was. I imagined it was in the city some place, far away so my friends could not find me. I could not understand how sending me to live some place with strangers would be better than dealing with me at home, but I guess they thought I was so bad they did not love me or want me around any more. I wondered why they thought that would be a positive way to keep me out of trouble, but the threat of it always made me behave, not out of love or respect but because Jesse and my other friends were all I had.

That is when Jesse and I became friends. He tried very hard to encourage me to stay out of trouble. He said he wanted me around and that he liked me. I think he really did a lot more than I could understand. He was real upset at us girls when we broke into the town hall and sprayed the fire extinguisher all over because then he had no place to sleep when he hitchhiked to see me. I did not even know he stayed there until it was too late to be sorry for what I had done. They had already changed the locks.

I was too young to understand that kind of love then, but I think I am getting a taste of what that must have felt like. To do anything you possibly could to be with someone. He would sneak into my back yard and talk to me sometimes when I was grounded when nobody else could even call me on the phone, but he would come. We spent hours and hours together in the back our yard by the fire pit watching the wood burn. We mostly talked and listened to the radio. Occasionally we would do some kissing and heavy petting. He gave me his leather jacket to wear. I had to hide it in the closet so my parents or sister would not see it, and I would wear it to school to show off to the other girls. Wearing someone else's coat was a symbolic sacrifice that someone had given you to show to everyone else you were not available to date. It was kind of like a promise ring or something significant.

He was the first boy I had intercourse with. He told me immediately after sex he loved me and asked me if I loved him back. I did not say a word but just looked in his big brown eyes. He said I probably did not because I did not know what love was and that I had not seen it before. He was right. My parents did not like him much, but if they had known he was the one keeping me sane then maybe they would have, but I could not talk to them about it because they would have thought I was too young.

Of course my parents tried to keep me from Tommy, too, because they thought he was a bad influence on me. I saw him at school every day anyway that did not work so well for them. He could not call any more, and I did not like that because I could not hear him say, "Good night," every day before I had sweet dreams of him.

The pressure got so difficult that we thought it best to break up for a while. Even though we were not going steady anymore he would still walk me to class. I would watch for him in the halls but he skipped school a lot. There were rumors that his friend may go to jail for selling drugs, but I did not know for sure because that was just gossip. I had not talked to him for a while.

I missed Tommy terribly, but my friends kept me occupied. It seemed breaking up was most likely for the best. I was going to try to be good again for a change because I had kept out of trouble for a while. I did not know for how long.

The Sleep Over

"Who is driving around on the dirt bike?" Lizzie asked, as we walked home after hanging out with the gang.

"I don't know," Abby said, as she looked for the bike behind us. "Maybe it is Jesse and Jackson," she suggested

I kept walking and was not paying attention to what they were saying. This was a rural town and we all rode dirt bikes around town when we were not supposed to. The cops did not bother us about it much, so we did it just because we could.

"Are we sleeping out tonight?" I asked them both.

"Yeah."

"Sure," they both responded.

"Meet me." I meant in the camper that my parents had in our laneway, but they already knew that, we had slept out in it so many times before. It was a habitual thing. It was summer holidays now so we were out of sync with any kind of regularly maintained routine. If they would have said no I would have slept out in it alone anyway. That seemed much better of a choice than staying in the house.

It was soon after that, they both went home to get their belongings I found out who was on the bike. It was Tommy and his friend Jeff, who, I had not met before, but had heard Tommy talk enough about.

"Hey," Tommy yelled from the back of the bike, "what's up?"

He had no helmet on, so I could easily see who he was. Jeff did because he was on the front of the bike, and the cops would see him first if they had spotted them. They would not be able to recognize him so easily if they had to outrun the police on the bike, driving through the fields.

They pulled in the laneway, and Jeff shut the bike off.

I looked bizarrely at them both before answering, "Not much. You?"

I was shocked to see Tommy. I had not seen him in quite a long time. I wondered what he was doing here now with his friend. Surely he must have someplace better to go than come and see me. We had not dated in a while, and I had thought he had forgotten all about it. I did not think I was important to him anymore.

"Just out for a ride," Tommy said, as he swung his leg off the back of the bike and sauntered toward me.

Tommy pulled out a bottle of some kind of alcohol and handed it to me. I wanted to stay out of trouble, but I knew this was not going to be easy. I could not refuse this offer because it had so much potential to become something fun. Adam had handed Eve the apple and again, and she could not resist.

I had not seen Tommy in a few months, and I missed him. As soon as he stood close to me I knew just how much. I missed his voice, his smile, his smell, his eyes, his kisses, his kindness, I missed everything about him.

I took the bottle and took a big drink, then handed it to Abby, who had just arrived. She looked at me, and I nodded. She tipped it up and swallowed as much as she could and then handed it back to Tommy. He hung on it for a while we talked and then passed it back to me. I drank again.

"You guys have been drinking?" Lizzie asked, as soon as she walked toward us. She could smell it that far away. Lizzie did not engage in drinking because she said she did not like the way it made her feel. She never thought it was a good idea that we did either but tolerated us when we did.

Lizzie also disliked Tommy almost as much as she did Jesse and usually had no problems telling either one of them how she felt. She was the typical best friend that hated my boyfriends because she thought they were not good enough for me. That was a good thing about Lizzie; she could see trouble coming a mile away where I sometimes could not.

We all piled in the camper and drank the rest of the bottle. It was about half empty when the boys got here so it did not take long to finish. We were all feeling pretty good by that time anyway, but Lizzie seemed annoyed with us as usual when we got drunk.

We were carefree and restless on this occasion until the knock came to the door. It flung open without hesitation, and to all of our amazement there stood Jesse.

"What is going on?" he asked just as he noticed Tommy and me sitting on the bed. He looked at the trio on the other beds, stood at the door for a moment to assess the situation, and then took his shoes off. You could have cut the tension with a knife.

69

Jesse looked directly at me and said, "I need a place to sleep tonight. Can I stay here?" Then he lay down on the bed beside me. It appeared he had already made up his mind and would not take no for an answer.

I wanted to die. *God, please make this go away,* I prayed in my head. I was a victim of my past actions that were now catching up to me instantly. I felt like my name was next on the docket to be hung. I would have felt better if I could have been.

I did not say anything to Jesse. I knew it was too late; all I could do now was wonder what was about to happen next. With Tommy and Jeff under the influence, I was not sure what they would do.

Tommy leaned over and whispered in my ear, "I am staying, too."

I looked at him and smiled. Was this some kind of joke God was playing on me to prove he has a sense of humour? I already knew that but I thought for sure it was. I did not know much but I did know that this was about to get very interesting. I wondered how the male pecking order would turn out this time now that Tommy and I had some kind of history together, too.

Abby, Lizzie, and Jeff were arguing about sleeping arrangements between the two beds on the other side. With our added guest this drastically changed what they had previously been planning in a hurry. I knew one thing for sure; I was not about to make the same mistake I had at the party. I did not want to play that game all over again. I had gotten used to spending some time with Tommy last year at school, and I was not about to let anything get in the way of that again. I had messed up at school and lost him again for a while, but he was here now, and that must mean something good was going to happen. Or at least I wanted it to.

Jeff crawled in the top bunk with Lizzie, but she made it very clear she was not interested in playing any games with him. He was too drunk to be any kind of trouble to her, all he wanted to do was pass out.

Abby convinced Jesse it would be a good idea that he shared the bottom bed with her. She was the little sister of his best friend so she felt no danger in that either. But we all knew he was not here for her.

That left Tommy and me on the other side in the big bed together. We had not seen each other since school was out and we had missed each other terribly. He had not looked down my shirt in a long time but I imagined he had much more than that in mind. It was not long after the lights went out and everything was dark I found that out exactly what he was thinking. I think he also had a point to prove to Jesse but that was just an added bonus.

Tommy started kissing me slowly and softly while he ran his fingers through my hair and touched my face. He opened my mouth with his tongue and slid it inside. His tongue was soft and tasted like cigarette smoke and the bottle. I did not care, since mine did too.

He swirled his tongue around inside my mouth. Slowly at first, then more vigorously, I drew my head back and began to lick his lips and touch them with my fingertips. He began sucking on them a bit, too.

With my other hand I pulled his shirt from his jeans and touched his skin. His chest was hot and sweaty under the thick blankets. It was getting hot. He pressed his body closer as I touched his neck under his shirt. I lifted it up and began to nibble and run my tongue along his salty skin. Every now and then I would bite him a little.

I liked to tease him. He liked it too. I could tell by the way he was breathing. He was panting. I could tell from his reaction whatever I did would satisfy him greatly he would take a little gasp of air into his lungs. I wanted to make him feel as best I could. I wanted to make him glad he had come here to see me. I wanted to remind him that he had once said he loved me. After a while he seemed like wanted that too.

It was not long until he was pushing the blankets that lay between us onto the floor so he could position himself directly on top of me. His weight was heavy yet I welcomed the warmth of his body with open arms and a fragile heart. He pushed my legs apart with his knees, and I had no chance to say no. I would not have anyway, and I was willing to give him whatever was not too shy to ask for.

I could feel his muscles flex as he supported his own weight on his upper arms above my body. He hovered over me being the most dominate species. At that point he had all the control to influence my body and emotions in whatever way he wanted. I was submissive to however he was going to behave. The instinctual animal rituals came flooding back from the time humans were created by God to procreate, felt like I was being led by the matriarch of time. I wanted him to plant his seed inside me, but only for pleasure.

Once again, Adam had given the apple to Eve and she had accepted it with pleasure. We were both failing at the game of temptation and we liked it.

I ran my hands over his chest, back, and buttocks and welcomed him closer. I wanted him to make love to me then. I did not want to wait a second longer. I had hidden my desire to love him but now I did not want to hide my emotions any longer. I wanted to let him know just how much I wanted him, but it seemed he already knew. We were teenagers in heat and had been teasing each other for a long time now. We did not want to wait any longer to reach heaven together.

The fact that we had an audience had escaped us for a while. It appeared as if someone on the other side had ESP or perfect timing. Just then we could hear someone on the other side roll over and make a noise to motion they were still awake and aware of what was going happening in our bed. I was not sure if it was Jesse or they all were conscious. I did not care this was the first time I had ever been alone with Tommy, well almost alone, and was not sure when it would happen again. Tommy, on the other hand, got the message and rotated himself beside me before he kissed me one last time before I drifted off to marvel in delight.

A New Date

As soon as I started school again in October I instantly looked for Tommy. We had not been in contact since our almost romantic night together, but I suppose it was just not our time to connect. If I had learned one thing from this profound connection with Tommy it was to be patient and wait no matter how long it took because sooner or later things always seemed to work out for us.

It did not take long for us to find each other again because our lockers were in the same place as last year; it was a habitual thing.

Tommy was in grade twelve now, and I was in grade ten. I did not know what to expect this year at school. I knew almost everyone around so it was much easier to start than it had been last year. I knew what all my classes were going to be like but I wondered about the social part of it all. It would be the last year for Tommy, Jamie, and Kayla. I knew that after this year things would be much different. I just did not know how so I thought I had better make the best of it because I knew they would.

Tommy and I were very good friends and talked on the phone every night after school. It seemed we both were interested in other things and our romantic flames had dwindled into barely a flicker. I still wanted to be his girlfriend but the timing did not ever seem right. We were both busy with other things and he skipped school a lot.

Kayla drove to school almost every day so I did not ride the bus much. I hardly saw Tommy at all. When I did see him he would say hi, but not much more. He stood in the smoking area with Jamie and their other friends but not usually with us. It seemed this year we were not going to be much of a couple.

I was still on the kick of trying to stay out of trouble at school. Last year was hard for me, and I knew I had made several mistakes. I was ready to focus on my grades and reminded myself I was too young for lustful desires. I had seen enough of the Y-chromosomes for a while. I did not have a steady boyfriend and was not looking for one either. If an opportunity came up I would assess the situation when it came but for now I did not think about it much. There were a few "steadies" around school but not many, as the year was still early.

Tommy and I had art class together. I think he took it just so he could see me every day, or at least I hoped he did. We did not sit together this year though. He sat at the table by the door with Luke and Terry. I sat at the other end of the table with Lizzie and Michelle.

Lizzie had a crush on Luke, so did every other girl in the school. He was new to our high school and he was attractive. I knew that I would never date him because he was a friend of Tommy's now so that eliminated all my chances. The boys all like to look at Michelle because she had a very mature body for being in grade ten. The boys did not care what grade she was in because they all had raging hormones. I was not quite as physically well blessed.

I would say Hi to Tommy when I walked by him in class. Sometimes I would write him notes and put them in front of him when I walked by. Luke always made a big deal about it and asked me where his was. I think he was just envious of Tommy. Although all the girls wanted to date him, nobody was. It was convenient for him to have Tommy as a friend and the other girls as mine. He would bring notes to our end of the table for Tommy but I think it was just to get close to the other girls. He would talk me for a while about Tommy but did not say much to the other girls until he got to know us better. Tommy was a good excuse for him. I knew that because before he was around Tommy would just give me the notes himself. We had nothing to hide because our chasing game was over long ago. Once we had been dating but we just did not know how to keep it together. We were young and our relationship proved that.

Tommy did not date anyone else, and neither did I for the first half of the year. We just talked and flirted. We talked on the phone often after school but that was about it. We would send each other flowers on Valentines Day and slow dance if we both went to the dances. It seemed we always found ourselves together sometime before the last dance of the night. I think that was the only reason why I would go to the dances anymore, to get drunk with my girlfriends and dance with Tommy a few times.

"Are you going to the prom?" Kayla asked me. I knew she was because she was finally graduating, and that meant Tommy and Jaime were, too. I was not sure who would be her date but I knew someone would ask her. She was

TOMMY'S FOREVER

focusing most of her attention on the other grade twelve and thirteen students anyway. I doubted much if she cared I went as I was only in grade ten.

"I am not sure."

"Tommy hasn't asked you yet?" It appeared that even though we were not officially a couple everyone assumed I would be his date to the prom.

"No." I sighed, "I asked him the other day if he was going, and he said that he did not want to get all dressed up and go sit with a bunch of stiffs from around here." I believed him; that was not his style.

"Is Jamie going?" I asked Kayla.

"I don't know."

I was not sure what a prom was all about. I thought it was a dance reserved for those students in their last year, but Kayla said anyone could go. I was not sure why you would want too but some of the other girls did. I knew you had to get all dressed up, Tommy told me that, so I guess it was a chance to show off if you wanted too. I was not sure if I wanted to go or not. I suppose I would if Tommy had asked me but I thought it was not something I wanted to attend alone. Since was getting closer to prom time and he had not asked I doubted I would go.

"I know someone who wants to take you to the prom," Lizzie told me.

I knew it could not be Tommy; he would not have told her that. Lizzie and Tommy did not really like each other much. She sided with my parents and thought he was bad news. She likes cleaner cut, more well-mannered boys than he was, anyway.

"Who?"

"Jim."

"How do you know that?"

"I sit with his friend in history class. He told me."

"Oh." I smiled, and wondered how true the rumors through the grapevine were. I did not believe her, and I barely knew who he was. I knew Tommy knew him from riding the bus, and we had said hi to him a few times, but that was all I knew.

"Would you go with him?"

"I don't know."

"Why not? Oh, are you waiting for Tommy to ask you? He won't. Why do you even waste your time waiting for him?" she said in a very sarcastic voice. I knew she thought that was a bad idea. She also knew he had not asked me and how much I wish he would have. If this was the last school dance he was going to be at, I did want to be with him at it.

"No," I lied "I am not waiting for that."

"Then go with Jim. He is cool; you would like him."

I wondered about that statement. I knew Jim's friend about as well as I knew Jim. They way I saw it was that I really was not that interested in going with anyone to the prom.

"Can I give his friend your number to give to Jim?"

"What?" I was lost thinking about the plan they may have already worked out.

"Can I give him your number?"

"Sure," but I doubted he would call.

The rumour must have gotten out quickly that I was entertaining the idea of being invited to the prom with Jim. It seemed to me the rumour was a bit different from the conversation I had had with my friend. It seemed to everyone that I had already accepted to go out with Jim, but he had not even asked or even called yet. I wondered if he would. It was later that day I found myself standing next to him in the smoke pit chatting it up. One thing was true; he was an okay person to talk to.

I only thought that until Tommy came out and stood with his friends. I saw the surprised and rather dirty look he gave me from between the crowds of people already out there. I was upset at him for not asking me to go with him in the first place and now I was even more upset at him for making me feel awkward for talking to someone else. How long did he want me to wait for him before I could talk to another boy? This seemed to be an issue that runs far deeper than what was really happening out there. I knew that if Tommy thought I was interested in Jim he would never ask.

Tommy did not stay outside long to smoke. I doubted that he really even wanted a smoke. I think he had just been walking down the hall and saw us outside and intentionally came out to see what was going on. That was something he would do, but from where he was standing he could not hear any of the conversation. That was a good thing; then he could wonder about it all day. The other part of me wonders if he even cares and thought maybe he had something better to do.

Jim found his way to my locker, and he was now waiting for me and leaving me notes and stuff. We were not officially dating but it was close to it. Everyone thought we were in a real big hurry and he sure was acting like it. I think it was the male pecking order stuff that I did not understand but I was having fun with him. The more I got to know him the more I liked him. He was always making Bobbi and me laugh. He was rather silly most of the time but he was very different than Tommy was.

"Are you going to the prom next week?" he finally asked.

"No."

"Why not?"

"I do not have a date."

"Will you come with me?"

"Ah, I don't know. Do you really want to go?"

"Yeah, it will be fun. We can get drunk and crash the prom party after. Come on, let's go, just for kicks."

"Sure." I knew that by accepting his invitation to the prom, although he did not officially ask, this would make me his girlfriend, or at least everyone would assume I was. I had nothing else going on at the time so I might as well see what would happen.

"Are you going to wear a dress?" He laughed as he pulled at the concert shirt I was wearing.

"If you are going to wear a suit," I smiled at him. "Us dressed up like that for sure would be the sight of the year."

I knew Tommy would be upset, but he had not asked me to go with him. I was not sure how I was going to tell him over the phone about what had just taken place. Maybe I would not tell him at all. I would just let him find out for himself. I am sure he will find out because this kind of official news travels fast.

I was right; it was that night on the phone when Tommy called. He had already heard the news, so it did not take him long to ask me about it either. "Are you going to the prom with Jim?"

"Yeah, I guess."

"Are you going steady with him now?"

"I don't know."

"You should; he is a real nice guy, and you will like him."

"Yeah, he is okay."

"I thought you were already going out with him. He is with you all the time."

"Yeah, we hang out a lot at school, but I had not thought you had noticed. Lizzie thought it was a good idea, so I thought I would give it a try."

"Lizzie? Who would want to go out with her?"

"Don't say that. A lot of guys would date her."

"I don't know why. She is a snob."

"Well, so are you sometimes."

"When?"

"Sometimes."

"When?"

"Sometimes."

"Give me an example?"

"Like, I don't know—when you won't talk to me anymore in art class."

"Because you won't let me look down your shirt anymore."

"We'll because you won't walk me to class anymore."

"If I talk to you tomorrow can I get a peek?"

"Maybe."

"Will you wear that pink shirt for me? I like that one."

"Only because when I bend over you can see my bra."

"No, because I like pink."

"Yeah, right."

"Yeah. I do."

"I got to go. It is getting late."

"Okay, see ya in the morning?"

"Night."

"Night, Hey."

"What?"

"The pink one."

"Nite, Tommy."

"Nite."

Tommy was waiting for me as soon as I walked in the smoke pit. He was always there first because his bus got to school earlier than Kayla drove. We did not like to be there much before classes started. We were much too cool to hang around school any more than we had to.

I walked right over to Tommy and hoped that he really was waiting for me. At least I thought he was because he was standing alone.

"Where is everyone?" I asked as I looked around to find his group.

"They went in already."

"Oh." I pulled a smoke out of my bag.

"You wore it." He smiled. "Now bend over."

"No." I slapped him on the back in a friendly kind of way. We both knew I would eventually while we stood out there just so he could get a cheap thrill.

Tommy and I were inseparable for the next few days. That was different for us this year. We were professionals now at the on-again-off-again roller coaster that our relationship had become. School was almost out, and I wondered what was going to happen next. I knew I would not see him every day, and I was going to miss that. I had imagined that he would move away to live with his sister to go to work or something. I did not think he would stay long living with his parents. His grandmother had died a while ago, and he missed her terribly. I think his grandmother did a lot of mediation between him and his parents. I do not think they get along very well, but he did not talk about it.

"There's Emmy and Tommy," Jim noted as he passed us in the hallway. Tommy smiled at him. "Hi."

I said nothing as I looked toward the floor. Tommy and I were talking the long way around to the bus today. It was strange to be walking with Tommy when I was sort of dating Jim. It was even stranger to hear him say our names together like that. As Jim said that, all of the sudden I missed being Tommy's girlfriend.

"How was the prom?" Tommy asked.

"Okay," my comment was brief.

"Are you still going out with him?"

"Yeah, I think so," but I knew for sure I was.

"Do you really like him?"

"You were right; he is okay. Are you okay?" I asked him. "You look different today."

"I have not been feeling well."

"Oh, what is the matter?"

"My arm has been really sore, and I don't know why."

"Did you bang it on something?"

"Not that I can remember. I have all these bruises all over me, too."

"Let me see."

He pulled up his sleeve and showed me a couple bruises.

"That is weird. It looks like it hurts. You look tired."

"I am. I have not been sleeping well. It has been so hot in our house I wake up with sweats and stuff."

"Do you have the window open?"

"Yeah, but it does not help. I even sleep with no shirt on."

"Well, I would like to see that." I smiled at him; he knew what I meant.

"I think I am going to get Mom to make me a doctor's appointment tomorrow."

"Call me and let me know what happens."

We were almost at the bus when he turned and looked me directly in the eye. I wanted him to kiss me. I stood, stuck in a moment of silence, waiting for him to say something. He stood there also.

"See you tomorrow." I smiled and walked away as I carried my disappointment in my heart. I hoped he would call me later tonight so I could tell him what I had wanted.

The Diagnosis

It was early spring when I was walking down the hallway of the high school at about three-thirty p.m. after classes had ended. I was walking to the bus alone thinking about Tommy because I had not seen him in a few days. The last time I talked to him was the other day at school when he had been making complaints that his arm hurt and he was feeling real tired lately. He said he had not done anything that he can remember that would make his arm hurt. He was going to go see the doctor about it. I missed him around the school since he had been off for a few days now. I had not talked to him on the phone. I thought he must have the flu or something.

Just as I was about to go downstairs a girl stopped me in the hallway. I had vaguely known her from some of my classes but she was not a friend of mine. She rode the same bus as Tommy and lived in the same small town as he did, so she knew him well.

"Have you heard about Tommy?" she asked, as we passed on the stairs.

"No, why? Is he sick?" I inquired.

"He went to the doctor the other day," she continued.

"I know that."

"He is in the hospital. He has leukemia," she explained.

"Oh." I was not sure what leukemia was, but I knew that could not be good news if he was in the hospital so quickly. I knew that anyone that went directly to the hospital was seriously ill. I wondered why he had not called and told me of any of this. Instantly my heart felt very sad. Standing there in the stairwell of the school hallway I had no idea what to expect out of all this and what the future would hold. After all, I was just a child of fifteen.

When I got home from school I asked my mother what leukemia was. She said it was cancer of the blood. That was all that she knew. That was not enough information for me. I wanted and needed to know more. I told her of

Tommy and she advised me that he having leukemia was really bad news but I did not know what that meant.

I dialed his number and waited for someone to pick up the phone. I wanted it to be him. I wanted the information that I had gotten a few short hours ago to be a rumour. The kind of rumour that was funny after you knew it was not true. The kind of rumour that you could make fun of the people that gossiped about it and talk about how stupid people were and how boring their lives were for making up things like that about other people.

I waited as the phone kept ringing and ringing on the other end. No one picked up the phone. Since it was still early in the day maybe everyone had something else to do. Maybe they were out grocery shopping or had gone to get gas in the car. Maybe they were out for dinner at someone's place. Maybe they were at the hospital but I doubted that.

I did not eat supper that night. The only thing on my mind was finding out the truth. I talked to my friends about what I had heard. They could not confirm anything. Nobody I knew had heard the news so they did not have any information. None of my friends was really his friends except through me. Maybe nobody at the school had heard the news either. I sat outside on the steps of the local church and smoked cigarette after cigarette wondering if I would ever see him again. I still did not know what it all meant but cancer of any kind of anyone you knew was the scariest thing anyone could have said. For cancer never had a cure and always eventually meant death.

I walked slowly home and again dialed his number. The phone rang, one time, two times, three times, four times, five times. I stood on the other end until I lost count. I do not know how long I waited on the other end.

"Hello," his mother answered the phone. She sounded tired.

"Is Tommy there?" I begged.

"No, he is in the hospital." She confirmed what I had already heard at school.

"Is he okay?" again I begged.

"They think he has leukemia," she informed me. "You can call him if you want. Here is the number."

"Thank you." I hung up the phone.

He has leukemia echoed in my head repeatedly as the tears welled up behind my eyes and the lump in my throat became so big it hurt. Leukemia? Is that what she said? It must be a mistake. I stared at the phone number on the paper. I was afraid to call. I did not want to hear him say it. I did not want him to tell me it again. I did not want to hear the truth.

Please, God, do not let this be true. Please let this be some kind of mistake.
I prayed out loud, for this was the first time in my life I meant what I prayed for. I did not want anything for myself. I swore I would never again ask for foolish things and waste God's time for frivolous things. I just wanted Tommy to be okay.

I slowly dialed the number to the hospital in the city. The city was a long way from the small towns in which we lived. I could not recall a time I had even been there. Maybe I had gone shopping with my Mom or to visit my aunt but I could not remember. I knew it was a very long way away, and I missed Tommy for being there already.

"Could I be connected to Tommy's room please?" I asked the receptionist that answered the phone.

"One moment, please." The voice sounded pleasant.

This had to be the longest wait I had experienced before. The tears fell from my eyes as I sat on my bedroom floor with the phone held tightly to my ear. I did not want to talk to him today. I was afraid for him. I did not know what to say but I did not want him to know I was crying. I wanted to be strong for him and pretend that I knew nothing about why he was there. I wanted it all to be a mistake. I wanted the girl to come back on the phone and tell me he was not there. I wanted his mom to be wrong too.

The phone began to ring again until I heard him say hello. I said nothing. "Hello," he said again.

"Hi, it's me. I called your Mom, and she said that you were there. How are you feeling?"

"How was your day at school?" he asked, avoiding my question.

"Okay, you know; it was just school. I wondered why you had not been around in a few days. How long have you been there?"

"A couple days." His answer was short.

"What are you there for? How are you feeling?" I asked again.

"They are running some tests on me. They say I'll be here a few more days, then I can come home." His voice sounded shaky. I had never heard that before.

"Oh. Can I come and see you?" I begged again.

"I won't be here long, so you won't have to." He tried to assure me things would be fine. I could tell they were not.

The tears fell down my cheeks like a soft rain in July. Again, I wondered if I would ever see him again. This was the start of something I could not understand. Maybe he was just there for tests but they must be serious ones otherwise they would have just let him stay at home. I knew nothing of anyone being sick and in the hospital. Since he was only eighteen, how sick could he be? His body was still young and healthy, wasn't it?

I did not sleep much that night thinking about Tommy. I did not know what it all meant. I just knew this was something bigger than both of us. I prayed to God with all my heart that everything would be okay. I prayed that Tommy's heart would be safe and that he was not as afraid as I was about what was happening. I wanted it all to go away. I wanted to see him at school tomorrow. School was almost out for the year and he needed to be there. I needed him to be.

I got to school in the morning and skipped first class. I went straight to the library and got all the medical books I could find. I looked up the word leukemia. It was a disorder of the white blood cells in your body. Something about the bone marrow making the cells incorrectly and then the cells cannot fight of infection. I wondered what that had to do with cancer. I looked up white blood cells in another book. It confirmed that they do fight off infections and were produced in the bone marrow. I looked up treatment and it stated, "chemotherapy and radiation," and listed hair loss, weight loss, and nausea, as some of the side effects. There were pictures of sores inside someone's mouth and throat as another side effect. I still did not understand. I sat at the table with my head in several books trying to figure it all out.

"Hey." I heard the voice of the boy who was calling me his girlfriend for the time being.

I looked up from my books that were scattered all over the table and did not say a thing. I could not. I closed my eyes and shook my head. I knew I must have been sitting inside of a dream. I was waiting to wake up.

"I was surprised to see you here in the library. I did not see you this morning, so I did not think you were at school today. What are you doing in here anyway?" he asked. Then he picked up a book I had opened to the pages that described leukemia. He directly looked me in the eyes and said, "Oh, you have heard."

I still could not say anything. I did not know what to say. I was lost. I sat there like a kitten someone had just taken from its mother with nothing left to hang on to for comfort. Again, the tears fell softly down my cheeks, and I tried to blink them away as I stood there in front of him. I nodded and handed him another book, the one with the pictures of the sores. He said nothing as he looked at the pictures until he closed it and put the book back out on the desk.

He took me by the hand and led me out of the library into a private area of the smoking pit. He put his arm around me as I sat on the step and cried. He said nothing as he listened to my heart breaking as I rested my head on his shoulder.

I was lying on my bed staring at the ceiling and listening to the phone ring. I did not attempt to get up and answer it. I did not care who it was. It rang and rang and rang and rang. I finally rolled over and picked it up.

"Hello?" This had better be important. I did not want to be bothered by anyone.

"What took you so long?" It was Tommy.

"Oh, I was sleeping," I fibbed.

"Want me to let you go, then?" he politely asked.

"No, I want to talk to you. How is the testing going? Did they say when you could come home?"

"No, they said I would be here at least for the weekend; that is about all they have said."

He had not yet told me they had diagnosed leukemia. Maybe he was hoping they would find something other than that which was making him sick. Maybe be hoped the same as I did, that it was not true. I did not know how he was feeling because he did not talk about it, and I did not ask.

We talked on the phone for a long time. We talked about school and other teenager stuff just as we had so many times before. If I did not know better he could be at home lying on his bed listening to the stereo. All seemed well, except for the stabbing pain in my heart as I tried to hold back the tears. He asked about my boyfriend. "How's Jim?"

"Good, I guess."

"What do you mean, 'good'? Are you still steady with him?"

"I am not sure; probably not anymore," I lied.

"Why, did you do something wrong?"

"What makes you think I did something wrong?"

"Just a guess."

"Well, it was a bad one."

"Then why do you think you will not be dating long?"

"I dunno. I guess I am just not that interested anymore."

"What are you interested in then?"

"I don't know, nothing I guess," I lied again. "Are you?"

"Am I what?"

"Interested?"

"In what?"

"In anyone?" I poked.

"I dunno; maybe."

"Who?"

"I can't tell you."

"Why?" I probed again.

"Because."

"That is not fair. I would tell you."

"No, you would not."

"Yes, I would. You know I would."

He paused but said nothing.

I knew Jim and I would not last long as boyfriend and girlfriend. I did not have those feelings inside for him. Tommy knew it. Jim was younger than I was and could not provide the intellectual stimulation I got from talking to Tommy every day on the phone or at school. Jim was fun to be around but the novelty of that wore off quickly and everyone knew it. We were friends that were playing the relationship game.

"Jim says they are coming to the city this weekend to visit his aunt with his sister. They said they would bring me to see you if that would be okay. I mean, you are still going to be there, aren't you?" I was hoping he would say no.

"Yeah. That would be okay. I would like to see you."

We talked some more about other things and then we had to end the conversation. It was long distance and cost money to call. Neither of our parents had much money so we had to make each call short. Not like the ones we used to have for hours and hours on the phone when he was at home. I wanted him to come home soon.

"It is you," he finally said.

"What is?"

"That I am interested in."

"Oh."

"Are you interested in me?" he finally asked.

"No."

"Why?" he got upset.

"Because, I love you." I told him on the phone. "I am beyond interested."

"I love you, too," he said back to me. This seemed like the first time I could really feel it in my heart that I loved him. I had said it several times before, but I did not know what it truly meant until now.

I understood that love meant I wanted everything to be well for him and that I would do anything I could to help him through this. I missed him, and I wanted him to come home. I wanted more for him that I did anything for myself. I remembered all the times I prayed for him to call me, to see him at school, to walk to home room with me or walk me to the bus. I remembered the first time we danced together and the first time he kissed me. I thought about all the times he had kissed me since and how much I wished I could have that right now. I wanted to reach through the phone and comfort him. *Please, God, let him get well soon.*

Jim let go of my hand before we walked into the pale blue hospital room. I could see Tommy lying on the bed facing the other direction. My heart hit the floor. It was quiet as he lay there alone. I wondered if he was sleeping.

Tommy rolled over as soon as I walked up to the bed. He tried to smile but I could see he was forcing it through. I tried to smile back but it was hard because I wanted to cry. He looked like he had every other day for the last two years that I had known him. He looked like he did the night of the dance that I met him. He was wearing a tee shirt and jeans and appeared as if he might be going somewhere. He did not look sick and he certainly did not look like he was going to die.

"Hi." He smiled again, then sat up on the bed.

"How's the food here?" Jim teased. "Better than the high school café?" The conversation began between friends just as it had if we were at school or any other place we might find each other together. I thought it would be weirder than this. I was glad I was not alone.

As we were talking the doctor came in. He was wearing a white jacket, had a stethoscope around his neck, and was carrying some papers. He picked up the clipboard that was attached to the bottom of the bed and looked at it for a few minutes. Jim and I were about to leave just as the doctor informed Tommy, "We have the results of your tests."

Tommy looked me in the eye and patted the bed as if to ask, "Will you stay?" I sat down on the chair beside him. The doctor waited for Jim to leave the room.

"We have found you have leukemia." He then began to explain to Tommy what I had already read in the books. I took Tommy by the hand and squeezed it softly. Tommy had tears in his eyes. This was certainly the worst news he could ever hear. This was the first time I had seen him this close to crying. His tuff exterior was all gone. I could see him for the eighteen-year-old, scared boy that he was.

"For the treatment we are going to give you is chemotherapy and radiation," he said. "This will make you very sick, and all your hair will fall out." The doctor was now talking about some other things that would happen, but I had to stop listening because it hurt so much in my heart. I closed my eyes while he was talking because I started to cry. He was not really saying those things about Tommy, was he? This was not true, was it? His voice was screaming in my head, "And you will get nauseated. You will have no immune system, and anything like a common cold could be a disaster for you." The doctor's voice became a whisper beneath my own thoughts.

"There is another treatment that you may be able to receive in a hospital called St. Anne's. It is quite a distance from here, but the specialist there can do a bone-marrow transplant. What happens there is you get a bone marrow donor, and they put it into your body and hope that it will take over, and you will grow the new and healthy cells. Before this is to happen we need to get your body into remission. You have to stay in remission for a few months before you will be accepted for a transplant. You have to be completely healthy before you go. We will set you up for that as soon as we can." The man in the white coat continued while we listened.

"We will do chemotherapy treatments here to rid your body of all the abnormal white blood cells in hopes that when yours grow back they will be normal, and then we can look at the transplant as another option. If it works we hope that is a permanent cure to this disease." He was talking to us about it like we already knew what he meant. Tommy and I just listened as he explained to us what was going on.

"We will start the treatments Monday," was the last thing he said, while he was writing something on the chart then he turned and walked out of the room.

I turned on the chair toward Tommy as he lay down to face the other direction. I was glad he did because I knew he was crying, and I did not want to see that. I had never seen him cry before today. I rested my hand on his shoulder, leaned over, and put my ear to his ear. His hair touched my ear as I laid my head on his. We stayed in the moment of silence for eternity not saying a word. There was nothing that could be said. We both closed our eyes, and I knew this time God had let me down. On second thought, even worse, God had let Tommy down. He did not save him. It felt like God had hand chosen Tommy to be sick right there in front of my own eyes. It was not fair.

"I love you," was all I knew how to say, so I did. He said nothing, but I knew he did, too.

The car ride back to the hospital the following day was long. I was on my way back to see Tommy. This time I was in the car with my mother. Her father was also in same hospital on another floor. My mother was chain smoking one cigarette after another. She had old country-and-western music playing on the radio and had been singing along with the melody. I was sure she did not know what to say to me and was covering up her own anxieties of seeing her father so sick, but I could only think of Tommy and what the doctor had told us yesterday.

Tommy had not officially met my mother yet. This was a very disappointing time to finally shake hands. She had talked to him on the telephone several times but it was only when he would call and ask for me. I knew she wouldn't like him, but I did not care if she did. Her thoughts and ideas were not my main priority any longer. I had much bigger things on my mind than making her happy. I was grateful she gave me a ride to the city so I could see Tommy again today. That was all I cared about.

The car stopped, and I opened the door immediately and jumped out. Mom stopped me because I had forgotten to tell her what room Tommy was in. I yelled out the room number from outside of the car while she parked and ran across the road into the hospital. I knew she would catch up with me after she saw Grandpa.

"Where are you taking those flowers?" the nurse asked me, as I walked down the pale, yellow hall. Everything was so quiet her voice rang out like a church bell on Sunday morning echoing through the hallway and into the waiting room.

"Ah," I stuttered, "they are for Tommy." I kept on walking.

I walked into the hospital room again where he was lying on the bed. I did not say a word because I thought he was asleep. I set the flowers down on the table beside his bed just as he rolled over.

"Hi," I smiled, "how are you feeling today?"

"Fine," he quietly replied.

I did not believe him this time. He looked pale and his skin was flush. The color in his lips had faded, and he looked like he had been suffering with a bad case of the flu. I pulled up a chair and sat beside his bed. I leaned through the elevated side rails and touched his arm. He was cold.

"Have you had any visitors today?" I was at a loss for words again. I did not know what to say.

"Not yet; they are coming up later this afternoon." His answer was only to the direct question and nothing more. He offered no more conversation than I was prepared to ask.

Just then the nurse from the hallway came in the room and picked up the two white carnations and the red rose which were still in the vase. "He cannot have these in here," she said frankly. "Would you like to take them back home?"

"What?" I asked.

"He cannot have these flowers in here." She paused. "They could cause an infection after he starts treatments tomorrow. Would you like to take them back home?"

I looked at Tommy in confusion, "No."

"We can set them at the nurse's station, and he can see them from there." She handed me the card that was attached. "He can have this." She took his flowers and left the room.

I handed him the card that had been signed, "Love Emily," and smiled, "Well, it seems this has to be good enough."

"Thanks," he said, as he looked at the card then laid it on the bed beside him. He said nothing else.

We sat in more silence. I finally stood up and looked out the window. I thought of anything I might say that was not ridiculous. I leaned against the widow seal and watched a bird eating the left-over sandwich that lay upon the top of the staff lunch table that was shaded by a big oak tree.

"Any squirrels around here?" I asked as I stared outside and began to look for anything as a conversation piece. I had seen what looked to be a babbling brook on the other side of the yard, yet I was not sure because I could not hear it. I could not hear anything except the air conditioner blowing air. The air did not even seem cold; it was room temperature.

"No."

I turned around to face him. He was still lying on the bed with a blank stare. I was not even sure what he was looking at. I began to rifle through some things that had been sitting on the window seat beside the night stand.

"Wanna play?" I asked as I held out a deck of cards toward him.

"No," he said.

I moved the ginger ale off the dinner table and swung it around to face him in the bed. I sat back down on the chair and shuffled the cards for a while. I dealt us eight cards each and pushed a pile toward him.

"Crazy 8s?"

"Crazy, all right." He picked up the cards.

"Yeah," I agreed. "You go first."

The cards snapped time after time as we played in silence.

"Last card," he said, as he put the queen of spades down on the discard pile. "Pick up five," he said, as he looked into my eyes and smiled.

I counted the cards aloud as I picked them up, "One, two, three, four, and five." I was playing as if I still had a chance to win the game. I laid down the seven of spades. I was wondering if he had a diamond or heart in his hand, and I might still have a chance to win.

"Pick up two." He smiled even harder as he laid the two of spades on top of the seven.

I threw the remaining cards I had in my hand at him. "You cheated."

He threw the cards back at me. "Loser deals."

I dealt the cards again. We sat and played several games of cards all afternoon. Playing cards was a distraction during the times the nurses would come in and out of his room to take his vital signs. Blood pressure, temperature, and ask the same questions, how much did you have to drink and how much did you pee? Then they would write it down on the chart. Every time a different nurse would come in she was make the comment, "Nice flowers." The nurses came and went just as the ticking of the clock on the wall, every hour. The motion became so second nature after the first few hours I hardly noticed them anymore. Tommy said they had been doing that every hour since he had been there.

"Hi, Tommy," my mom said, as he came in the room and kissed him on the cheek. "How you feeling today? You're looking good." She patted him on top of the head.

I did not want to see her so soon. I knew that by her presence we would have to leave and go home shortly. I had not had enough time with him yet. I was not ready to leave.

After a short visit with Tommy my mom looked at me and said, "I am going for a coffee in the café downstairs. I will meet you there in a few minutes; then we have to go."

I wanted to kick and scream and have a temper tantrum like a toddler right there in the room but I knew it would not do any good. I knew that would not enable me to stay any longer by his side, and I would have looked very silly. If it had worked I surely would have tried it. *God, let me stay, let me stay, let me stay.*

I put the cards back beside the table and sat beside him on the bed. I hung my head until my chin touched my chest. I did not know what to say but I was sure that I did not want to say goodbye. He put his hand on my shoulder.

"It was nice to see you today. I am glad you came." Tommy lifted my chin with his other hand and looked directly into my broken soul. He leaned forward and kissed me on the lips. His mouth was dry and cracked from the air that was pumping into the room. The air conditioner was still all I could hear while I kissed him back.

Comes Home

"How's Tommy?" Jim asked, when I saw him on Monday morning arriving at school after the bus had dropped him off. "Did you talk to him yesterday?"

"He is fine," I answered. I watched the ground as I walked into the doorway of the high school. I felt all alone and the rest of the day at school was lost. My heart was in the hospital with Tommy. I could not wait to get home so I could call him on the phone. I wondered if they had started his treatments yet. Would his hair all fall out the second the treatments started, would he puke, what did he look like, how did he feel, did he miss me, when could he come home?

"Emily," I barely heard someone call my name, "Are you okay?"

I looked up from a book I was holding on the bus. I looked around the bus again. I did not remember getting on. It was hot through the window, and I started to sweat.

"Are you okay?" It was Lizzie.

"I'm fine." I noticed I was sitting in a seat by myself, and she was already walking down the aisle just before she walked down the steps. I understood what it was like to be *fine*. It was not a good feeling. It felt empty, lonely and a lot like a disaster.

"Are you coming?"

"Yeah, " I sighed, then grabbed my backpack. "I was just reading this book."

"Oh." Lizzie nodded and looked at me quizzically. "You have been reading that all day, even during math class, English class, at lunch, and in geography. It must be a good one." Just before she rolled her eyes in the back of her head and raised her brows.

"Oh." I looked at the cover of the book, then turned it right side up. "It is."

I tossed my book bag on the floor of my room before I lay down on the bed and took the remote control for the stereo in my hand. I turned up my favourite song as loud as it would go. Today it just did not have any meaning to me, so I shut if off just in time to hear the phone ring.

"I'll get it." I reached over and picked up the receiver. "Hello?"

"Hey, how was school today?" It was Tommy.

"Okay." I wanted again to cry as soon as I heard his voice. He sounded as if he was trying to be happy. I could tell behind that his fake voice he was also holding back the tears. I knew him much better than that. I may not know I was holding the book upside down on the bus but I knew my best friend was sad.

"What did you learn today?" he attempted to make cheap conversation.

"Nothing," this time I was giving short answers. I wanted to be with him, but I could now understand the silence behind trying to hold the tears back from drowning us both in the flood. It was quiet for a moment.

"You start treatments today?" I finally asked.

"Yeah, chemo," he said quickly.

"How was it? Did it hurt?"

"Not bad, they put it through the IV line, so it did not hurt at all."

"Are you sick yet?"

"No, I feel fine." I knew he was lying; he did not feel fine.

We talked for a while on the phone and then he had to go because they had brought him supper. I hoped he would eat something, but I doubted it.

"Are you off the phone?" Mom yelled from the kitchen. "Supper is ready."

"I am not hungry." I yelled back from my room.

"Come and eat anyway." I heard her say as the door pushed open of my room.

I got up and filled my plate with food that I already knew I had no intention to eat. My stomach was in knots. The smell of the pork chops and potatoes was making me ill. I cut up the meat into small pieces on my plate and crushed the potatoes. I reached across the table for the butter and put a dash of salt on top.

"How's Tommy?" she asked in between bites.

"Fine. How was Grandpa yesterday?"

"He is really sick. They said he has throat cancer. He cannot eat, and they are putting a tube in the esophagus to feed him. They said he will never eat again, but they might let him go home like that. I think it is just to die. I am not sure he even knew we were there." She appeared very sad. I could not understand her pain.

I thought about my grandfather for a moment and wondered what he was like. I had spent some time with him as I child, but I barely remember. I thought about how I felt when I thought about him. I remembered him being very nice to me and growing a big garden in his back yard. One year he let me bring home the biggest carrot out of his garden I had ever seen. I ate it for weeks, and I kept putting it in the fridge when I was done with it for the day. I thought about his cherry tree out in front of his house. I wondered if they were ripening on the tree yet or if they were already out of season. I thought about when I used to tap dance on his deck out back by myself while I was playing in his yard under the white trellis that divided the yard from the garden. I thought about the sweet smell that surrounded his house from the scented flowers around the yard.

"I hope he is going to be okay."

My mother looked sad. "Me too," but she knew he did not have much longer to live here on earth.

I waited until she was finished eating and then I emptied my plate into the garbage. I started to do the dishes in that had been in the sink. I looked out the kitchen window toward the neighbour's house. Nothing was happening next door either. It appeared the entire town was still. I decided it would be a nice night for a walk. I could use the alone time to think.

I found myself surrounded by trees, and I was walking down the road. I had walked a few miles already. I looked at my watch. I had been walking much longer than I had realized and it was getting late. I wondered where the time had gone. I thought about school tomorrow, maybe I would skip classes. If I did I wondered what I might do. School was ending in a few weeks, and the teachers were preparing us for our final exams. I did not care much about that either. It was most likely a good idea if I went. It would be another good distraction or so I thought.

I put the headphones on and turned the music up again. My hair was still wet from the shower I just took. I opened my eyes in the dark and stared at the ceiling. If I could be anywhere in the world right now, where would I be? With Tommy.

"The phone," Rose said, as she was standing over me. "It's Tommy."

"Hey," I greeted him. I tried to be happy and pretend nothing was wrong. "How you feeling?"

"Fine, you?"

"Fine."

"How is Jim?" he asked unexpectedly.

"I don't know. Okay, I guess. He asked about you today, and says to say hi."

"You still going out with him?"

"I don't know." I had not officially broken it off with him yet. Any fool who saw us knew where my heart really was. I had not thought about Jim at all. I had forgotten he was even supposed to be my partner. I guess he was still my boyfriend. I thought back to this morning when I got off the bus when I was talking to him but that seemed like a long time ago. I remember that he carried my books to homeroom for me. I guess I was.

"You don't know? What does he think?"

"I don't know. I didn't ask him. I guess we are." I did not want to tell him that. I wanted to be his girlfriend again.

"Did you tell him you kissed me yesterday?" He must have been thinking about it too.

"No." I wondered why I would do that. Tell Jim I had kissed Tommy in the hospital. I did not tell him that I told Tommy I loved him either. "Did you like it when I kissed you?" I hoped I already knew the answer to that.

"Did you?"

"No," I lied.

"You did so." He laughed. It was good to hear him laugh. I could almost see him smile. For a second I felt good inside. I felt like I could feel his heart right next to mine. I closed my eyes and thought of the kiss.

"No, I didn't. I think you need to do it again sometime soon so I can see for sure that I hated it." I laughed along with him. The teasing helped the fear go away. "Did you?"

"No, I didn't like it either." He laughed softly.

"Good, then. We are even."

We talked a while about nothing. Everything for a moment seemed okay. I forgot where he was for a second until I heard the voice in the background saying, "I'll be back in a minute to take your temp since you are on the phone." It was the nurse.

"I miss you," he said. "I want to come home."

"I want you to come home, too," was the last thing I said before I hung up the phone, and I finally fell asleep.

We talked on the phone every day sometimes twice while he was in the hospital for a little over a month. There were seldom days that I did not talk to him at all. I was not able to make the trip to see him in the hospital again because I did not have a ride. He never asked me to come. We just talked on the phone as if nothing was wrong. He did not complain about being sick, and I did not ask. It was better that way. We could both pretend he was not sick. In the back of my mind the idea never went away. I remember seeing the pictures in the book of the sores in the mouth. I wondered if that was happening to him yet. I was afraid to ask. I did not want to know. He did not want to tell.

The next time I talked to Tommy it was terrific news.

"I get to come home today," he sounded very weak, but his voice sounded excited over the phone.

"Can I come and see you?" I wanted so badly to kiss him again. I wanted to show him that I loved him.

"No, they said I could not have company for a while because my immune system is so low; they said I have to stay away from lots of people in case I catch an infection or a cold or something. I do not care what happens anymore. I just want to come home. I am tired of all this hospital stuff already. I just want to see you."

I did not understand what he meant by getting an infection and how important that was to him, but if the doctor says he cannot see anyone then I will wait.

"But you get to come home! That must mean you are doing better, and you will be okay now."

"I don't know," his voice trailed off into the distance. "I got to go; the doctor is here to talk to me again. Bye." He quickly hung up the phone.

Steady Again

Jim and I were still dating. We were having as much fun as we could have together, regardless of my state of mind. We were developing a friendship between us and it was nice. He would write me nice letters that made my heart feel warm and fuzzy. It was my birthday, and he hand carved my gift out of a piece of wood. He gave it to me one hot night in July for my birthday while we watched the sun set on the deck of his swimming pool. I was turning sixteen years old.

Tommy came home from the hospital and seemed to be doing well physically, but he had changed. He said things that I could not understand. Tommy said he did not care what was going to happen to him. It scared me to hear him say things like that. He had to find a will to live. He had to get better. What was going to happen if he does not?

Tommy also said he still liked me, but I wondered if he wanted me to be his girlfriend again. I had deep feelings for him, but I did not know how to show him. It was hard because of Jim, but he knew all about the history that Tommy and I had. I could not hide those feelings any longer. Jim was not a fool; he could see through my disguise.

Jim and I had lots of fun together. His parents let me stay over at his house for the weekend and took me camping up North with them. It was the first time I remember being on a trip anywhere. My parents took me once to Florida when I was a child but I was too young to remember much of it. I felt I was gaining some independence away from my parents while I was spending time with Jim and his family.

His family was much different from mine, and they would let us get away with much more than mine ever would have. I enjoyed being with Jim and everything was good when we were together but the second I was alone I started thinking about Tommy. I was torn between the two of them.

I was thinking about, dreaming about, talking about Tommy. I could not seem to control my thoughts. I could not help it. I was sorry, but Jim had moved into the second position in my heart even though I knew how much he loved me. I was scared to fall in love with Tommy yet I thought it is too late for that. I thought I already was.

It was apparent to both Jim and me that our relationship was ending. He knew as well as I did that my mind had been preoccupied with something else. I could not hide my feelings and my desire for Tommy. Jim and I had finally agreed that it was time to stay friends for the summer, and it was time we could no longer avoid the inevitable break up. We both had ideas that we would resume our relationship after the summer when we went back to school in the fall. After all, we were both young and trying as hard as we could to be adults about the situation we were facing. Jim was as supportive as he could be, and I respected him for that. I was grateful for his friendship and understanding. We both had desires for one another and being with him was fun but my heart was somewhere else, and Jim knew it.

It was then I learned that part of loving someone was letting him or her go. Sometimes you have to let something go because you are the one holding them back from something else more important to do that you are. As hard as that was for us to understand at such a young age Jim knew he needed to let go. We agreed that it would not be forever but I was sure it would be for a long time to come. Love is not fair for anyone one of us. We did not ask for this when we asked for love and we certainly did not expect the pain to come along within, no matter which corner of the triangle we were on.

I felt sad and it seemed I could not see the forest for the trees. I had to let go of one thing and hoped to step into another. It was all messed up in my heart, with Tommy being sick and everything. People told me every day he would die but I did not want to believe them, I just wanted to love him again. I wanted to hold his hand and kiss him again. I wanted to dance with him again. I wanted everything to be okay despite the fact all the odds were against us. I wanted to try in the face of adversity even if I might lose in the end. I had more faith in God for that to happen anyway.

I am supposed to see Tommy tomorrow. I have not seen him since the day that Mom and I went to the hospital a few months ago. I cannot see Tommy today because he is going to the hospital for a check up. I hope everything is going to be okay with him. I hope he does not have to stay there again. Then I will not get to see him.

I wondered how he was going to do at the check up. He does not deserve all this pain he only deserves the best of everything. I will try to give that to him if I can. I am not sure what the best of everything is but I can only give him what I know how. I am not sure how to love him but I am going to try. I do not know how to support him but I am sure God will show me the way to do what is best.

I picked up the phone and dialed his number. It rang and rang and rang and rang until he finally picked up the other end. "Hello." He sounded happy. I had heard him say hello a million times, but today this seemed different.

"Can I come and see you today?" I had asked this question a thousand times before. I already was anticipating another excuse and the answer to be the same as the last. The doctor said...he had to go away...he was not feeling well...but I asked anyway.

"Not today; I have to go back to the hospital for a checkup this afternoon, but you can come when I get home."

"For sure?"

"Yeah, I will call you."

"Promise?" I did not believe him.

"Yeah."

I waited all afternoon in agony and anticipation waiting to hear from him to say that I could come over. When I talked to him again it was much different from what I had expected.

"They kept me," he said, with more disappointment than I had in my own heart.

"At the hospital?"

"Yeah."

"Why?"

"They said the leukemia came back, and they said I only have about three or four months to live; maybe six."

"What?" *Three or four months; three or four months; he did not really say that.* My knees buckled, and I fell to the floor. The silence itself was deadly. "What?" I repeated myself.

"They said the leukemia came back, and I had three or four months to live."

"Do you believe them?"

"I don't know."

"They are wrong. I know it. They are wrong. How do they know that? How can they tell? They don't know what they are talking about." *Oh, God, please, please, please, this cannot be true, and I begged and begged again.*

"They are going to keep me here for a while, but they said not as long as the last time, a week or so. Maybe you can see me when I come back home."

"I want to see you now." My heart ached while it felt like it was lying beside me on the floor after he had just ripped it out. The only thing that would make it feel better is if I could see him again. If he only had a few more months to live I wanted to be part of it. I was not going to back out now. Talking on the phone to him every day was not enough.

"I got to go. I will talk to you soon." He hung up the phone before I had a chance to say goodbye.

I sat on the floor and "Three or four months" ricocheted in my head, surrounded by the sadness of his voice. If they were right that would mean he would be gone before Christmas. That just would not do. That would not be acceptable because he could not die at Christmas. Christmas was a time for miracles, not death.

I did not talk to Tommy again for the next few days, but the next time I did he was able to come home again. I wanted to see him so badly that this time I was not having no for an answer. All I wanted was to be with him. He said he wanted to be with me too but he would never allow me to come. Why? If this was love I wanted no more of it.

"Can I see you today?" I begged.

"Okay," he agreed. "Will you come alone?"

"No, I can't. I cannot drive myself yet. I will ask Kayla and Lizzie to come with me, but they do not have to come in to see you if you do not feel like company." I pleaded, "I really want to come."

"Okay."

It was a long drive to his house as Kayla drove my father's truck. I did not care what he would say because I was going to see Tommy one way or another. We pulled in his lane and my stomach turned inside out. I had never been to his house before, but Kayla said she was sure this was where he lived. I had flicked the last smoke out the window and gathered all the courage up I could. I walked around the house and heard the dogs barking from inside as I knocked on the door. I could hear footsteps coming closer and closer. I was soon to see him. I was shaking. Then I had seen the stranger come to the door.

"Is Tommy around?" I asked.

"No, he is not here right now." The person who answered the door was older and looked like Tommy. It must have been his father. He looked tired. No wonder it had taken him so long to come to the door.

"Will he be back soon? Can I wait?"

"I am not sure where he is; you shouldn't wait, but I will tell him you came."

I hung my head and walked back to the truck with my friends. *He said he would be home. He said I could come. He promised. Where did he go?*

I climbed back into the truck and asked Kayla to drive me home. It was a longer ride home than it had been a ride there. My friends had asked if I wanted to do anything else while we were out but I just wanted to go home. I did not want them to see my cry. I could not believe he only had a few months to live and did not even want to spend any of it with me. If the doctors said that he could not go out then where was he? Had he been lying to me all this time because he just did not want me to come? Does he not like me as he said he did? Does he really have no emotional investment in our friendship? Did he think I was pretending all this time?

He had asked me a week ago to spend the night at his sister's house with him so we could be alone together, and I was so excited about that, but it never worked out for us either. He made up some kind of excuse that I could not come. He went along without me and called me from there saying he wished I had been there with him. I doubted that to be the truth now. I doubted anytime he said he wanted to be with me as the truth.

I was not home long and the phone rang. I did not want to answer it because I knew it was Tommy. I was angry, hurt, confused, I did not know how I felt, but I did know one thing for sure, I did not want to talk to him. I did not want to hear one more excuse from him as to why I could not see him.

"Hello."

"Hey," he sounded happy again. "Dad said you were here." He sounded almost like he was bragging.

"Yeah, I was." That was all I could say. I wanted to cry, and he sounded like he was on top of the world. Maybe it was I after all. If I was doing something wrong, I did not know what it was.

"I was with Jeff at the store."

"Oh, your Dad told us not to wait."

"Yeah, then we went for a drive in his old man's car to take a movie back."

"Oh." I did not know what to say. He had known I was coming.

"I got to go, I am cooking supper." I was not but I did not have the energy anymore. I was glad he was feeling better, but I was not. I did understand the nice thing about the telephone because you could lie your ass off and get away with it to cover up the way you really were feeling inside. I did not agree with lying but at times like these I was not sure what else to do. I wanted to see him, and he stood me up.

"Wait…will you come with me next weekend and stay overnight at my sister's?"

"Sure," but I doubted that would happen. Now I was lying again to make him happy. I knew he would back out. I knew he did not want to be with me. If he only had a few more months to live he was sure going to string me along the entire time.

"I really want you to come. I hope you don't change your mind."

"Ha, no, I won't." With that remark he made I became even angrier. I think he meant he hoped I was not like him and that I would not stand him up. I do not think it was about anyone changing minds rather than finding something better to do than wait for me.

"I got to go." I knew I needed to get off the phone before I said something that would intentionally hurt his feelings. I did not want to make him feel as bad inside as I was feeling inside. I would just have to accept that whatever he wanted had to be fine; after all, it was his life, and he should be able to spend it however he wanted, even if it was different from what I was asking for. I sat and cried for a while after I had hung up the phone. I was so angry at him.

"What is wrong?" Mom asked.

"Tommy would not let me come it see him again today. I went there, and he was gone. I have made plans with some friends to get his stereo from another friend from a party that was at a while ago. Then I can have an excuse to take it to him, but I do not think he wants to see me. I don't think he likes me anymore." I cried until there were no more tears.

"All I want to do is see him. Why won't he let me come?" I asked my mom questions that even she did not have the answers to.

Mom left the room, and I again did not understand why she would leave me in my time of need. She dialed the phone, and I could hear her talking to someone on the other end of the line.

"…You will never find another friend like her again. She really wants to see you, and I am not sure how much longer she can hang on. It is not fair that you make her wait any longer. What is it that you want her to do? If you don't want to see her, then let her go. Then don't call anymore, but you cannot keep her in this agony any longer." Then she was quiet for a while. "I understand but if you do not let her come you will lose her as a friend. She does not deserve it." Then she hollered that the phone was for me.

"No thanks," I replied because I was still crying. I understood what she was trying to do, but I did not think it would help. He clearly did not want me around anymore.

"It is Tommy. He wants to talk to you," she called again. "He already knows you are crying. He doesn't care."

"Hello," I said as I tried to cover up the tears.

"I am sorry. I will let you see me if you come alone."

"We're you home when I was there?"

"Yes."

"Why did you not want me to come in? I came to the door alone. They would not have waited outside."

"I did not want them to see me. Emily, I am dying. I do not want to see anyone right now. I want to see you so badly, but I do not want you to see me like this. I do not look very good, and I do not want to scare you away. I have lost all my hair."

"I don't care. I want to see you anyway."

"I want to see you, too."

"Can I come now?" I begged again.

"Yeah."

"Will you stay home?"

"Yeah."

"Promise?"

"Yes, I promise."

"I will see you in thirty minutes." I hung up the phone as quickly as I could.

By law I needed a licensed driver with me, but this time I went alone. If I ever had any excuse to break the law it was right now. I raced all the way to his house. I had told him it would take thirty minutes to get there, but I knew I could make it in less time. I did not want to give him time to abandon me again. I wanted to see him today even if I had to wait outside of his house all night. He said I could, and I was determined I was going to.

I knew from the pictures in the book what was happening to him. I knew all his hair would fall out. I had heard the doctor say that to him. I did not care.

I did not believe he was dying. I would not accept that as the truth. I need him every day to keep me sane here in this world. He cannot leave me alone. I will die with him. He does not understand that for the past few years he was all that I have had.

My sister is tired of playing my mother whenever she has to. My sister has a life of her own now, and I am here with no one. I am lost and alone. Tommy cannot leave me. Who would I talk to every day on the phone for support? Who would help me through my problems? Who would be there for me? This is not fair.

My thoughts raced faster than I could drive. I had a million things on my mind but most of all Tommy. I could not get to his house fast enough.

"God, please let him be there when I arrive at his door this time. I want to see him so badly."

I turned the music up as loud as the stereo would go so I could drown out the thoughts in my head and the feelings of fear, anger, and anxiety in my heart. The words in the music were ringing in my ears yet I heard nothing that the singer had suggested. I wanted to get there as fast as I could. I took all the back roads to his house as fast as I could. I knew there would be no cops there.

The closer I got to his house the more my hands started to shake. Maybe I was not quite ready for this. I started to sweat and my heart felt like it was going to jump out of my chest. There was going to be a big hole under my shirt and blood would be dripping all over my pink shirt I had picked out to wear especially for him.

"God, please, please, please do not let me cry. Please give me the strength to walk into this situation with more wisdom and understanding than I had ever had before. I want to go, God, but I am terrified of what will happen. I am anxious about what I will see. I am angry that he left the last time I came. God, please help me get through this one," I prayed out loud.

I could not do it. I needed more time. I needed another lifetime to prepare for this, so I pulled into the store and went in to get a pop. I slowly strolled toward the cooler and opened the door. The cool air that was coming from inside the door felt good on my burning face. I waned to crawl inside the freezer and stay there a while. I stood and stared aimlessly at the selection of drinks before me, but I could not choose one. I heard someone behind me say, "May I help you?" It was the man behind the counter. I imagined that he knew Tommy already, since the store was only a few blocks from his house, and wondered if I could ask him what I could expect I might see.

"No, just looking." I grabbed the first bottle I could reach. I wondered how long I had been standing there looking at the refreshments.

I returned to the truck and lit another smoke as I opened the pop. I fumbled around in my purse for some gum. My mouth tasted like a wet ashtray because I had been smoking too much today. I was starting to feel sick. I knew another smoke was not what I needed, as I took another drag and felt the relief of the nicotine run through my veins. My head started to hurt. I felt like I was going to puke. I did not want to go any farther. I wanted to turn around and go back home, no, I wanted to go anywhere else but face to face with leukemia and the destruction it had caused for Tommy this far. I leaned my head back on the headrest of the seat and began to pray again. After all, prayer was all that I knew how to do.

I pulled into his lane and quickly got out of the truck. I have procrastinated, this long enough and it was time to put my emotions in my pocket and go knock on the door. Regardless if I was scared of seeing him and feeling this way, this is what I had asked for.

The dogs were barking louder this time, the sky was darker, and the wind blew harder. Now there was a big orange cat sitting on the step waiting at the door. I bent down and began to pet it on the head and just behind the collar where cats seem to like it the best.

"Hello," I greeted the cat. "Are you as nervous as I am to go in?" The cat looked up toward me and began to purr.

"Well, how about you come in with me so I do not have to go in alone?" The cat sat on the step and enjoyed the attention. He stood up, turned around and put his paw against the door to scratch against it.

"No, no, no, I am not ready." I took a deep breath, closed my eyes, crossed my fingers, and prayed again for help. I guess if the cat thought it was time to go in, I would follow his lead. It did not seem in this moment I could trust my best judgment, the cat's judgment surely must be better than mine right now.

I raised my hand and knocked on the door. No one came.

"I thought you said it was okay?" I patted the cat on the head again. I knocked again, then heard the footsteps coming closer to the door. I wondered if it would be Tommy to answer this time. In a few seconds I would see him. *Run,* I heard in my head, *run before it is too late.*

The door opened, and it was the same man who opened the door before. He greeted me with a smile, but he looked as if he had gotten no rest from the first time I was here.

"Come in." He smiled as he held the door open for me. "Tommy and Jeff are inside."

I followed the old man through the door and into an entryway where I took my shoes off then down a hallway and into the kitchen. He held open his hand toward the living room but I could not see Tommy yet. I turned the corner and there he was sitting on the couch. Jeff, Tommy's mom, and younger sister were also in the room. I smiled as I stood frozen in the doorway. He looked very different.

"Come in; sit down," Tommy's Mom offered.

I started to walk toward the couch, but Tommy stood up and walked toward me first. He looked weak and unstable when he tried to take each step.

His skin was pale white, and his lips were very soft and pale pink. His hair was all gone, even his eyebrows. His clothes were baggy because he had lost so much weight. He looked sicker than anyone I had ever seen in my life.

"No, let's go into my room." He walked past me expecting I would follow.

My eyes hit the floor, and I wanted to cry as I walked behind him. The pictures in the book had not described this. They did not say that the leukemia and chemotherapy would make him look as if he was a walking dead man. The book did not tell me that I would hardly recognize him. It did not say the treatment would be worse than the disease. It did not say he would deteriorate so much that he would want to hide from those he loved.

I hoped his room was far away so I could gather my emotions before I had to speak aloud. I do not think I could say a thing because my words hid behind the swelling in my throat. I was not good at dealing with these intense emotions. I did not know what to do with myself. Now I was here all I wanted to do was run out the door.

I understood why he did not want me to come to see him. I understood why talking on the phone was easier for both of us. I understood why he wanted to give up and why he kept saying he was dying, because he was, or at least he looked like it. All of the sudden everything hit me like a ton of bricks. I saw leukemia right there before me, and I did not like it. I did not want this to be happening anymore. It was no fun.

I wondered what it must be like for him to have to look in the mirror and see himself deteriorate like that. I was sad for him not for me. For the first time I wanted to give someone else life. I would take his sickness upon myself if it would make him okay again, even if it could be only for a little while.

"Want something to drink?" he offered, as we walked back through the kitchen.

"No thanks." I held up the pop. "I stopped at the store before I came."

He led me back down the hallway where I had just come from and into his bedroom that was near the outside door.

"This used to be my grandma's room before she died, but I am glad I have it now." He opened the door to a small room. He had a single bed, a night table, a dresser, and a small TV on a night stand at the end of the bed. The furniture all matched, and the bed was made perfectly. The TV was off, and the only sound I could hear was muffled talking from the people in the other room and the hum of the TV they were watching.

"It is quieter in here," he said. "I will be right back. I need some water." He left the room.

I held back the tears as I sat down on the end of the bed. Was this a good idea? *God, send me a sign that I am doing what is right.* I looked toward the door toward the movement in the hall. The big orange cat slowly swaggered into the room, jumped up on the bed, and put its head on my lap. I began to pet the cat again and smiled.

"Thanks."

"That is funny," Tommy exclaimed as he walked back through the door, "that cat never comes in here." At that moment I knew that everything I was going for was for the greatest good.

Tommy sat down at the other end of the bed and sipped water out of a glass cup. He set the cup down on the night stand beside the bed. Everything was in its exact place in this room and it was perfect. I looked around the room some more in trying to find some kind of conversation piece to this most uncomfortable situation.

"Nice cowboy curtains." I started to giggle. I did not really find the curtains that funny but the giggle came from pure nervousness. "You don't strike me as a cowboy-curtain kind of guy. Spiderman maybe, but not cowboys."

He laughed in agreement, "Yeah, I know. They are kind of odd. My mom picked them out."

"Oh, right. I bet she did!" I teased him some more, "I bet you asked her to."

"Wanna listen to something?" He handed me a case full of the latest recordings of all our favourite bands.

"I see you got your stereo back." I motioned. "It is nice." I looked through the case he had handed me.

"Yeah, Jeff took me there when we went to the store. I just got it back today."

I could see the pole light was on outside his bedroom window and the warm breeze blew through the cowboy curtains into the room. The lamp was dimly lit with a low-watt bulb, and I was trying to pick out tunes that might fit the mood. Nothing seemed to be appropriate right now to fit the crazy feelings I had inside and the moment did not at all feel romantic. I never dreamed of being inside his room, but this seemed to be a nightmare.

"Anything you want to listen to is fine with me. Help me pick something." I pushed the case toward him.

He flipped through the music in silence for a few minutes; then we both agreed it was best to listen to the radio. He stood up again and turned in on softly. The song that had been playing was better than one I would have picked anyway. This conversation dragged, but I was feeling more comfortable each moment I was with him. He seemed nervous, too.

He sat back down on the bed and took another drink of water and handed me the cup. "Sure?"

I shook my head no.

"Got a smoke?" he asked. "Mine are out there."

"Are you sure you should be smoking?" The idea of him smoking did not register in my brain as a good idea.

"What? Is it going to give me cancer?" he smiled. Then he took out a cigarette from the pack I had handed him and lit it with the lighter that was already on the night table. He put the lighter into his pocket and handed me back the smokes.

"Thanks." He took a long hard drag and blew out the smoke from his lungs.

As I sat on the bed beside him I looked at him, and I wondered about the experience that he had been through in the hospital and how sick he must have gotten. I wanted to touch him, but I wondered if it would hurt him because he still looked so ill. I watched every move he made as he took one drag after another off the cigarette as we made cheap conversation about nothing. Talking about nothing was much better than not talking at all.

The time had passed quickly, and I had been there for a few hours already. I could have stayed forever, but I knew I needed to get going home soon. I did not want to leave his side. I wondered if I did if I would ever be able to come back. I wondered if he would want me back. I did not know for sure and he had been so unpredictable lately I was not even sure how to ask. I wondered what he was thinking and if he wanted me to leave. I wondered if he had even really wanted me to come. In deeper thought I reminded myself that if he had not wanted me to be here to see him I would not be here now. He would have left again before I got here, not answered the door, or whatever other kind of game he could think of to play so that I would go away. I reminded myself that I was finally here, and I had come this far; he must have wanted it, too. How could I be sure he would want me to come back? How could I trust him even if he said that he did?

I looked into his eyes which glistened with joy in the dim light. I knew inside somewhere he was glad I was here. I wondered when the last time he felt that emotion was. I bet it had been a long time for him to see any kind of pleasure. I knew he wanted me there, and I was being silly for thinking he would not want me to come back. The hardest part of seeing him for the first time was over. How could not get any worse? He had not sat beside me, had not touched me, had not kissed me, but I was at least there in his room with him, that was a big step forward from where I stood a few hours ago.

"I have to work tomorrow, and it is getting late. Tommy, I need to go soon," I explained.

He looked saddened by my comment, but I could not stay here with him much longer even if I did want to. "And I think your friend is still here." I motioned toward the living room. "I am sure he wants to see you, too."

"Nah, Jeff is here all the time; he won't care," he said as he stood up. Then continued, "But if you have to work and get up early I understand that you need to go. You can put your shoes on in here." He reached around the door and handed my shoes to me while he stood by the dresser and waited while I tied the laces.

I stood up beside him looking him directly in the eye. We did not say a word as we stood together looking beyond the fear, beyond the pain, beyond the confusion looking straight into love. I wanted to tell him how sorry I was that this was happening to him and how much I did not want him to die in three or four months yet I did not want to ruin this perfect moment so I said nothing.

He took me by the hand and then kissed me softly on the lips as he pulled me closer into his body. I could feel the warmth coming from under his shirt and the color came back in his cheeks a bit. As he kissed me he slipped his tongue inside my mouth. The more we kissed the harder he pushed against me. I had kissed him this way so many times before but this was different. This time I could feel more than this tongue inside me. I felt his heart melting, his soul connecting. His face changed as if nothing mattered anymore but that moment right there in his room between us. As he kissed me he began to pull up my shirt and touch my breasts over my bra. I wanted him to touch me more. I wanted him to kiss me all night long.

"Way to go, Tommy!" Jeff said as he poked his head through the open window as he was walking out the door off the deck. "See you tomorrow."

My cheeks were instantly hot with embarrassment. I wondered if Jeff had been standing there watching us, but I did not care. I was trapped in this moment of eternity and was feeling good about it. In that instant I could see through the leukemia and the damage it had done to Tommy. I could see him again for all that I knew he was. For all that I knew we were together. *Thank you, God, for letting me come here tonight; thank you,* I said inside my own head.

"Walk me out. I really need to go." I smiled as I pushed away from him.

"Are you sure you can't stay for a while longer?" he asked.

"No, if I leave now, I will be sure you will ask me to come back," I smiled and unwrapped his arms from my body as he was still trying to feel my ass. "I really got to go."

He walked me out to the truck and opened the door for me to get in. I turned on the key and went to start the engine after I had gotten in the driver's side door.

"Have one more smoke with me?" he begged, with his big blue eyes and smile that shone through the darkest hour.

As the music on the stereo played, "Heaven can wait," by Meatloaf, I agreed. "Only one." I stepped out of the truck and left the key on so we could hear the music.

"I am glad you came," he said, as he looked directly into my eyes.

"I am glad I came, too."

"I am sorry it took me so long. I was afraid that when you saw me you would not want to be around me anymore." He was looking at the ground now.

"No, all I wanted was to see you. I would have waited forever if you would have made me."

"I know," he said, while his eyes were meeting mine.

"Will you go out with me?" He looked again at the ground, and was making designs in the gravel with his foot as he was leaning on the truck with one hand and dragging off a smoke with the other.

"Yes," I agreed. I wanted to be his girlfriend. Now that I saw him I understood more about what he was going through. I wanted to help him in any way I could. I loved him sincerely, and I knew no disease could take that away.

He kissed me again then pushed me toward it the open door of the truck. "I'll see you tomorrow." His shadow followed behind him as he turned and disappeared around the corner of the house.

Tommy and I saw each other every night after that for about a week. I went to his house every day, and the cat waited by the door. I was there so often that the dogs did not bark at me anymore when I went into the house. When I knocked Tommy would always call to come in from his room. He did not even get up anymore to open the door. I would go in, take my shoes off just outside his door, and enter his room. I would engage in whatever he was doing without asking a word. There was no discomfort between us anymore, and I had finally found somewhere I had belonged. I wanted to be with him every second I could, not because he was sick but because we wanted to be together.

"Are we going to Street Dance?" I asked him. Going without him was not an option. Street Dance was the biggest harvest celebration around. Without a word we already knew everyone from school would be there, and neither one of us had seen much of any of our friends all summer. Not seeing our friends was fine between us, as we had each other for company, but it was always a big celebration.

"Sure, pick me up later tonight, and I will be ready."

"Are you sure you are feeling up to it?"

"Yeah, I am feeling better and better all the time. I think it would be okay to go for a little while. It will be nice to see some people from school again."

As we drove together in the truck on the Labour Day weekend I was optimistic of everything being okay. I was anticipating Tommy and me to have fun since he was feeling better now. We had not had fun like this in a long time and we were going to attend the street dance. I wanted to dance with him again. It had seemed like it had been a long time since we swayed together with the beat of the music. I wanted him to hold me close and make everything go away.

"I hear Luke has an apartment uptown someplace. Want to try and find it first to see who is around and what is happening?" he invited.

Luke was a friend of Tommy's from high school. They would sit together in art class. I never did see any masterpieces either one of them accomplished but they always seemed they had fun. From where the girls and I sat across the room it looked like that was all they did.

"Sure," I agreed.

After we had found a parking spot for the truck we got out and walked across the road holding hands. Tommy was kicking the pylons out of the way because he thought they were a nuisance.

"Hey, guys!" We heard a familiar voice calling toward us. Tommy turned around and began to have a conversation with a boy who was also his friend from high school. At first guess, Tommy was glad to see him.

"So how have you been feeling?" Tim inquired.

"Good," Tommy responded, as he still held onto my hand. I was not paying attention to the conversation. I did not like Tim that much anyway, so I was looking for any of my friends I thought might be around. I wondered if I would see Bobbi soon.

"I was going to come and see you in the hospital," Tim advised Tommy, "but I was not sure where you were."

"That's okay," Tommy informed him. "I have been home for a while now anyway."

"What are they doing to you in there?"

"Chemo, but there may be other treatments to help me later on." Tommy was talking about the bone marrow transplant, but he knew Tim would not understand. We did not really understand because we had not been given that much information about it yet.

"When did they say you were going to die?"

"What?" I gasped for air. Did he really ask that? I pulled on Tommy's hand because I wanted to drop this conversation and deck Tim right where he stood.

"When are you going to die?"

"When are you?" I sarcastically asked him back.

"They gave me six months unless I can go for the other treatment in the city." Tommy responded and pulled back on my hand to not let me leave his side.

"That is too bad. I suppose I will not see you again then."

"No, maybe not." Tommy all of the sudden looked grim.

Tim held out his hand in offering to shake with Tommy. "I hope everything goes well for you then."

Tommy let go of my hand to shake with Tim. "Thanks."

"I wish you all the best."

I took Tommy's hand again and pulled him away. I did not want to be witness to that conversation any more. I could not believe how insensitive he could be. Of all the supportive things as a friend he could have said to Tommy, why would he say that? Why now? Why today?

"That guy is an asshole, Tommy. I don't know why you like him."

"He is not that bad. I have not seen him since school." Tommy was quiet.

"Well, I hope not to see him again." I was very upset. "Do you want to go home?"

Tommy looked at me like a lost puppy. I knew that he would rather leave now. I knew he did not want to have this conversation again with anyone else, and neither did I. I squeezed his hand.

"I won't be upset. I think it is a better idea if we just leave now." I tried to pull him hard enough to turn him around and go back toward the truck.

"Nah, we just got here; let's go see if we can find Luke."

I was hoping that when we at least found Luke that would offer us some comfort. I knew that Luke would not be that ignorant. Even if Luke had those thoughts in his head he would not say them aloud. Luke would not hurt Tommy's feelings like that. Luke would have more consideration for what Tommy was experiencing. He would not be that honest.

Splash, went the water balloon directly in front of us that had mysteriously dropped from the sky.

"What the hell?" I was instantly mad. Tommy started laughing as he turned his head in another direction.

"Look," he pointed toward the window on the second floor above the street.

"Get the hell up here; this is a blast!" Luke yelled from the window. "I could have hit you guys!" He pointed the way to the stairs that led to the door.

We entered the apartment without knocking. It was filled with empty beer bottles and garbage all over the table. Tommy walked in and grabbed a beer out of the fridge without asking. I found more balloons beside the sink and began filling them up with water. Luke was yelling something at someone else from the window and Tommy went over and began yelling something, too. I stood back and watched the pair half hanging outside in the boiling sun that was beginning to finally rest for the night.

"Fill them with cold water; it'll be more fun when we hit someone," Tommy shouted at me from across the room.

I shook my head in amazement. "Okay."

Luke and Tommy and thrown all the latex out the window that I had given them, and then Tommy came and sat at the table with me while Luke was doing something else. More and more of our friends were gathering in the small apartment and it was getting rather crowded fast. Someone had thrown a bag of weed on the table beside the rolling papers that were already there and told Tommy to start to roll. Without question Tommy began rolling joints while I watched in admiration. I was not the only one who did not see Tommy as sick anymore. None of our friends did either.

Luke came back into the kitchen, lit a joint and passed it to Tommy. "This one is for you guys." Tommy took the joint and toked on it a few times then handed it to me. I did not want to take it. I did not think getting high was a good idea right then. I thought about what Tim had said and wondered if it was the truth. Was this the last time I would be out with Tommy at some kind of party? Tommy was having fun in this environment. It certainly was a switch from what it must be like in the hospital. Did I want to be the one who nagged, "No,

I cannot smoke that, it is not good for my health?" Did I want to remind Tommy he was sick right here, right now? I did not. I took the joint from him and gave him an accepting smile. Even when I did not want to I did it anyway for him, for me, for our friends, for all of us. I wanted to be part of this experience with him, especially if it might be the last.

We stayed at Luke's apartment for a while, then we decided to go for a walk. Tommy was looking like he needed some fresh air and an escape from the party. Drinking a few beers and a few joints were fun but much more intoxication for either one of us may end us both in trouble. I was not sure how I could explain to his mother bringing him home all messed up from a party that we never intended being at in the first place?

We walked and held each other up through the crowd until we ended up at the end of the pier at the lighthouse. The moon was on the raise and it was bright orange in the sky. It was the second full moon of the month and that meant it was a blue moon. We wondered why it was orange.

"This is beautiful," I said, as I looked at the reflection over the water to break the silence that we had been sitting in.

Tommy leaned over and began to kiss me. I was not sure if it was the alcohol or the moon that was affecting him so strongly, but I did not ask questions I just kissed him back. I liked it when he kissed me. We kissed a lot. If there was anything that made us both feel better about anything, it was kissing. It made us feel connected. With the hormones running through our bodies it made us feel alive, invincible.

"It is getting chilly," I stated. "Shall we go back?"

"Luke said we could stay there tonight. Do you want to go back to his place?" I knew what Tommy was hinting about. We had been kissing and petting each other on the end of the pier in the moonlight for a while now, so I assumed what he really meant was, do you want to go back to Luke's and have sex with me?

"No, there are probably so many people there by now we could not be alone together anyway, and I have had too much to drink. I have to work tomorrow, and it is getting late."

I did want to be alone with Tommy but tonight was not the right night for that. I was sure we would get more opportunities to make love. I was sure he was not going to die even if some of his other friends were not.

Do You Want My Leather Jacket?

"I have to go to the hospital to stay on Monday," Tommy told me over the phone. "It will be for about a month." He sounded very sad. "They are going to give me more treatments."

"Oh." I did not know what to say. I wondered why he had not told me before.

"When did you find out?" I finally asked.

"The other day they called me."

"Why didn't you tell me before?"

"I did not want to upset you. I wanted to have a nice weekend with you."

"Did you?" I asked.

"Did you?"

"Yes, I did. You never answered me. Did you?" I asked again.

"I had the best weekend that I have ever had."

"Thank you."

"For what?"

"Telling me that. I think you are just making it up to make me feel good, though."

"Would I do that?" he asked.

"Yes."

"No, I wouldn't. I would tell you the truth."

"You would not. You would not tell me if it sucked."

"Yes, I would."

"No, you wouldn't. You would just not do it again."

"But it didn't suck. It was the best weekend I have ever had."

"Oh, yeah? Why?"

"Because I was with you."

"Yeah, mine too, because I was with you."

"Are you coming over tonight?" He finally changed the subject.

"Yeah."

I arrived at Tommy's house just like I had all the times before. This time was different. It was the first time I had been with him when he had to go into the hospital. I had talked to him on the phone before his trips and treatments but was not physically there to comfort him. It was awkward I did not know what to do or say because I knew he was sad.

I watched him as he packed his bags to go. He wanted to get it all done as soon as he could so he did not forget anything once he got there. I wondered what he needed other than PJs and his toothbrush. I was naive as to what was going to happen to him there. He knew what would happen as this was his third trip for chemo treatments.

"Do you want to take my stereo and all my tapes home?" he asked.

"No, won't you take it with you?"

"No."

"Do you want my leather jacket?"

"Won't you take it with you?"

"No. I won't need it."

I did not understand.

"Is there anything else you want of mine?" he asked, as he looked around his room.

"No," I said. "You will need everything when you come home."

"Just take it with you today, okay? I want you to have it all."

"I'll just have to bring it all back, but if you want me to, I will take anything you want to give me."

"Okay." He gathered this stereo, tapes, leather jacket, and a few clothes by the door of his room. Once he had everything in a pile he carried it out to the truck and put it all in the passenger's seat by himself. He did not want any help. I wondered what he was doing, but I did not ask any questions. I did not want any of his things, but I did not object because this seemed what he was determined to do.

He gave me a kiss goodbye then said, "I'll call you when I get there." He closed the door after I had gotten in the truck, quickly turned and walked away.

I watched him walk around the corner of the house and waited a few minutes before I started the engine of the truck. I hoped he was going to come back out to fetch me to come back inside with him. I had not planned on coming over to his house to have him give me his stuff and leave. I wanted to be with him. I wanted to make him happy. I wanted to see him smile. I did not want him to be so sad. I wanted to lie on his bed with him and watch TV until we fell asleep like we always did. I wanted this to be the same as always. I did not understand why he was pushing me away so quickly.

I cried as I drove home with all of his stuff in the seat of the truck beside me. I wondered what he was thinking although I thought I knew. He did want have to say it aloud. He did not think he was going to come home again.

The Hospital

Tommy was in the hospital about two weeks before he came home again. I could not make the trip to see him as I was working every day in the harvest and was about to start school again. I would talk to him almost every day on the phone, and I wrote him letters during my lunch break at work. He wrote letters for a while also until he became too weak to keep writing. I wondered if going out to the party at Street Dance, and being around all those people in the unsanitary environment contributed him to becoming ill again. I hoped not. I hoped it was not my fault for taking him there with me. He said he did not think it did. He said would have gotten sick again anyway. He said he was glad that he went and it was the best weekend he had ever had. I still wondered if it was true.

He returned home from the hospital but he was not feeling well yet. I tried to convince him to call the doctor but he would not make the call. I wished I could call for him but that would do no good unless he will go for a check up himself. He is afraid that they will put him back in the hospital and does not want to go back there again. I am scared for him but I do not know what I can do to help him. I know he does not like to go to the hospital but if he is sick they can help him there. He does not think they can.

Harvest has finished now and the traditional finishing party is coming soon. Mom has left home again but she works with me so I see her every day. Tommy says he wants to go to the party also but I doubt he will have the strength for it. I would not go without him there is no sense. If he is not there it will not be any fun. It will be a waste of time. People at work will ask about how he is, and I will tell them he is fine. He would tell them that himself if they asked him. He would not tell them how he is really feeling. They really do not have any reason to know any different. It is not as if they would deeply care, they would just ask to be nice or phony. I will save myself the grief and not go. It will be easier that way.

I will be going in to grade eleven this year at school. I have already missed two weeks, and I will have a lot of schoolwork to catch up on. I do not want to go back to school yet. I want to stay home and hang out with Tommy. I know my parents will never let me stay out of school any longer than I need to for work. Work is the most important thing to them, but it is not for me.

"I went the doctor today," Tommy informed me.

"And what did he say?"

"That I needed to go back to the hospital."

"When?" I was afraid to ask.

"Monday."

"Oh, already? You just got home."

"I know. They say that I will have to stay a while this time."

"How long is that?" I asked.

"I don't know."

It seems that after all Tommy's fear he was right. He knows more about what is going on in his body than any doctor does. I can only imagine how he feels, although he does not tell me about it. I wonder if he tells anyone about it. I doubt it, but I wish he would. I know he does not want to scare me, but not knowing what is going to happen with him is almost worse than knowing. I never know what to expect anymore. I wish he would make me part of his illness as much as I am a part of the rest of his life. I know he wants to protect me however he cannot protect me from the truth. I only want to help him along the path through all this. Maybe he does not want any help. Maybe I am not good enough to help, not smart enough, not strong enough. Maybe I am just not enough.

Every day mom says that he is going to die and that I should not fall in love with him. It is too late for that, I already am. I am tired of everyone asking me all the time how long does he have to live. That is not fair. Is that the only thing people are concerned about is his death? What about his life? What about all the things we do together every day? Can everyone not see him for beyond his sickness? Can they not see how wonderful he is? Can they not see the hope that things will get better and maybe things will be okay? I wish they all could. I can.

One day I wish I would wake up and Tommy would tell me, "I am better now; the leukemia is gone. I am not sick anymore." I would hug him and we would jump for joy in celebration of his health. His hair would grow back, he would gain weight, become healthy, and all would be well again. We could get married, have children, and live in a big house with a cat and a couple of dogs. Dad could walk me down the aisle and give me away to him and he would take me as his wife. That is a simple dream for anyone, is it not?

I cannot picture life without Tommy in it. I am scared of life without him. I love Tommy more than I have loved anyone before. It is hard to stay strong for him but I have to. Tommy has to stay strong for me. He has to fight this thing and not listen to what anyone has to say. If that means not listening to the doctors because they are wrong, then listen to something that says he is going to live. They are mistaken. He is not going to die. I am not going to listen to that. If I do not have faith that everything will turn out okay then what do I have to hang on to?

When I am with him it is easy to pretend he is not sick and nothing is wrong. We have fun together, we laugh together, and I listen to his voice say good night to me each day on the phone. I do not want anyone else to take his place. I want his hands to touch me forever. I wanted his lips to be the only ones that kiss me or his arms to be the only one to hold me. His face to be the last thing I see each night. I want to be happy with him, for him.

When I am not with him I feel like crying. I cannot actually cry though if I do I fear everything will fall apart. If I cry I may never stop. I cannot show that kind of weakness. I cannot show him I am afraid or he will be afraid. I cannot show him I doubt our love or he will. I have to show the strength I have so he will. He cannot afford to doubt love and life or the idea he will get well. He will become well; I know it. I have asked God to help him and He will.

I wish God would make him well and take me instead. I would go to the other plain if I knew Tommy could stay. He is a much better person than I am he deserves it more. It seems God has already made His choice, and I can do nothing but love Tommy despite that fact.

Tommy is in everything I do now. I cannot get him off my mind no matter how hard I try. Sometimes I try to think about other things but it does not work. I soon find myself thinking of Tommy again. I need relief from this fear I am feeling but I do not know where to find it. I only find relief when I am with Tommy because I can see it in his eyes that he is not afraid or in as much pain when we are together. When I am not with him all the pain in my heart comes flooding back. Every person, every place, every thing brings back thoughts of Tommy. Being with him is the only thing that makes me feel better.

Tommy went to stay in the hospital again today. We did not go to the harvest party. I went to see him in the hospital instead of going alone. I knew I would not have any fun without him.

Tommy is very sick. He sleeps a lot and does not eat anything. It is always quiet there. The nurses are very nice to us. We play cards when we can but mostly I just sit by his bed and watch him sleep while I hold his hand. I watch his chest go up and down to reassure myself that he is still breathing. I wonder what it would be like if he stopped while I sat beside the bed and watched.

When I let go of his hand to change positions or stand up for a while he wakes up. Sometimes if I leave the room to eat or have a smoke his family comes find me because he opens his eyes and asks where I am. I do not leave his side very often though. I sit there beside him and wait for him to get well.

I watch the nurse poke him with needles, take his blood pressure and his temperature. They give him special medicine to wash out his mouth so he does not get the sores he does not like it but it does help, for a while. I rub lotion on his back and legs so he does not get bedsores and he likes foot messages but I think that is just a personal thing.

They try to encourage him to eat and drink as much as he can. Then they measure his pee in a hat thing in the toilet. Sometimes they even make him pee in a blue jar thing beside the bed if he is too sick to get up. They record all the fluid that went in and all that came out. They come in every few hours and do it all again and write it on the chart. They are quiet when he was sleeping and make casual conversation when he was awake. They all already know him by name because they had all taken care of him before.

"See you brought your girlfriend this time," they would tease him.

He would smile and nod.

"Maybe we can get her to do some of this stuff, too, for you so we don't have to." They would smile at him. "You're a lot of work."

They taught me how to do the easy things and told me it would not hurt him. I played nurse to him. It gave us both something to do, and he liked it better when I did it anyway. When we were alone I could give him more attention that was "special."

"Spit." I would say, then hold the cup to his mouth after giving him the red mouthwashes through a syringe that had no end on it. Then I would take the yellow one. "Open," and give the other to him. Then he would open his mouth, and I would put the other stuff on with a little pink sponge on a stick, that he did not spit out.

"I hate that kind," he said, three times a day, because that was how much he had to take it.

Tommy's mom would sponge bathe him so the nurses did not have to do that part either.

"Rub my feet," he would ask, so I did.

"Cream my back," he said, as he handed me the lotion, so I did.

"Help me up," so I did.

"Hand me that drink." I did that too.

We took care of him as best we could. When he did not need anything I would sit by the bed. Tommy's mom would do crossword puzzles, word searches, and read the paper while he slept. She had much more experience at keeping herself busy than I did. Sometimes when he was awake I would read him the newspaper aloud; that at least gave us something to talk about. We ran out of things to say after a while. I would also read him books, but he could not stay awake that long. I did not read anything without him.

I was staying with my mom's sister while I was in the city while Tommy was in hospital. I stayed with Tommy all day long. I would arrive at the hospital as early as I could sneak in the side door, and I was staying as long as I could before I fell asleep. I usually went around ten or eleven in the morning and came home around midnight. Visiting hours did not really apply to me because the nurses let me stay as long as I wanted. Even if he was sleeping, I could still stay all day.

I took a cab back and forth to my aunt's. She lived alone and worked a lot or whatever she did. I was there by myself, so I could sleep in her bed at night. She also had a cat. I think the cat liked my being there because she would curl up on the bed and sleep with me. I think she must have been lonely, too. I would get up in the morning, feed the cat, shower, and take a cab back to the hospital. I hardly ever ate.

I had to come home because I needed to start school. I had already missed the first few weeks. I told Tommy I would be back on the next weekend to see him if he was still there one way or another. I would not let him stay in that awful place alone. I understood why he hated it there. I did too.

Tommy finally came home again after two weeks. When he did come home he was still very sick. I wondered if he came home because he wanted to or because they let him. I was not sure. I did not ask. He said he would call the doctor to tell them how sick he was but he did not.

Tommy finally called the doctor after a lot of prompting. He had to go for x-rays now to see what was wrong with him. He did not seem to be getting better this time he was home. I was scared for him. I wanted him to get better so he could go get the transplant. I thought he wanted that too. I thought he wanted to get better.

Tommy had been out for ten days. I had seen him every day while he had been home. He was still sick. The doctors were putting him back in the hospital. He did not want to go. He was not packing anything to take with him this time. They said he had some kind of infection that needed immediate attention. *God, please let them help him get better.*

I was not going to stay at the hospital this weekend because of school, but Mom is going to take me to see him on Sunday. I have not talked to him since Tuesday. That is a real long time. I wonder how he is doing and why he has not called. I am worried about him.

It was a long night Friday, because I was waiting for Tommy to call. My friends wanted me to go out with them but I said no. I would only be a drag anyway. I want to talk to Tommy on the phone. I would wait here at home.

"Come with me babysitting tomorrow night," Lizzie asked. "I do not want to be alone. It will be fun, and we can play games and watch movies and stuff."

"Nah, I have had a long day already."

"What have you done?" she asked.

"Today I hung out with Dad. We were shooting the pellet gun and throwing knives at caterpillars and stuff. It was fun. Now I am tired and just want to wait for Tommy to call."

"You waited for him to call last night and did not want to come out. Come with me; you will see him tomorrow when your mom takes you to the hospital. Come on; it will be fun. It will take your mind off of things."

"Okay," I agreed. Fun was the last thing on my mind. I knew she was well intentioned trying to support me through this time of trouble. I did not need a push to do anything but wait for Tommy; I needed a shove. I did not want to go but I would.

Sunday was finally here, and I could go see Tommy. I imagined Mom would go visit Grandpa while we were there. I just wanted to see Tommy, but I thought about going upstairs to see him also while I was there. It will be a good change from sitting beside Tommy's bed and watching him sleep and Mom said Grandpa would like it if I did. I did not want to waste my precious time there with Tommy doing anything else but I thought I would.

I was greeted by the nursed on shift when I walked into the cancer ward at the hospital. They all said hello but there were no smiles on their faces. They knew already where I was going. Tommy's mom was already in the room when I got there. She did not say anything when I came in the room and stood beside his bed. I was not prepared for what I would see this time.

Tommy was sleeping on the bed when I went into his room. When I looked down at him I noticed a rash he had all over his body. I did not ask his mom what is was from. He had sores all over the outside and inside of his mouth just like the ones in the pictures I had seen. I did not need information about that. His stomach was so bloated you could see it sticking out from underneath the blankets. I looked at the monitors that he was now hooked up too. I had not seen that before. The monitors were constant recordings of his vital signs that the nurses had taken manually the last time I was here.

Tommy's mom said nothing. She and I stood alone by the bed and listened. Beep, beep, beep, beep, was all that I could hear. I wanted to go anywhere but see him lying in the bed like that. He slept. After a few minutes of my being there Tommy's mom left the room for a smoke. I wondered how long she had been standing there, probably for a week now. I knew why he did not call. He could not.

I sat down in the chair beside the bed and took him by the hand. I rested my head on the raised side rail they had up so that he would not fall out of bed. I doubted he would fall anyway because I doubted he could even roll over by himself. Beep, beep, beep continued on.

I closed my eyes because I did not want to cry. I did not want to see him like this anymore. I wanted him to be well in that instant. I prayed, *God, please send him a miracle right now. Send him an angel to carry him up, and take him away from all this pain.* I waited for one to come while I listened to the morbid lullaby of the monitor.

I left the room and went upstairs to see Grandpa. I sat by his bed and talked to him a while. He asked how my friend downstairs was. I told him Tommy was fine. Although Grandpa was in the hospital he looked better than he did last week. He said they were sending him home soon. I smiled and told him how happy I was for him. I sat with him a while when everyone else went for a smoke. It was nice to talk. I wondered if he would get sick again, too, as soon as he got home and have to come back. I hoped not. I wished him all the best with a hug and a kiss and told him I would see him again soon before I left and went back to Tommy's room. He understood why I could not stay long.

When I went back to Tommy's room his mom had returned. She had a strange look on her face. It was a look of panic and fear. That was the first time I had seen that look on someone else's face. I knew how she was feeling in that moment; I was feeling it too.

Tommy was still asleep, but he was breathing very hard. Between breaths he was mumbling something, but I could not understand what it was. I stood by the bed for a few minutes, then I left again. I could not hold back the tears any longer.

I went to the café, got a pop, and lit a smoke. I sat alone and tried not to cry aloud. I did not want anyone to know how scared I was. Mom came into the café, and I described to her what was happening with Tommy. She convinced me to go back upstairs so she could see for herself. I went with her.

When we got back to the room he was awake. He seemed to be doing better than when he was sleeping. He was talking coherently and understood everything that was going on around him. I wondered if he knew how he just was. I was not going to tell him I was just glad he was awake.

I was scared again and Tommy sensed it. He asked me to sit on the bed with him. I did not want to. I just stood there looking at him not saying anything. I was frozen in my own fear. He really was dying. He was dying right now, right there before my own eyes. He was dying today. I had never seen anyone dying before. I understood now why I could not see him before and how important it was he stays well. How a common cold could kill him. It was killing him.

"Sit." He patted the bed again. "Sit beside me for a while."

Everyone had left the room, and it was only he and I there now.

"Okay." I sat on the bed. I did not move. I did not want to hurt him. I did not want him to fall back asleep. I did not want to touch him. I did not want to do anything. I did not want to be there anymore. I wanted to spread my wings and fly us both away. I did not know what to do.

"It is not catching, you know," he said, as he looked into my eyes then smiled at me.

I did not see Tommy anymore; I saw the leukemia and the chemotherapy. I saw death.

"It isn't catching," he said again. He slid his hand up my back as if he was Braille reading my thoughts until he rested his hand on my shoulder. He took my chin in his other hand and turned my face toward him. Then he wiped the tear off my cheek that had found the way out of hiding. He was comforting me when I needed it most, but I should have been comforting him. I could not. My thoughts were scrambled, my heart was broken, and my body was drained. This was not what I expected.

"Well, that is a good thing." I tried to smile back and pretend that everything was going to be fine, but I knew it was not. I am sure he had seen this look before on the faces of those he loved that stood and looked at him.

TOMMY'S FOREVER

This was the first time he had seen it in me. This was the first time I had felt anything like this.

He took my hand and put it on this stomach. "It feels better if you rub it." He continued to look me in the eye.

"Like this?" I began to rub his abdomen area as I looked back at him. I did not want to hurt him. I guessed that it did. Every part of his body must be in physical pain right now from the way he looked.

I slid my hand to his face and touched him gently. I wanted to kiss him, but I was so afraid. He looked like a stranger; this was not who I knew as my love. This cannot be real. I am dreaming. I want to wake up. *God, please wake me up!* I screamed in my head as I sat on the bed beside him, looking into his eyes touching his parched lips. I leaned over and kissed him on the mouth.

"I love you," was all he said, before he closed his eyes again to rest, while I continued to wait.

I wanted to tell him it was okay, but he would know I was not being truthful, so I did not say anything while I watched him fall back into the slumber toward death.

I felt sorry for him. No one should ever experience that much pain. I was sad inside. The hurt inside me was so strong I wanted to collapse. I had never before felt the crushing pain of watching someone I loved suffer before. I thought when I had found out he was sick was hard, but this was a thousand times worse than I could have imagined. I realized sitting there beside him that I could not beat this thing. I knew why he wanted to give up. When I first saw him all skinny and without any hair, that was the easy part. Now I understood why everyone was asking me when he was going to die, they knew something that I did not. I imagined they had experienced something similar before. I walked into that room a sixteen-year-old teenager, but I walked out a hundred years old. In my heart, I knew that Tommy would live forever because that was all I had to hang on too while I watched him trying to breathe.

Mom drove me home in silence. I wondered if I would ever see him again.

127

Back at School

Tevin went to school today. I had not seen him since I was barely a child. His family was my neighbours across the street a long time ago. I could not remember where they went after they moved away. I just did not see them anymore. I was not sure why he was back in high school. He is older than I but was in some of my classes. Lizzie said he asked her if I was still going out with Tommy. I do not know if he knows Tommy is sick. I am not sure if he even knows Tommy.

Tevin was waiting at the outside doors of the school when I was going to get on the bus. He asked me to show him the way around because this was his first day at school. He asked me if he could sit with me on the way home, and I agreed. I was not sure exactly what he was thinking because he had other people he knew that he could have asked for help. I was not interested in anything more than being his friend. The distraction was good and at least I had someone new to talk to for today.

It was raining when we got off the bus. Tevin took the long way and walked all the way home with me. He even carried my books. That was nice of him. He said that he was now dating Victoria, a girl I knew from around school but she was not really my friend. I wondered what she would think if she knew he walked me all the way home. I could feel the attraction between us yet I knew in my heart nothing would ever become of it. I had other things on my mind, and I was not interested in a light, casual relationship now. I think he knew that and was just being nice. I wondered what the rumors would turn out to be the next day at school from the other kids that watched us walking home together. I did not care. I did not have time for silly high school games anymore.

"Are you going to the welcoming-back dance next week?" he casually asked.

"Probably not," I admitted.

"Oh, why not?"

"I will have to catch up on homework."

"Homework," he laughed, "you, staying in to do homework? That is funny. Why don't you just save it for the weekend and go to the dance?"

"I will be busy on the weekend."

"All weekend?"

"Yes."

"It must be a pretty hot date," he laughed.

"Not quite like that." I did not laugh back.

"What then? What can be so important that you need to skip the first dance of the year to do homework so you can be busy on the weekend?"

"I will be at the hospital."

"Oh, my gosh, are you sick?"

"No, it is not me."

"Oh, a friend of yours?"

"Yes," was all I said. I did not feel like talking about it today. Words could never explain the idea that, "a friend of mine was sick." I just wanted to think about the good things that my friend had to offer, not the bad. I needed something to hang onto.

My focus was on trying to stay positive for Tommy when everyone else is saying he is going to die. I understand now why they think that but saying it all the time will just make it happen quicker. If they really saw him so sick they would not talk about it so much. They would see how cruel they are being and it would not be so amusing to them. I know those that talk about it do not intend to be cruel but they are. I see no room for that kind of negativity because it only makes a bad situation worse. I choose not to talk to them anymore about it or anything else for that matter.

Maybe things will not be okay. Maybe things will turn out all wrong. Maybe Tommy will die. The only thing for sure that I know is that he is very sick and in a lot of pain. I need to look on the bright side because there is no other side to look on. Somehow in my heart I know things will be okay, somehow I know I must try to make things okay for him. I know that whatever I do now I am going to get hurt over all of this. If I stay with Tommy now I will end up hurting a lot more than if I would if I left him. How can I leave him knowing what is happening to him now. I cannot leave him alone. I love him too much for that. He loves me too much for that. I have made the decision to love him, and I must stick to that for as long as I have with him. I will love him forever.

Maybe he wants me to leave him alone. Maybe he does not want me to watch him die. Maybe he will not die. I want to make things as nice for him. Is that not what you are supposed to do when you love someone? I did not think you were supposed to abandon someone during the time you needed him or her the most. Is that not something like what you say when you get married, in good times and in bad? Well, this was certainly bad, and I am not sure how it could get any worse. I am hoping that there are more good times to come. I hope he comes home, I know he will. My time with him cannot be over yet. I am not done with his love. I cannot give up now.

It is strange being back at school again. The summer was long and all my friends have separated ways. Lizzie has found new friends at school and Kayla moved out of her house since she has graduated. I have missed so much time at school already that everyone is already formed the cliques, and I am trying to find my way. I am not interested much in joining anyone's social activities, and it is very strange without Tommy at school every day. I just want to be with him. I do not want to be at school at all. My mind is always on Tommy and how he is doing. I do not like it here anymore. I wish I could quit. I am still friends with Bobbi, which is one good thing. Since Tevin has been dating Victoria I have become friends with her, too. We all stand together in the smoking pit before classes and meet each other at lunch.

I received a letter today from Jim through one of our mutual friends. I did not see him around today, though. I had almost forgotten that we had made plans to start dating again now school was back, but so many things have changed for me. The letter was nice, it said some sweet things that made me feel warm and fuzzy inside. I will write him back even if it is just to say Hello. I have missed his friendship but I know now that is all it was. I cannot return his feeling of affection.

It is Thanksgiving weekend. Tommy is still in the hospital. He is still sick. He has an infection, and the doctors do not know what it is. They do know that it is causing fluid on his lungs. They inserted a tube in his side to draw the fluid out. It was not working so they had to move it and put another one between his ribs to hit another spot. Now he has two big gaping holes in his side. One with a tube out of it that drains into a bag beside the bed, the other is covered with a bandage. It looks ugly when the nurse changes it. They let me watch. They say he will either get better or worse from here. I am not sure how much worse he can get.

The doctors say that things are getting a bit better for him. His liver and blood count is getting back to normal. I am not sure what normal is anymore for him. They also say he is in serious condition. That I do agree with: having fluid on your lungs, a hole in your side, having not eaten in months, sores all the way from your lips into your stomach, bed sores, oxygen to breathe, and let us not forget the leukemia. They make us wear sterile masks, gloves, and slippers and sanitize our hands each time we come and go inside his room. I would say that is serious condition. Do they need to put that label on it and say it aloud? Does it make them smart because they have the authority to say that, as if I could not make that diagnosis myself?

Sometimes it seems the smart people like doctors seem very stupid to us regular folk. I thought that he just had the flu. I thought I was just sleeping in the hospital chair for days on end were because I had nothing better to do with my time. Of course I would rather not be anyplace but in the hospital all weekend, every weekend for a month now.

I came home from the hospital for a break, as I had been there almost a week. When I got home Mom was drunk and started in on my again as soon as I walked in the door.

"Tommy is dying you know," she slurred.

I said nothing. She must have been talking to those brilliant doctors again. It seems they both have an expert opinion. I guess since either Mom or the doctor sits by his bedside all day and night long that gives them a pass at having manners. They may be physical experts, but they sure know nothing about anyone in emotional pain. She talked to me like I could not see it for myself.

"He does not have very long to live," she repeated herself. I wondered if she really thought that because I did not say anything the first time if I heard her or not. I just wanted her to stop. I was not sure why drunken people think this is a good time to make any kind of conversation, especially a personal hurtful one at the time of their own drunken painlessness. It sure did not help me any.

I thought this was a perfect time to pour my heart out to her. I thought this was a much better time to chat about my boyfriend dying than when she was in a better state of mind. In my head I commended her on her choice of timing. I was glad she was my mother at that moment. I wanted her to keep talking and reminding me I was in the most painful situation of my life. I thought this was a real supportive way to handle the situation. I was glad I came home for the support of my family. She was doing a real good job at being a mother right then. I hoped she would help me through every hardship I ever had. She knew just what to say at all the right moments especially when I needed it most. I was being sarcastic in my head.

Dad finally made her stop. I wanted her to go away and not come back this time. Again, I knew I was just being mean but she deserved it, or so I thought.

Dad invited me to sit on his lap, and he put his arms around me while I buried my head in his shoulder while I cried. He said nothing and just held me tight. I felt like a small child that was begging for protection from the big bad world. I did not ever want him to send my out into the world again. I did not like it there. I wanted to be small again and try life again. I wanted it to be different next time around that I tried. I wanted Dad to make all the bad stuff go away just like he did when I was a child. I did not want to move from that chair. For one moment I knew someone loved me and someone cared.

He took me for a long walk outside in the dark. He told me several things about his personal life he had experienced before I was even a thought. He told me of a son he had that died at a few years old because he was sick. He talked to me about the brother that I did have and how much he wished he could have been part of our lives. He told me that life throws many hardships your way sometimes and it all does not seem fair but somehow you have to deal with it and do the right thing.

He said that the right thing meant to do the thing that was best for your heart not what everyone else thought you should do. He also said that even though we can see bad things coming for ourselves ahead we should not give up no matter what it is. He thought we would all be better people for being good people. I knew what he meant, and I knew what the right thing for me to do was, no matter how hard it was going to be. I would not give up. I would not give up for me or for Tommy.

As we walked he also talked of how proud he was that I was his daughter and how much we are alike. He said that he lived for me as his child and that he did know how hard it was for me even if he did not say it in words. He said since he was my father and knew me better than anyone he could see it in my eyes and in my heart how much I hurt inside. He said he would do anything for me I needed him to do. He told me he loved me and then he asked me to quit crying and reminded me that I needed to be strong. I did.

After we went back home Dad took Mom and me out for supper. I was very hungry after spending all that time with Tommy in the hospital. I never eat much when I am there. I cannot force food to stay in my belly. I always feel sick, and when I do eat I throw up anyway. Therefore I avoid it altogether.

My thoughts fell toward my father's life as I tried to sleep. I thought of how he grew up in a family with nine children. I had heard various stories of my father's childhood over the years, but it was mostly how they had had to work on the farm and how poor they were. It seemed that in those days the children left home to find a life for themselves at a very early age. By the time my father was sixteen years old he was already making a life for himself as a man, just as I was trying to find my own way.

I thought about my own entrance into this world, and the first thing I remember in my own consciousness is standing outside in the dark alone. I could faintly hear the voices of several people engaging in some kind of adult activity. I remember feeling scared, alone, and second to everything. I was not prepared to hang on to these feelings for a very big part of my life.

I recall a few other fragments of my early childhood but my real vivid memories do not start until I was about four years old.

We lived in a house in which I had a bedroom at the top of the stairs. I was always terrified to go up the stairs in the dark. It was a very long way to the top, and I always felt as if someone was following behind me. I had an invisible friend named Lola. She played with me every day out in the yard and accompanied me to places I did not want to go alone. She would be there whenever I called on her to come for me. Lola would help me to walk up and down the stairs when I was afraid.

My sister and her older friend would babysit me when my mother was out and my father was away. They would tell me I was adopted because I was born in a cabbage patch. My sister would tell me our parents were not my real parents and some day the men in the white coats were going to come and take me away. My sister and her friend would then leave the house and return dressed in raincoats with hats on in disguise. They would tell a story that they were the men coming to take me away. I would cry and panic in fear. Once again I was scared and alone. I would call on Lola to come to rescue me.

While we lived in the house with the stairs I remember my father being around quite often doing various physical things like restoring a boat and having several pets. I remember my brother would occasionally visit us, but he did not live there. The men in the white coats must have already taken him away, but they let him come home occasionally to see us.

We had a hound dog in a pen in the back of the yard. Her name was Grey. She was on a chain as well as in a kennel because she had escaped several times. She had several puppies; she was nursing them. I went outside one day and the dog was hanging from the collar over the side of the kennel. She was dead. She had hung herself. I recalled telling my father of what I had found.

We had an above-ground swimming pool in our yard. My father had caught a catfish that appeared to be larger than I was, and put it in out in the swimming pool. My sister told me she was going to put me in the swimming pool with the fish. I knew that was not true because Lola would never let her do that. She would be there to protect me. I stood and watched my father retrieve the fish, cut its head off, take its internal organs out, and cook it on the barbeque. I knew then that I was safe.

Lizzie and I had also been friends forever. In fact, I never remember not knowing her.

Lizzie's mother was my father's cousin. Therefore, we are related by blood. Her grandmother and my grandmother were sisters. Her grandfather and my grandfather were brothers. We have a lot of the same genetically makeup, but it was funny how we were really quite different. One thing was the same; we knew we would always be best friends. I felt some comfort in knowing that.

Do You Love My Son?

The next day Mom took me back to see Tommy. The specialist had been there and said Tommy had an infection, but Tommy was not sure what he had said. The rest of his family was there too, but they did not know either. I looked on his chart and found some notes that said phenomena.

Tommy slept most of the time while I was there. That was okay because he needed the rest for his body to heal. At least now he was resting a bit better than before. I wondered if they were giving him a new kind of antibiotic to fight the infection although I forgot to look for that part on the chart. I wondered if they were if it was helping. Something seemed to be for now. I sat beside the bed and listened to him breathing while he slept, and waited for him to get better.

I walked down the hallway and went into the room that had the word, "Chapel," on the door. I was not sure if I had ever been in such a room before but it was not like what I expected. I expected stained glass windows, Bibles, statues, and other church stuff. It was not like that at all. It was a small room with a pedestal at the front and a few bench seats. Once I got inside and sat down I forgot to look for a Bible. It was quiet in there, and I was not sure if I had to pray to God out loud because I was in the room, like I saw on TV or if praying in my head was good enough. Sometimes Tommy talks to the pastor of a church that is down the road from him. I will need to remember to ask him when he wakes up. He would probably know more than I do about that, or at least he could ask someone about it. I had no one to ask. I thought it probably really would not matter how I prayed in that room since it was only a room in the hospital with a sign on the door. I knew the faith had to come from inside myself. It did not mean I was any closer to God sitting downstairs than I was sitting by Tommy's bed on the second floor.

I almost could hear Tommy's voice in my head say something like, "You would be closer upstairs since it is fourteen steps closer to heaven." Then I imagined him telling me something else like, "If you want to get closer to heaven then maybe you should go up to the roof." The funny thing is if he said that I would have.

So I prayed in my head, just in case someone else walked in and heard me talking. My thoughts of God were private, and I did not want to let anyone else know that I thought Tommy really might die.

God, I do not know where I am supposed to be to pray. In fact I know nothing about you at all. I know I never go to church, and I find myself sometimes doing things I should not. For that I am sorry. However, I ask that you take a moment of your time to listen to me anyway because today I am not praying for myself. I am willing to take any punishment that I deserve for the wrongs I have done, and I am willing to take any punishment for the wrongs Tommy has done, if it can work like that. I ask that if I can I could take his pain from him. I wish that I were sick instead of him. I ask that you make him well again if only for a little while. I need him. I have no one else here. I want him to live. I do not understand what is happening. I am not that smart. I just ask that you help Tommy to get well again. That is all. I know I have asked very silly things from you before, I am sorry I wasted your time. Please, please, please, help Tommy, Amen.

I stood up walked out of the room and went into the coffee shop. I stood at the cooler and looked for a drink. I really did not want a drink, I was not thirsty. I did not even know if I would puke it up if I tried to drink it anyway. I dug in my pocket for change. I was not sure if I even had any money to pay for it.

I pulled out five quarters and a dime. That should be enough money. I stood there and looked some more. Juice was the best option. At least that way if I were not going to eat I would get a bit of nutrition. I was trying to be as healthy as I could for my body. I thought if God answered my prayers and made me sick to make Tommy well I wanted to have a good start. Although I knew that would not happen and even if it could Tommy would not let me do that for him anyway.

I gave my money to the cute boy behind the counter. I had given him my money several times before. He smiled and said, "Hi." At that moment I found comfort in any familiar face that did not seem to be as sad as I was. I wondered if he would be working again next weekend when I came. I was sure I would be here.

"Hi." I smiled back.

I was not sure how much money he asked me for, but I gave him all the change I had. I knew that would be the last thing I bought today, and Mom or

Dad would give me more money the next time. Dad always made sure I had enough money for whatever I needed but I usually did not spend much on anything while I was in the city. I usually had his credit card if I needed money anyway but I did not use that either.

I sat down at a table with Tommy's Mom and sister. They were eating a sandwich and some chips. I opened my juice, lit a smoke and looked down at the ashtray that needed to be emptied. It looked as if they had been here a while.

"Can I ask you a question?" Tommy's Mom asked.

I looked up at her and wondered what she wanted. Even though we were together in Tommy's room a lot together I hardly ever talked to her about anything. I did not respond to her question. Tommy's sister kept eating.

"Why are you here?"

I was shocked. What did she mean, why was I here? Why did she think I was there?

"Mom!" Tommy's sister joined in. It seems she was as shocked as I was. "She is here because she loves him."

Tommy's Mom looked at me straight in the eye, "Do you love my son?"

I felt the tear again in my eye before I could answer, "Yes." If she only knew how much I loved her son. I knew I could not tell her. I could not tell his sister; I could not tell anyone. Tommy knew how much I loved him, and that was enough.

"Of course she loves him. Why do you think she is here?" Tommy's sister spoke on my behalf. I was glad she was there. I am not sure what I would have done without her advocating for me. I turned toward her but I could not say a word. I just wanted to cry. How could she doubt my love for him? Did she think I was some kind of morbid teenage girl that had nothing better to do than come here and watch him in so much pain? Did she think this was fun for me? Didn't she know he had told me he feels better when I am here with him? Didn't she know he asked me to be here? I quickly decided in my head that I did not care why she thought I was here. I did not need to justify anything to her. I knew why I was here, and Tommy did too; that was all that mattered.

This time Tommy was very sick. Mom said that I could stay at my aunt's again for a few more days before I came home so I could be close to Tommy. I really did not want to go home. I knew she thought it was because he was for sure not going to make it through this infection this time. I had doubts, myself. If he really was going to die I wanted to be there when he did.

Being close to him was the only place I felt anything. When I was not with him I felt nothing. I walked around school like I was a zombie anyway; I might as well be here with him.

I knew his mother did not like me. I did not care. Tommy did not care either. I knew he would want me close to him, although he could not say that anymore. He did not say anything. He just slept.

The Call

I was sitting in math class writing Tommy a letter. It was uncertain if he would ever get it or not. I wrote him letters all the time anyway. I would give them to him when I went every weekend to see him at the hospital if he was feeling well enough. I would also read them to him the phone when he is feeling well enough to call.

Today writing him a letter was much better than doing grade ten math in grade eleven. Since I had failed the class last year I had to take it over again. Grade ten mathematics was a mandatory credit to graduate. Although it seemed a long way from today, I did want to graduate someday.

"Dear Tommy," I wrote at the top of my page. I put the paper right inside my math binder so everyone would think I was really doing the assigned work. I had nothing to do when I got home anyway, so I could finish my math then. Maybe later I would be able to better concentrate than I could right now.

"I hope you are feeling better today. I am sitting here in math class, but I would rather be thinking about you. Thinking about you always makes me feel better even when I cannot be with you. I hope you are doing well. I am going to be able to come and see you this weekend. Mom says she will either give me a ride or I can use the car to get my friend to drive me there. I will come on Saturday and maybe I can spend the weekend...."

"So that is why he was always late for homeroom every day last year." Miss Bell, the grade-ten math teacher, said as she was standing there reading my note over my shoulder.

My face went all red, and I thought for sure I was in trouble. The next thing I thought for sure she would say was something like "And you wondered why you failed this math class last year?"

I was going to flip over the page so that she could not see the note, but it was already too late. I knew that even if she had not read the entire thing there were enough words on the paper to prove I had not done any math work at all. I thought for sure I was going on another trip to the vice principal's office to see God.

I looked up at her and smiled, "Well, every now and then he would walk me to class."

"Every now and then?" she smiled back at me. She knew I was not telling the complete truth on that one. "Tell him I said hi," she told me, just before she put her hand on my shoulder and continued to check other students' homework.

"Oh, by the way, Miss Bell says hi; she just caught me writing his letter. I will tell her you say hi back because I know you would." I continued writing until the bell rang at the end of class. She did not come back around to check on me again, Thank God.

As I was packing my books to leave for lunch she called me to her desk. She asked me about Tommy and how he really was doing. I told her he was in the hospital and was very sick. She always guessed at how sick he really was by how much time I missed from class. When he was very sick I only went to school a few days a week. Just enough to catch up on a couple lessons, get some notes from the other kids, get homework assignments and then I would go back to stay at the hospital for another four or five days.

I did not have many friends anymore because I was hardly ever at school. I still hung around with Bobbi, who had started to hang around a few other girls when I was away. They were all good friends, and they welcomed me hang out with them, too. Jeff had already quit school, but Victoria and I were still friends. I hung out with her a lot, too. I focused most of my attention toward my personal life away from school and kept a low profile. It all seemed to work out better that way.

I had several chores at home that were my responsibility, too. I fed the dogs, helped cook supper and every now and then had to drive to the laundry mat to wash and dry the clothes when we did not have enough water at home to do it. I really did not mind that as it got me away for a while and I could drive the car. Some times I took the long route just to be alone.

I thought it odd when my sister came to the laundry matt and told me I needed to go home right away because Mom needed the car for something. I wondered why she did not just use my sister's car or why she had sent me in the first place if she has something to do. I did not care because that meant my sister had to stay and finish the work.

When I got home, Mom had told me that "they" had called from the hospital. Tommy was very sick, and "they" did not think he was going to live through the night. She said I had better pack some clothes in a bag, and she already called her sister, so I could stay there as long as I needed. Mom had also already arranged to meet one of Tommy's sisters and her husband in a nearby town, and we would go together to the hospital to see what was happening. It all happened so quickly I was not sure how I felt or what I thought.

I went into my room and started packing clothes into a bag. I did not know what I would need or how long I would be staying this time. I stood at the end of my bed and closed my eyes for a moment. Was this the end?

By the time we arrived at the hospital Tommy's family and a couple close friends were already there. They were the most silent group of people I had ever seen. They were all just sitting around in the waiting room in chairs staring at the floor every now and then someone would say something or go get coffee. I sat down and stared at the floor for a while, too.

Tommy was in his hospital room where he had been before. He still had the tube in his side, was hooked up to several monitors, and was breathing oxygen from a mask. I stood again at the side of his bed and looked at him in silence.

He was sleeping, but his eyes were open. He did not have any focus and was staring into space. I knew he was not there.

He was talking, but it was all mixed up. He was not making any sense. He was talking to many people all at once. He was moving his arms and hands as if he was doing something, but I could not tell what. If I tried to talk to him or ask him questions he did not respond as if he understood. I just stood by the bedside alongside of whatever family member came, went, and watched him.

He was yelling at his sister about her peeling an orange for him. He was yelling at the dog. He was driving a car. He was mumbling soft words under his breath. I wondered what kind of a trip his mind was taking him on. I wondered if this was his way of having his life flash before his eyes but it was taking longer than a moment. I wondered if he would ever wake up. I was afraid. I did not understand.

The doctors and nurses told us it was hallucinations from the infection. They said his blood pressure was very high, and that was what was causing all the trouble. I did not know about all that kind of stuff, but I wanted him well. I wanted him back.

I stayed at the hospital as long as I could handle it there. Mom had gone back home already so I took a cab to my aunt's. She was home this time, and her daughter was there, too. They took me out for something to eat. It was nice not being alone there this time. I really needed the support of someone who did not know Tommy and what was happening. They asked me a few questions about it but the conversation drifted quickly toward other things. For a moment, I felt relief.

My aunt suggested I shower before bed that I would feel better, and I could sleep with her instead of on the couch. She said the rest would do me good because I would have a few real long days ahead of me. I did not know what she meant but I enjoyed her trying to comfort me and bring her good ideas forth. It seems I had fallen asleep before my head even hit the pillow that night.

I awoke to my aunt talking on the phone to someone. I looked out the window and it was still dark out. I did not know what time it was but it was not morning yet.

"Okay, I will have her there right away." My aunt hung up the phone, and then I heard her call a cab and give them her address.

I knew something was wrong at the hospital and got out of bed and dressed before she was off the phone. I went into the bathroom and brushed my teeth. I put my hygiene stuff into my purse and ran a comb through my hair. I knew it would be a while before I was back at the apartment.

"It is bad," she told me. "They do not think he is going to make it much longer," was about all she said before she asked me if I had enough money and if I needed anything else.

"No thanks." I smiled. "I'll be fine."

I was not fine. I was shaking inside. I did not want to go to the hospital. I changed my mind; I did not want to be there when he died. I did not want to be there because I did not want him to die. I wanted to do anything to make this all go away.

"I'll pray for him." She hugged me.

Pray for him? I already did that. God was not listening. God did not care. God did not help Tommy. God had allowed Tommy to get worse and now he was going to die. What good would praying to God do? I had already received the answers to my prayer, and that answerer was *No*.

"Okay, thanks." I tried to smile as I put on my shoes. "I will wait outside for the cab."

The doctors had moved Tommy upstairs in the hospital to the critical care unit. It had a buzzer on the locked door and you had to be accepted to go in. The more experience I had with this hospital the more the protocols did not make much sense to me. Who would want to be here if they did not have to?

I felt dizzy as I stood outside the door and waited for something to happen. I felt like I was going to be sick. I felt like I was going to fall down. There would be no one there to catch me. I supposed if I passed out eventually someone would come. After all, this was a place where they took care of people was not it. All I wanted to do was see Tommy now. I did not think I was going to have to say goodbye to him I just wanted to hold his hand or rub his feet, or something. I wanted him to know I was there for him.

Finally a volunteer came to the door and let me in. I could hear the voices of Tommy's family as soon as I got close to the waiting room. I took an inventory of who was all there so I knew who was in the room with Tommy.

"We cannot see him yet," someone said. "They are still doing tests."

I wondered what good more tests would do. "Okay." I sat in the hard orange chair and waited.

"Here." Tommy's brother-in-law handed me a cup. "I bought you a coffee."

"Thanks," I said as I took the cup. I did not drink coffee. In fact I hated coffee. I could not even stand the smell of it. I took the lid off. It appeared as if it had cream and sugar already in it. In my head I could hear Tommy say, "You don't have to drink it," but I took a sip anyway. I waited some more.

A nurse came out and told Tommy's mom that she could go in to see him now. They said she could only take one other person with her. She asked if they would make an exception so three could go. They asked who, and she told them she wanted her husband and Tommy's girlfriend to go. The volunteer did not say anything at first; then Tommy's dad said he would not stay long and promised we would all be quiet. Then they said it would be okay for all of us to go.

Again they made us wear masks, gowns, slippers, and stuff. We already knew that as soon as we saw them sitting close to his bed when we walked in.

He looked different from how he had just a few hours ago. All the words were gone, his eyes were closed now, and he had tubes out of every place they could stick him. He had heart monitors, breathing monitors, blood-pressure cuffs, and all kinds of other gadgets I had never seen before. If I had not known for sure it was Tommy I would not have recognized him at all.

We stood by the bed in silence. Tommy's mom was rubbing his head and said a few words to him. Tommy's dad stood beside his wife and watched his son lying there in that bed, dying. I stood at the foot of the bed like an outsider. I did not know what to say or do. My heart was so broken it did not even hurt anymore. I watched him. I waited some more, but this time I was not sure for what.

"I will go tell the others how he is," Tommy's dad said, just before he left the bedside.

I moved over closer to Tommy's mom. I took Tommy by the hand as a tear ran out of my eye and soaked up in the mask I was wearing. I felt sorry for Tommy as I looked down at him lying in the bed. His mom reached down and pulled the white sheet up toward his chest.

"He feels cold," she said, without looking at me.

"Yeah, I think he is, too." We finally agreed on something.

I woke up in the chair in the waiting room where I had fallen asleep. Everyone else was already gone except Jeff, who was still asleep a few chairs to my right. I wondered where they were. I sat up and fixed myself as best I could and waited.

Finally Tommy's eldest sister came back with more coffee. This time I took it willingly and thanked her greatly. Now I knew what coffee was all about. It could be as much your best friend as any other substance people used to sustain normal functioning in critical situations.

I was able to go back in and see Tommy again for a while. For a moment Tommy's words had returned, but it was obvious when he was trying to pull out his IV line and was trying to get out of bed that he was still in the hallucinations. When I asked him where he was going he stated, "I am fucking going home." That was just before they made me leave his room again.

Tommy would go between waking up and falling back asleep. He was still covered in tubes and IVs. At one point he had a tube up his nose and into his stomach that they were feeding him green stuff through. He did not like that much, because he pulled it out himself as soon as he could. The nurses gave him trouble for it, but he did not care. When they asked him why he pulled it out he told them because he simply did not like it. They did not try to pull it back in.

I stayed at the hospital all day. I mostly sat in the same hard, orange chair. Shortly after supper hour I went back to my aunt's to shower and change my clothes. I was not there long this time and went back to the hospital.

By the time I returned they had moved Tommy out of critical care and down to his regular room. I was not able to see him again until much later that night. At least down in his regular room the nurses would let us stay as long as we could handle the pain inside.

That night I stayed in a nursing resident's room with Tommy's mom and sister in a room they had given us across the street. The room was small, had two beds and thin blankets. I did not care. I only lay awake all night long waiting to see Tommy again in the morning anyway. I did not want to leave him to even go get any sleep at all but the nursed assured me they would personally come and get us if anything changed during the night.

I was up, showered and back at the hospital by seven a.m. I wanted to see Tommy as soon as I could, but I did not get to see him until almost lunchtime. I stayed for as long as I could. Mom was back in the city so I went back to my aunt's with her for a while before she left for home again. We had supper and she gave me a ride back to the hospital where I stayed with Tommy from around seven until almost midnight before I left again. I slept in the same room with Tommy's mom and his aunt from out of town.

I was up early again and went across the road via the tunnel to see Tommy again. I stayed beside him until Mom came and got me around two to get my belongings from my aunt's place. This time she was taking me home. I was not sure why, and I really wanted to stay here with him, but she said it was for the best. I did not believe her but I did not have the energy to argue about it. I just followed along what anyone told me was the best for me because I did not know anything for sure myself.

I forgot my note that would explain why I was away to take to school on Monday because I had been away so many days so I got a detention. I did not try to explain to them where I was because I did not want to relive the last few days even in my head if I did not have to. I did not care much about the detentions anyway, since I had no place special to go.

Tommy was getting a bit better, and he was awake enough to call me from the hospital. I do not think he is thinking that clearly yet according to our conversations but at least he feels good enough to call at all.

"I could scare you if I wanted to," he said.

"Oh, how?" I questioned his comments.

"I could tell you that I see cats and dogs all the time here in the hospital room with me."

"Still? I thought you were feeling better."

"Still? Don't you think that is weird?"

145

I did not think it was as weird as he thought it was. "Yeah, a bit I guess." I lied to him. I did not think that was as weird as what was happening to him before he started to feel better. It was clear he had no idea what he had been through. I was at least happy for him that he could remember seeing anything at all. He might not think he was getting better, but those of us that slept in the waiting room in the orange chairs sure knew he was.

I was glad he was feeling better now even he if could not see it for himself. I was happy that the doctors had been wrong and he did make it through the night. I did not ever want to go through that again. I did not want him to get that sick ever again. I was glad he could not remember. It seemed that no one had told him what we went through, and I was not going to be the one to do it.

"They said I can come home in a few days."

"They did?"

"Yes, they said that I am doing much better and as soon as my blood pressure comes down a bit more I can come home."

"I am glad to hear you say that," but there was no way he could know how glad I really was. My heart beat with joy. It had been a short week ago they thought he was not going to make it through the night. We all thought for sure he was going to die but he did not. Now he is telling me he gets to come home, that is wonderful news.

"The bad thing is that they said I could not have any company because my immune system is so low. Any kind of cold or flu I could catch my body would not be able to fight it, and I will be back in the hospital."

"That is understandable."

"I want to see you when I get home, though. I think you should come anyway; it is worth getting sick to see you."

"No, I will wait until they say it is okay to come." The last thing I wanted was to be the one to bring him a cold and he gets sick again. I would wait a lifetime to see him if that is what the doctor said to keep him well. I knew he did not understand how much we had just watched him suffer through because he could not say those things if he did.

"They do not know anything. I want you to spend the night with me as soon as I get out."

"No, they are right. I am back at school, and there are too many things I could carry and bring to you. We can talk on the phone instead. Besides, you know as soon as you are well enough I will come."

"But I want you to come to see me the second I get home. I don't care what they say."

146

"No, I won't. I can't. I don't care how badly you want that; you are just going to have to wait until you get better. You *have* to get better before I come. It will give you something to get better for. You will just have to wait. Period."

"But I want you to come and see me," he begged.

I closed my eyes and remembered him at the hospital. The lump came back in my throat, but I did not want him to know how much I wanted to see him too, but I couldn't. I could not be responsible for making him sick again.

"No. I can't." I sobbed a bit. "I am sorry."

"I know. I am sorry for asking."

"See, you did not scare me at all. It is not because of the infection you are seeing things. I think it is just because you are plain crazy," I joked.

"Nah, you are crazy. You are the one that is in love with me."

"No, I am not."

"In love with me?"

"Crazy."

"I think you are crazy."

"Why?"

"The nurses told me how much you loved me today."

"How do they know?"

"Because they said when you were here you never left my side. They said you were in my room even more than my family. They said you must love me a whole lot to sit beside my bed and hold my hand for so long." He paused. "They said I must love you too because any time you went to the bathroom or something I would wake up and ask for you. They said they assured me you would be right back, but I did not fall asleep again until you were there. Is that right?"

"Do you think they are making that up?" I asked.

"No. They said you were here until they kicked you out at night and were here first thing in the morning."

"Yeah, would you rather I hadn't come?"

"No. I wanted you here."

"And so I was."

"I knew you were here."

"You did not."

"Yes, I did."

"How did you know?"

"I could just tell you were."

"Okay. You could tell."

"Thank you."

"You do not have to thank me, Tommy."

"Yes, I do. I know what it is like when you are not here. I hate it here without you. Thank you for being here with me even if I did not know it all the time."

"You knew it. In your heart you knew I was there all along. It was just like you said, you just knew."

"Yeah, I guess I did."

I said nothing.

"I miss you." He finally broke the silence.

"I miss you, too."

I was amazed. Ten days after being in the critical care unit Tommy came home. Mom had made comments toward the idea that she wondered if they just let him come home to die because he was so sick. I doubted that. They let him come home because he is well enough now.

Tommy called every morning before I went to school. I would call him on my lunch hour to see what he was doing which he was usually watching something on TV or in his room listening to the radio. Sometimes we would talk again after school and always before we went to sleep. I could not see him yet, but we certainly kept in touch all day long. I understood that life could change in an instant and an hour could seem like eternity. I had never put value on time before but when you are not sure how much more you are going to have of it you learn in a hurry what is important to do with it when you can.

He said he was feeling better and asked me to spend the night with him at his house. I was not sure if that was a good idea yet but he had been home a while and assured me he was feeling fine. He said he even asked him Mom and she said it was okay but I did not believe him on that part. On the other hand I knew his Mom would certainly not have allowed me over if it would not have been fine. So I agreed.

We both slept in his single bed together in his room. I think it was more like he slept, and I lay beside him all night, awake, thanking God to have this chance to be with him again.

Eric

"Tommy, I need to tell you something, and I do not want you to get mad at me."

"What?" I could tell by his voice he already was. I might have chosen a different delivery line, but it was too late for that now.

"I met someone a while ago, and we have become friends."

"You have a boyfriend?" he was sarcastic.

"No." I could not tell him the truth. "Not really a boyfriend."

"Tell me about it."

I could not tell what he wanted to know but I knew he deserved to know everything I had been doing in last little while. "What do you want to know?"

"Everything." He was upset, and he had every right to be. He was sick in the hospital, and I had met someone else although purely by accident.

"Like what?" I was trying to play as stupid as I could, but it was frustrating him more.

"Tell me how you met him."

"My friend and I were standing at the store one night, and I was standing by the telephone wishing I could call you. It was when you were real sick, and I could not talk to you at all. I was missing you terribly." I was not trying to candy coat the situation; that part was true.

"Yeah?"

"This guy came up and started talking to both of us while he was waiting to meet this girl that lived down the street a bit, his girlfriend. We told him that she would not be allowed to come and hang out with him because her parents did not allow that to happen. The more Eric waited for her the more he knew we were right. He works with her in the harvest on a farm a few miles up the road. He is a French guy that is only here for a while."

"So."

149

"Then I saw him a couple times after that but not much because I was at the hospital with you. When I saw him again he said I looked sad all the time and asked me where I had been. He would try to cheer me up and did not care why I was unhappy, just that I was."

"What did you tell him about why you were so sad?"

"At first I did not tell him anything, but he kept asking where I went on the weekends because I was not around. I told him my boyfriend was very sick and in the hospital."

"Oh."

"He said you must be real sick because I was always gone away and was always so sad. I told him you were and that you almost died."

"Did you have sex with him?"

"No."

"Have you ever?"

"He is done with the harvest and has caught the bus to go back home."

"Where is he from?"

"Up North."

"Have you had sex with him?"

"Yes."

"Do you love him?"

"No, I love you."

"You do not."

"Yes, I do."

"How can you love me and do that?"

"I don't know."

"You were just here last weekend with me. Were you with him then?"

"No, I was with you." I was breaking my own heart now. "Can I come to see you right now?"

"No."

"FINE."

"FINE." He hung up the phone.

I knew I was responsible for tearing Tommy's heart in half. I do not know why I told him of Eric. I knew why I liked spending time with Eric. He was an escape from all the terrible things I was watching Tommy go through. Eric makes me laugh, we can have fun, go for walks together, out for dinner, to the show, or just hang out, and everything is not always so serious. When I am with Eric everything seems better for a while. For a few moments I forget how cruel life is and there is still some goodness left. When I am with Eric I feel

God has not forgotten about me. God has given me Eric to keep me sane. Eric is alive and well, and I need him for that, even if it is only for a while. I could not tell Tommy all those things, after all, Eric was really an escape from the horror I was living in every day while I was watching Tommy slowly fade away.

Mom said she thought it was a good idea I dated Eric but I already knew why she thought that. She thought that dating Eric would lessen the blow to my heart when Tommy died. She did not say that out loud but she did not have to.

"Get the phone before you go." Mom yelled from the kitchen.

I picked up the phone to say hello. It was Eric. I had not talked to him since last week when I took him to the bus station to go home. I had missed him. I wished he was here right now. I could tell him Tommy was mad at me, and Eric could make me feel better, but I knew that would not be fair to him, so I did not say anything about being upset about that.

"What are you doing?" he asked.

"Nothing. I was just about to go to out."

"Where?"

"For a drive."

"You sound sad again."

"I am."

"Why?"

"I told Tommy about you, and he got real mad at me."

"Oh, did you break up with him?"

"I don't know." I was crying.

"Can I help?"

"No." I knew he could not help this, even if he was the cause.

"What are you up to?" I changed the subject. Eric could do nothing about it anyway, and I did not expect him to have to listen to me cry over it. I did not want him to feel bad for what I had done to Tommy.

"I worked today. I am buying a car this week."

"Oh, good for you."

"I wondered if you wanted me to come down to see you as soon as I get it."

"Sure."

"I thought that if I came down next weekend, then the weekend after that I would bring my stuff and come down there to stay."

"Stay?" I wondered what he meant.

"Yeah, stay. You know, move down there to be closer to you."

"Stay? For how long?"

"I don't know: as long as you wanted me to."

"Oh." I paused.

"I miss you," he admitted.

"I miss you, too."

"I keep your picture beside my bed. I kiss it every morning before I go to work. I lay it down on the bed when I leave so it is the first thing I see when I come home."

"That is nice." I did not know what to say to him. This was starting to sound like love.

"I wrote you a letter today. I will send it in the mail. Will you write me one back?"

"Yeah."

"I cannot wait to see you again."

"Me too."

I did not want to fall in love with Eric, and I did not want him to fall in love with me either. I was falling hard or had tripped into it by mistake. This is not what I expected when I said hello to him the first day. He said so many nice things to me and it always seemed like he meant them all. Being with him was easy. Talking to him was easy.

I did miss him. I wanted to see him. I wished he was here. I did want him to come here to stay so he could be close to me but I was not sure how that would affect everything with Tommy. I had been honest with Eric and told him that no matter what happened Tommy would be my first priority and that I was not going to ever break up with him. Eric said he did not care because he just liked being with me no matter what else I had going on in my life. I had told Eric everything about Tommy long before he ever kissed me. I did not want to tell Tommy that because I did not want Tommy to think Eric, or anyone else felt sorry for him. Tommy would be much more upset at that than anything else.

I think Eric and Mom had conversations that I was not aware of because although Eric never said it, he thought Tommy was going to die soon, too. Maybe he thought that because I was so sad all the time. I am not sure what he thought

"When are you coming?"

"Next weekend. I thought we might go see my sister for the weekend. Do you want to come with me?"

"Sure, sounds like fun."

"We can spend the night at her house together. Would you like that?"

"Yes, I would."

"I cannot talk long; I just wanted to call you and see if you wanted to go with me there. I will call you again in a few days when I get my car. We can make more definite plans then."

"Sure."

"Bye."

"Bye."

I got in the truck and thought I might go see Kayla. I needed to bounce some ideas off someone that would understand my reasoning. I am not sure if she would agree with it but she would understand it. I was not sure if telling Tommy was the right thing to do or not. I had remembered what my father had told me about keeping secrets. I knew that keeping secrets was not a good idea. I only imagined if someone had seen Eric and me together and told Tommy about it before I did. I did not want that to happen. I think that would break his heart even more. I supposed it did not matter how much I justified my actions dating someone else seemed all wrong. I wanted to make it better now, I just did not know how. While I was driving I had changed my mind. I was going to go see Tommy even if he did not want me to. I needed to see him. I needed to tell him I was sorry again for all that I had done.

I went to his house despite the fact he had told me not to. His dad answered the door and told me he was not there. I was angry. It was just like him to leave because he thought I was coming. It was just like him to know I would come. Did he not see I could not stay away from him no matter how hard things were between us? Did he not see that nothing had changed? I was with Eric when I came every day to the hospital, I missed school for him, I missed work for him, I missed my friends for him, and he left. He had a lot of nerve.

I got back in the truck. All of the sudden I did not want to go to Kayla's anymore. It was getting late, and I did not want to drive that far into town. I decided I would take a drive around the block and see if Jim was home. It was not far to his house from Tommy's.

I had gotten to Jim's just in time to talk to him for about fifteen minutes before he left with his friends. I wished he would have stayed and hung out with me yet I knew I would just be a depressant for him. I knew the value in being with your friends when you were up. I did not tell him about my hardships, I wished him fun as he left.

I went back home.

I was still angry at Tommy for not understanding what I needed. If he wanted me not to treat him like he was sick, I would not. I refuse to feel sorry for him because he has an illness I cannot fix. Just because he has leukemia gives him no right to be a jerk to me. Does he not see that? Does he not see that I have feelings, too? Does he not understand this is hard for me, too? Everyone else has someone to lean on, to cry on, to talk to, to have fun with, to make them forget, and I do not. I have Tommy and he is the one that is sick. I cannot forget that because I see it in his eyes every day. I hear it in his voice over the phone. I am the one left waiting for to him to call, waiting for him to get better, waiting for him to wake up. I am the one waiting for him. I am not going to wait any longer for Eric. I have lost the fight for Tommy. I cannot make him well again and it is unfair that he asks me to. I do not want to try. I have had it. I am done with Tommy.

Eric called again. It was nice to talk to him. He said he just called because he missed me and could not wait to see me next weekend and wanted to talk to me before he went to sleep. I wished him sweet dreams to come to him in the night because I knew I would not have any. I knew falling asleep with Tommy mad at me because of some terrible mistakes I had made would only bring me nightmares. I was not exactly sure what my biggest mistake was: dating Eric in the first place or telling Tommy about it.

I was right I did not sleep well. I woke up feeling more tired than before I had gone to bed. When the alarm rang for me to get up and go to school I felt sick to my stomach. I did not want to get up. I did not want to go to school. I did not want to see anyone. I had broken my own heart and now someone else's. I did not want to do anything but set my wrongs right. I was not sure how I could.

I stood in the shower for several extra minutes. I tried to wash away all my inner pain with the soap on my skin but it did not work. I scrubbed and scrubbed but it would not come out of my heart. I sat down in the shower and cried. I wished a million times I could turn back to the clock so that I could change my decisions from a few moths ago but I knew I could not. I knew what I needed to do even if that meant it was going to be the hardest thing I had ever done yet. Even if I did not want too I needed to see Tommy and somehow make this right.

I got out of the shower and dried my hair. I could not face myself in the mirror today. I hung my head to avoid my own eyes. I asked myself one more time trying to figure out what I had done. Why did something that felt so good for me feel so bad? Why was God torturing me with both the good and bad of love at the same time? If Tommy was not sick this would not happened. I would not have broken his heart. I may not have his heart to break. If Tommy was not sick, I wondered if I would even still be dating him. I wondered if he would even want me as his girlfriend anyway.

You are stupid to do a thing like this to him. You love him. He is your best friend. He does not deserve this crap from you. He would be better off without you. He is sick and is dying, and you did this to him. You should have not told him about Eric. You should have not been with Eric. You should have not let Eric fall in love with you. You should not fall in love with Eric. You are lying to Eric, too, because you are letting him believe you love him. You do not want to be with Eric. You want to be with Tommy. Eric is not the one for you. You should break it off with Eric right now. You should call him and tell him you do not love him. Tell Eric not to come back to see you ever again. That would be the best for everyone. The voices in my head were ringing so loud the next thing I knew I was bent over the toilet heaving up the last thing in my stomach that was left of what I had eaten last night. It felt like whatever was coming up from inside of me was coming from my toenails. The more I heaved the more it hurt. My body was hardly strong enough to hold myself up from falling in my own vomit. I must have the flu.

I lay on my bed in the fetal position with the wet towel still wrapped around my naked body. I was not sure how it stayed intact after all that puking. I was too sad to cry, and too weak to stand. I knew I could stay home from school and tell Mom I had the flu, but staying in bed all day would not make my mistake go away nor would it make Tommy not be mad at me anymore. I could get dressed and go to his house instead of school. I doubt he would see me anyway if I did that. It would certainly be a waste of time, so I had just better get myself dressed and face the day. I was not sure what it would bring, and I could see it not bringing anything good, but I had to do something. I would lie here a few more minutes before I went.

God...I have made a mistake. I have been handed a situation that I had thought I could make the best of, and I did not. I broke Tommy's heart more than I have broken my own. I do not want him to be mad at me. I want him to understand how hard this is for me, too. If he does die I will have no one. I do not want him to die, but I think he is going to. I do not know what to do. I do not know how I am going to get through this. I do not know how to help Tommy anymore.

I woke up again to the phone ringing. I had fallen asleep praying to God. I was not even sure where I left off. I did not want to get the phone because I did not care who it was. I let it ring as I rolled over and looked at the clock. I was officially late for school. I got out of bed and went into the bathroom and started to vomit again. I certainly must have the flu for sure.

The phone kept ringing and ringing. I wanted it to stop. The high pitch hurt my head, even more than it already did. Now to go along with this stomach issue, I had a big headache.

"Hello," I said, even though I had been puking and was still naked from my shower.

"I am sorry for getting mad at you."

"I am more than sorry for what I did."

"I know you need other friends than me, but I want you to know I love you."

"I love you, too." I started to cry. I knew for sure I loved Tommy, and he was the only one that I wanted to be with.

"You don't sound so good. Are you okay?"

"I think I have the flu," I said as I held back the tears.

"You should stay home from school if you are sick," he suggested. "Do you want me to get Dad to drive me over so I can be with you?"

"No, you cannot come over if I have the flu."

"I will anyway."

"No, I think I will be okay, as long as I know you do not hate me anymore."

"No, I do not hate you; I never did."

"Good." I felt the instant relief run through my body, and I closed my burning eyes so the only thing that was real to me in that moment was his voice. "I love you."

"I love you, too. I hope you feel better soon."

"I am sure I will."

And I fell back asleep on my bed.

No Matter How Long It Takes

Eric finally arrived just after midnight on Friday night. I had been waiting for him all night to get here. I knew he was going to be late when I went out with Bobbi shopping but the distraction was not enough. It had been a long wait.

Eric and I stayed up until four a.m. watching movies, talking, and catching up for lost time missing each other. I was really glad he was here.

We slept for a few hours and then we got up and went to town to see Kayla and do some more shopping. Eric wanted to buy a stereo for his new car before we went on the road trip together to see his sister. He was looking forward to seeing his sister and his aunt but it was a long drive from my house and he had just spent six hours in his car getting here to see me the night before. I did not care what we did, I was glad he had made the trip here, and I agreed to go with him. I was looking forward to spending time alone with him away from here for a few days.

We started our voyage shortly after we had supper. Eric was tired from driving so far yesterday so I took a turn for a while as he relaxed. We listened to tunes on the radio and he held my hand as I drove his car while dusk began to fall. I wished we could drive forever and things would always be like this. I felt peace in my heart and for a few moments I thought life seemed good. I felt as if nothing could hurt me now while I was with Eric. I felt safe.

Eric drove the car once we got into the city where his sister lived. His sister would not be home for a while yet as she was still working. Eric thought we could go visit his aunt first. It seemed like a good plan until he got lost and kept driving around in circles. I did not care he had gotten lost because I was anxious to meet any part of his family anyway.

It all worked out, and we got to his aunt's house, but she was at work also. Eric's uncle was home, so we had a pop with him, and Eric played their piano while I sat on the bench beside him and listened. We then went to the club where his aunt worked and visited with her for a while there before going to Eric's sisters and ordering pizza.

It was finally time for us to retire to bed for the night, and it was the plan that Eric and I would sleep together in the same bed in the spare room. Eric had spent the night at my house a few times, but we had never had the opportunity to share the same bed all night long together. We had also been intimate, but I had never been able to wake up in the morning beside him.

We had gotten into bed and had been fooling around for a while when I pushed him away from me. "I don't want to have sex tonight."

"That is okay; I don't either."

We fooled around some more until I moved away from him because the way he was touching me did not match the idea that we were not going to have sex. I knew he was a teenage boy with raging hormones and this teasing and touching each other was not telling his body he was not going to get what it wanted.

"What is wrong?" he asked.

"Nothing," I replied.

He rolled over and faced the other direction and would not talk to me anymore. I did not understand. If he said he did not want to have sex with me and it was okay to say no, then why would he not talk me now?

I began to cry. The truth hit me like a ton of bricks. *"What do you think Tommy is doing right now?"* I heard in my own head. I wanted to go home right then. I put my hand on Eric's arm and pulled myself closer to him.

"I don't hate Tommy, you know." It was as if he knew what I was thinking. "I know it must be hard for you. I understand what you must be going through. I wish I could help you."

"You are."

Eric got up out of the bed and stood in front of the window and looked outside as if there was something he was watching. I knew there was nothing on the other side of the glass. It was too late at night for that. I lay by myself in the bed trying not to cry and cover up the hole in my heart with the soft blanket that covered my body. I should not have come here with Eric. Now I am hurting him, too.

He did not say a thing as he got dressed and went outside. I did not know where he was going and wondered if he would leave me here. I looked out the window and saw him sitting in his car. I again wondered if he was leaving me. I wrapped a blanket around my naked body and thought going outside with him was a good idea. I knew Eric better than that. I knew he would not leave me there, so I sat on the couch instead and waited for him.

Eric finally came back in the house and sat beside me. We sat in his sister's living room together for a long time without saying a word. I did not know what to say to him. The only thing I wanted to do was go home but I knew it was too late at night to make the trip. I also knew if I asked him he would take me home but that would most likely be the last time I saw him. I wondered what he was thinking. I wondered if he also wanted to take me home and throw in the towel to this relationship that should not be. I was too afraid to ask him in case he said that was really what he wanted, to end it all now.

He finally stood up and went into the bathroom for what seemed like forever while I waited on the sofa for him. When he came out he took me by the hand and pulled me toward him.

"I love you," he said and then picked me up and carried me back into the bedroom and sat me down on the bed. We both sat in silence and looked out the window. I knew Eric was not mad at me anymore, but I wished he would say something. I wish I could think of something to say. I am not sure how I feel. I think I love Eric back but I do not want to tell him that I do. How can this thing ever work? I love Tommy. I have a lot of fun with Eric. He makes me laugh. It feels good when he touches me, and he has life in his eyes, in his smile. I never wonder if this will be the last time I see him again every time I say goodbye. He tells me nice things, and he likes to be with me, not because he needs me, but because he wants to be. Eric and I can do whatever we want together. We can play around together, and I am not afraid he will get hurt. I am not afraid if he sneezes that he is getting a cold or the flu. Eric can comfort me when I am ill. He can hold my hand when I am sick and go for long walks on the beach late at night with me. He can go into a public place and not be afraid of whoever may have sat there before him, leaving germs. It is okay to be with Eric. I do not have to worry about him.

He finally broke the silence. "What are you thinking?"

"What?" I had forgotten for a moment where I was. My mind was running wild with thoughts that I could not control. I closed my eyes for a moment and the pictures of Tommy being in a hospital bed came behind my eyes. My heart broke once again.

"What are you thinking?"

"I was thinking how nice it is to be with you. And I think I am falling in love with you, too," but I knew I already was.

"Do you mean that?"

"Yes, I do mean that. I am not sure how all this is going to work out, though. I love Tommy for sure, and I cannot leave him now. I will not leave him ever, and I am not sure what is going to happen when he gets better. I cannot see myself ever letting go of what I have with him."

"Do you think he is going to get better?"

"Yes."

"Are you sure? You said before he gets real sick and almost died last time he was in the hospital. I remember how sad you were."

"I was sad, but things have to turn out okay for him. I am not sure what will happen if they don't."

"I will help you through it."

"How can you help me?"

"I love you, and I will be here for you and give you whatever you need."

"I need Tommy to be okay. You cannot give me that."

"No, I cannot give you that, but I can be here to give *you* what you need. I cannot help him get better."

"I know. I am sorry."

"He will probably die, you know that?"

"Yes." In my heart I did know that sooner or later that would most likely be the outcome, although I was not prepared to admit it.

"Then it will be just you and I."

"Yes."

"Then we can have all the things we want together. Then we can spend our lives together. Who knows what will happen?"

"I do not want Tommy to die," and I certainly did not want to think that when he did I would live happily ever after. I knew that would not happen.

"I know he has your heart right now, and I have a small part of it, too. I do not hate him for that. I know why he needs you, and I know why he loves you. You are a wonderful person. I am just saying that I hope someday you and I have a future together. I know I want to be with you no matter what happens."

I sat in silence for a while. I did not know what to say. The things he was saying to me sounded really nice but before my future could really begin in this blossoming relationship something else would have to end. I was not sure what the bitter sweet part of that was. Eric was wrong anyway Tommy was not going to die and there would be no future for us together forever. There was no such thing as forever and all I knew was we had this moment together and it needed to last for forever. Who knew what tomorrow would bring? Who cared?

"Like I said, I love you, and I will wait for you for as long as it takes."

"Thank you." I hoped in that moment that he meant it.

I lay back down on the bed. I felt better. *Thank you, God, for sending Eric my way. He is just what I needed.*

Eric lay back down beside me and kissed me softly. I kissed him back.

I woke up in the morning with Eric kissing me as he held me in his arms. If this was what it was like to wake up next to him I surely wanted to do it as often as I could. This kind of forever I could get used to. He felt good.

"Last night when we were fighting and you thought I was sleeping, I wasn't. I just did not want you to see me cry."

"Oh." I rolled my body into his and looked deep into his green eyes, "I am sorry."

He kissed me again and without many more words we fell asleep again in the comfort of each other's arms.

The next time we woke up he said his goodbyes to his sister and we left for home. I drove because Eric got too stoned in the car. I did not smoke with him. The last thing I needed was artificial substance to confuse me more than what I already was. I was glad Eric smoked though, at least then we did not have to engage in any serious conversation on the drive back home.

Once we arrived back at home around supper a friend of mine came over and we played cards for a while. When Eric and I were alone again we I fooled around some more. If it was one thing that Eric and I know for sure, fooling around sexually with each other was fun, and the sex we shared was terrific. I was learning that no matter how bad I felt inside the physical attention from Eric made me feel better. When I was physical with Eric it took all the other things that life had to offer off my mind. I could be myself with him. I could pleasure him physically the way he pleasured me emotionally. I could make him feel as good as he made me feel for no other reason other than because he wanted to. There were no obligations with Eric. If we liked something we did as much of it as we could and fooling around and sex we liked a lot. Eric wanted me as much or more than I wanted him. For a short time we were both found something in each other that no one else had to offer. We had found a connection between us that for whatever reason made us both feel good. I did not want to ask why anymore I just wanted as much of it as I could get.

I got up at seven a.m. and had a shower. Eric and Mom did not get up until eight. We sat around the kitchen table and chatted while Mom made us breakfast. It was nice that I did not have to go to school because it was Thanksgiving Monday. I doubted we would have any kind of family dinner today. Thanksgiving was not a holiday we usually made any kind of big deal about.

After breakfast Eric and I went back out town and stopped in at Kayla's for a while. It gave us some place we could go and not have any other people bothering us. It was nice to see Kayla because since she moved to town I didn't see her much since she graduated from school and now had a full-time job in a factory, and I was busy with my stuff. Our schedules did not mix very well. She did not like Eric much, though she was as nice as she could be when she was around him, but I think it was only to be nice to me.

Eric and I hung out together for the rest of the day and of course smoked a bit. My friend Len and Eric fixed some things in Eric's car later that afternoon while I sat in the driver's-side seat and watched them. It was soon going to be time for Eric to make the long trip back home by himself. It was going to be an awful long drive for him.

As I sat in the car and watched Eric working in the seat beside me I wished he would take me to his house with him. I wished we could have our own place together. I wished every moment could be as sweet as this moment right now. I wished there were no more pain and suffering in the world. I wished Eric and I could hide away forever. It occurred to me right then that there was no hell, because what we live in every day must be it. I wondered why with all the horrible things in the world already why people wanted to hurt each other. I wanted to be with Eric because I knew he did not want to hurt me and was sure if I asked him to take me away he would have. My father would not have liked that very much, and I knew I could not leave Tommy.

"What are you thinking?" Eric asked me as he looked up from taping some wires together under the dash as he was hooking up his stereo.

"I was wondering what time you were leaving today."

"I need to go soon but not quite yet. Why?"

"*I wondered if I would have time to pack my stuff to come with you. No, on second thought, I did not need any of my stuff. I could leave in the car right now and come as I am.*" I looked into his eyes and wondered if I actually asked him if I could really go with him, but for now I knew I had to keep that question in my head.

"Just wondering." I tried to smile but my heart was sad again.

After Eric kissed me goodbye, I went into my room and lay back down on the bed. I was really tired from the weekend. I was trying to put all my thoughts together and all that happened between us in some kind of sequence that I could comprehend. I knew in my heart I would never leave with Eric but it was nice thinking about it.

I woke up with Tommy on my mind. I had not seen him since last Tuesday, almost a week. I wondered how he was. I wondered if he wanted to talk to me. I wondered if he had a Thanksgiving dinner with is family. I wondered if he cared at all what I was doing. I wondered if he had called me over the weekend, but I doubted it.

I picked up the phone and called him. I talked to him about an hour and a half. It seems he has missed me, too. He says I can go to his place after school tomorrow, but he says he will call me first. I bet he won't call. He says he is not mad at me about anything but I know in my heart he still is. It has never been this long that I have not talked to him before and he did not even ask me what I had done over the weekend since I was not with him. It seems he never tells me how he feels or what he really thinks. If he is still mad at me then I wish he would just tell me; but I will pretend he isn't because that is what he says.

I was sitting in class wondering how Tommy was doing at his doctor's appointment. I wish I could have gone with him. I knew he did not want me to go. He says it is just a routine check up but sometimes I do not think he tells me the truth about it. I think he tells me that so I will not worry. I wonder if he will call me after school and if I can go see him.

"Hello?" I picked up the phone.

"Hi." It was Eric.

"Oh, hi. I am surprised you called." I was hoping it would be Tommy to tell me about his day.

"I could not stop thinking about you today. I just wanted to call and say hi."

"What were you thinking about?"

"Oh, you know," he laughed a little.

"What? Our time alone together, in the dark when we played touch tag under the covers?"

"Is that what you call it?" he laughed again. I could tell he was smiling.

"It is for today."

"I was thinking about how much I liked spending time with you and that I had a really good time this weekend. Did you?"

"Of course I did. I did not want you to leave."

"I know. It was a long drive back home thinking about you."

"What did you think?"

"I wanted to turn back around and come and get you."

"Yes, I wished that too."

"I cannot wait to come to see you again already. I want to move down there so I can be close to you all the time."

"Are you sure that is what you want to do?"

"Yes. I do. I am sure I want to be with you. Are you sure you want me, too?"

"Yes, I want you, too. I wish you could be here all the time, too. Just like when you stayed here for a few weeks after harvest."

"Yes, I liked that too." He paused for a moment. "I wish we could be together every day."

I listened to him breathing over the phone, "Yes, I know; you already said that."

"What I mean is, I called to say that I love you."

"How do you really know that?"

"I know that because I cannot stop thinking about us when we are not together, and nothing seems right when I am not with you."

"Oh."

"Do you love me?"

"Yes."

"Then how do you know?"

"I know I love you because when I am with you I feel better than when I am not. I feel like I never want our time to end together, and I do not want to face the world alone without you in it with me. I hated it when you said goodbye, and I had to watch you leave. I wanted to come with you."

"You did?"

"Yes, I did."

"Would you want to move here with me?"

I thought seriously about what he was asking me. "I can't."

"Oh, yeah, right." His voice became somber. "I am sorry I asked. That was not fair."

"That is okay. Nothing is really about being fair anyway."

"I will not be able to come back and see you for a while. I have to work here to make some money, and then I can come again."

"I understand."

"I will write you letters every day. Will you write me back?"

"Yes."

"Will you send them?"

"Yes." I laughed because last time I didn't when I said I would.

"I have to go now. I really just called to say I love you."

"I love you, too."

"I wish I could be with you and hold you in my arms as I said good night."

"I will close my eyes and pretend you are. I am good at pretending."

"Okay then, good night."

"Good night."

Tommy finally called, but it was too late for me to go to his house. He said the appointment took longer than he thought it would. He said he had to wait in the waiting room all afternoon. We talked quite a while on the phone. I am not sure why, but he always seems to like that better than seeing me. Maybe he is sick again and he cannot have people over. If that is the case I wish he would just tell me.

It was a boring weekend. I stayed home Friday and Saturday nights watching TV. Sunday I finally got to see Tommy again. I have missed him a lot. I wish I could see him more but I think he is tired a lot. I do not think he is feeling that good but he did not really mention it. Sometimes he does not have to.

Eric called again. He says he thinks that I do not want him to move down here to be with me. I do want that but I am not sure how much time we can spend together. I have to go to school every day, and I need time to spend with Tommy. Eric says that I can spend as much time with Tommy as I want to and he will not get upset. I do not believe him. He does not really know how much of my time I choose to be with Tommy. Eric is talking about silly things like getting married or moving in together when I am done school in June. Mom says that she does not think I love Eric and that I am just using him. She does not understand. I love Tommy. I guess I do not have the same feelings for Eric as I do Tommy but it is different. Eric says he has the same feeling for me as I do Tommy but I do not think he can. I do not think Eric understands what I am talking about when I say I love Tommy. I mean, there is really no other for me. Tommy says he loves me, but I do not understand the things he does either. Everyone is crazy when it comes to matters of the heart. Love is certainly blind because I cannot foretell anything the future will hold for any of us.

Eric is moving down this weekend. I am not sure if I am excited he is coming or anxious of not really wanting him here. I do not know what I want but if Eric wants to come here he is making that choice for himself. I hope all goes well for us but this seems to be like a big step that I am not sure I am ready for. I wish he would stay living at his house with his parents and only come and visit me once in a while. Maybe living with his parents is not that great for him. He never talks about it. All he says is that he wants to come here and be with me.

Eric moved in to a house with some strangers and is renting a room off the back. It has his own bathroom but he has to share the kitchen with the woman that owns the place. The woman has an adult son that has some kind of disability and she needs the extra money that Eric gives her so that he can stay there. I think he said the meals were included in his rent. It is not a very big room but since he does not have that much stuff he does not need that much room. It has a bed and that is all that matters to us.

Eric was very happy the first time he took me there. He wanted me to stay the night but I couldn't. My parents would not allow that. We had our usual sexual rendezvous and he took me back home.

It was a few weeks before Christmas already. The snow had already fallen on the ground, and Eric and I had fun decorating my parents' house outside for Christmas. We also made a snowman and snow angles in the front yard. Lizzie came over and we bombed Eric with snowballs as he was trying to hide behind his car. I liked the snow and playing with Eric in it was so much fun. We sat on the couch and looked out the window at the lights we had put up once it got dark. The reflection of the lights made the snow glitter on the ground in little spots of red, yellow, blue, and green.

"I bought your Christmas present today," Eric told me before he asked, "Do you want to see it?"

"No."

"You will like it a lot."

"If you show it to me now then it will not be a surprise."

"You can wear it, and I can get you something else for Christmas morning."

"I guess if you want to give it to me."

"Guess what it is."

"You said 'wear it.' I think it is a sweater. Eric, did you buy me a sweater? I hope you got someone else to pick it out for you. I bet you don't even know what color it is." I started laughing. Eric is color blind. The last time he went shopping for himself he bought a grey pair of jeans that he thought was blue and a purple shirt that he thought was grey. I guess the good thing about being that color blind is you are always wearing whatever color clothes that you want, despite what everyone else can see.

He was laughing at my joke. "No, it is nothing to do with color. I am sure you will like the color it is already."

"I don't know what it is, show me."

He pulled a small box out of his pocket, and I knew right then what it was. It was some kind of a ring. *"Okay, I take it back; I did not want his gift. Not right now,"* I said quietly in my head.

He looked me in the eyes and said, "I told you before I wanted to marry you, and this ring is a promise that I will wait as long as it takes." He took my left hand and slid the diamond ring upon my finger.

"I love you."

The tears began to well up behind my eyes. This time it was not because I was instantly happy. What would I tell Tommy? I did not want to tell Tommy anything. We had not talked about Eric since the first and only time I told him about it back in the summer. As far as I knew Tommy knew nothing of this other relationship I had built without him.

"I love you too, Eric." I hugged him as hard as I could. I did not want to let him go nor did I want to get this serious this soon. I know we had talked about marriage and kids and our future, but this was becoming too real for me. Eric was my fantasy and escape, not my reality, not yet.

"You promise you will wait?"

"Yes."

"No matter how long it takes?"

"No matter how long it takes."

All the Things We Could

Things have been going very well between Tommy and me. We have been spending almost all of our time together. He also spends as much time with his family and with his sisters as he can. It is almost like we are all competing against each other for his time. I wonder who he likes spending time with the most. I wish I could be with him more but I have been sick a lot with the flu and tonsillitis. The doctor keeps putting me on antibiotics but it only helps for a little while then I get sick again.

I have a hard time sleeping. I keep having nightmares and sometimes I am even afraid to go to sleep. The other night I thought it felt like someone grabbed my leg and tried to pull me right out of bed. I wanted to get up and turn on the light but I was too scared. I think it was the devil coming to get me for all the wrong things I had done. Tommy said I was probably just dreaming. He said he thought it was my fear of death sneaking up on me. I still thought it was the devil. I told Mom about it, and she got me some kind of dream book, but it did not help much.

I was doing well in school. I had a B average so far. Nothing much changed for me around school, though. I was not that interested in the social crowd and still only hung out with my few trusted friends. It seemed most days we were all just plugging along and hoping to stay sane while we made it through the week until the weekend came around again.

I bought Tommy a cross and necklace for Christmas this year. I hoped he liked it. Mom bought me a pendant that said, "I love you," on it for me to give to him. Mom also bought him a bunch of clothes, a video game and some other stuff, too, but I forget exactly what, there is so much of it. He was having Christmas dinner with our family this year.

He had not been feeling well either. He went to the doctor the other day and he told me they said he was fine. He did not look fine. He had not gained much weight back yet and his skin was really pale. He also said he got night sweats and sometimes even had to get up to change his PJs before he could go back to sleep. He said he did not sleep much at night, yet he felt tired all the time. His hair was finally starting to grow back, but he still hates the way it looks because it is too short. He always had long hair before he was sick. He says he will never get it cut again, and will let it grow as long as he can. His Mom says she likes it short.

Tommy bought me a diamond birthstone ring for Christmas. He says he would ask me to marry him if he was not sick. I told him I would say yes if he did, whether he was sick or not. He did not ask. I do not think he wants to. Maybe someday we will get married, but he cannot have children because he is sterile from the chemo. He did not ask the doctor if that would be a lasting effect or not. I do not think we should have children; anyway we have too much other stuff going on, and I am not done school for another year yet. All that is certainly out of the question right now.

I wish I could quit school now and be with Tommy. He says I need to graduate and go to college so I can get a good job later on. I am not sure what I want to be when I grow up. Growing up seems a long way from now. I can only imagine one day at a time and dread when the night comes. Mom says most people die during the night, and I believe her. Night time is when the bad things happen.

I wonder what it is like to die. Tommy says he wonders, too. He says if he dies he still will not leave me. He says he is going to scare me if he can. I asked him not to do that. He sees a minister from the church down the road a few miles from his house. Every now and then he reads the Bible, too. I am not sure how much, though. The preacher tells him that he does not need to be afraid to go to the other side. I am sure if he does he will go to heaven. He does not think he will because he thinks getting sick was his punishment for being bad. I told him I did not think God was that cruel, but sometimes I do have to wonder.

I wonder what heaven is like. Tommy says he is not sure about what heaven is like but says he sure knows what hell is about. He says he is there now. He says this life here is hell, and there must be a better place than this to spend forever in. I am not sure I know what hell is like, but I sure know it is real hard watching him go through it. He says he is glad he has me because he does not have to do this alone.

It does not seem like he really knows how alone he is when he gets so sick he almost died and we could not reach him anymore. I wonder where he went inside his head when he left for a while. He says he just sees a lot of cats and dogs and other weird stuff. He does not remember much about it though. I say not remembering is a good thing because I see it every time I close my eyes. I am glad God has given him relief from at least one thing.

I asked Tommy what he wanted to do if he ever had a chance to. He thinks he would like to go skydiving. I say he is crazy for wanting that. He says he has never been in an airplane and would like to try it. I have been up in a small one once with my Dad and his cousin. Dad says that he will call that guy in the summer and see if he will take Tommy up.

Dad also showed Tommy some game birds and how they will fight one another until dead if you let them. Tommy was impressed when Dad brought them into our living room and let two of them go. Mom was not so happy about it all but she did not mind really since it was too cold for Tommy to go outside.

Christmas had come and gone and it was Valentine's Day. Tommy came to the high school dance with Bobbi and me. We had fun. Tommy and I got to slow dance together, just like we had when he was still in school.

Tommy and I also got our pictures taken together. That was my idea. I tried to take lots of pictures of him myself, but we both could not be in them then. He liked it better now his hair is growing back nicely.

He was feeling better now. I spent the entire weekend at his house. It was the most special time I have ever had with anyone.

Eric and I had broken up. It seemed we do not have much that keeps up together except sex. I told him I felt like his personal slut. He does not say much about that. We decided it was a good idea to break up. I need the rest from him anyway. It was almost a relief. He got mad when I spent all my time with Tommy, and said he felt second in my heart. He was, and I told him that from the start. He also got mad when I wore Tommy's ring instead of his. I should have seen that coming a mile away.

Tommy had been in a bad mood lately. He thought his best friend is going to jail for selling drugs. It would be a real shame for Tommy to have to lose out on his friendships at this time in his life. I told him people do not understand much about what they do affects others around them and that most people are very selfish. It seemed some people do not realize what they have before it is gone. I hoped that would not happen to us.

I knew Tommy would snap out of his moods soon. He just got like that sometimes and felt like he had to blame everything around him because he is sick. I did not like it when he was in a bad mood so I tried to cheer him up as much as I could. I liked to hear him laugh and see him being playful. Sometimes we got silly together. In those times it did not seem like he was sick anymore. We did not talk about him being sick much; we just talked about the good things and how much we love each other.

Eric and I got back together after a few weeks. He said he was sorry for getting upset at me over Tommy. I said I was sorry for feeling the way I was about sex with him. The sex we have is terrific, and I did enjoy things with him I have never done before. I did like making him feel good because it seemed he was always in a grouchy mood anymore. I told Eric I needed him because he helped me so much get through the hard times. I reminded him that he said he would wait as long as it took for me, and that he needed to be patient. He agreed, but I think he is regretting ever moving here to be with me. I think he thought it would be different from how it is. I think he thought he could see me more, but he does not ask me about it.

Eric moved to a new place, and this time he lives by himself now. It is a real small but it is all he can afford right now. He is working but I guess it is hard paying for all the stuff alone. I wonder if we will ever live together. He says he wants me to live with him but I can't right now. He says he understands but I doubt he really does. I like being with him but for him, I think it is not enough. I know he wants to be with me every day, but I have a long way to go before I am ready to consider anything like that.

Tommy goes back to the hospital tomorrow for a check up. He thinks they will want him to stay. I asked him why he thought that because he said he was feeling better. I wonder if he is telling me the truth. I hope he does not have to stay and take more chemo treatments. He says he does not want that either because all his hair will fall out again and he is just starting to look handsome again. I told him he is handsome anyway and at least that way he would not have to worry about a brush. He laughed.

I know I will not see Eric at all if Tommy gets sick again. All my time will be taken up at the hospital. I am sure things will fall apart between Eric and me again soon anyway. He gets mad at me a lot especially when he comes over and I talk to Tommy on the phone. One time I asked Eric to leave because I was going to Tommy's. He got mad and would not talk to be for a while and spun his car tires out of the driveway. I did not care. I went to Tommy's house anyway, that was much more important to me.

Tommy was right. The hospital says they want him to come to stay for treatments again. They said he could wait until Monday and spend the weekend at home. I asked him if there was anything special he wanted to do and he said no. He just wanted me to spend the weekend with him at his house so we could sleep together. He also wants to pack up all his stuff and give it to me before he goes back in. I told him he should take his stereo and stuff with him to the hospital but he says no because he will get too sick to use it anyway. I guess he is right about that, too.

He said they also told him he did not even have to go for treatments this time if he did not want to because he only had three or four months left to live. They also said that if he wanted to try the transplant he needed to go within the next six weeks. He does not want to go there because it will be too far for his mom to travel. I told him that was the last thing he should worry about because we would all go with him no matter where he needed us to be. He says he does not want to have the transplant anyway because he thinks he will not be strong enough to make it through. I told him if he kept thinking like that he for surely would die. He says I am right this time and he will try to cheer up but what he really meant was that he would just hide it from me better.

The weekend before he went to the hospital was nice. We necked a lot. We touched a lot. We talked a lot. I did not sleep too well though. I woke up a few time soaked in his sweat during the night. He kept saying he was cold and then hot. He would kick the covers off, and then pull them back up. He would get up during the night and go to the bathroom, then get back in bed. It is really no wonder he is always tired if that is what he does every night. Then when he does finally fall asleep I lay awake and listen to him breathing. I even put my head on his chest sometimes to hear his heartbeat. I get real scared listening to him because it seems like I am waiting for it to stop. I am not sure if he knows that secret or not.

Tommy is the only person that can make me feel so much inside. He makes me laugh and makes me cry. He makes me feel good, and he makes my heart bleed. When we are together I wish time would stop forever. I wish the sun would never set and the moon never rise. I wish this moment was eternity. I wish I could look into his beautiful blue eyes and stoke his hair forever. I wish God would never take him away. I wish I could let the world know how much I love him. He says he feels the same way.

"Are you awake?" he whispered quietly.

"Yes."

"How did you sleep last night?"

"Good," I lied.

"You?"

"Okay," he lied too.

"You want something to eat before we go to the hospital?" he offered.

"No, I don't feel like eating right now, but you can."

"No, I don't either."

"Tommy, you should eat something; you need your strength."

"So do you."

"Okay," I agreed. His Dad was already making bacon and eggs in the kitchen anyway.

"It is going to be a long day today," I said, as I rolled toward him and slid my hand up his chest onto his heart.

"Yes, it will," he agreed, and closed his eyes.

We lay together in silence for a while until he said, "I don't want to go today."

"I know. I don't want you to go either."

"I hate this. I wish it was all a bad dream, and I would wake up, and someone would say it was all over."

"Me too."

All got quiet again for a while.

"Tommy, I love you."

"I love you, too."

Silence.

"I am not afraid to die. I am just afraid of what will happen before that."

"Me too." I was trying not to cry. I wondered if this would be the last time I would wake up next to him.

"Tommy, can I do anything else for you?"

"You already are by being here and coming with me today."

"Are you sure you want me to come?"

"Yes."

Silence.

"BREAKFAST!" his Dad called from the kitchen.

Tommy lay silently on the bed.

"I don't want you to move. I don't want to start this day. I want to stay here," I admitted.

"BREAKFAST," his Dad called again.

Tommy kissed me softly on the lips and tried to smile, "Me either." Then he got out of bed and began to get dressed.

"Okay, I AM COMING!" Tommy yelled back toward the kitchen to his father; then he left the room.

As we sat on his bed and tried to eat the bacon, eggs, and toast we chatted more about all the things we needed to say. He told me that he loved me again and that nobody else knew him like I did. I told him it was easy to love him because he was so beautiful inside and no matter how hard it got while he was in the hospital I would not give up the fight for him. I told him I would be strong enough for both of us when he could not do it himself. I told him I never doubted his love and that he had better not give up on us just yet. I told him I was not through with loving him yet, and I knew he was not through with me. I told him we needed more time together to be happy so he needed to fight as hard as he could to get well again and that I knew he could if he tried real hard. I am not sure if he believed all that, I am not sure if I did but it sounded good and it made us both feel better thinking we would have more time together after today. Tommy says he will die smiling because I love him so much; I say he will not die at all, not this time.

Tommy turned the stereo up real loud to his favourite tune as we got dressed and ready to go. It seemed we were all done talking. I just do not think either one of us knew anything more we could say.

The car ride into the city seemed to take a real long time. Tommy and I sat in the back and held hands while his Dad drove and his Mom sat in the front. Tommy slept off and on during the trip while I closed my eyes and rested my head on his shoulder.

His admission to the hospital was quick because they knew he was coming and he had been there a few times before. He always stayed on the second floor because that was the cancer clinic part of the hospital. There were mostly old people in there and us.

It was always quiet in that ward, and the hallways always seemed so long. My feet felt heavier every time I got close to the big oak doors that led into his room. Some of the doors creaked when they pushed open. Tommy says he liked those one the best because he could hear when the nurses were coming and they could not catch us kissing. I don't think they minded because they always just smiled when they walked in. The nurses also let us sneak outside when we wanted to or go up to the roof in the rain. They never asked us why we were wet and Tommy would just change his clothes before he got back into bed. They would just hook him back up to the monitors when he came back.

I hated the hospital room at night. The big windows would turn into mirrors, and you could see in the hallway the people walking by. Sometimes you could see people crying as they left the ward. I was always the last to leave. The visiting hours never applied to me. Tommy always wanted me to lie down on his bed with him before I left so he could fall asleep. Once in a while I would fall asleep beside him and would wake up when the nurses came in. They still did not say I ever had to go but I did anyway. I knew Tommy would not get any rest if I we tried to sleep in the same hospital bed. I did not care where I was, because I hardly slept anyway. Sometimes I would fall asleep while I was sitting in the chair beside his bed while I hung on his hand. I did not want to waste my time sleeping, and besides, inside my head was horror when I closed my eyes.

So far Tommy was doing okay. He does not talk about how he is feeling, but neither does anyone else. We just go through the motions every day.

Eric came to the city to see me at my aunt's. He brought me some stuff to take my mind out of reality for a while. We do that every chance we get now. He always brings it to me and then we fool around for a while and have a few laughs. I do not hear much laughter where I go anymore. At least I can sleep when Eric is with me. I think it is because he makes me feel safe for a while. I am not sure if we are still dating or not but at least he comes to see me. He says things are harder here than he thought they would be and he is thinking about going back home.

"You know I love you, but things are not the way I thought they would be."

"Yes, I know."

"I feel lost here, and you are so busy with everything that you do not have much time for me."

"I am sorry."

"I know. You told me that it was going to be like this, but I hoped once I got here it was going to be different. I am leaving because I do not love you; I am leaving because I need to go home for a while. I cannot take this anymore."

"I understand. I am sorry that you could not have had things the way you wanted them to be." I paused. "I am sorry I cannot be with you every day. I wish you could get a bigger place, and I wish you had some more friends around here. I wish you were happier here, Eric. I understand what it is like not to get what you want, and I understand what it is like to be homesick."

He said nothing.

"I do not like the way things turned out either. I am homesick, too. I want to go home, and I want all this to be over, but it is not. I will stay here in the city as long as it takes for Tommy to come home, too. I do not want to come home without him. I am sorry I have to tell you that, but I think it will be for the best for you to do what you need to for yourself. I wish I could spend more time in this relationship with you, and I know lately I have not. I can't right now. If you want to go home I understand."

"What will you do without me?"

"I will do what I have done before. I will be fine."

"No, you won't. You are so sad."

"Yes, I am sad without you, but I am not sad because of you. Things for me here will not change for a while, and I hope they don't. I want Tommy to get better. I want him to come home again. I hate it here more than anyone else does."

"What do you do all day?"

"I sit by his bed and wait for him to get better."

"One of these times he is not going to come home, you know."

"You are wrong. He is going to come home this time. He is not going to die today. He can't."

"He will not always be well."

"Eric, if you want to go home I understand, but please don't make me feel bad because you are leaving by saying that Tommy will die sometime soon. Don't you think I know that? Don't you think Tommy and I live with that every day? You have no idea what it is like knowing that today may be the last day you have, thinking that this may be the last time we see each other, hearing the doctor's say you only have a few months to live, and as each day passes you pray to God that they were wrong. That out of a few months, each day is a long time, and you learn to be happy because today is all you have. You are leaving soon to go back home to the ones you love, tomorrow, but I am going to stay here and pray that I can make one more day last as long as it can, because that may be all I have left. I hope you never understand what I mean when I say those things. I hope for your sake you are never in love with anyone that when you look at them all you want is for them to never go to sleep. I hope you are never afraid to close your eyes for a moment because you are afraid for what you will see when you do or what has happened while you passed out for a while. I hope you never know the honest fear of death. Not the death of yourself, but thought of living life after death has taken something away from you. I hope you never know pain of watching someone suffer."

"I am sorry." He looked at the ground. He wiped his eye without saying another word.

I feel like Eric is waiting for the wrong thing. He is waiting for Tommy to die so we can be together. I feel guilty for Eric thinking like that. Although Eric has never said that out loud I am sure he knows that would break my heart way to much to hear that. I think he knows I would get real mad at him yet some things do not have to be said out loud, you can just tell.

Eric said goodbye again while I watched him drive his car away which was packed with all his stuff. I knew he had a long drive home but this time I did not cry. Letting go of him for now was easy. I did not know when or if I would see him again but I knew I needed to let go. I knew he needed to let go. I did not know if things would ever be the same again, and I knew my life would be different without him in it but this was for the best, for all of us, even if I did not want to admit it.

Tommy is finally home from the hospital. I told him I was glad it was not as bad as he thought it was going to be. I told him I was right about us needing more time together and that I was not done with him yet. He said thanks for believing in him and believing that he would come home again even when he could not believe that for himself. I told him that is what I thought friends did: believed in you when you could not imagine good things ever happening to you. I told Tommy that I had asked God to be with him, and He was; that was all I needed to know.

Tommy says he is feeling fine but I know he is not. He gets a lot of headaches and he is always cold. I am not sure what I can do to help him though. Every now and then I get him some medicine to help him feel better but he says just being there with him makes him feel better. He his getting real good a faking feeling well, but I can tell he is not.

It has been exactly one year now since he has been diagnosed. This anniversary is certainly nothing to celebrate. I am glad he had made it this far. I did not ask him how he feels about it. In fact I did not even mention it to him but I am sure he already knows what day it is I do not need to remind him.

Tommy has to go back to the hospital again. He says he thinks there is something wrong with him but he will not tell me what. He never tells me what is wrong. He says he is sorry for making me sad and says he feels empty inside. I do too.

He says he can freak me out by telling me he sees cats and dogs out the window when there really isn't any. I think he is lucky if that is all he sees because he should see the monsters I see when I close my eyes all the time. At least he has an excuse and can blame his hallucinations on the treatments. I am just going crazy. I do not tell him that though. I tell him that I did not think anything he could tell me would scare me. I wonder if that is why he thinks there is something wrong with him but I think it is just some kind of lasting effect from when his fever was so high. If I was him I would ask the doctor if that is what could be the cause instead of thinking I was crazy.

It is July 1 weekend and school is finally out for the summer again. I wonder what this year will bring for me. I know a few things for sure, that I will work in the harvest and hang out with Tommy.

Dad made arrangement to get Tommy and me up into the airplane. Once we got up there Tommy was scared and said he did not want to jump out anymore. I laughed at him and called him a chicken shit. I knew he would not jump. I told him he would not have to worry about the leukemia; he would die long before that if he threw himself out of the plane. I told him I would follow him to the end of the earth and back as long as we were walking. He said he would push me out anyway and make me go with him to the ground, and he knew I would if he really wanted me to. I told him he was crazy enough for both of us, and that at least I needed to make the sane decisions because he was not thinking with his right mind, or what was left of it. He laughed at me and called me a chicken shit back. Neither one of us jumped out.

Tommy and I were having as much fun as we could. We went to get our pictures taken together again. We had them taken once before, but Tommy did not like them. He thought he looked too sick in the first ones. Now his hair was growing back, and he thought he looked good, so he wanted to do it again. I told him I loved him no matter how much hair he had, and the first pictures were fine. I said I did not think we should spend the money because I was sure there were other things he would want to do to have fun other than pay for that. He said he wanted to do it because he wanted a picture of me with a better haircut so that he could remember me when he was not with me. I said I would if he wanted to, but I loved him no matter what, and I always remember him in my heart. I did not need a picture. We went and got them done. Bobbi came with us.

We would spend lots of time at the beach together. I think I liked it there more than Tommy did. When I am at the beach I feel free. I feel like if I had wings I could fly forever across the open water as long as it was not too windy. If I could breathe under water I would jump and splash in the air as long as the sun was in the sky as long as I did not swim into a net. I liked to watch the butterflies dancing in the sand and the waves sweeping away the grains. The sun was always warm on our faces. The air was fresh and damp. We could smell the flowering weeds.

One time we went mini golfing with Shelly and Sandy. Tommy cheated so he would win. He really did not even care that we caught him, he kept cheating anyway. He was the one keeping score, so we believed he was really winning right up until the end. It seemed like he enjoyed tricking us. I do not think he would have told us the truth if we could not have caught him. He said he was trying as hard as he could, but he was not good at doing the math. I argued with him that he was smart enough to add numbers like two and three together, but he said he wasn't. He stuck to his story, but I still do not believe him; neither did the other girls.

While we were playing it started to rain. Tommy wanted to keep playing anyway, so we did. We thought it was a good idea to get in the car when it started to thunder and get windy. The balls were too hard to hit in a straight line on the wet cement. Once the wind came up there was even less of a chance to get it in the hole, so we quit. That is also when we caught Tommy cheating, so he wanted to stop the game even more than we did.

I was falling in love with Tommy even more than I thought I ever could. We spent all of our spare time together. When I was not working I was with Tommy. My friends were also finding their paths in life, and I was now only hanging out with Bobbi and a few of her friends.

Kayla has moved to town so I did not see her as much. She was also working full time in a factory and had more adult friends than I was. After all, I was still in high school. I missed having her around every day, and I saw her when I could.

Lizzie had been dating John for a while now. She spends all of her time with him. Along with John came an entire set of new friends. She was enjoying it all and seemed to have finally found what she was hoping high school would bring.

Jesse was already a daddy. I did not ever see him anymore. I used to talk to him at least once in a while but time has moved on for us both. We have very different lives now, and I guess fate has its own agenda, which was not bringing him and me together.

The rest of the group was scattering apart as well. Some of us had jobs, children, school, and partners. Life was happening for all of us and it was not keeping us together.

I wonder if Tommy and I will ever have children. I wonder what we I would name them. I wonder if we would take them camping if we did. I wonder what else we would do with our kids. I wonder if Tommy and I will get old together. I wonder if he will still love me when I am old. I wonder what he is going to be like when he is not sick anymore.

"Tommy?" I broke the long silence as we lay together side by side on his bed.

"What."

"When we have kids I want to name them after you."

"Why?"

"Because I love you."

He then rolled over and softly touched my cheek with his warm soft hands and looked into my eyes. I looked back into his soul and put my hand to his heart. I wondered if it was going to beat forever. I closed my eyes for a moment to hold back the tears.

"I love you, too." He kissed me softly, then closed his eyes, too.

I got a letter from Eric. It seems like a long time since he has been gone. He writes to say that he is doing well and is still working hard. He wants to come down soon to visit me. He says he misses me and calls me sunshine. I hope he is doing well, and I would like to see him. I miss him, too, but I have been spending all my time with Tommy, and nothing much has changed since he has left.

Tommy is mad at me again. He got mad at me when I took him back to his sister's house while we were camping with my friends on the July 1 long weekend because he was getting drunk. That was not that part that bothered me so much but he was getting loud and boisterous toward people. It was like he was angry at something, and I felt as if it was my responsibility to take care of him. I guess he should just not drink rum. It was all getting rather uncomfortable for me so I asked him if he wanted to go home and he thought I wanted him too. I did but it was not because I did not want him there it was because I did not want him so drunk, but it was too late for that. I was trying to tell him that but he was not listening. As long as he was there behaving like that how could I have fun. After all these were my friends and it was my birthday.

I finally took him back to his sister's. I think he let me take him only because he was going to pass out soon anyway. It appeared he was drinking more than any of us were and was drunk way too early in the day.

It was after I got back that I almost made my mistake. I held strong for a while, and I overlooked the sexual invitations for the first few times. I was not interested in any kind of game like that until I met up with a boy I knew from high school last year. He had come to see us camping with a mutual friend. The list of visitors was endless and it seemed everyone I knew had come to see us there. It certainly was turning out to be quite a party. Some other kind of college group was there too that weekend, so we found lots of action wherever we went.

I am not sure how I ended up in the tent with him almost naked and him not being able to get it up. He assured me it was nothing I was doing wrong and that he had too much to drink. He also said it was all the people outside of the tent making him nervous. It turned out that of all the invitations I could have accepted during the night I picked this one and look how that turned out. I did not want to make him feel bad by leaving him there alone, for sure the guys outside would make fun of him then, but I really did not want to stay here any longer with this deadbeat. I suppose it was a good idea I stayed where I was, as I had probably had more than enough to drink myself.

I was the first one out of the tent in the morning. All the others must have crashed with us sometime during the night. I was still sharing the covers with the deadbeat, so I guess at least he could lie about what happened. I did not care. I just wanted to get out of there. The people were scattered every which way, and I think we had a few more than tent capacity is stated for. It was really hot, and I needed fluid.

I looked in the cooler and only found yesterday's watered-down milk. That was not going to cut it. I looked in Bobbi's cooler, and she had two beers left. I raided all the other open-sided coolers and found a few more beers, but nothing else to offer. I drained the excess water out of the coolers and put all the ice in mine, and then added the beer.

Susie, a girlfriend of Bobbi and mine from high school, was the next one to crawl out of the tent and sat beside me at the picnic table. She looked worse than I felt. I handed her the smoke I had just lit and reached in the cooler.

"Ready for another one?"

She looked at me like I should be pushed off the other side of the planet if it really would have been square.

"No," was all she said.

Pssst. The beer fizzed a bit when I twisted the cap off. I took a big drink. The beer almost hurt as it forced open my throat. It felt good hitting the bottom of my stomach though.

"Look what I found." I showed her the joint someone had left on the table last night.

She did not look up until she could smell the smoke after I had lit the pot. "You gotta be ready for this." I handed it to her.

We sat on the bench of the table until the zipper slid open again. This time it was Bobbi. She immediately joined our dope-smoking session as soon as she realized it was there.

"Fuck, it is hot in there."

"Here." I handed her a beer from the cooler.

Susie and I sat on the bench until the last straggler rolled out of the tent, and everyone else woke up. Bobbi was busy gathering all the beer she could find and putting in our coolers. We told everyone we had a case in the car from last night. I tried not to laugh when the deadbeat took his turn coming out. I turned around so I could see him directly but he did not make eye contact. I tried not to laugh as I remembered all the things he had said last night. He wanted me to move away to the city with him when he went to college; he loved me and he wanted to be with me forever. That is what I thought was so funny. One night of a few too many beers and a sleepy cock is love? I do not think so.

Tommy was still mad at me a few days later and asked me if I wanted him to go so my boyfriend could come later. I told him that my boyfriend was already there and had gotten too drunk and was being an ass, so I had to take him home. I told him I had wanted him there and was looking forward to having fun with him, but he ruined that for himself. His drinking had nothing to do with me. I was not the one that had to leave the party before it got started. I thought if Tommy would have just acted normal things would have been perfect. He could be mad at me if he wanted, but I was not going to be held responsible for his acting badly. I asked him if he even remembered what he was like, but he did not answer the question, so I assumed he had not. He was still mad at me only because it was easier than being mad at himself.

Sometimes I wished Tommy could have more fun with us. I wish he could have stayed and not have gotten so drunk. I get tired of his dependence on me, and I just need to be myself for a while. We are always together, and I love being with him, but he makes a bigger deal out of being different than anyone else does. He does not understand that we know that he is sick, but everything does not always need to be focused on that. We can have a good time and be somewhat normal for a while if he would just let us.

Tommy went to the doctor today for a check up. I have not heard from him yet. I wonder what they said. I miss him. I have not seen him in a few days because I have been sick with the flu again.

Tommy finally called to tell me that the doctor said he was fine. He says he is really hungry and wants to go eat. He will call me later.

Here and Gone Again

"Hello," I answered the phone.

"Hello." It was Eric.

"Hi, I got your letter the other day."

"Why didn't you write me back?"

"Oh, I have, but I have not mailed it yet," I lied.

"What does it say?"

"A bunch of stuff."

"Do you miss me?"

"Yes," I did. "I wanted to talk to you about something."

"What?"

"I am pregnant."

"Is it mine?"

"Yes."

"Oh, my God. I am so happy. I cannot wait to see you..." Eric's voice faded in my head.

I am not sure why I just lied to him like that. I was not pregnant. I did not want to get pregnant. I had no intentions of getting pregnant. Why did I lie to him like that? I will tell him the next time I talk to him I am not.

Eric and I talked on the phone a lot over the next few weeks. I did not tell him the truth yet. He is so happy. His parents say I can live with them if my parents will not allow me to live here anymore. His dad says I should not work in harvest this year because he does not want me to lose the baby. He is really taking this entire thing to serious. I wish I was really pregnant with his child now. Maybe that would be my way out of here. Maybe then I could make the change that I had been waiting for. In reality I know I cannot keep up this lie, but the attention it is getting me from Eric is wonderful. I feel special to him. I feel wanted. I feel as if someone wants to take care of me now. I know lying was not a good thing but for now it feels better than telling the truth but soon I know I will have to come clean.

I have started work in the harvest anyway. I am not pregnant and no one but Eric thinks I am. I told him my parents said I have to work for money for the baby. I see now that one lie leads to another lie, and now I am going to do what I have to do. I have been lying to him almost three weeks now and it is time to fess up.

I was just getting out of the shower when the knock on the door came. I was not sure who that could be. I was sure it is not for me anyway as I was not expecting company.

I could see the bike in the laneway before I got to the door. It must be one of dad's friends or something. I did not know anyone with a bike like that. I opened the door and it was Eric standing there.

"Surprise!" he hugged me tightly.

I stood there limp. It sure was a surprise. The biggest part of the surprise is that I had plans for a date, and it was not with him. I had been invited to go for a dinner with a boy I had met while working on the farm. He was making me dinner tonight.

"It sure is," I agreed, for my own reasons.

"Is that your bike?" I motioned out the window. "It's nice."

"Yeah, I told you I was getting it the other day on the phone."

"Oh, right." But I must not have been listening.

"So I thought I would go for a ride."

"Eric, a ride is not six hours on a bike."

"I missed you."

"I missed you, too."

"Get ready, and we'll go for a ride."

"Don't you want to rest?"

"No, I want to go to the beach with you."

"Okay."

I knew today was the day I would have to come clean about my lie. How could I keep going like this? I feel really bad inside because I started this in the first place. Eric has done nothing except show me what it is like to be happy again. He has shown me not to give up no matter how hard things became. He said he would wait for me as long as it takes, and I repay him by lying. I am horrible.

He stopped the bike, and I got off the back. That was the shortest ride I ever took on the bike. It was now time to fess up. My luck if I did not tell him the truth soon he would ask me to marry him. Even though I wanted that it could not happen.

"I need to tell you something." I took a deep breath.

"What?" He tightened his grip on my hand and began to walk more slowly.

"I lost the baby," I lied again.

"What?" he stopped walking and faced toward me.

"I lost the baby." I looked down at the ground.

"Why?"

"They said stress."

"Are you okay?"

"I am now but I was kind of sick for a while."

"You are okay now?"

"Yes."

"I am glad at least you are okay. Why didn't you tell me before?"

"I guess I just did not want to disappoint you. You seemed so happy with it all, and I was not sure what I would do. I wanted to tell you but it came up rather suddenly and it just happened a few days ago."

"You are okay?"

"Yes, you do not need to keep asking me that. I am fine."

I had gotten myself out of that one but I did not feel any better about it. It was a big mistake in the first place. Eric did not deserve my head games. I wondered why I wanted to play them anyway. I knew life was too short for that but it did feel good to have his attention even if it was only for a little while.

"…was going to move down here to get a job in harvest."

"What?" I needed to hear that again because I was not listening the first time. I was thinking he was upset at me.

"I wanted to move down here for a while to get a job in harvest. What do you think?"

"Harvest has started already."

"I know, but I bet I could get a job. Do they need anyone where you work?"

"Actually, we do."

"Would you like that?"

"Sure." My mouth and my words are saying the same thing. I wanted Eric here with me to stay. My life was easier with him here. My head knew this was not a good idea. He had just been here over the winter, and it had not worked out that great for him. Why did he want to come back now? I thought it was because he thought he was going to be a daddy, but now that he is not, why would he still want to come? I was not sure what good it would do after he had just left here and went back home. Maybe home for him was crappy and being away from there was better. I did not understand why he wanted to try again now. After all, nothing had changed around here with me.

We immediately went and talked to my boss, and Eric got a job at the farm where I was working. He could start work in a few days. He needed to first go home and get his stuff. He was then going to stay in the bunk house with the other farm help until the end of the season. We did not have any plans other than that. It was going to turn out okay after all. He said he wanted to come back here to be with me and work for a while, and I had no reason to believe anything different.

Eric and I spent the night together. It had been a long time since we had seen each other and things were going better than I had imagined. I was happy he was here, and I had almost lost the guilt of my lies. He was happy that he was here, too. We expressed our fondness for each other and vented all other emotions together through our second natural behaviour together, sex.

I got up in the morning, and I was almost happy to be alive. I was happy the way things were turning out and maybe there was some bright light at the end of this tunnel after all. As long as Eric could wait for me, maybe his love would make everything better. He kissed me goodbye, and I was on my way to work. He was going to sleep a bit longer before he was on his way home again. He would return in a few days for work. All was good.

"Did you hear we got a new labourer starting soon?" The lady I worked with advised me.

"Yes, I heard." Matthew acknowledged her question. He was ignoring me.

"He starts on Saturday," she continued.

"Yes, I heard."

I was wondering if Eric had left yet or if he was still at home in my bed. I thought for a moment about what he looks like while he is sleeping. I wondered if he would make the bed when he got out of it. I wondered if he had eaten something before he left or if he would stop on the way. I wondered how long it would take him to get home today. I wondered how long he was going to stay at home before he came back here. I wondered how long it would be until I would see him again.

"…Some French guy from up North is going to stay in the bunk house with Chris and me," Matthew was saying.

"Yes, I think he is," I added. I was not sure if he would talk to me yet or was still ignoring me from skipping out on dinner last night.

Matthew and I had been doing some serious flirting since work had started. It was only the three of us that worked in the kiln yard; everyone else worked in the fields. We had a lot of time to socialize. The other lady that worked with us spoke a different language so she did not talk to us much. She sat by herself a lot. She was nice but the conversations were all mostly between Matthew and me.

"Oh, you're going to join the conversation." He was being sarcastic.

"Well, if I am invited to."

"Well, it seems like you do not do so well with invitations and you stand people up."

"What?" now I was being sarcastic.

"I made you spaghetti last night."

My mouth dropped open. My heart hit the ground. I closed my eyes for a second to catch my breath. *God, please help me get out of this one. I did not mean to hurt him. He will not understand. I don't understand sometimes how quickly things turn out to be different from what you had planned on.*

It was right about then I heard the rumbling of the bike. I knew the answers to all the questions I had a few minutes before. Eric must have gotten up when I left and got ready to leave because I could see his bike coming down the road towards us.

"I was not feeling well; I told you that yesterday, and I had a surprise."

"What kind of surprise."

"Oh, just a surprise." This flirting was a little game that we played, but it was soon to turn out bad.

"Tell me about it."

"No."

"Tell me about it."

"Are you sure you want to know?"

"Yeah, " he was almost begging, "I want to know."

"Good."

Eric pulled up and turned off his bike. Time stood still as both Matthew and I watched him. He put the kickstand toward the ground, and I stood in silence. I remembered that I had met him just about this time last year. I had thought about all that he had helped me through and how much I did miss him.

He took off his helmet and balanced it on the throttle of the handle bars, then swung his leg off the bike. He walked toward me as if we were the only two people in the world. He kissed me on the lips just like we had last night while making love.

"I wanted to see how you were feeling before I left." Eric felt my forehead as he looked into my eyes.

"I am okay; it is just a cold." I popped a cough drop in my mouth as I pushed him away from standing so close to me. All of the sudden I could feel Matthew's eyes burning through my skin. My gaze dropped to the ground.

"I am leaving now. I am going to spend tonight at home. I will start back in the morning. I should be back here sometime tomorrow night." He put his hands around my waist and pulled me closer to him and kissed me again.

Now I remembered why I was in love with this man. "Call me when you get home?"

"Yeah."

"Drive careful."

"I will."

He led me by the hand back toward his bike. I waited beside him while he prepared for his long ride. I did not want him to go. I wondered if he would really come back. I tried to smile as I watched him leave, again. If it was one thing that Eric was good at it was driving away while I stood and watched him.

"I love you," he whispered in my ear, before he kissed me goodbye.

I heard the door slam shut a few minutes after Eric left. Matthew was returning to work. He must have left sometime while Eric was here. I had not noticed. As I watched him walk across the grass he did not appear very happy.

"What is wrong?" I asked.

"I had to make a phone call, and it was not pleasant."

"Sorry to hear that. Was it bad news?"

"Yeah."

"That was my surprise."

"I figured that one out myself."

"Is he the one coming to work with us and live in the bunk house?" the lady asked.

"Yeah, " Matthew answered. I knew from the expression on his face that he had not made a bad phone call. I knew in my heart he was upset at me for not coming to dinner, and now all the chances that he thought he had in getting together with me had vanished. I was sorry for anything I caused him to feel on my behalf; I did not intentionally mean to set him up for any kind of disappointment. He walked into that himself. After all, it was not like I had planned for Eric to come here, but now that he had I was happy about it. I knew it would create many more problems for me in the long run than anything Matthew could imagine, but God must have directed him here for a reason.

The next few days came and went, and soon Eric was back. Matthew did not talk to me much now at all. I think he was jealous of Eric, but he did not ever say that he was. I could tell, though, things were different between us now.

"What did you do last night?" Matthew finally asked.

"Nothing."

"Nothing?"

"No, I am still sick. I talked on the phone with Tommy for a while, took some medicine, and then went to bed. I am not feeling well."

He handed me a cough candy from his pocket, "You left them in the bunk house yesterday when you came in for lunch."

"Thanks."

"You didn't see Eric?"

"No, I was sick."

"He went out on his bike."

"He has lots of friends around here. He was here last year and then lived here for a while in the winter."

"He was all dressed up."

"He likes to look nice."

"He goes away a lot. I though he was coming to see you."

"No, I only see him once in a while."

"I thought he moved back here for you?"

"I am not sure why he came back. Eric does a lot of things I am not sure of."

"Aren't you dating him?"

"Sort of, I guess. It is complicated."

"Does he know about Tommy?"

"Yes. He always has."

"He does not care that you have a boyfriend?"

"I am not sure. I guess not because he keeps coming around."

"You said he moved here last winter because of you?"

"Yes."

"Why did he leave?"

"For the same reason as he came: because of me."

"How long was he here?"

"I am not sure."

"This is crazy. Your boyfriend moved here for you, and you don't know how long he was here or why he left?"

"No." I paused. "I mean yes."

"Yes, or no?"

"Matthew, I am not sure of anything with Eric. He is here, then he is not. He does what he wants, when he wants, and if we can get together in the meantime, we do. We try to keep it real simple. He knows I am not in any kind of position to make any serious commitment to him."

"Wow, I guess being your boyfriend is not an easy thing to do." He smiled.

I was not sure what kind of seed Matthew was trying to plant in my head about Eric. I knew that Eric went out a lot. That was no secret. I would like to know where he goes, but I do not ask. After all, how much worse could he do to me than I was already doing to him? Matthew did not know even half of the story to be making any kind of judgments on how Eric and I treated each other. Neither one of us was too stupid to know what the other was doing. If he was finding romance someplace else so was I. I already had Tommy, and Eric knew about that all along.

"Why are you so interested in what Eric and I do?"

"Just curious."

"You live with him; you would know better than I do what he does. How often does he go out, anyway?"

"Often."

"How often?"

"Every night. And you said it was not with you?"

"No."

"I wonder where he goes."

"I wonder, too."

"What do you do then, if you are not with him?"

"I have been sick; you know that. So I stay home."

"You don't go see your friend?"

"No, I can't while I am sick. He cannot get the flu."

"How do you protect someone from getting the flu?"

"You don't go see them when you are sick."

"But you have a cold."

"Same thing, to him. Sick is sick, and germs are germs. Anything at this point can send him back to the hospital, and he could die then."

"Is he really that sick?"

"Yes, he is."

"And he is your boyfriend? How long have you been dating him?"

"About three years now."

"And how long has he been sick?"

"A little over a year."

"And you love him?"

"Yes."

"And Eric knows about him."

"Yes, Eric has known about him all along."

"And what does Eric say about your dating him?"

"Eric does not say anything about it."

"Nothing at all?"

"What can he say? He can either be with me if he wants to, and if he does not want to then he doesn't."

"No wonder he went back home."

"What?"

"Nothing. You are right, it is confusing."

We worked for a while in silence.

"Can I ask you one more question?"

"No."

"Do you love Eric? I mean really love Eric, like you must Tommy?"

"It is different."

"How?"

"I don't know. It is just different."

"Does Tommy know about Eric?"

"You said one question. I am not answering that."

"Does he?"

"He did. I told him last fall, I guess. After the first time Eric left."

"How many times has Eric left?"

"A lot."

We worked for a while in silence.

"What did he say?"

"Who say?"

"Tommy."

"He said he has to go to the hospital today for a check up."

"No, I meant what did he say about Eric?"

"He said he loved me, and that was all that mattered."

"He did not want to know anything about him? Was he mad at you?"

"Matthew, you are asking silly questions. Tommy has leukemia; he is not stupid. Of course he was mad at me, of course he wanted to know everything, and of course he wanted to dump me. Wouldn't you? I would. But sometimes in the face of adversity you find what is really important to you even when it is hard. Even when people make mistakes and do things they wish they wouldn't have, or you wish they would not have done, you love them anyway. If you really love someone it is not conditional on a few things they do, good or bad. At the point when you are faced with something hard in a relationship you can do two things: keep trying or give up. It took a little while, but Tommy chose not to give up. We chose to move through it, and we did."

"Oh." He paused. "Does he know Eric is here now?"

"No. We talked about Eric once, and that was it. He never asked about him again, and I never mention it. Eric does not affect my relationship with Tommy."

"So Eric is last in line."

"Last in line?"

"Yeah, you know, plays second fiddle?"

I shook my head at his silliness. "Oh, believe me there is no fiddle playing in this orchestra of love. And I think no matter what song you play the last note will be more like the child's game, Ring around the Rosie. Husha, Husha, we all fall down."

I left work at lunch to call Tommy's house, but the phone rang and rang. He must not be home from the hospital yet. I wondered what they are doing to him today. I wondered what they are talking about today. Are they talking to him about the transplant? Does he want to? Will he be home soon? Has he seen the doctor yet? Is he just sitting in the waiting room looking at magazines? Has he had lunch? Will he call me when he gets home? I will try to call him again after work.

"Are you going out tonight?" Matthew asked, when we came back from lunch.

"Are you going out tonight?" he asked again.

"What?" I was thinking about Tommy.

"What are you thinking about? Didn't you hear me?"

"No."

"Are you going out tonight?"

"Maybe."

"Are you feeling better?"

"It was just a cold; it is not like it can kill me or anything." The tears welled up behind my eyes. "It could kill Tommy, but I am okay. It is just a cold. I will be fine."

"I was just asking."

"Sorry, I did not mean to snap."

"Are you going out tonight?"

"Maybe I will go see Tommy, if I can."

"Oh."

"Did you mean am I going out with Eric? Probably not."

"Why not?"

"I don't know."

"Wanna go to the beach or something after work?"

"I want to talk to Tommy. He went to the hospital today for a check up. He just went last week. He tells me everything is fine all the time but I don't believe him. They want him to go for a transplant. He does not want to go. So, no, I think I will just stay in tonight. Why, did you want to go to the beach?"

"No."

"Then why did you ask?"

"I don't know, just wondered what you were doing."

"You did so. That is why you asked. You wanted me to go with you."

"I did not."

"You did so."

"I did not."

"Oh believe me, you don't want to play in this band; it is crazy enough already."

"That is not what I meant."

"Then what did you mean?"

"Nothing. I meant nothing."

I worked for the rest of the day just listening to the radio and trying not to think about what Matthew was finally putting together in his head. I did not know why Eric was here. I did not know if he went out every night because he had a girlfriend, and I did not care. I did not want to start anything with Matthew. In a different time, under different circumstances, maybe, but not right now. He did not understand my life. He was a traveler on vacation just passing though. He may think now that dating me was a good idea but once he knew how crazy I really was in my head he would bolt for sure. What he thought he seen on the outside looking in was certainly not what my life was really like. The insanity in the mirror was much closer than it appeared.

I got home and Tommy had already called so I called him back. He says they say he is fine again. He is happy today. I believe things are fine today for him. They must have told him good news at the hospital. When I asked him what they said he just says he waits around there all day to talk to them, and then they don't say anything to him at all. I say, they must say something. He says they don't. He also says that as long as they do not say anything they are not saying anything bad. I agree.

I went to Tommy's house to see him. He said that he felt good enough and did not think he would get sick from my being sick. He told me it would be worth it if he did because he missed me so much anyway he would take the risk. He also said that he thought I was sick from working outside all the time, and I should just quit my job so I could come and hang out with him all day. I told him life was not that easy for me, and I needed to work even if was making me sick. I told him I wanted to come and see him but I did not think it was a good idea. I told him his voice on the phone was enough and all I really wanted to do was sleep anyway. He said I could sleep at his house; he did not care. He just wanted me there with him, and he would take care of me.

I ended up going to Tommy's for the night and fell asleep beside him on his bed while he was reading some kind of book to me. He is right about one thing, when you are not feeling well you do feel much better beside the one you love even if it is doing nothing at all.

"Did you see Eric's bike?" Matthew asked as soon as I got to work the next morning.

"No."

"He hit a ditch coming home last night. I think he was stoned." Matthew laughed a bit.

"Is he okay?"

"He is in the bunk house now. I think his parents are coming today to get him."

"What?"

"Eric got in a bike accident last night, and his parents are coming here today to get him."

"Is he okay?"

"He is banged up a bit, but it is not like it killed him or anything."

I gave Matthew a dirty look. "I'll be right back."

I went through the door and Eric was lying on the bed. It appeared that he already had packed his belongings and was ready to go home. I was not sure if he was sleeping or not. I did not want to wake him up if he was. After all, I was working, and I could not stay long anyway.

I walked in and sat on the bed. He opened his eyes.

"Did I wake you?" I put my hand on his chest. I looked at his body to see all the bandages he had taped on.

"Non, j'ai seulemeur pris des medicamaurs," he said, in French.

"Are you okay?"

I heard the outside door open and the water tap turn on. I knew Matthew had followed me into the house.

"Ouis."

"Are you going home today?"

"Ya, mes parents vienneus me cherdier 'a euviron quarve heuves," he said again, in French.

"Today?"

"Ya."

"What happened?"

"J'ai frappé une calvette avec ma motocyclerte hier soiv."

"Where were you?"

"Coming from town, it was late," he said in English.

"What were you doing there that late?"

"I went to see a girl."

"Your girlfriend?"

"No."

"A girl?"

"Yes."

"What kind of girl? What are you trying to tell me?"

"I met a girl, and I was going to see her. I was coming home and hit a ditch on my bike because I did not see the stop sign."

"Why did you not see the stop sign?"

"I was thinking."

"About the girl?"

"No, about you."

"Oh, Eric, don't give me that. I don't care if you were seeing a girl and were stoned and whatever; just don't lie to me about it."

"I am not. I have nothing to hide. I was thinking about you and that all I wanted to do was be with you and not with anyone else. Can you understand that? I only want to be with you. I hate the way things are right now."

" Eric...don't. Please don't do this. Don't start getting mad about the way things are. I don't like it either, but they are as they are. If you want to date someone else, date. I cannot or will not change the way things are. Desoleé."

"Desoleé. I know you are sorry, but that does not make things better." I was not sure if he was getting frustrated at me or at himself for ever dating me in the first place.

"I love you," he continued. "I came here for you, to see you, to be with you. I wanted you to love me again. I want to be with you and nothing else."

I could see his tears. I wondered how much medicine he took or if this was real. I did not want to see his tears. I did not want him to tell me he loved me. I did not want him to have a broken heart. It was easier if he didn't.

"I love you too, Eric." I wiped my own tear and then his.

"I know, but you can't. Well, I am going to say it. I cannot wait until you can love me with all your heart. I cannot wait until I can marry you. I cannot wait until the world can see how I feel."

"The world does not need to see anything as long as you know."

"That is not enough."

"It is always enough, Eric. When you know in your heart that you are sure of anything, that is enough."

Eric closed his eyes again, and I could hear the tea kettle boiling. Matthew was still in the kitchen making coffee. I had forgotten for a moment where I was and what I needed to do. It was time I went back to work even if I had rather not.

"Well, I am glad you are okay. Tell me when your parents get here, and I shall say goodbye. If they are not here by lunch I will come back in and see how you are." I kissed him on the cheek. He lay still then I pulled the covers up over him.

I went back to work with few words to speak. I was glad Eric was okay and did not get hurt. I was a little disappointed that he went to see a girl. Matthew was right in planting that seed. It is not as if I am surprised by it all. After all he did originally come here because he thought I was pregnant because I lied to him. Then once he got here I was sick and focused on Tommy. He deserves to find someone to make him happy. I would not expect otherwise. He deserved a better girlfriend than I, and I hoped he found one for himself soon.

Tommy is really sick again. He has a cold now, too. He got news back from the doctors from when he went to the hospital the other day. The doctors said that St. Anne's would not take him for the transplant because he has a cold. They said his immune system would be too low and the cold might kill him first. I asked him if he thought me coming over the other night made him sick but he said no because he went for the check up before I saw him. He said that they found it in his blood work when he was at the hospital. He said I could come over anytime now because he has a cold so he cannot get any sicker. I say he is wrong he can always get sicker, and besides we can talk on the phone like we always do, but he says that is not enough. He says if this cold is going to kill him he would rather it be with me. I told him I did not want him to die in my arms, but he said he would rather die no other place. I told him we did not need to talk about this because he was not going to die today anyway. He said he would see me later after I showered and hoped I would not be long getting to his house after work.

Matthew did not come with me to Street Dance with me even though I asked him to. He said that he was going to go and would meet up with me there but I knew he wouldn't. I really did not care if he did or not but since he had been trying to ask me on a date this long I thought it would be a good excuse to finally get together. Harvest was almost finished so what harm could there be now.

Tommy could not go because he is too sick. He probably would not have gone even if he was not sick because he could have gotten sick. At this time he really has to be very careful about what he does. It is hard for both of us because he always wants me to come over but I can't. He gets frustrated and says he does not care anymore but I do. I told him if all he wanted to do was make bad decisions for himself then I would have to be the one to make good ones for us. Even if he did not care much I still wanted him to be around a little while longer. Even if he wanted to give up I was not going to, and I was going to stand strong in that, even if he did not like it, he agreed.

I met up with Bobbi, Susie, and the rest of our friends from school at the dance. It was the usually end of the year get together and school was about to start again in a few days. Anyone who was anyone went to the street dance and got drunk in the park for the last party of the summer.

I had a few beers with my friends but soon needed an escape. Everyone else has all been drinking all day, so they were well on their way to drunk. I, on the other hand, did not feel like I had much to celebrate. I decided to make my great escape and go for a walk alone on the pier.

I put a couple beers in my pocket and started off. I met a few people I knew along the way to the end of the pier, but all I really wanted was to be alone. I needed to reflect on all that was happening to me and the way my life was changing. It seemed like everything was going so fast, and I just wanted to slow life down for a while. I wanted to hold on to what I had before it all slipped away. It seemed that I could not hold onto things tightly enough. It did not matter how badly I wanted things to happen for myself or someone near, they always went away.

I missed Tommy. I wanted him here with me at the pier this year just like last year. I remembered that last year at this time they only gave him a few months to live. He outlasted their predictions. Despite all the bad news they gave him he stayed alive. I was glad he was still here. I am not sure what I would do without him. I wished I could talk to him right now. I wished I would have not come here. I wished I would have listened to Tommy and went to be with him instead. I knew he would be asleep by now but I wished I could talk to him anyway.

God, please send Tommy my love. Please let the wind carry my heart to his heart. Please let his eyes see the same moon shining above his head just like it did last year when we stood here together. Let him hear my voice in his dreams, let him hear me say, 'I love you,' and make him understand I mean it. Please, God, tell him how much I miss him and that I wish I was there. Tell him I am sorry for all the rotten and unkind things I have done. Please, God, help him to understand I will never leave him. This will be until death do us part. Just don't let it be too soon. I do not know what to do for him or to help him anymore. I feel like he is giving up, and I am the only one that is hanging on. He needs to hang on for himself. He needs to hang on for me. I will not let him go that easy. I will not let him give up and die. Please, God, give me strength to be strong for him.

I drank both beers as I prayed out loud then decided it was time to go. I did not want to say goodbye to my friends. They would think I have disappeared with a boy for a while anyway. It would be easier than trying to explain why I wanted to leave. They would not be mad if I did but it would just be better for me. It was probably better that they thought that anyway. I would not want them to think I was sad. I would not want to ruin their fun. I will just go home alone.

The next person I saw was Shelly. Her boyfriend, Kayla's younger brother, Jackson, who had gotten together when they met when we were camping, had gotten taken off to jail for resisting arrest. She wanted me to drive her car to bail him out because she was too intoxicated. I had nothing else to lose. I was not having much fun at the fest this year anyway.

After several attempts at finding him she finally went in the police station to get him out. I thought this was a silly plan, but I knew what lengths people would go to for love. Shelly came out empty handed, and back to the party we went. At least I did not waste my time alone and feeling sorry for myself. She was passed out anyway, so I just drove along the highway and listened to the tunes.

"Shelly, Shelly, wake up," I said as I shook her. "Shelly, I think there is something wrong with your car."

She raised her head and moaned something, but I was not sure what it was.

What was I going to do now? I could lock all the doors and leave her here. I am sure she would be fine. People pass out in their cars all the time during Street Dance, and they are okay. I was not here to babysit her. I did not even come with her here. She is a big girl, and she can take care of herself. I am leaving because it is two a.m., and I have to work in a few hours.

"Shelly, wake up. I am going to get my car. I will be back for you in a minute." But she did not respond. I knew it would take longer than a minute, but I was sure she would be okay.

I locked all the doors, took the keys, and got out of the car. If she did wake up she was in no shape to drive until she found me anyway. It looked as if most everyone had left the party. There were only a few people left walking around.

"You looking for somebody?" I heard an unfamiliar voice say. I kept walking.

"Are you looking for somebody?" he called again.

I turned around and vaguely remembered who he was. I think he was talking to me. "Not really." I stopped a moment.

"What are you doing out this late?" he asked.

"Long story, but my cousin is here in the car, passed out, and I was going to get my car to come back and get her."

"Oh."

"But the trouble is, there is something wrong with this car, so she cannot drive it, and she is too drunk anyway, but I do not want to leave it here." I was wondering why her boyfriend had gotten in trouble in the first place and wondered if she was part of it. I did not want the cops to come back now and give her a hard time.

"How far do you think the car can make it?"

"I don't know. Maybe to my house, but she lives in town."

"Oh."

"I will just go get my car and take her to my house and she can do whatever she wants in the morning."

"Do you think the car can make it to your house?"

"Maybe."

"You drive her car to your house. I will follow you, then I will pick you up and bring you back to get your car. Then you can go home."

"Why would you do that?"

"Remember when you and Lizzie gave me a ride home from school last year, with that guy in that blue car? And I said I did not have any money to give him so he said it was okay that I could give him a ride sometime. Now I can give you a ride in repayment, because I never see him around anymore."

Now I remembered who he was. He had just started our school near the end of the year. Lizzie wanted to get to know him so we checked him out for a while. Everyone else thought he was some kind of narc looking for drugs at school. I thought that was funny because Tommy and all his friends were already done school. If he was a narc he was a year too late. I had said hi to him in the halls a couple times and listened to him sing a few tunes for some kind of drama class or something. Funny how life helps you out when you need it the most. I really did not need it this time, but I could pass on the favor to Shelly.

"It is getting late."

"Yeah, that is why we should get going."

"No, I mean it is getting late, and you do not have to do this."

"I owe you one, almost." He smiled.

I unlocked the car door again. "Shelly, wake up."

"Where are we?"

"Your car is broken, and we are just going to take it to my house. Just go back to sleep."

She sat up, looked around a bit, and laid her head back down.

The car made it all the way to my house. Once we got there Shelly decided that she wanted to go all the way home. I said I would take her there once we went back to get my car but we would be a while yet. Our friends in the car behind us followed us all the way to make sure we did not have any trouble and so we could go get my car. It was a nice thing for him and his friend to do.

"She wants to go all the way home. Do you mind if she gets in the car, too?"

"No," he motioned to his friend to get in the back seat of the car with Shelly. I knew his friend from around school. He was rather a social outcast, one of those wiz kids without any friends.

"Hey," I smiled at him when he got in the back with Shelly. "Don't take advantage of her; she is pretty drunk." I smiled again.

I got in the front of the passenger's side of the car. He lit a smoke and tuned the tunes down low so we could talk.

"I am sorry. I don't remember your name."

"Kodi."

"Thanks, Kodi; this is a really nice thing for you to do for us."

It was not long after our informal introduction he suggested the idea that we all take Shelly to her house from here. He said that it would make the trip much shorter for me. He also said that he needed to take his friend home which was on the way to town anyway. He said that we could drop his friend off first and it would not be much farther to take Shelly home. I agreed. I had nothing better to do.

He drove quickly to town and it did not take us long to get there at all. Shelly was sobering up by the time we arrived at her house and we were well on our way. We did not go in once we were there. I was not in a hurry but I would have rather been alone in bed a long time ago. I wondered how Tommy was feeling.

He drove much slower on the way home. We were listening to Pink Floyd on the stereo as loud as it would go. I already had a headache and really was not in the mood for any more parties.

"Light me a smoke," he demanded, as he threw the pack on my lap. "I am driving."

"Okay." What is with this guy? Can't light a smoke and drive? Let me out of the car if his skills behind the wheel are that bad. What did he do when he was alone?

Kodi stared directly at the road while we transferred the smoke from his hands to mine. He put his hand on top of my hand touching me gently. He left his hand there for a second too long, and I could feel his energy rush through me like a breath of fresh air. I wondered for a moment if this was some non-verbal way of saying he was enjoying his time with me. I overlooked the insight and chalked it up to his concentration of being as tired as I was and keeping us safe on the road.

I had a rough couple of days, and I really just wanted to go home. I wanted to sleep. My throat was getting sore again, and I was not feeling well. That would mean I cannot go see Tommy if I get sick again. I was missing him terribly.

Kodi and I rode the rest of the way home without talking. We just listened to the songs on the radio while he sang along. His voice sounded as if it came from angles. I thought about the first time I heard him singing in the café. I now remember just why Lizzie thought he was an interesting character. I agreed with her now; maybe she could see something in him then that I did not see. Although he was not the type of guy she was looking for, she was right, he seemed like he was worth getting to know.

As he pulled into my laneway to drop me off I was only thinking of my bed. I wanted to make the great escape. Although I thought he might be worth spending some time with, tonight was not the time that I wanted to get to know him. I was not sure if I would see him again because he had already said he was not returning to school in a few days. I knew that if fate was to bring him into my life I would see him again. I had made an awful lot of mistakes lately and sparking an interest was something that I had better leave well enough alone. I just wanted to say a quick goodbye and get out of the car.

"See ya around." I put my hand on the door and opened it. "Thanks for the ride, and I am sure Shelly thanks you, too." I laughed a bit. "Even if she did not say it out loud."

"When?"

"Pardon?"

"When will I see you around?"

"I don't know; sometime I am sure."

"Soon?"

"Maybe. I am kind of busy these days. I have to work tomorrow, and there are a few other things I need to do."

"Are you busy after work?"

"Ummm, I don't know." I wondered what he was getting at.

"I have to work tomorrow, too, but they are playing all-night movies at the drive in. Would you like to go?"

"Tomorrow night?"

"Yes. I could pick you up, and we could go get your car after work, then go out."

"Ummm, no, you do not need to do that. I can use my dad's car tomorrow, and he will help me go get my car. You have done more than enough already."

I was not sure I wanted to accept that invitation. My heart was already in turmoil from Eric leaving and Tommy being sick. I was sick too, and I really needed the rest. If I declined I wondered if he would ask me for another time. I wondered if he would disappear, and I would not see him again. I wondered if this was fate unfolding right in front of me. I thought about how it felt when he briefly touched my hand. It felt good and although I was not sure what I wanted right then; I knew sooner or later I wanted more of that feeling.

"I can call you after I am done work or you can just come to my house when you are finished work yourself. I can get ready and just wait for you there."

"Ummm," I thought to myself for a moment. Was this really a good idea? Probably not. Was Adam trying to hand the apple to Eve? Would she take it?

"You already know where I live, where you guys dropped me off. Do you remember?"

"Sort of. I think I can find it. I will see you then?" I am not sure if that was a question or a demand.

"I am not sure. I will think about it. Thanks again for the ride, though." I opened the door and got out of the car and sighed with relief that I was finally home again.

I went in the house and fell asleep instantly. I did not give any further thought to my date or anything else. I knew Shelly was home safe, I was home safe, and that was all that mattered in that moment.

The next day at work Matthew was asking a lot of questions about my night. I was telling him what happened and that it was a good thing he did not come with me there. He said he was there and had been keeping an eye out for me and he wondered why I had not been around. I did not tell him I was sitting on the pier alone, I just told him I had met up with some friends before the night had started and my plans changed more quickly than I had thought with the other stuff that happened with Shelly. I did not mention the other part.

"What are you doing tonight then? Going to see Tommy?"

"No, I thought I would just stay in and rest for a while. I am real tired from being up so late last night. Why?"

"Just wondering?"

The rest of the day we worked in the hot sun with our usual conversations. Matthew did not ask any more questions about my personal life. There were so many things he did not know about me. I was sure if he knew the real me he would not be interested anymore anyway. It seemed that he just wanted sex with me anyway. I had enough of that and besides, it seemed like those relationships did not ever turn out for the best for me. Harvest would be finished soon and Matthew would be going back to the city where he came from and where he belonged. I was in no mind to have another long distance relationship and for God's sake I surely did not want him to move around here because of me. I had enough of that, too.

I went home and sat on the bed after my shower. My body hurt from the flu, and I was tired from working all day. I did not want to go out on a date with anyone, not even someone new. I wanted to go see Tommy, but I could not. I called him on the phone instead.

"Hey, how are you feeling today?"

"I am sick," he responded.

"I know. I wish you were feeling better."

"Me too. I wish you could come over."

"Me too."

"How was the Street Dance?"

"It sucked without you."

"Oh?"

"I wished you were there. I wished I did not go at all. I went to the pier and sat there for a while and remembered last year when I was with you."

"You did?"

"Yeah, then I drove around with Shelly a while and came home."

"Sounded like it sucked. Didn't you see anyone you knew?"

"Yeah, but I did not feel like being around them. I wished you were there."

"Me too."

We paused for a bit. Being in silence with Tommy was a natural thing. We did not always need to talk. Sometimes when we were on the phone I would do homework or he would watch TV. We spent hours on the phone together. It was the next best thing for us when we could not be together.

"What are you doing tonight?" I asked him.

"Nothing," he paused, "Jeff might come over later."

"Ah. Does he have the cold, too?"

"No, he is safe. It won't kill me to see him."

"What?"

"It won't kill me to see him."

"Why do you say things like that?"

"Because I can die at any time."

"So can I."

"What?"

"So can I. So can anyone. I could get hit by a bus tomorrow, and that would be it for me. But I do not think about it."

"But it is different."

"No. You could get hit by a bus too, and die from that, and you have then spent all your time worrying about being sick, and that is really not what killed you."

"Yes, but it is more likely to happen that way."

"You do not know that."

"Yes, I do."

"Why, because they told you a year ago you would already be dead by now and you are not? They were wrong. So now every day that you have is a blessing."

"To you."

"Yes, to me. Is that not enough? Did you want it to be a blessing for anyone else but me and you?"

"Well, no, I guess that is enough."

"Then use it like it is a blessing instead of always worrying about it all. If you tell yourself you are going to die, you surely will sooner than later."

"What else am I supposed to do?"

"Think of something else."

"What?"

"I don't know, anything but that."

"That is easy for you to say."

"Is it?"

"Yes."

"You think it is easy for me not to think about your dying?"

"Well, no."

"Well, then I do not want you to think about it all the time either. What good is it doing you to always be depressed about it? It does not change anything."

"Well, no."

"Well, use your blessing then. Don't waste it or you might as well already be gone."

"Will you be happy when I am gone?"

"No. I will be sad."

"What will you do?"

"I will love you anyway."

"How?"

"In my heart."

"Will you think about me when I am gone?"

"Every day."

There was another pause.

"You sound tired."

"I am."

"Okay, I will call you later."

"No, I think I am just going to sleep anyway. I will call you tomorrow after work."

"Okay, Bye."

"Bye."

"Hey."

"What?"

"Thanks."

"For what?"

"Cheering me up. I love you."

"I love you, too." I hung up the phone.

Kodi

I sat on the side of the bed for a while longer before I got dressed. I did not know what to wear on an actual date. It had been a real long time since I had been on a real date with a boy that I did not already know well. Tommy never cared what I wore as long as I was with him, and Eric never cared what I wore as long as it was easy to get off.

I flipped though my clothes and nothing seemed right. I thought I must be real tired and this was a way of procrastinating getting ready. I thought about calling Kodi and canceling but thought again. I knew if I did that there would be no second chance. A tee shirt and a sweater would be fine with a pair of jeans, impressing him was not what I was in the mood to do anyway.

I arrived at Kodi's and did not want to go to the door. I wondered if it was too late to back out. I did want to see him again just not right now. I wondered how I was going to be on my best impressive behaviour when I was this sick with tonsillitis. My throat hurt, and I could barely swallow water. I was hungry from not being able to eat for days on end, and I was tired. I was just about to pull out of the lane when I saw someone look out the window. It was too late to back out now, I had better go inside.

Kodi appeared to still be getting ready when he opened the door. He was wearing white jeans and a white shirt that was all the way unbuttoned. I wondered if that was an intentional thing. I did not care much, but I liked it anyway.

"I got home late from work today. Can you wait?"

"Sure."

He led me to a couch in the living room and he disappeared upstairs. I was feeling a bit nervous to be there alone. I looked around and wondered where everyone else in the house was. There did not seem to be any other signs of life around here at the moment. I looked out the window at the birds in the tall grass that led out into the bay as the sun was just about to set. I stood up and walked to the patio window and gazed at the pinkish orange and blue sky that melted against the deep blue water. It was beautiful here. I wished I lived in a house like this.

It was not long before Kodi came back down the stairs. He was almost fully dressed this time and he appeared as if he was ready to go. We did not make much conversation while I waited. He seemed like he was in a hurry to leave.

We got to the drive in and both thought it was a good idea to sit outside beside the car while the movies played. We were not that interested in the shows, but spending time together was nice. We talked a while and made cheap conversation. It was when he started asking me if I was comfortable. I should have guessed what he really wanted.

"Here, you can lean on me." He motioned for me to sit close to him while he leaned against the tire of the car.

"Okay." I really was uncomfortable. I was not sure why we just did not stay inside the car like everyone else, but I guess that would have been too easy. There would be not much of an excuse for him to touch me either.

I moved over and sat between his legs, and I leaned back toward him. He put his arms around me and asked if I was cold. I wasn't cold at all, but the affection was nice. As soon as he touched me the same energy sparked between us as it did last night. I knew from that moment on this was going to turn out to be much more that I had wanted to get myself into. I should have listened to that inner voice earlier and stayed home.

"This is uncomfortable," he stated. I was glad he did because it was not all that great for me either. I did like his arms around me, but sitting on the grass was not what I had expected to do.

"Yeah, it is," I agreed.

"Do you want to sit in the car?"

"Yeah," I agreed. I wondered what kind of excuse he would use to touch me then.

He opened the door and motioned that we get in the back of the car. "It will be more comfortable back there."

I smiled and thought to myself, *This I cannot believe. That was a very forward come on. He did not even try to pretend to make an excuse to get me in the back seat. That I like, a no-game-playing kind of guy. I'm not sure what I'm getting myself into, but why not get in the back? I have already gotten myself this far.*

It was not long once we were both in the back of the car and comfy before Kodi started to kiss me. I was not surprised by that at all, after all, I knew what to expect when he got me in the back seat.

His lips were soft and so were his hands when he started to run them under my shirt. I started to touch him under his shirt, too. I understood now exactly why he had picked that shirt to wear. It seemed like he dressed for the occasion.

I started kissing him back and touching his skin. I was kissing his neck and noted that he was less than responsive. That is when I noticed he had fallen asleep. Well, it looked like I was batting a thousand now days with my charm.

I laid my head down on his chest and watched a bit more of the move. That is when I fell asleep, too. I have not been sleeping well the last couple of days and it did feel good to be in someone's arms for a moment. Even if I only slept for a while, it would be better than most nights. I did not blame him for falling asleep since it had been a real long couple of days. I understood how late he was up last night because he was running around with me. I also understood the physical demands of working all day long in the hot sun, I had done that, too. If he was half as tired as I was it was okay for him to sleep.

I woke up before the movie was over and before Kodi. I do not think he knew I was sleeping. I guess this would be a good time to get out of this new beginning before it even started. I could tell him I was upset and offended for falling asleep on our date. I could tell him he was inconsiderate of my feelings and that I just wanted him to take me home. I could tell him that I thought he only wanted one thing from me and that I was not going to give him that. I could tell him a million things to get out of this now but I knew none of them would be true. After the last lie and how that turned out I think I will stick to the truth this time.

"I am sorry, I fell sleep. It was really not you. I was just really tired from last night and working all day." He was scrambling for excuses. It was cute.

"That is okay. I understand. I am tired, too."

"I am sorry. I am really sorry."

"That is okay. I understand."

"Can I make it up to you?"

"It is okay. You do not need to make anything up to me. I understand."

"Will you give me another chance?"

"I don't know."

"You need to give me another chance; that was not a fair date."

"Fair," I laughed a bit, "but since when is anything fair?"

"Come to my house tomorrow. I will make you dinner."

I remembered my dinner plans I had made a while ago as a date. I was not that good at showing up for a home made dinner. What is it with guys these days wanting to even make dinner as a date? I drifted off thinking about the last plans I made and my surprise visit and why I had not shown up. I wondered how Eric was feeling after his accident.

"Tomorrow?" he asked again.

"Sure," I accepted the invitation. I would give it one more try. I would make my choices after one more date. He did not need to know I had spent my time sleeping, too.

As I pulled into the lane, I could smell he was making dinner already. I hoped he was almost finished because I was hungry and had still hardly eaten. I do not usually go to a dinner date hungry but I was late getting home from work. I did not want to be late for our date. I was not sure what the rest of the night would bring but I hoped he was at least a good cook.

Kodi yelled from the kitchen to just come in the house when I rang the bell. I thought that was a bit odd but went in anyway. He could have at least greeted me at the door.

I walked into the house and looked around and again it seemed like we were the only ones there. He told me his lives with his parents and had two brothers but I had not seen any of them yet. He said his parents worked a lot at the restaurant they owned down the street. He said his younger brother worked there some days too when they needed help and his other brother he said was not home much. It appeared we had the house to ourselves.

Kodi's dinner was a nice treat. He was a good cook and made a wonderful meal even though I could not eat much of it. I was sorry for that but he understood or so he said. I accepted his offer of ice cream and apple juice for desert because he said it might help me feel better.

It was not long until he was showing me around the house and into his parent's bedroom. This was surely the nicest room in the house. The balcony overlooked the bay and as it was getting dark out the moon was starting to shine through the window. It certainly was romantic. I wondered how many other girls he had up here before me. I was not sure I wanted to ask that question. I was not sure I wanted to ask any question because I may not want to know what was on his mind.

"Sit," he motioned for me to sit beside him on the bed.

I did.

We started kissing where we left off in the car last night. In my head I was not sure if this was a good idea but my heart was saying something else. Eve had once again taken a bit of the apple.

When he touched me I felt alive. I felt like his desire for me was just that, desire to be with anther human being just because you wanted to. It seemed like he had no hidden agenda, he was letting me know just what he wanted. I liked it. I was nervous though. I was not sure how far I wanted to go with him. It seemed funny that it was only a few days ago I could not even remember his name.

We kissed, touched and petted each other for a while and then he began to take off my shirt. That is when I got a bit more nervous and thought we needed to add a bit more conversation to out date than just physical interaction. Although I had been with him a few times already, talking was not something we seemed to be doing much of.

"I am not sure this is where I want to go on this date." I stopped him from going any farther.

"Okay," he agreed. Then he removed his hands from under my clothing. "What is it that you want to do?"

"I am not sure, but I think this is going too fast too soon."

"When is it not too soon?" he asked.

"Well," I thought for a second, "at least the third date."

"This is." He reminded me.

"Well, it is not really; the first time was not really a date."

"But it could have been."

"Yes, it could have been."

"Will you come over tomorrow?"

"Maybe."

"Then what difference is one day if it makes us feel good?"

"I do not want you to think I am that kind of a girl."

"I won't."

"Yes, you will."

"No, I won't. I have known you before, from school. I know you are not that kind of girl. I remember, I saw you with that guy that had that blue car. I did not ever see you with anyone else. I never heard anything bad about you around school. In fact I did not hear much about you from around school."

"There is a lot about me you don't know."

"Maybe, there is a lot about me you don't know."

I thought for a moment. "You are right. I know enough already."

212

We talked for a while longer and began kissing again. As much as I did not think it was a good idea to procreate with him upstairs in his parent's bedroom I got carried away with how good he was making me feel. I fell into the temptation of him handing me the apple. I made love to him.

Kodi and I saw each other every day after that. Once school started again he would pick me up after school and give me a ride home. We spent all our time together doing whatever we wanted to do. We would hold hands while we walked on the beach, he would sleep at my house while I was doing homework, and we would pick apples and pears to bake deserts. We very quickly fit like a pair of old comfy running shoes.

My mother hated him with a passion. She allowed me to date him but disliked his sense of style. What she despised most about him was the way he dressed. He was more into the grunge outfits that my mother did not understand. I suppose I did not understand it either, but I knew if it drove her insane it must be good. She did not say I could not see him anymore but certainly gave me a hard time about it. Kodi was nothing like Eric at all.

I wrote Eric a letter saying that I thought we should see other people. I also said this long distance thing was getting too hard and although I would like to see him again I thought it was time we gave ourselves a chance to discover who we really are and what things we might want for ourselves.

Eric wrote me a letter back which said he agreed but that was not really what he wanted to do. I was not sure how much of that was the truth when I answered the phone one day for his voice asking for another girl.

Tommy called today. He was crying. He said his family is not getting along to well and it is driving him crazy. I did not know what to say to him about it all. My family drives me crazy every day, at least he had one to get frustrated about.

I feel out of touch with Tommy these days. I have focused my attention on Kodi. When Tommy asked me about why I had been so distant I told him I was still not feeling well and since school had started again, and I had been busy. He said he had been busy too, but I doubted that. Tommy says he feels like he is part of my past now, and that I do not care as much about him as I used to. He says that because I do not call or come over all the time anymore; he is wondering if something is wrong. I tried to tell him there was not but he could tell I was different.

He is right, there is something wrong. Kodi and I are getting close. That is wrong. I do not understand why God gave me something that makes me feel so good yet makes me feel so bad at the same time. When I am with Kodi he takes everything away. My pain goes away, my fear goes away, and my insecurities go away. It is nice to be in love with him. He says he is in love with me, too. I can feel he is. I believe he is. When he makes love to me I know that he is. He touches me in a way no other can. It feels like somehow he has melted my soul, softened it. When I wake up in his arms I feel safe. I want to be with him but I can't, this is all wrong. Since Tommy pointed out the changes in me, it must be wrong.

I know I need to make a life for myself but not yet. Tommy still needs me to be there for him. He is fighting for his life, and I am out making love to another. Tommy is struggling each day to stay alive, and I am having a good time with someone else. The last few months I have forgotten his struggles and how much he needs my support. I love Tommy even more than I love my life. I would give half of my life for half of his. If I could give some of my days to him or take away half his pain I would. Tommy knows I would. I can't.

The only thing I can do is be there for him and make his days as happy as we once were. I know Tommy must be scared with all that he is going through. He has some other supports but he says no one knows him like I do. He says that he cannot cry in front of anyone else. He says he cannot talk to anyone else. He says he cannot tell anyone else how he really feels inside. He says that I am the only one that makes him feel good inside. He says he wants to be with me forever and that he is glad I am his friend. He says he would have died a long time ago if it was not for our love.

I tell him that I love him, too. I tell him that he has to be strong for himself because I cannot always be there for him. I remind him that I still need to go to school and get good grades if he wants me to go to college. I tell him that I doubt I will go to college but he tells me to try anyway. I remind him that if he wants me to be a nurse then I need to study. He says he knows, but he misses me anyway.

After talking with Tommy it was inevitable that I needed to tell Kodi it had to be over with him. I did not want to. As much as I loved skipping school and spending the afternoons making love to Kodi, I needed to get out of that fantasy world and back into the real world. Behaving like that was only going to sooner or later get me into trouble.

I knew Kodi was not going to take the news well, if he only understood why I must break up with him now. The longer I wait to tell him this relationship needs to be over the harder it is going to be when it is. If Kodi really knew how much I wanted to be with him he would never go away. I only want him to go away for his own protection. Loving me at this time in my life is not a good idea for him. It is not a good idea for anyone but Tommy to love me right now.

"Kodi, we need to talk."

"About what?" he asked, as he held my hand.

I looked him directly in the eyes and squeezed his hand. "I am sorry to say this, and it hurts me more than you know. But it is time. I need to say goodbye to you."

"What do you mean, goodbye? Are you going somewhere?"

"No. I am saying that I can no longer be in this relationship with you."

"What?" I don't think he could believe that I had just dropped the bomb.

"I need to say goodbye to you."

"Why?"

"You would not understand."

"Try me."

"I just cannot do this anymore. I need to let go."

"Why?" he questioned me. "Why would you want to let go of something that makes us both feel so good? I thought we were getting along very well. I want to spend more time with you."

I knew that I could not explain all the reasons why I needed to let go. I knew that I could never tell Kodi that I had never intended to get this close to him. I could not tell him that falling in love for me was a very scary thing. I could not tell him that because the time I spend with him is so wonderful, that is why I need to walk away from it. I know it was not fair to either of us, but for now, that is just the way things need to be. I know he cannot understand it, but it will be for the best for all of us.

Kodi says he wants to keep trying. He says that he will wait as long as he has to and that we should not throw away all the good things we have together. He says that feeling as good as we do together is not a bad thing. He thinks we must have found each other for a reason and that reason is not to let it go. He also thinks that we need to fight for what we have to keep us strong and that I can draw all the strength I need from him to keep me going. I said I do not think that it is fair to him to not be able to give him all that I can right now because my heart is someplace else. I am not sure I have it in my heart to keep trying but Kodi sure does not want to let go. How could I tell Kodi that I had been through all of this before and it will not work out? I know he does not understand, but I do not have the energy to go through it with him. I need to save myself for something else.

Dad is upset with me again. He is telling me that I should be responsible and not play games like this with these boys. Dad and Mom both say I used Eric and that he really did love me. Dad has no feelings toward Kodi, but Mom still dislikes him. I think she thinks he does me good to take my mind off of Tommy, but that is about all she can see that he is good for.

I am crying now in my room after my disagreement with my father over my personal life. Can he not see that I am trying as hard as I can to be responsible? Can he not see that every now and then I need an escape, too? He is not the one that has ever sat in the hospital and watched Tommy dying, how does he know what it is like? How does he know what it is like to talk to the one you love several times a day on the phone because you cannot go there because you are sick with a cold? How does he know what it is like to cry in the pillow every night and pray that the only one you truly love makes it one more day? How does he know what it is like to fall apart inside? How does he know what it is like to have nightmares each time you close your eyes and sometimes it is not even to sleep. How does he how what it is like to hold on each day by a thread of any kind of sanity? How does he know what it is like to watch someone die? He doesn't.

My father is not being fair. Is he not supposed to keep my best interests in mind? Is he not supposed to want me to find happiness? Am I not being responsible enough to save a life? Can he not just let me mess things up for a while? I am sure I will get back on my feet again as soon as all this is over.

It seemed that whenever I needed him most he would call even when I did not expect it, he just somehow knew.

"I bought some stuff for our place today." Eric told me over the phone.

"You did?"

"Yeah, I bought some really cool lamps."

"When are you coming to live here?"

"Not for a while, but I thought if I started getting stuff now it would be better for us when we live together."

"I thought from the letters that our plans had changed? I thought that we were going to date other people?"

"I know, but dating other people for a while does not mean I have given up on us or that I do not want to still be with you."

"Then what does it mean? What if you do fall in love with someone else?"

"I won't."

"How do you know?"

"I love you. I know I won't. If I somehow did it would not be the same kind of love."

"Yes, it would."

"Could you love someone else like you love me after this last year?"

"Well," I thought about Kodi for a moment, "I guess not."

"See, that is why I bought some stuff for our place. I know that even if you dated someone else for a while you would not be able to date him very long. They might fall in love with you, but you would never fall back in love with them. Not real love anyway." I could tell he was speaking from experience.

"Yes, I guess you are right. I have no stuff to bring." I changed the subject.

"I know, you are still in school, and I am working, so I will get the stuff for us."

"I know but that is not fair."

"You need to focus on your studies first; you only have one year left of school, and soon we can be together."

"Are you sure that is what you want?"

"Yes."

"How do you know?"

"I just know."

"What about your other girl?"

"There is no other girl."

"I am sure there is another girl someplace."

"Well, I do not want to live with her. Not like I do you."

"So there is another girl."

"Sort of. I don't love her."

"You do not need to tell me about it. You do not need to feel guilty. I did not expect you to come here again after you left with your bike. I do not expect you to come back or wait for me."

"But I said I would."

"I know, but you don't have to. I am not worth it."

"I think you are. It is my choice."

I did not know what to say.

I wish that Eric would have taken me with him when he left. I wish he would have asked me to marry him after all. I know even if he would have asked me too I would have said no. I could not have done that anyway. Leaving Tommy for Eric was not an option. I should not even think it is. Thinking those thoughts just makes it harder. I should have not talked him but I do miss him. I guess Dad was right, maybe I am I leading Eric on to believe things will come true that I cannot give him just yet anyway.

When Will the Pain Stop?

It was the beginning of October; the summer had gone fast. I was settled in school again and was doing well. Grade twelve this was finally our last year. I was anxious in wondering what kind of changes this year would bring for us, as I did every year when school started. Well, mostly for Tommy and me. I did not care much about school that was just my duty to perform. Tommy wanted me to graduate and go into nursing. He said that I would make a good nurse with all that I already knew from being with him. I vowed that I would try my best to get good grades in biology and chemistry so that I might apply in a few months to go to college. I asked Tommy about what changes that would bring for us if I left and went to school in the city. He just said we would worry about those things as they came along.

"I have to go to the hospital for a checkup. Would you like to come with me this time?"

"Do you want me to come?"

"Yes."

"Why this time?"

"I want you to come every time, but I know you cannot take time off work."

"Oh, sure." I paused for a moment. "Do you think they will tell you anything about the transplant?"

"No, probably not."

"Do you still want to go if they say you can?"

"No."

"Why not?"

"Because I do not think it will work anyway."

"What kind of thinking is that?"

"They have already said my chances of making it are low because of all the chemo I have already had."

"And if you don't go what are your chances of ever getting better?"

"None."

"Well, then?"

"Well, then, what?"

"Well, then, why don't you go?"

"It is too far to go away from you all."

"I will come with you."

"You can't."

"Why not?"

"You have school."

"So, that can wait."

"No, it can't."

"You don't think I would want to be with you?"

"Your parents won't let you go."

"Yes, they will. I will go anyway."

"I don't want to go."

"I don't want you to go either, but what else can you do?"

"I don't know."

"I am scared I will not make it."

"I am scared, too. Well, how about we wait and talk about after they tell you something. There really is no point in talking about it now because we don't even know anything at all about what the decision is going to be. Let's talk about something else."

"How was your day at school?"

Tommy was right again. The doctors did not do anything to him at the hospital. They did the routine tests and sent him on his way after we waited there all day. I did not like it there. We had to sit in the waiting room with a lot of sick people. Most of the people looked sicker than Tommy. It is no wonder he did not like to go there. I am glad I went with him for support though. I think it made us both feel better.

I sat and watched the people come and go. While we were in the waiting room we were sitting beside another guy that looked about the same age as Tommy. He kept looking at us while we were reading a magazine together and talking about what we saw. I thought Tommy was going to ask him what he was staring at for a moment but then I think his kind heart kicked in. I wonder what he was thinking. I wonder what he was there for. I wonder what kind of cancer he had. I wonder how long they gave him to live. Everyone in the room looked very sad. Now I know why Tommy had never asked me to come here with him before. I think he was trying to keep me from the pain.

I wonder when the pain is ever going to stop. I try to be strong for Tommy and he tries to be strong for me. Sometimes everything gets to be too much. It seems at times I just want to wake up from this bad dream. I want it to be one of the nightmares I suffer from each time I try to sleep. I want the phone to ring and hear Tommy say hello, it is nice to hear from you, I have not seen you in a while, what have you been up to? I can say to him, I had the weirdest dream about you.

I want the pain to stop hurting for Tommy. I want to see the happiness in his eyes again like I used to before he got sick. I do not ever want to hear the sound of fear in his voice. I do not want him to ever lie to me and tell me things are okay when they really are not. I do not want him to hide anything from me. I do not want to feel like I am going to be sick every time I hear the words, "I have to go to the doctor tomorrow." I want Tommy to hold my hand forever. I want to walk down the aisle with him in marriage. I want his face to be the first thing our child sees when it opens its eyes for the first time. I want this to be over. I want Tommy to get well soon so we can start our lives together. I do not want to cry myself to sleep again tonight because I am scared of what might happen when he is gone.

When will the pain stop for all of us?

I wonder why God gave us all life. I wonder what my purpose is here on earth. I wonder what Tommy's purpose is here. I wonder why God showed us this much love and now is threatening to take it away. What are we supposed to learn from this? I wish someone could point it out to me so that we can get on with it. It gets hard standing strong every day for Tommy. It is hard watching him go through these struggles every day. I know we cannot give up. I will be strong enough for both of us even when I do not exactly know how.

I find my strength in my friends. I find my strength in my lovers. Kodi and I are becoming friends now that we have stopped dating so much. It is nice to get to know him on the other side of the sheets. He is starting to see how messed up my head really is and he says he will help me through it any way he can. I wonder if that is true. Eric told me those same things once, but when I needed him most he needed someone else.

I have not known Kodi as long as I have known Eric. I know it is not fair to compare the two lovers I have, but if it were a contest, and I could only have one to love, I think they would both be out of the running. Tommy and I have been together for four years now, and I cannot stop loving him no matter what. I do not think of there ever being a second in line because that is just not fair. Some days I am madly in love with Eric and wish he was here and other days I am glad he is not. Some days I feel like Kodi and I will have a future together, but other days I do not. I am not sure what I am doing, and I can understand my father when he tells me I need to treat them differently. I am not sure how. They all know what I am about and they keep coming back, do they not get what they deserve?

It seems that no matter how hard I try neither of them fill the empty spaces that Tommy being sick leaves. It seems like Eric is waiting for Tommy to die but Kodi keeps one foot in front of the other and pushes forward with the crap I hand him. Kodi and I spend a lot of time together. He is much more of a thinker than Eric.

I love all three of them for different reasons. I am not sure I will ever have to decide on what it is I want to do. I think time will just take care of that anyway. When Tommy goes to the hospital for the transplant nothing else will matter. Maybe my father is right, and I am just playing wicked games of the heart that is making us all insane.

The First Attempt

Kodi and I are fighting a lot now. I do not think our fun will last much longer. I am not sure how to put it all back together again. I am not sure if I want to. I feel I have been lying to him for so long about Eric that he will hate me forever if I do tell him the truth. I know what keeping secrets and lying does to people, and I do not want to be one of those people. It is just that Kodi touches a place inside of me that no one else can. I do not want to let that go.

I let Kodi read my journal today. He read about Tommy and Eric and all the things I was hiding. I thought he would want to leave and never see me again but he didn't. He stayed. He asked me to try again with him but this time with no more lies. I wonder if I can do that. I wonder if I am worthy of that kind of love from another. Kodi says I am, but I do not think so. I think I get all the pain I deserve because I am dishing so much of it out. Kodi deserves someone who can give him back as much love as he has to hand out. He says he already has that.

I am sick again with kidney infection. It is awful but at least I can still see Tommy. I went to the doctor the other day and they told me I had to have surgery on my throat. I have to get my tonsils out right after Christmas. A friend from biology class has to get hers out the same day, too. I hope we are in the same room because at least I will have someone to talk to when I am alone. Tommy says he will come and stay with me. I wonder what it is like for Tommy to be sick all the time. I hate being sick even for a while.

Tommy has been in the city for a few days now. I miss him a lot. He had to go there for check ups and to set a date for the transplant. I think he will do it. He has to. He says he is scared being there but he has some family he is staying with to comfort him. He says that I can stay there with them while he is in the hospital. I guess I will have too since I have no other place to go.

"How are things today?"

"Fine."

"Did they tell you any more?"

"Yeah, they said a few things."

"Like what?"

"They said they were not sure if they are going to do it now."

"Why?"

"Because of all the trouble I had before with the chemo, you know, when I almost died."

"Yeah, I know that part of it."

"They said they would tell me Tuesday, after the weekend."

"So you are staying there until then?"

"Yeah, " he paused, "but I want to come home."

"I want you to come home, too." I was trying not to let him hear me cry.

"How is school going?"

"Okay. What else are you doing up there?"

"We went out for dinner and around the city for a while the other night."

"Are you having fun?"

"Yeah, I guess. We are going out again on the weekend with my aunt and some other cousins. You know, the one that stayed with you and Mom at the hospital."

"Yeah, I remember."

"I think I will be home Tuesday night if they do not keep me."

"Good, I cannot wait to see you."

"I love you."

"I love you, too."

"Bye."

I got off the phone with Tommy, and I could not stop crying. Could they really say no to him? Would they just let him die? This was the most awful joke God has played on us yet. I was angry at God for letting this happen to Tommy. Why Tommy? Why me? Why leukemia? Why now? Why not when he was older and had already lived a life? Why not after he had loved a lot and given his heart away to someone good, someone who deserved it. Why was God punishing him? This was not fair. I hated God for all of this. I hated Tommy even more.

I hated the way he touched me. I hated the way he looked at me. I hated the way his voice sounded on the phone. I hated the way he said, "I love you." I did not believe that he did love me. Why would he put me through this if he did? Love is letting go, not dragging someone through the hardship of it all.

Love is not this painful. This is not love. This is a sick game that someone up in heaven wants to see me lose. This is not fair. I am only seventeen years old. I want a normal life with normal friends. I want the worst thing in my day to be wondering what clothes to wear to school or what my friends think of my new boyfriend. I want to care what they think of my boyfriend. I do not want them to ask me if he is okay anymore. I want them to ask us to a party or the beach with them. I want to be a normal girl with normal friends. I want it all to stop.

I hate fighting with Kodi. I broke up with him for the last time. I do not want to try this anymore. He does not understand me. He does not love me. He is immature, and I want him to leave me alone. It is best for him to find some other pet project to make rescue when they are down. Kodi cannot make this better, and he cannot take my pain away. He is just hanging out with me to make himself feel like he is doing something good. I do not need his charity. He can give it to someone else for a while. I do not need it anymore. I am strong enough. I can stand on my own two feet. I do not need a leaning post anymore. I do not need a crutch.

I wrote Eric a letter today. I told him I had been seeing Kodi. I wrote that I did not want to see him anymore and that I did not want to move in with him. I thanked him for everything we had shared together but I hoped he found what he needed in someone else. I wrote I hoped he had a good life and all that was left in it. This relationship was sucking to much energy out of both of us, and I needed a rest for a while. I needed to know what it was like to not hang on to something you cannot have. Eric deserved to be able to not hang onto something he did not have. He needed to be free from it more than I did.

The phone rang again and again. I sat at the kitchen table and chose it ignore it. I did not care who it was. I did not want to talk anymore. I wanted it to stop ringing.

It rang again. I did not answer.

The phone rang again. Whoever it was must really want to talk to me. "Hello?"

"They said yes." Tommy sounded sad.

"When are they going to do it?"

"They said soon, but I can come home for a while first."

"Are they going to wait for Christmas?"

"I don't know. I hope so."

"When will I see you?"

"Soon."

"Soon today?"

"Yes, I will call you when I get home. Will you come over?"

"Yes, I will come as soon as you get there."

"See you soon."

"See you soon."

It was finally here. They are finally going to do it. I wonder if Tommy is strong enough to pull through it. I wonder if they just think there are no other options for him. I wonder how he is feeling. I wonder if he will really go. I wonder if I can go with him. I wonder if he wants me, too. I wonder if God is going to take him away from me.

Christmas came and there were no signs of the transplant yet. Tommy kept going for checkups and trying to prepare himself for what might happen next. I tried to help him forget as much as he could about what was to come for him. I tried to cheer him up so he was not always thinking about the worst things. We did not talk about the future. We stayed in the moment as best we could. We did not look to far ahead because we were not really sure how much future he had. One day at a time was usually more than we could handle.

Our Christmas was very nice. We had a couple of celebrations. We had dinner with both our families but the one we had together was the nicest.

"Do you want to see what I got you?" I asked him.

"Okay," he said, as he handed me the gift he had gotten for me.

"I hope you like it."

"I do."

"You have not even opened it yet."

"I like it already."

"Open it."

"Open mine at the same time."

"One, two, and three…" but he waited until I opened his first. I knew he would.

It was a high school ring. It had our school emblem on it with my birthstone on each side. I could not stop smiling. It was the prettiest thing I had ever seen.

"Maybe someday it will be for when we get married," he said as he looked into my soul, "but for now, promise me you will graduate."

"I promise." I hugged him without letting go for a second.

"Promise me no matter what happens you will go to college."

"I promise."

"No, I mean if things get hard for you, promise me you will still go."

"What do you mean?"

"If I die. You still have to go to school."

"I will."

"No, you need to go."

"Stop saying that. I will go."

"I wonder what is going to happen to you when I am gone."

"You are not going anywhere."

"When I die."

"Tommy, it is Christmas. You are not dying today. Please, do not talk to me about it. I do not know what is going to happen to me either, but you have to trust I will be okay."

"You will not be okay."

"I don't know how I will be, but today I am great here with you, and I would not want to be anywhere else in the world. That is all that matters to me."

I gave him my hand. "Put it on," I smiled, "beside the other ring that you gave me last year." He did.

"Open mine now."

He opened the box slowly. He smiled when he saw what was inside. It was a pendant for his necklace that I had gotten him last year. It said, "I love you."

"Now you can take my love with you wherever you go."

"I already do." He smiled at me.

He rode in the back of the car with me when I went for my operation two days after Christmas. He held my hand all the way there. My dad drove, and my mom sat in the front with him.

My surgery went fine. I had a lot of scaring so they had to cut deep into my throat, and it felt like I had swallowed razor blades, but Tommy kept telling me I would be fine. I believed him.

Kodi came to see me at the hospital but he could not stay long because Tommy was with Mom and Dad in the café. I was glad he was there even if it was only for a few minutes. He gave me one of his shirts to wear to make me feel better because he could not stay just before I had to ask him to go.

Eric called while I was at the hospital, too. I could not talk to him because my throat hurt so badly but it was the thought that counted.

A couple of the guys from our gang also visited me. The nurse kicked them out and gave me more medicine to sleep because we were caught in the smoking lounge. I was trying to have a smoke but it hurt too much; then they had to leave.

I was in the hospital four days. Then I got to come home. The day I got home from the hospital I started to vomit. I puked all over the floor in our living room because I could not get up to get to the washroom. Dad said it was okay and Mom held my hair while I was sick. It was awful. I wondered how Tommy handled it all so well.

I have made three resolutions this year. I want to quit smoking, find out who I am and just be myself. I am not sure what being myself is but I think I need to try to figure it out.

I have become lost in this intertwined bond with Tommy. Everything I think about is for him. I ask myself what he would do if he were in the same situations. I talk about him to my friends, see him every day, and talk to him on the phone, usually twice a day or more. I do wonder what life will be like without him, but how can I know? How can I try to understand something I do not understand? How do I know what I do not know? I do not want to find out.

Tommy goes to the hospital soon for his transplant. I wonder if he asked them to delay it this long so he could be with me while I was sick. That is something he would do.

I am scared that when he goes I will not ever see him again. I do not want him to go but I do not want to tell him that in case he changes his mind about it all. It is the only chance he has left and no matter how afraid we are, he has to do it anyway. I love Tommy and not even death will change that. In my heart I know all our simple dreams will come true. We have gone through so much that it has to. I am not sure what I will do if it doesn't.

"Dear God," I said out loud, "I am sorry I was angry at you and at Tommy. I feel that this life is unfair for Tommy. I am not praying for myself this time. Well, I guess I am in a way. I am praying for Tommy. I am praying that you give him a miracle this time. He does not deserve this pain and suffering. He does all he can to stay here with us in this life but the odds are always against him. He does try to be nice to everyone, and he has the kindest heart of anyone I know. He wants to live and he tries every day to be strong. This is not fair to him. Please help him. Please let him stay a while longer with us. Please bless his heart and keep him safe. Please let us win this cruel game. Please stop all the pain. Amen."

I went to Tommy's house. We sat in his room and talked and listened to the stereo like we always do. We did not talk about him being sick though, we talked about that already on the phone. We were just spending time together being a normal teenage pair together sharing each others company.

I watched Tommy as he sat on the edge of the bed and lifted weights. He has started doing that so that his body will be strong for the treatments. I teased him about how big his muscles were getting. I told him that if he kept it up all the girls would be after him. He said he did not want any other girls that I was more than enough.

I sat on his bed and did some homework while he was flicking through the stations on the TV. I was not sure how he expected me to get smart with all that noise. I closed my books and watched TV with him instead. The homework would be there tomorrow.

"Are you done?" he asked me.

"No."

"Then open them up again and finish it."

"I do not feel like it."

"So, do it anyway. I will help you."

"Here, then you do it for me. It should be easy for you."

"That is cheating."

"So."

"You are smarter than I am. I never took chemistry."

"So it is all kind of like math. You are smarter than me in math."

"No, I am not."

"Yes, you are. I failed grade-ten math, remember?"

"Yeah, but now you are in grade-twelve math. You are smart; keep working."

I sighed and opened my books again and started to work while he turned off the TV.

"What is nine times six? Fifty-four or fifty-six?"

"Fifty-four," he said without looking up from something he was trying to fix.

"Are you sure?"

"Yes."

"If I get that wrong then the rest of it will be wrong, too. Are you sure?"

"Ten times six is sixty, minus six, for six times nine. It is fifty-four," he explained it to me.

"Oh, yeah. Right." I tried to follow his logic.

I kept doing my homework while he was fiddling with something else now.

"Are you staying overnight this weekend with me?" he finally said.

"Sure."

"Wanna get some movies?"

"Sure." I did not care what we did as long as we were together.

"Did I tell you what I heard at school today?"

"No, what."

"Do you remember my friend Steve?"

"Yeah, the dark-haired kid that you always said hi to. The one you said you had known since kindergarten?"

"Yeah, him. I was talking to his brother today, and he said Steve was not feeling well. He said they took him to the doctor and they did blood tests. Guess what he has?"

"I don't know, what?"

"He has leukemia."

"No!"

"Yes."

"That is awful."

"His brother told me what hospital he is in, and I wondered if you would come with me to see him on the weekend."

"What would I say?"

"What did I say to you?"

"That was different."

"Do you think it is any different for him getting sick than it was for you?"

"No."

"Would you have liked it if someone you knew with the same disease came to see you?"

"Yes."

"Then will you go with me?"

"Yes."

"Thank you."

I fell asleep in Tommy's arms while we were watching TV. I slept for a few hours without the horrid thoughts in my head tormenting me. It was a relief.

The next week Tommy and I spent all of our time together hanging out and being silly. We both tried as hard as we could to be free and in love. We tried to forget all the bad things that hung over our heads while we waited for the news to come about furthering his condition. We did not want to talk about it but it was always there haunting us.

"Happy Valentines Day." I greeted Tommy with a kiss.

"Thanks." He kissed me back. "I got you something."

"I got you something, too."

"Here." He handed my a dozen red roses.

I took them in my hands, then put them up to my nose. "They are beautiful."

"I got us something else. Hang on."

Tommy left the room for a few minutes. I set my bag down and took out the chocolates and the other gifts I had gotten him and set them on the bed. I was sure he would see them as soon as he came in.

I looked around his room and saw he had put candles on the bedside table. I lit both of them before he returned. I wondered where he got them from. I had never seen candles in his room before.

"I got us this," he held up a bottle of pink champagne and two wine glasses.

"Oh, that is so nice!" I was speechless.

He poured the pink liquid into the glasses and turned out the lights before he sat down beside me on his bed.

"Cheers," he said just as he handed me the glass.

"Cheers." I took a sip at the same time as he did. "To what?"

"Love," he said.

I watched him without saying a word.

"Lovers like us," he continued. "I think this day is for lovers like us, people that cannot live without each other. People that make each other so happy that not even death can take their happiness away. I will love you even after I die."

"I will love you after I die, too. Even when I die I am not going to leave you."

"Yes, you are."

"No. I am going to come back and be with you all the time. I am going to haunt you."

"Haunt me?"

"Yes."

"Promise not to scare me?"

"I promise, but I am not going to leave you, ever."

"I will love you forever, I promise."

We sealed the deal with feeding each other a chocolate and more kisses to follow. We watched the roses wilt by candle light until we were so overwhelmed with being together we made love.

I woke up the next morning in his bed and in his arms. I wanted to stay there forever. I wondered if this was real love. I wondered if this was the love that kept people together for their entire life. I wondered if love like this was real. I wondered if Tommy felt the same way.

Sometimes Tommy and I argue about the silly things. Last week I had some school functions to attend and he did not want me to go. He thought I should spend my time with him instead of staying after school to help out with the drama club. I told him I liked the drama club and that he should not pick on or make fun of the things I like to do even if he doesn't. He says that is a waste of time. I do not think it is.

We have been together four and a half years now and we still argue. I wonder if we will ever stop. I know that he is sick a lot and he gets frustrated and miserable because of his medication and the leukemia but I am on his side. It seems that whenever things do not go his way he blames it on me. I guess I blame things on him that are not his fault either.

I am glad that most of the time we are happy together. I do think this is that kind of love.

Tommy and I are going to the city today. We are going to St. Anne's Hospital. I know they are the best doctors and nurses. I know they will do all they can to help him. I know that if anyone can help him, they will do it there. I know he will get the best care possible. I know all there is to know. I also know one last thing. Tommy does not want to go.

It is going to be a long trip. Tommy is taking all his belongings with him because they said he might have to stay for the transplant today. I hope he can stay. I hope he does not stay. I think he has given up hoping for anything although he does not say that he has.

We rode in the back of his father's car in silence. It was like we were driving on the highway to hell. Maybe we really were.

We all wondered if we were going to be making the trip back home without him or not. He did not say anything about it though. I think he was holding his anxieties inside because he did not want to scare me. I wondered if this would be our last trip.

We got to the hospital and there was more waiting. The nurse took Tommy into the room for a check up and this time he asked if I could go with him. She said yes so I did.

I watched once more as they stuck needles in his arms, took his temperature, checked his reflexes, asked him questions, and assessed his brain function. "Hold your arms out like this. Count backwards. Spell backwards. Stand on one foot. Touch your nose." He did all that they asked without one single complaint. He never complained.

We waited in another room for another doctor to come.

We sat in the chair together and played games like I spy and told knock-knock jokes, and Tommy looked in the drawers to see what he could take home with him. He did not want anything, though; he was tired of all the medical stuff around him and wanted nothing at home to remind him of the hospital. We talked some more, then sat in silence and waited.

"You two look like twins," the man in the white coat said when he came in the room. "Are you married?"

"Not yet." Tommy answered him.

"You two look good together. You look like you are in love."

We smiled and said nothing as we looked into each other's eyes.

"Well, it looks like we are going to go through with the transplant. Are you ready to stay today?"

"Yes," Tommy said quietly.

My heart hit the floor.

"Do you have any questions?"

"What is going to happen?"

"Well, first you will take a series of radiation and chemotherapy treatments. You already know what that is about, but this time it will kill all the white blood cells in your body. More than you have ever taken before. We need to make sure everything is gone this time. That will last for about the first two weeks. Then we will give you the transplant. The bone marrow transplant itself is simple. We will have already taken the donation from your sister, and then we will give it to you through IV, just like a blood transfusion. You have had lots of them, so you know what that is like. It will take a few hours; then we wait, and we should know if it takes or rejects itself in a few weeks after that. You will probably become very sick for a while, but then when you feel well again. We hope the new marrow will grow, and you will be in full remission for a long time."

"What are my chances?"

"Well, you have taken so many treatments already that your chances are about fifty percent of surviving the radiation and chemo."

"And if I do not do this?"

"Your leukemia will surely come back. We cannot give you many more treatments of chemo. If we do it will keep deteriorating your brain and the rest of your organs."

"Oh."

"In the next few days we will be doing lots of tests on you. We will give you an MRI so that we can see how much brain damage you already have from the chemo. We will do lots of blood tests. We want to insert an amyia in the top of your head that will allow us to take brain fluid samples directly from your skull instead of doing spinal taps. We will also insert a Hamelin tube, which is like an IV that goes directly into your heart. This way you do not have to have one through your arm. Your veins are really weak, and this will be easier for you."

"Oh."

"This will take a few days to get all this done, and then we will start the treatments. You can have anything you want to eat or drink until the chemo and radiation starts. After that you will not be allowed anything that is not given to you by the hospital. You will have no immune system so you cannot have anything that is not cooked. No fresh fruit, nothing brought in from the outside, nothing. Do you understand?"

"Yes."

No, no, no, I do not understand. You are going to kill him and then hope he gets better again? No. I do not want this to happen. I want Tommy to come home. I do not want him to stay here. TOMMY, SAY NO! The thoughts were screaming in my head.

"What do you think?" Tommy squeezed my hand, as he asked me the question.

I looked at the floor as I wiped the tears from my eyes. This time I could not hide my fear behind the walls I had built within myself. I put my head on Tommy's shoulder. I could not answer the question.

The doctor left, and we waited in silence for the nurse to come and get Tommy and take him to his room within the hospital. We followed her to the white, sterile room. This was the coldest, ugliest, palest room I had ever seen. I did not want him to go in. I wanted to hold him at the door and scream at him not to go. I wanted him to change his mind. He was right: this was awful.

"You can put your things in here. This is where you will be for the next few days. After the transplant we will give you an isolation room, but this is it for now."

"Thanks."

Tommy stood by the window while his mom put his things away in his closet. I sat in the chair beside him. We said nothing.

"It is time we should get going, Tommy," his father informed us. "It is getting late, and we have a long drive back home."

233

"Yes, I know."

Tommy walked us to the front door of the hospital where we said our goodbyes. His father walked on ahead while Tommy and I stood in the entrance way.

"I have to go with him."

"I know," Tommy said, as he hung onto me as tightly as he could.

"I don't want to go. I will be back with your dad on the weekend when he comes."

"I know."

"I will call you every day."

"I know."

"I don't want you to stay."

"I don't want to stay either."

We kissed as we waited for Tommy's dad to pull up with the car.

"I love you."

"I love you, too, Tommy."

He held my hand until I got so far away he had to let go. I walked in body toward the car but I left my heart with him. I held my breath as I turned around to wave goodbye to him. He was standing in front of the window at the hospital looking out of the glass. He had tears running down his face but this time he was not trying to hide them. The entire world could now see our pain or whoever cared to look.

I was already crying. I stood in front of the car for a moment and watched him through the window. This was the saddest moment we have ever shared together. I did not want to leave him. I wanted to stay.

I did not want him to stay. I wanted us to run away together. I wanted his pain to end.

Dear God, please stay with him until I can see him again.

I waved goodbye and got into the car.

The next afternoon I got a call from Tommy. "Hey, how are you?" I asked, as soon as he said hello.

"Good. I get to come home."

"What?"

"I get to come home. Dad is going to come and get me tomorrow. Are you coming?"

"Yes, but why are you coming home?"

"I do not want to stay."

"Tommy, you are already there; you should stay."

234

"The leukemia is back."

"Oh."

There was a long pause on the phone. I was not sure what to say.

"What happens now?"

"I don't know."

"Didn't they tell you anything?"

"All they said was that I might have to go back for more treatments before the transplant."

"Did they say you were strong enough for that?"

"They did not know."

"What do you think?"

"I think," he paused, "that I am tired of it all."

"Yeah."

There was another long silence on the line.

"Are you coming with Dad to get me?"

"Yeah."

"Okay, see you then."

I sat beside my bed on the floor after I hung up the phone. I did not know what to think. I did not know what to do. I did not know what to say to Tommy anymore. I did not know how to help him through this. I felt numb.

I knew this was very bad news for him. I knew that the doctors were not sure if he should take more treatments because the last time he almost died. I do not think he is strong enough to pull through this time. I wonder what they are going to do. I wonder if he is really going to die this time. I wonder if he is going to die sooner than I thought. I did not think he was going to die at all. I want him to get well.

I sat and stared at the floor for a while. I felt so helpless this time.

"Did I tell you about Mom?" Tommy asked when we rode in the car while his dad drove us home.

"No, what?"

"You know that she has not been feeling well?"

"Yes, I know."

"She went to the doctor today, and they told her that she has some kind of disease."

"Oh, what kind?"

"I don't know the name of it, but they said that she would be paralyzed within about six months, and after that it will start to attack her insides and stuff, and she will die."

"Oh."

"I feel sad for Dad."

"Me, too."

I wondered how God could throw any more horror at this family. I wondered why He was being so cruel to them. Did God not know that Tommy needed his mother and Tommy's dad needed his wife? It was hard not to be mad at God all over again for things I could not possibly understand. Where was the miracle in all of this now?

"I have to go to the hospital tomorrow to stay for a while," he finally said.

"Oh, what did they say?"

"They said I would be in there a month, then home a month, then I could go back for the transplant. They said that this would decrease my chances to about thirty percent, and they think it will do some serious brain damage."

"Oh."

"I am going to ask them if I can stay out until Monday."

"Why?"

"Because they will not do anything over the weekend, and this way I can spend it with you."

"Okay."

"Is there anything you want to do special?"

"No."

"You don't have to come tomorrow."

"Okay, I was going to go with my sister to town for some stuff. Call me when you get home, and I will come over."

"Okay."

My sister and I returned from a shopping trip out town, and our mother was sitting at the kitchen table. She had a rather sad look on her face. I was pretty good at picking out that emotion in people.

"What is wrong?" my sister asked her.

"I went to the doctor today. They said they thought I have skin cancer."

"Oh," we both sat down at the table and listened to her talk about what the doctor had told her. It did not sound that serious, but cancer is cancer, and that is a word I do not care to ever hear again.

It seems there is no good news anymore. I am walking around numb and afraid to talk to anyone. Everyone only has bad news. What can happen next?

I have not slept in several nights. I hate the nights. I just want to be with Tommy for a while. That way I can at least get some rest. I do not like being away from him. It seems that every time I go away from him even for a while the bad stuff happens. I think we should always be together, that way we will be safe from the world. That way we can hide from the world together.

I think I am getting sick with the flu again. My stomach is sick, my head hurts, and I am very tired all the time. I hope I am not getting sick; then I will not be able to see Tommy this weekend before he goes in.

I have to get myself functional so I can go to the school and do some stuff for the drama club. I do not feel like it. I used to like doing technical things for the club but now I just want to quit. Tommy was right about that too, this is really just a waste of my precious time. I know I have to go because they depend on me. If I do not go no one else will. I have been on the tech crew for four years now and it is time I trained someone else to do it. My time there is almost done anyway because I only have a few months left before I graduate.

We took Tommy to stay in the hospital today for more treatments. They say he will be there about a month. I wonder if it will be longer. He says he is not sure what he thinks will happen. I wish I could stay there with him, but I can't this time.

It has been another long night. I have been awake since five in the morning waiting for Tommy to call around quarter to eight. He calls me that time every morning, even when he is not in the hospital. I cannot wait to talk to him.

I feel so alone without him here. I wish I could skip school today and go see him but I know that will not be good for either one of us. I know I will see him on the weekend but that seems like a long time away from today.

I feel like crying all the time now. I hardly talk to anyone at school. I cannot stand the simple things people say. I cannot stand one more question about how things are going with Tommy. If people want to really know then they should go see him for themselves.

I hear all the things my friends are doing at school on the weekends, and I am jealous. I want to be the one having fun and parting. I want to be the one without a care in the world, getting drunk and being silly. I want to find some way to numb this pain. I am not sure how anymore, nothing works.

I had another night mare last night. This time it was different. The monster was attacking Tommy instead of me.

We were walking in the woods and a bunch of people were there that had some dogs. There was a German Shepherd, a terrier, a mutt, and some kind of small white dog. The little white dog started attacking Tommy. It was biting and tearing at his face. He was bleeding and his skin was ripped as he was trying to cry for help. The people just stood there and watched him.

I grabbed the dog off of him, and I started beating it with a stick. I kept hitting it and hitting it until it was almost dead. I am not sure if it was the crying voices behind me, but something told me to stop, so I did. I turned around and looked at all the people standing there. They were all crying and pointing at the dog. They were all sad for the monster that had just torn Tommy's face off. I rushed over to Tommy, who was watching me become psychotic. As soon as I got to his side the bleeding stopped and all the scars went away.

I woke up in a cold sweat.

Tommy finally called. He reports that the doctor says he can come home in a week. I hope that is still the way it is then. I hope nothing changes this time. I miss him a lot.

Dad is mad at me again because I am always on the phone. That is not my fault people call me. It is nice to talk to my friends sometimes. I almost feel normal.

Dad did not get upset when Tommy called from the hospital, nor did he get upset when Bobbi called, but he did get upset the third call I got, which was from Jim. It was nice to chat with Jim. I have not talked to him in a while. I thought he must have ESP because I was just looking at a tape he had given me a long time ago.

Jim and I talked about when we went to the prom a few years ago when we were dating. He asked me if I would be going this year to my own. I said I doubted it because Tommy was too sick to go. He said he was sorry for that and asked if I wanted to go with him again this time. I laughed and told him I thought it had been enough the first time around. I know he would have really taken me if I wanted to go but I think he was just asking to be nice.

It is Good Friday today. The only thing that is good about it is that Tommy did come home from the hospital. He is losing his hair all over his room and is complaining that it is making a mess. He says it gets all over his pillow case and it bothers him when he is trying to sleep. I think he should just get a new pillow case, but he says it gets in the laundry. If that happens then it gets all over his clothes, and he hates that, too. I told him he should just not wear any clothes and he would not have to worry about it then.

I tried to clean the hair out of his room for him, but he just got mad at me. He said I did not need to take care of him. I told him I had to because it was better than listening to him complaining about it. He finally gave in and let me help him, but he did not like it. He is too sick to put up much of a fight with me today because he knows I would have done it anyway.

238

Eric called today. He is in the hospital now. The other day at work he got his hand caught in some kind of a machine and crushed it. The doctors said they may have to take it off if it does not get better soon. I hope that does not happen to him. I wonder what his parents must be going through after they have already lost a son to some kind of an accident. I forget what now.

Eric says he misses me and that he wished I was there. I wonder if that is the truth because I have tried to call him a few times, but he never calls me back. I stopped calling.

He says he still loves me, too. I think it is only because he has too much time to think about things, and I am much too busy for that. I do miss him, though.

I do send him best wishes and all the love I have though cards and letters. I pray that it helps him get well. I am not going to hold on to the fake dreams of the past. I am not sure if they were really my dreams in the first place or just his. I think those dreams faded for him as soon as the next girl came along. Maybe I should not be so hard on him. Maybe he is real.

Kodi was around this weekend asking for me. I do not want to see him either. I do not need any more crazy stuff to mess my head up. I need my time to focus on Tommy. Although it would be nice to see him for a while I do not have the energy for his head games.

Kidnapped

I heard Tommy's voice while I was behind the stage doing some work on the lights for the upcoming plays. At first I thought I was dreaming until I heard the drama teacher call my name.

"Emily, there is someone here for you."

I turned around, and it certainly was Tommy. "What are you doing here?" Everyone was looking at him like he was an alien from outer space. I wondered what they saw that I did not. Was it his short hair, pale skin, or the fact that they had heard gossip and had thought he was already dead?

"I came to get you."

"For what?"

"Come with me. Tell them I am sick, and you need to go."

"Tommy, have you been drinking?"

"Tell them I am sick, and you need to go."

"You should not use that as an excuse."

"Then don't tell them anything. Just come with me."

"I can't."

"You are." He was not asking anymore. He took me by the hand and pulled me away from my work. I followed out behind him while I was trying to think of what excuse to make. This was one of those moments that I was wishing he had not known exactly where I was.

I said nothing as I walked out from behind the stage after him while he held my hand.

"She won't be back today," he said in the general direction of the drama teacher, who was Tommy's old English teacher. Nothing else was said.

"Where are we going?"

"Shelly and Sandy are in the car. We are going to see her boyfriend in jail."

"I don't want to go."

"So."

He led me out to the car anyway. If I was ever kidnapped this was it. They seemed to already have a plan.

It was obvious from the smell in the car they had started the party without me. It was nice to see Tommy having some fun. For a moment when I looked into his eyes he was happy. I saw the glisten of the light behind the illness. I saw Tommy again.

"What the hell?" I greeted them, in an untraditional way.

"Come with us," Sandy said, and she handed me a beer.

"Get in." Tommy pushed me into the back seat.

"What the hell are you guys doing?"

"We picked up Tommy to go for a ride and then we had to come and get you. He said he would not go without you."

"Yes, he would have. He just wanted a reason to get me away from school." I smiled at him. I knew he would not have gone with them without me.

"Let's go."

Sandy, Tommy, and I were not at all interested in seeing Shelly's boyfriend in jail. We were along simply for the ride. I was not sure why they thought going to visit a jail drunk was a good idea but I never seemed to know a good idea if it hit me in the head.

I followed Shelly into the jail to visit anyway. I was the most sober and sane one of the bunch. After all, he was part of our group, and Kayla's younger brother, so I at least could go say hi. It would have been a long trip for nothing. It would be good to see him again but not like that.

Sandy and Tommy stayed in the car while Shelly and I went in. After a few moments of talking I did not want to waste the time those two devotees had to share, so I went back out to the car with them. We listened to the radio and had a few more beers while we waited. Life seemed ordinary for a moment, and Tommy was happy. Tommy was free of worry for a while, and that was all that was significant to me.

Shelly and Sandy had to pee on the way back home. It was dark out now, and for some reason urinating beside the road was not a stable plan for them. I am not sure who came up with the better idea to stop at a stranger's house, pretend to use the phone for an emergency, and then ask to use the bathroom. Tommy and I thought it best to stay in the car while they carried out this brilliant plan.

Shelly pulled into a driveway, and they both went to knock on the door. I could see Sandy trying to ring the bell in urgency, but no one came to answer the door. They both went into that garage and tried the side door. They rang the bell and knocked on the door again but to no avail.

It was Sandy that spotted the freezer in the garage, and Shelly was the one that opened it. Tommy and I sat in the back of the car and wondered what bright idea they had next.

From where we sat we could only see the bottom of Shelly's feet as she reached to the bottom of the ice box. She is so short that she was falling into the freezer as she was reaching into the bottom for something. Tommy and I started to hysterically laugh at her.

Out she comes with a frozen ice cream cake and a box of ice cream sandwiches.

Both the girls ran back to the car in laughter themselves. Shelly is about to put the car in reverse until Sandy has another idea.

"Get the turkey."

Shelly agreed, "Let's go get the turkey in the freezer."

"No. Let's just go."

"It will only take a second."

"Stay here," Tommy whispered in my ear.

They both jumped out of the car again, and away they went. This time Sandy had her feet sticking out the top, and Shelly was holding the lid open.

"Shit. Hurry up; here they come!" Tommy yells out the open window. We again begin to laugh at the sight of two barely adult women stealing frozen cakes and a turkey out of a stranger's freezer because they stopped to use the bathroom.

The Break Up

I applied to go to college for the nursing program. I am still waiting for a letter on the outcome of that. I wonder if I will get in. I wonder how I am going to pay for the schooling. I wonder what will happen to Tommy if I go. I wonder where I will live. I wonder if I will even get accepted.

I heard through the grapevine that Kodi was back around this weekend. He was supposed to have been looking for me but I did not see him. I wonder why he is here now. He has been gone for a while since we last broke up. I heard that he had moved to the city someplace but I do not know for sure. I guess it is none of my concern now. I need my time to focus on other things than some kind of dysfunctional sexual relationship with him, although I do miss him at times.

Eric keeps calling me again. I think it is only because he is not working because of his hand. He needs something else to do than hang onto me. I bet he is sleeping with another girl anyway. He says he misses me and wants to move down here again for the summer. I think he is just board and it is that time of year again for him he is getting ants in his pants and needing a change of scenery. I guess he wants to make sure he is all hooked up with some kind of plans before he comes. Maybe he really does love me but he has a weird way of showing it from where he is. I do miss him, too. I miss the fun we shared but for now I am glad he is where he is. He would get mad at me anyway for spending so much time with Tommy.

Tommy and I had a disagreement today. He was talking about one thing, and I was talking about something else. Tommy told me what he felt like when I told him about when I was seeing Eric. He said that he thought I was going to leave him for someone else. I tried to tell him a million times that it does not matter who else I see, romantically or not, he is the most important thing in my life and that I would never leave him. I do not think he trusts me when I say that no matter how many times I reassure him. I do not blame him but if he only knew all that I have given up for him already he would know for sure, but I cannot tell him that.

I cannot tell him that Eric calls me on the phone all the time and wants to come down here to live with me. I cannot tell him that Eric tells me he loves me all the time and wants a wonderful future together someday. I cannot tell him that Eric has been at my house, and I have asked him to leave so I could go see Tommy. I cannot tell him that Eric has waited all week and weekend to see me while I was at the hospital with him. I cannot tell Tommy how many times I have told Eric that he is second in line and that if he wants to be with me he will have to wait. I have told Eric that there may be no future with us because of all the things I am doing with Tommy. I cannot tell Tommy how Eric must feel being second. I do not think Tommy would care much about the way Eric felt anyway. Tommy would feel Eric was just waiting for him to die, and I guess he would be right. I could never explain to Tommy that I do not want him to die and Eric will always be second to anything that Tommy needs. It is best to keep it all from Tommy and assure him that no matter what happens I will be there for him even if he believes me or not.

I am getting tired of waiting for Tommy to get better. I hope it happens soon. I feel like I am losing my fight to keep holding on. I am not sure if Tommy and I will be together forever even if he does get well. Sometimes I wonder if it is his illness that keeps us strong and together, yet I cannot leave him now. I do not want to, but sometimes it gets hard. Sometimes I need a shoulder to lean on, too. I wonder if sometimes I am missing opportunities to be happy.

I got a ride home from school from a new boy in our chemistry class today. I had seen him around a bit but he is older than the rest of us and seems to have no interest in making many new friends. His name is Tristan, and he is attending some classes at our high school before he goes to study out West in the fall. He is going to be a geologist. I wondered who would want to study rocks, but I guess he does. He seems to be a very nice guy.

Tristan says he thinks I am smart because I answer lots of questions in chemistry, and he has looked at my test papers when the teacher handed them back the other day. He asked me if I would like to study with him. He is also in my math class and wants to study math together, too. I said I was not sure because I was getting good grades as it was and did not have time for the extra study sessions.

I do not want Tristan to think I am putting him off and that I am not interested in him. He seems to be a very mature, smart guy. I would like to get to know him better, but he is leaving as soon as school is done, and I really do not have that much time to spare. I do not want to tell him about Tommy being sick. That part of my life is none of his business. I do not want to make the same mistakes with Tristan that I have with the others. I do not need another boy standing in line but I could use a friend. Maybe I am pulling the cart before the horse. After all, he only asked if I wanted to study with him, but I do know what boys are like.

I went for a long walk tonight after school. I needed the fresh air to clear my head. I starting thinking about life and all the things I have been handed. I was thinking about the things that are unfair, like Tommy getting sick and all the good things, like the love that I have found in Tommy. I was thinking about the bittersweet relationship love hands us. I wondered if I did not have Tommy how my life would be right now.

School will be out again soon and since this is my last year, I wonder where I will end up. I am not sure if I want to be a nurse or not even though everyone else thinks it is a good idea. I am not sure if I want to dedicate my life to people who are always sick. I wonder what kind of pat on the back a nurse gets after a long day of taking care of people. I bet they don't.

I do not want to get a job in a factory. That seems to be like a lot of hard work. I do not want to just be a clock punch number or a production amount. Life has to be more than that.

I know I will need to work at something to support myself. I cannot see living at home much after I am done school. Mom and I argue all the time, and Dad would never allow me not to contribute to supporting myself. If I can move out I wonder if Tommy would come and live with me if I could get a job. Maybe getting a job in a factory is not such a bad idea; then I can support us until he gets better. Maybe I could buy us some new lamps or dishes or something after I get a job. I wonder if Tommy would like that.

As I lie on my bed after my long walk outside, I began to reflect on how I felt inside. I did not want to think about Tommy or my future anymore, just how I felt. It was hard to put a label on what was going on inside my body. I did not know how I felt, there were no feelings there.

I stared at a picture of myself that had been taken only a few months ago. If I did not know how I felt now, how did I look like I felt in the picture? I looked like I had it all together. I looked happy. I looked safe. I looked sane.

I looked like I had emotions. I looked like I knew what I wanted. I looked like someone loved me. I looked like I had a purpose. I looked satisfied.

The tears fell from my cheeks onto the glass of the frame. The picture was wrong. I was lost. I was scared. I was uncertain. I was unhappy. I was afraid to fall asleep. I was afraid to wake up. I was afraid to answer the phone. I was afraid to talk to Tommy in case he was sick again. I was afraid not to talk to Tommy in case he was sick again. I was terrified what would happen if Tommy died. I wondered what would happen if he didn't die. I was afraid to get accepted to college. I did not know what I would do if I did not get accepted. I was lonely. I wanted love, but I was afraid of that, too. I felt like I was making myself love Tommy because I was afraid of what would happen if I didn't.

I grabbed the picture off the night stand and threw it up against the wall. The glass shattered and fell onto the carpet of my room. The picture landed upside down on the floor on top of the broken glass. Now the picture looked exactly how I felt: upside down and broken. I wondered if it was going to be the last night that I cried myself to sleep or into a nightmare. I asked God once again, *When will the pain ever stop?* I wondered if he was listening.

"Hey, what ya doing?" Tommy asked over the phone.

"Nothing. You?"

"Nothing."

"What did you do last night?" he inquired.

"Nothing. Went for a walk outside."

"Did you wear my coat?"

"Yeah. What did you do?"

"Jeff came over."

"Oh."

"He said that he was talking to Sandy and they wanted to know if we wanted to barbeque that turkey for my birthday and have a party."

"Where?"

"At Sandy's next weekend."

"Sure. Do you feel like it?"

"Yeah. It will be fun."

"Okay, if you want to."

"Are you coming over in an hour?"

"I just got woke up."

"How did you sleep last night?"

"Fine," I lied.

"You?"

"Okay." He probably lied, too.

"Are you staying over tonight?"

"Do you want me to?"

"Yes."

"Then I will bring my stuff when I come."

"Do you want me to rent movies?"

"If you want."

"See you in an hour?"

"No, see in this afternoon."

"Okay."

I went to Tommy's later that day and spent the night and stayed with him all the next day. He has an awful time sleeping, too. He gets up a lot during the night. He sweats a lot. He said it was just because he was hot because his dad had the furnace on too high but the window was open, and I was not that hot. I did not sleep well either because he kept waking me up, but it was better than both of us being alone.

After school on Monday Lizzie was talking to Tristan on the phone. He called me because he had some questions about our math homework, but she ended up talking to him about other things. She seems to like him and their conversation went well. I did not talk to him much because I was trying to study while I had the time. I had to utilize my phone time so that I could talk to Tommy later tonight.

Tristan asked Lizzie to ask me if I wanted to go out for lunch tomorrow during our school break. I said I would although I wanted her to come with us. She said she thought he wanted me to go by myself. I wondered if Bobbi would come if Lizzie did not want to. I did not want to give Tristan the wrong impression although the flirting was funny. It was funny that he was so scared to ask me himself. I wondered how the lunch would go if he could not even ask for the date.

"Did you study last night?" I asked him as soon as we got in his truck.

"A bit. Did you?"

"Yeah, while you were talking to Lizzie. How did you think you did on the test today?"

"I am not sure. You?"

"I think I did okay."

We drove to the restaurant in silence. I did not know what else to say and this seemed to be an awkward waste of my time.

247

RUBIE ANN GRAVES

"I do not see you around school with anyone. Do you have a boyfriend?" Tristan finally broke the silence.

"Yes, actually, I do."

"He does go to school?"

"No."

"What does he do?"

"Not much of anything."

"Doesn't he work?"

"Not right now."

"Why not?"

"He is sick and gets a pension."

"Oh he is just off work now because he is sick? Did he hurt himself?"

"No."

"Why doesn't he work?"

"You ask too many questions."

"Sorry, I just wanted to know if you had a boyfriend." He pulled into the restaurant parking lot. "Do you want to get lunch to go quickly so we can talk more?"

"Not if you are going to keep asking so many questions?" I laughed.

We ordered lunch and stayed at the restaurant to eat. We only got soup and that was fine with me. I had not eaten much more than that in a while. My stomach had not been feeling well again, but this time I did not think I had the flu. I think it was stress.

"Would you like to go for a walk before we go back to school?"

"Sure."

We walked a while in silence before I started to give him the answers he was looking for but I did not want to start the conversation.

"Tristan, if you really want to know about why my boyfriend does not work I will tell you."

"Okay, I would like to know all about him."

"Well, he is twenty years old, and he graduated from school a few years ago. That is where I met him. His last year of school he got sick, and they found out he had leukemia."

"That is sad. Is he going to die?" There was the haunting question again.

"He is going for a bone marrow transplant soon, and the doctors think that may help him get well again. He has about a thirty-percent chance to make it."

"That is not much of a chance."

"Sure it is. You are good at math."

"Emily, if there is a thirty-percent chance that it is going to rain, it usually doesn't."

"This is different."

"How?"

"Because he will die if it does not work."

Tristan and I returned to the school. We talked a bit more until he sat down at the piano in the café.

"Sit," he said as he patted the bench beside him.

I sat down, and he started to play a song for me. I closed my eyes and listened to him play. The music he was making rang through my soul, and I knew he was playing just for me. I smiled inside.

"How was your day?" Tommy asked.

"Good. Yours?"

"Good."

"What did you do today?"

"Lifted weights."

"Oh, anything else?"

"Waited to call you. Are you coming over after supper?"

"Okay."

I went to Tommy's house, and as soon as I got there I handed him the letter I had gotten from the college. I was not sure if I wanted to show it to him or not. I was not sure how he would feel about it. I was not sure how I felt about it.

"You got in!" He was happy.

"Yes, I did."

"You are going to be a nurse!"

"Maybe." I was not sure if I was or not. I was still not sure if I wanted to be. Mom said I was too irresponsible for that.

"I am happy for you."

"See, I told you I would go."

"Do you love me?"

"Yes."

"Like I love you?"

"How do you love me?"

"I want to spend the rest of my life with you. I want you to be my wife. I want to be with you forever. Do you love me like that?"

"I am not sure how I love you. I know I love you as my best friend. I know that I do not want to ever live without you. I am not sure how a man loves a woman like a wife. If that is it, then I guess I do."

"Do you ever want to be with other people?"

"Sometimes."

"When?"

"When you are not feeling well, and I cannot see you or when you are in the hospital. I get lonely."

"Do you have another boyfriend?"

"No."

"I know this might sound weird, but I would not care if you did."

"I don't."

"But if you did."

"I don't."

"Why don't you ever want to make love to me?"

"I don't know."

"I want to do that with you."

"I know."

"Is it because I am sick?"

"Sometimes. You are sick."

"I know, but I could do that."

"I want to make you as happy as I can, and sometimes we do that."

"I know but I want to do it more."

"I know."

"Are you doing it with someone else?"

"No."

"Would you tell me if you were?"

"Yes. I just think that is not the only way to show I love you. Maybe when you get better, then all that will be better for us."

"Maybe."

"I love you like I love no other. You are my best friend. Nobody else knows me like you do. There is no one else in my life that comes close to how I feel about you. Sex has nothing to do with that."

"I know. I am sorry I asked."

Tommy and I have lots of conversations about sex and love. We have lots of conversations about everything. I know he wants to be sexual, but it does not seem right for me. I do not see Tommy in that kind of lustful way. I am not sure how I see him anymore.

Eric called tonight when I came home from Tommy's. I thought it was bizarre that after Tommy and I were talking about relationships and love, Eric calls.

We talked for a while about old times and how long we had been together. He said it was the longest time he had ever been with a girlfriend. He said that he felt like I was always pushing him away. He asked me if I was happier that he was not around anymore and that way I could do what I wanted. He said that if was hard to hang on to something that he did not know if he could ever have. He said loving me was not a choice for him because he loved me whether he wanted to or not. He said that he loved me even when he did not want too and that being so far away from me was hurting him every day inside.

I did not know what to say to him. I loved him, too. I loved him in a different way from how I loved Tommy, but how could it ever work out between us? I told him it would not work out anyway because I was going away to school in the fall, but he said that he wanted to come with me. I told him that I did not think that was a good idea, but he thought it was the chance we had been waiting for.

He talked about all the empty nights he spent alone thinking about me and wondering if we would ever be together again like we were when he lived here for a while.

I told him that I thought about him often as well, and I was lonely for his company, too.

I knew it would not work out for us yet. I knew that although I loved Eric I was not ready for the commitment he was asking me to make. I did not know what else to do but tell him how I felt and hope that he would understand. I was not sure if he could understand but I did respect the fact that he was trying.

The one thing that we did agree on was that the nights were hard being away from each other, and we could not wait until the day we could wake up in each other's arms again. We agreed that no matter what life handed us it was easier when we were together in love, but we were not sure when that was even going to happen again.

I fell asleep thinking of Eric. My mind was trying to sort it all out and as it tried it became another bad dream. I was walking toward Tommy in the dream. I was not sure where we were but he was standing in this big house where Tristan had lived. I walked through the house, and I was afraid. I was searching in each room of the house for Tommy as I was calling his name. I never found him.

I went outside and Tommy was there waiting for me to come closer to him. We went for a ride in his truck and he told me he was Kodi's brother. I was thinking about Kodi and how I must have forgotten about him in the last while. Tommy was telling me how Kodi must have felt with all that we shared and how I dropped Kodi's heart in the gutter.

In the next part of the dream I was at school. I was standing outside of English class with Tristan but I was ignoring him. Tommy was standing in the distance. I could see Tommy but I could not talk to him because he was too far away from me. I was trying to talk to him but I could not reach him.

All of the sudden Sam, my faithful dog, was getting trampled by wild horses. I was trying to save him but I had no help. I was trying to turn to someone who cared for my dog but there was on one there. The strangers that were surrounding me were laughing and telling me that it was my fault he had been in the corral to begin with. I kept calling his name but I could not help him out. Finally he ran under the other side of the fence and found his way out without my help. He did not need me. I woke up.

I think the dream means that I am afraid to be alone. I think it means that I will not know what to do with myself when no one needs me anymore. I have made many mistakes when it comes to love and because of those mistakes no one really loves me back. I deserve to be alone. I think the dream means that Tommy and I love each other on different levels, and I am searching for the love he sees in me in someone else. I am searching for that love, but finding that it is only causing me more pain because I cannot let go of what I have with Tommy. I want to love Tommy in that way, but it is hard. How can I love Tommy as my husband who will be with me forever when he cannot even make plans that encompasses the next few weeks? I need a future to look forward to.

I want someone to love, but the searching is killing us all inside. It is not the right time for me to look any farther than what I already have. None of this is fair to me and it is even less fair for Tommy. I am not sure I can give him what he needs.

I do know for sure that no matter how bad things get I always feel safe when I am with Tommy. I know that when things fall apart he is always there for me even if the things that are falling are because of him. He talks with me about it, he listens to me when I am unsure of what I need to do, he holds me when I am scared of life and cannot find the strength to go on. If it is all wrong then why does it feel so good when I am with him?

We had Tommy's birthday party at Sandy's. It did not go as well as I had hoped. It was too cold outside so the turkey did not cook right. It kept catching on fire. Sandy ended up cooking the rest of it in the oven.

Most of Tommy's friends showed up. That was good for him. The problem I found with that was his friends thought it was a good idea to feed him a lot of beer and dope. Of which he took all that anyone gave him. After all, he was turning twenty one.

I had to take him home after a while because he was too intoxicated. Like any twenty-one-year-old boy, Tommy thought he needed to get laid for his birthday. That turned into an argument.

"Why won't you have sex with me?" he whined in a drunken slur.

"Because you are drunk."

"So. I bet you fucked your other boyfriends when they were drunk."

"That is not fair, Tommy."

"I bet you have sex with them when they want to."

"I have no boyfriend."

"Have sex with me."

"No."

"Why?"

"You are drunk."

"But what about when I am not?"

"I don't know."

"You do not love me. You do not want to be with me anyone. You are only here with me because I am sick."

"I am not. I am here with you because you are my best friend."

"If I am only your friend and you feel sorry for me maybe you should not come here anymore."

"What?"

"I want to break up with you."

"On your birthday?"

"Yes."

"You are just saying that because you are mad at me."

"No, I am not. I do not want to you come here anymore. I do not want you to be my girlfriend."

"Are you serous?"

"Yes."

Well, I did not know what to say. The idea that he was breaking up with me for real never crossed my mind before. I thought that he needed me, and breaking up would not be an option. My heart broke even more than it had ever before. I started to cry. "Are you sure?" I was almost begging him to say no.

"Yes, I want you to go and not ever come back."

"I love you."

"Go."

I walked out the door of his room and thought that I would never see him again. I picked up my shoes and carried them outside under my arm. I did not want to stay in his house a second longer. If he really wanted me to go, I would.

I threw my shoes in the car and started the engine. I was still crying. I did not want to leave. I did not want to say goodbye to Tommy like this.

I backed out of the lane and put the car in drive, but my heart was still in his room. I drove by Sandy's and there were still some people outside at Tommy's party. I wanted to stop there and tell them what happened. I wanted to tell them why it was not a good idea that they got him drunk. I wanted to show them how they had broken my heart. I kept driving.

I kept crying. *God, if I ever needed your help it is right now. I am not sure what is happening, but I know I am not done with Tommy yet. I know he is drunk, and please forgive him for that. He does not know what he is saying. He does not mean it. He cannot really mean that. What am I going to do without him? God please let him call me and say he is sorry. Please, please, please, this time it needs to be for me.*

Tommy never called all weekend. I never called him either. Maybe it was true. Maybe he did know what he was saying. Maybe he did want to break up with me for good.

I tried to hold back my tears as much as I could. I did well as long as I was at school and thinking about other things. I did not tell anyone what happened because I did not want them to ask me about it. I knew if they did I would just cry anyway. Crying was doing me no good. It did not bring Tommy back.

I wondered if he was crying, too. I wondered if he was happy to get away from me. I wondered if he thought I was just smothering him or just trying to take care of him. I wonder if he thought I ever wanted to be there with him. I wondered if he missed me. I wondered what he was doing. I wondered what he had for supper or if he lifted weights today. I wondered if he was getting along with his family. I wondered everything about him. I wondered if he would ever call me again. I wondered if I finally had gotten what I deserved.

Karma, I Think They Call It

Tristan and I have been spending some time together, but it is not the same. I like being with him, but he asks too many questions. He was raised in a Catholic home, and I was not. He has a very different outlook on life than I do. We get along fine but it seems we do not have much in common.

Tristan comes over after school once in a while. I think it is because he would rather be at our house than home alone. It seems he does not have much of a family there. Everyone at his house seems unconnected to each other. I often wonder what kind of family that is. Where is God that he talks about in that?

We take long walks on the beach even though it is quite cold out for that yet. It is nice just being with him talking. He says that things between Tommy and me will get better but I do not think he understands. I told him that I wondered if Tommy really thought he was dying and maybe thought he would rather die alone than break my heart. Tristan said that could not possibly be true and that Tommy must love me and probably just feels stupid about hurting my feelings. I said I doubted that, and I really think he meant what he said when he told me to get lost. Tristan just said I was being foolish, and I needed to give it a few more days, and my heart would feel better, although I doubted that.

We also go watch the local ball games together. I really do not like baseball, but it gives us something to do together. We usually talk through the game, but at least it is a bit of a distraction when the conversation gets dull.

Tristan was supposed to come over and spend the day with me, but he went canoeing instead of coming over. I was not surprised

He said he wanted to get together to study, but I doubt he will do that either. He is leaving in a few weeks, and it seems that he is pulling away from our friendship. Now I know how Eric feels. Funny how what comes around goes around when you least expect it, karma I think they call it.

Tristan was right. Tommy did call after a few days. I was still so upset at him I started crying as soon as I heard his voice say hello.

"You have not called me," was the first thing he said.

"No, you said you did not want me around anymore."

"But I thought you would call me anyway."

"No." I thought for a second. "I will give you what you want even if it breaks my heart."

"I am sorry I was mean to you."

"Mean to me?" Is that all he thought he was?

"Well, maybe a bit more than that."

"Do you really want to break up?" I was not sure if I wanted the real answer to that question.

"Do you?"

"No, these last few days have been hell for me."

"Me, too."

"Then why did you say that?"

"Because I thought you wanted another boyfriend. Someone told me they saw you at school hanging around with this guy, and he was giving you rides home and stuff."

"I am."

"See, I was right."

"He is a friend. He says he would like to meet you. He says you are crazy for dumping me. He said he would never have done that to me if he was you."

"You told him about me?"

"Yes."

"All about me?"

"No, just that you dumped me. He said I was sad all the time and wanted to try to cheer me up."

"Did it work?"

"No." I started to cry again. "No, it did not work."

"Do you love me?" he asked the stupid question.

"Yes."

"I love you, too. I am sorry. Will you be my girlfriend again?"

"Are you going to dump me again?"

"No."

"Promise?"

"Yes."

"I cannot do that again Tommy that hurt too much. If you do not want to be with me anymore you do not need to explain to me why, but I cannot go through that again. If you do not love me or want me around I will leave you alone if that is what you want."

"No, I do not want that. I made a mistake."

"So have I, but that hurts."

"I know; it hurt me, too."

"Then stop doing that and we will be okay."

"Will you come over today?"

"Okay."

Tommy and I talked a little more about what happened between us. I instantly felt better as soon as I saw him. I was still upset about the idea that he could say those things to me without thinking that it would hurt. I think now he can understand that I am not just in this relationship because I feel sorry for him. I love him and now maybe I can see I love him like a wife.

We also talked about Tristan. I told Tommy that we met at school and he gave me rides home sometimes. I told him Tristan and I studied together at lunch and that he was helping me with my grades so that I could do well to go to college in the fall. I told Tommy that Tristan was leaving in a few weeks to go to school. Tommy said he was glad I found a friend but he did not want to meet him.

All was well again between Tommy and me; therefore, all was well in the world.

Mom and I were arguing because I told her I was moving out as soon as school was finished. I told her if I was accepted to college then I wanted to go to the city as soon as I could to look for a place to live and get a job. She said it was a bad idea and that I would never be able to do it on my own because I was not that responsible. I told her if I did not leave as soon as school was done I wanted to get a job in harvest again and work until I could save some money to go. She did not like that idea either.

I told her I had applied for some grants at school, and I was likely to get them, so that would give me money to get started on my own. She still did not believe me and thought I should stay home and not go anyplace. I thought it was too early to discuss this situation and no matter what I did she was not going to be happy with what I wanted to do.

"I went to the hospital today."

"Oh, yeah? I did not know you had to go. What did they say?" I asked. I wondered why he did not tell me about it yesterday. I wondered if it was bad news. My heart hit the floor. "What did they say?" I asked again.

"I can go for the transplant in about a month."

"You can?"

"That is what they said."

"Do you think you will really go this time?"

"I don't know."

"I am scared. I want you to go, but I don't want you to go."

"Me, too."

"I wonder what is going to happen."

"Me, too."

"I wonder if you will really get there this time."

"Me, too."

The lack of words brought along anther one of those comfortable silences.

"What else did they say?"

"Nothing, they just took some fluid out of my brain thing in my head and said I have to go next week for a check up. At St. Anne's. Will you come?"

"Sure, if you want me to."

"I do."

"Okay."

"Are you coming over tonight?"

"I have school in the morning."

"You can stay overnight here and go to school from my house."

"Okay."

I was surprised that Tommy was in such a good mood when I got there. I am not sure what happened to him lately, but even though he has been dealing with so much stuff he is doing very well.

His mom is so weak now she uses a walker to get around. That bothers Tommy to see his Mom sick, too. Tommy's dad is always sad.

Kodi came to school to see me today. I wanted to see him while he was there but I did not talk to him long. I knew it was too dangerous for me. I knew that if I was with him too long I would quickly remember all the good times we shared, and I cannot do that now. I need to hang onto what I have with Tommy.

I felt as if no time has passed between him and absence has really made my heart grow fonder. My heart felt warm when he touched me. My lips wanted more when he kissed me. My body wanted to go in the car with him so we could escape to our own secret world and no one could find us. Everything in my body and soul wanted to go with him and be as connected to him as we always were. I wanted to say yes to every question that he asked me. I was willing to be whatever he wanted. I knew he could make me feel good.

I told him I could not stay long with him because I had to write an important test in the next class, but I lied. I went to class and wrote him a letter that said I did not want to see him anymore. I lied in the letter because I knew it was for the best. I knew I could not allow myself to be overcome with him because I needed to focus on Tommy. I knew if I told him the truth he would claim to understand and want to support me through it but I think it would have been just trying to convince me not to leave him. I was sure Kodi did not understand the love Tommy and I had, and ruining that at this point because of a mistake I had wanted to make was not an option. I needed to keep a clear head with all that the near future held in store for me. Kodi could not hold any piece of my heart right now. The pieces that he already held I needed to hide away as deeply as I could. I could not get overtaken by lust. I would not accept any apple that he handed me.

I gave the letter to Bobbi to give to him in the parking lot while he waited. I did not have the heart to do it myself. I knew as soon as I saw him I would not give him the letter and end up making a decision I would regret later. I knew I would have had sex with him and he would have told me he loved me and how he wanted to start it all again. I did not want that to happen for either of us. I knew that we would have just had to let it go again, and I did not think either one of our hearts could handle that right now. I was more fragile now that I had even been I did not need his help in messing my heart up more.

I watched from the second story window of the school as Bobbi handed him the letter. He did not look shocked to see her instead of me, but he did look disappointed. My heart ripped open wide as I watched him get in the car and drive away. I was as sorry as I had ever been for hurting his feelings. I wished he had never fallen in love with me a long time ago because I can only imagine how it must much hurt. Eric tells me that all the time, I could not bear to hear it from Kodi, not now.

There are only ten days left of school. Tommy goes for the transplant in twenty days and Tristan is leaving sometime between those times, too. All the things that have been important in my life are coming to an end, and I all I can do is wonder what is going to happen next. I am afraid of everything and all I feel is numb to it all. It seems when you live one day at a time it sneaks up on you and is here before you know it.

I have talked to Eric once a week for the last while. He is planning on being here when Tommy goes for the treatments. I told him it was not a good idea because I will go to the city with Tommy. Eric says he will come with me if I want but this is something I need to do alone.

Tommy has made plans for me. I can go and stay with his cousins that live down the street from the hospital that he will be in. He says he wants me there with him.

I am not sure how I feel about going to live with strangers in the city by myself when Tommy is sick. We both know he is going to get very sick again before he gets better. I looked at the sky and remembered what Tristan said about thirty percent when it rains. In all honesty, I did not want Tommy to go, and I did not want to go either. It felt like we were walking straight into hell and the outcome did not appear like we would end up somewhere over the rainbow where the skies were blue.

I would go to the city for him, and I would not complain about it. He was the one who was going to endure the hardship. I was only going to be there to support him through it. I was only holding his hand while he walked through the shadows of the valley of death. Pray was all that we could do now, in hopes that he comes out the other side still standing.

I felt helpless. I was helpless. Tommy was helpless, too. Any kind of outcome now depended on others' knowledge of what was best for him. I am not sure the doctors even knew what was going to happen, but they had some kind of educated guess. I was not sure if I wanted to know what they thought or not.

Tommy was like a log drifting in a rapid creek, and I was the bridge. All I could do was stand still and watch him floating by. I cannot stop him. Everything is floating by quickly, and I am at a stand still. I am just the cover from the hot sun for a short while but the journey he has to take is on his own while I watch. I see God as the water holding him up so he does not sink and eventually carrying him away.

I do not know if Tommy believes in God. That is not something that we have ever talked about. He sees the reverend from the church down the road a few miles from his house. I see a Bible on his night stand, but I do not know for sure what his ideas on that are. I am not sure if he has clear ideas about what happens when you die. We do not talk about that either. I do not want to think the unthinkable, let alone say the words out loud. After all it is Tommy's life, and it will be Tommy's death. If he chooses to talk about it we will.

It Was Finally Here

Tommy and I were sitting on his bed getting ready for his father to drive us to the big city for the transplant. Tommy had to go a few weeks before the actual date because the doctors wanted to do so many tests and insert a few things into Tommy to make things easier for him. This is the second time we had been through this so we knew this part already.

We had done that same routine as any other time he went to the hospital when he knew he was going to have to stay. He made me take home all his stuff. We cleaned his room out, put everything in its place, and listened to his favourite songs on the ghetto blaster before we went. I would always stay overnight with him. We kissed a lot, and sometimes if he was feeling well we even made love.

"What do you think is going to happen?" he asked me while we sat on the bed and waited for his dad to get ready.

"I don't know. What do you think is going to happen?"

"I do not know either."

"Do you think you are going to come home again?"

"I am not sure."

I was trying to be strong. I was trying not to cry. I was trying not to show my weakness, but I could not help it.

Tommy took my face in his hands and looked deeply into my eyes as he brushed away my tears. He was trying not to cry, too.

"I want to thank you for all that you have done for me. I could have not made it this far without you. I promise that I will do whatever I can to be with you again."

"I know. I just want you to come home."

"I do not know if I am going to make it this time or not. I want to tell you that I am not scared to die. I am only scared of what is going to happen first."

261

"Well, I am scared of everything. I do not know what I am going to do if you die. I will die, too." The lump in my throat became bigger.

"I know you will. I wish I would have never put you through this."

"I would not have stayed away, Tommy; you know that."

"I know. I tried to keep you from this, but you would not listen. I am glad you didn't. No matter what happens I want you to always remember that I love you, and you were the one that kept me strong. You were the one that kept me alive this long. You were the one who stood beside me when everyone else disappeared. You were the one that was at the hospital with me and my mom all the time. For all of that I thank you."

"Tommy, I would do it all over again for you."

"I know you would."

"I love you. I do not want you to go. Promise me you will come back."

"I can't promise that, but I can promise if I die I will still be with you forever. I am not sure how or why, but I know I will be."

"I know."

I hugged him as hard as I could. I did not want to start this day. I did not want to go anywhere. I wanted to stay right here for forever in this moment in time. I wanted to die right here with him, right now, so that neither one of us had to endure any more pain, fear, or sadness. I prayed so long for all this to be over for us, and now the time has snuck up so quickly. I changed my mind. I did not want it to be over. I did not want it to be this close to the end of whatever was destined to happen. I wanted to take it all back. I wanted more time.

"You can let go. I am not going to die today." He smiled at me and again wiped away my tears.

The hospital seemed so big when we walked into the lobby. The floor was shinny and the marble on the elevators was gleaming as the florescent lights burnt above the door. Tommy knew exactly where to go and what he had to do. He led me by the hand, and I followed behind him holding on.

"I don't like it here," I whispered in his ear.

He turned around and looked at me as if I was crazy. "I do," he replied.

"Sorry," I was not thinking about how much he must hate it here, too.

The nurses took us to his room where he would be for the next while before the transplant. It looked exactly like the room he was in before. I imagined they all looked the same.

Tommy did not want to unpack his things while we were there. As soon as the nurse left he wanted to leave to go get me arranged at his cousins. He wanted to go out for supper before we left. He wanted to go anyplace but hang around in there. He said he would have lots of time to unpack his things later that night after we had left. He said he did not want to waste our time.

We arrived at his cousin's, and it was not far at all from the hospital. I thought I would be able to walk there in about fifteen or twenty minutes. It was directly down the street, so it would be easy for me not to get lost. I was sure I could figure that one out.

"This is my son; he is six. He and I will share his bed. You can sleep here in my bed. I know they are in the same room, but Corey lives here with us, too. He sleeps in the living room on the floor or on the couch. I know it is crowded, but we will be fine." Tommy's cousin showed me around.

"Yes, this is fine. Thank you," I lied. I did not want to stay here. I did not want to sleep in her bed. I did not want to be in the city. I did not want any of this.

"You can help yourself to anything you want while you are here. Make yourself at home."

"Thank you."

"This is from my mom." I handed her the envelope full of money. "She said this would help with the costs while I was here."

Tommy and I stood on the balcony and looked out over the city lights. It was the first time I had ever seen anything like it.

"This is beautiful." I tried to make something positive out of this.

"Yes, it is." He turned and kissed me under the stars and into the city. "I am glad you came." He knew I really did not want to be here at all.

"Me too," I lied.

We stood outside as long as we could. His dad was ready to give us a ride back to the hospital so he could make the trip back home. I was the only one staying here with him this time. Tommy's mom was getting very sick, and she was using a walker now to support herself to even go as far as the bathroom. I am sure he wanted to get back to his wife because it seemed that she might not have much longer to live either.

I stayed at the hospital as long as I could. It seemed that the hospital did not go by any kind of visiting hours as long as you were quiet. I sat on the bed and pretended to read the newspaper while Tommy said goodbye to his father and unpacked his stuff.

As soon as Tommy was done he lay down on the bed beside me and patted the pillow.

"Lie down," he demanded.

"No, that is for sick people."

"Well, you are." He nudged my ribs. "You are here with me, aren't you?"

"Lie down," he demanded again, but this time he pulled on the back of my shirt.

I laid my head down on the pillow beside him and looked into his eyes. There was nothing left between us to say anymore.

I woke up when the nurse came in the room for shift change just like they did in the other hospital. They would always come in to greet the people and say good night or see if Tommy needed anything before bed.

"I see you don't need much," the lady in white smiled at Tommy.

"Not right now." He smiled back and rolled over to put his arm around me.

"I am sorry." I apologized for being on the bed and falling asleep. "I will go."

"It is getting late. It is after eleven," she said, as she looked at her watch, "but a few more minutes to say goodbye is fine." She turned around and left the room.

Tommy started kissing me like nothing was wrong, as if we were lying at home in his bed. I kissed him back for a while but even when I closed my eyes and tried to focus only on him I knew where we were. I could not hide the smell of hospital, the sounds, the lights, the stiff bed, and the footsteps behind the door. No matter how hard I tried I could not make it go away.

"I've got to go, Tommy. I will see you in the morning. I will be here as soon as I shower and can get here."

"Make sure you eat before you come."

"I will."

"Make sure you take a cab home. You do not want to be walking here at night. Did you see that hostel down the street by the park for the homeless?"

"Yes, I did."

"Make sure you take a cab."

"Okay."

I walked down the hallways of the barren, cold, silent institution. I wondered how many others were here for the same thing as we were. I wondered how many have walked this path before me. I wondered how it turned out for them. I wondered if anyone ever left here happy. Tonight I was not one of those people.

I stepped out of the elevator and into the marble lobby again. The lobby had been cleaned up and it looked very different now because it was there was no hustle and bustle of people coming and going. The magazines were all in place waiting for someone to look through them in the morning. There was a beautiful flower arrangement on one of the tables that was neatly placed beside a couch made for two. I knew in my heart that the flowers must have been taken to someone's room that was ill who could not have them so they were put in the lobby for everyone to see. I found that sad because that meant someone that someone loved must be very sick.

I waited for the cab outside by the curb. This was the first time I had ever been alone in a city this big. I felt nothing as I stood there and lit a smoke. I wondered what tomorrow would bring.

As I lay on the bed and stared at the ceiling in this strange room I could not sleep. I could not close my eyes. Even though I wanted this day to end I was afraid of my dreams. I was afraid of tomorrow because it was one day closer to hell.

I must have fallen asleep because I woke up to the sound of the almost strangers getting ready for work in the kitchen. I knew if I was quiet long enough they would not hear me and not expect me to get up. I did not want to talk to them. I did not want them to ask me how Tommy was doing. I did not want anything from them but a place to lay my head until I could go back and be with Tommy. I waited for them to leave.

I arose, showered and got ready to leave again. I put on my shoes and remembered that Tommy had told me to eat. He was right, although I doubt he will eat much today either. If I hurried I could be there before the hospital served breakfast, and I could make sure he put something in his belly. I decided I would try to eat at least some toast because I said I would, for him.

I gagged down as much of the cooked bread and a small glass of milk as I could. It was hard because my stomach thought it would have been better on the floor in front of me than ingesting any kind of nutritional value. At least I tried.

It was a nice sunny day outside, and I thought it would be a good morning to walk back to the hospital. The exercise would do me good because I would most likely spend the day sitting and waiting for something to happen. I wondered if Tommy would want to go out for a walk today. I think he had some kind of plans that his aunt and uncle were coming to see him and maybe take him out for a while, but I was not sure. Whatever happened I am sure he will make the best of it.

The store on the corner was selling fresh fruit. I thought I would pick some up for Tommy. He liked fresh fruit and the hospital usually did not serve him what he liked the best. I went through all the oranges, apples, grapes, plums, bananas and cherries to find him the best ones. I waited in line with my basket to pay and realized this was the first time I had ever bought groceries, in a strange sort of way, for him. I hoped he would like my gift.

"Would you like that in a double bag?" he store clerk asked.

"Pardon?" I was not listening.

"A double bag. Do you have far to carry it?"

"Oh yes, that would be nice, thank you." Actually I was not sure how far I would have to carry it. The distance did not seem far in a car.

The sun was hotter than I had expected as I was making my way down the street. It seems much warmer here in the big city with all the cement and tall buildings. Where was the grass? Where were the trees? Where was the shade? The smell of the pavement burned my nose. The rush of the traffic and the car exhaust hurt my eyes. I felt like I was almost running to keep up with the other people walking on the street. I sure was glad the guy had double bagged my stuff because the walk was a bit farther than I had anticipated. I was not enjoying this much, and I wished I was already there.

"Good morning." I smiled as Tommy was coming out of the bathroom. He had not known I was there yet.

"Good morning."

"Are you just getting up?"

"Yeah." It was sort of like I never really left then.

"How did you sleep?" I inquired.

"Fine, and you?"

"Fine." I wondered if we lied to each other to make the other person feel better or ourselves.

"What is in the bag?"

"Look," I opened the bag to show him what I had brought.

"Oh, good." He opened the oranges and laid the rest on the bed. "Did you see this crap they want me to eat?" He pointed to the oats and dry toast on the tray.

"Yuk," I agreed.

"You even got plums and cherries? Thanks."

He sat on the bed quietly and peeled the orange.

I read the pamphlet the nurse must have left in his room last night explaining the procedures he should expect. It was the same one he had been given before from the other hospital, so I already knew what was in it but I read it anyway.

"Here." He handed me half of the orange.

"What does it say in there?" he asked.

"You know, it is the same one as before. I got a newspaper too," I handed it to him.

He opened the paper and read the comics first. He read the funny ones out loud to me while we ate the oranges.

"Have some toast. I put butter on it for you." I gave it to him. "Eat it."

"You eat the other one," he handed one slice back to me.

The nurse entered the room and looked around at what we were doing.

"Where did he get that fruit?" she demanded to know. "He is not supposed to have that in here; he should not eat that. It could make him very sick." She sounded very upset.

Tommy and I sat together and looked at her like we did not know what she was talking about.

"Did you bring that here?" she asked me.

"Yes," I admitted.

"He cannot have that." She began to gather up what was left on the bed.

I opened up the papers I was hanging onto and read it aloud to her.

"It is suggested the patient receiving the bone marrow transplant eat fresh fruit and vegetables as much as possible before the radiation and chemotherapy is received. This will allow for one's body to enter the process in a healthy manner. After the treatments have started, the patient will not be allowed any other foods except what is provided by the hospital dietarian." I looked up at her for a moment. "Shall I continue?"

"No, I will be right back. Do not eat any more until I come back."

"Okay but if you would like to know, his treatments have not started yet," I informed her as she was already walking away.

Tommy sat on the bed and continued to eat what was left of his orange and read the paper.

"Banana?" he opened one and gave me half.

Another nurse appeared within a few minutes pushing the cart full of needles, bandages, thermometers, and various paraphernalia that we were already very familiar with. Tommy ignored her until she was finished looking at his chart and getting her stuff ready.

"This looks like a better breakfast than what I had this morning." She made cheap conversation while Tommy held out his arm while she cleaned it with an alcohol swab.

"It looks good."

"Want an orange?" Tommy offered, "they are awesome."

"No thanks."

"There is more than we will eat in the next few days; you might as well try one, and they will just have to go in the garbage anyway."

She finished up her work and began writing his name on the vial of blood she had just taken, "Sure," she said, as she popped another vial onto the end of the needle that was already sticking out of his arm.

"Do you know what is going to happen in the next few days?" she asked him.

"Not really."

"Today they want to run these blood tests to make sure everything is okay. Tomorrow they will do some more tests. You are scheduled for an MRI, then they will put in a Hickman line. Your radiation and chemo will start after the weekend."

"Oh, I thought I already had that?"

"You think so? Let me see."

Tommy lifted up his shirt and showed it to her.

"So you do. Then I guess we did not need this." She pointed to the needle that was still drawing blood out of his arm.

"Do you know what all this is?"

"Not the Hickman line."

"It is like an IV, but it goes directly into your heart. It does not hurt at all. It is so that any meds that we give you pump right into your blood quickly, and so you do not have to keep getting IV lines. Your veins are getting weak."

"I know," he agreed, as he held the cotton swab on his arm. He held his arm out straight so she could put a bandage on it before she even asked him.

"You know that you can go out and do whatever you want until the treatments start. Then you will have to go into an isolation room and will not be able to leave."

"Okay," he said.

"There is a real good burger joint just up the street and a park nearby you two might enjoy," she said as she was still writing something down on his chart.

"We will have to try that."

"You are lucky to have good company with you." She paused to write something down. "A lot of people come alone for this part." She looked up at me and smiled. "I heard about last night."

My face turned red, I knew she meant when we had gotten caught sleeping on the bed together.

Tommy smiled at her. "I know I am."

We had to wait until the doctor came to see Tommy before we could make arrangements to do anything outside of the hospital. He doctor reinforced all that the nurse had already told Tommy about what was going to happen in the next few days. He said that the blood tests had already come back and everything looked good to start the process. He also informed Tommy that he would be in each day to see him if he had any questions he could either ask the nurse or wait until he came in.

Tommy had made plans with his uncle to go downtown in the city. We had never been downtown before. His uncle suggested that we wait until it got dark because it was much different when it was all lit up. Tommy's uncle was a limousine driver so he said he would stop around and pick us up in one of the fancy cars from work. We thought that was a fun idea.

"Let's go to the hamburger joint," Tommy suggested. "I want to get out of here."

We walked a few blocks down the street and found the place the nurse was talking about. Tommy ordered two burgers, one French fry with gravy, and two pops.

"Let's play." He pointed to the race car game in the corner.

We went over and sat down on the seat. "You steer, and I will run the gas and the brake," he suggested. I was not sure that was such a good idea.

"I will shift, too." He pulled on the gear shifter that was located on his side of the car.

He dropped the coins in the slot and the car began to move slowly forward. Tommy held his foot all the way to the floor because he wanted the acceleration to go as fast as the game could.

"Slow down, slow down!" I was yelling at him. I was trying to steer the car around the other vehicles on the road. "Slow down!"

"You crashed our car!" He laughed at me.

"Let's play again." I dug more money out of my pocket. "Switch me sides."

He drove the car this time, and I pushed on the gas and the break at the same time. "Let's see if we can make this thing do a brake stand and smoke the tires." We were both laughing at the game while we sat together in the seat that was really only made for one person.

"Your burgers are ready." The guy behind the counter yelled loudly over the noise we were making playing the game.

We sat in the restaurant and ate the food that Tommy had gotten. We were stuffed and could not eat mine at all.

"Next time let's just get one," I suggested, assuming there would be another time.

Tommy and I fooled around outside in the streets for a while and went for a walk to the park. We sat in the sun on the bench and played silly games as we watched the people walk by.

"Watch this." He threw a quarter on the sidewalk. "How long do you think it will stay there before someone picks it up?"

"Three," I guessed.

"What?"

"I guess three people will walk by before someone notices it. What is your guess?"

"Ten."

We watched the quarter on the ground and counted the people walking by.

"Seven," he said, just before someone bent down to pick it up.

"I wonder if we put more money there if someone will notice it sooner?"

"That can be the game for tomorrow. We should be getting back soon."

Tommy's uncle came and picked us up right on time. Tommy and I rode in the back of the limo as if we were real important people. We were important just in a different way than most people that ride in the back. It was exciting to be in the city with Tommy looking at all the lights and sounds we had never seen before.

After the ride uptown we went to Tommy's uncle's house across town where his aunt had supper waiting for us. Tommy's cousins were there too, even the one I was staying with, and we all had a nice meal.

After the meal the beer broke out, and Tommy began to drink a few. No one said anything to him about it fact it may not be the best idea. We all felt the same way, at this point he could do whatever he wanted to.

"Give me a smoke," he said.

"I am not sure about that, Tommy; you have not smoked a cigarette in a long time. Are you sure you should?"

"What do you think I am going to do? Die of cancer if I do?" He was sometime sarcastic like that after he had been drinking. Sometimes it seemed as if he was almost angry.

"Here, you can die of cancer if you want, but that line is getting a bit old." I handed him my smokes and opened another beer for us to share. I knew we would be there for a while yet to come, and I wanted Tommy to have as good a time as he could. It seemed to me at this point in his life he should be able to do whatever he wanted. Who was I to tell him what to do now?

When we arrived at the hospital the doors were locked, and we had to ring a buzzer to get in.

"Name," the security guard asked.

Tommy told him our names.

"Where have you been?" the guard asked Tommy.

"What?"

"Where have you been? The hospital has been looking for you. They said I was to call the nurses' station as soon as you arrived. If you had not have come back soon they were going to send the cops out looking for you."

"What did they think? I was going to die or something?"

"Tommy, let's just go," I begged.

"Visiting hours are over. I cannot let her in."

"Then I am not coming in either. You might as well just call the cops now." Tommy was getting even more rude toward the guard.

Tommy pulled my sleeve and started to walk over toward the curb. "Give me a smoke."

He lit the smoke and leaned against the wall.

"What are you doing?" I asked.

"Waiting for the cops to come."

I lit a smoke for myself and leaned against the wall beside him. "Okay."

We stood there a few moments until I noticed the security guard trying to get our attention by waving his arms at us.

I nodded my head to acknowledge his attempts and nudged Tommy with my elbow.

"She can walk up, too." He notified us of the change of heart.

Tommy stood by the wall and finished the smoke and flicked the butt away from the wall.

"Thanks," I said to the guy, as I looked him in the eye.

"It is just that we have never had anyone stay out this late before; it is after midnight."

"Sorry." I tried to smile. I really just wanted to get Tommy into his room before he managed to get us in any kind of real trouble. Tommy ignored anything the guard was saying and went inside.

It was getting very late, but I decided that I was going to walk home tonight anyway even though I had told Tommy I would get a cab. I had nothing to hurry home for. I did not feel like I had a home. I had a place to stay while I was here. It was someone else's home, not mine.

271

I could hear someone walking behind me. It sounded like he was saying something in my direction but I was trying not to pay any attention to it. Almost every time I walked on the streets here someone would make some kind of reference to me. Sometimes it would be bums asking for money or a smoke because I had to walk by the hostel where they live and the park where they waited but tonight it was much to late for the bums to be out. I think most of the time people would proposition me for sex because they thought I was a prostitute. I understand now why Tommy said I should always take a cab.

"Hey, baby, where ya going?"

I kept walking.

"Want to come up to my place for a drink?"

I was trying to walk faster, but he was catching up to me.

"Can you flag me a cab? They won't stop for me. They do not like me tonight."

"Can I walk with you?" he continued to try to get my attention. "What is a pretty young girl like you doing out this time of night? Do you know who you could meet out here on the streets in the dark?"

He was walking beside me now. I slowed my pace a bit because I was getting tired from almost running, and my head was a bit dizzy from the heat and the party. I still said nothing to him.

"Where are you going?"

I said nothing.

"You do not need to be afraid of me, sweet pea. I only asked where you are going."

"Home."

"You do not live around here. I can see that. I doubt you are going home."

"No, I don't. I am only here for a while, and then I will be gone."

"Where are you going, then?"

"Home," the words echoed in my ears. I wish I really was going home, my home.

"What is your name?"

I ignored the question.

"Where are you going?" I asked.

"Home. Come with me. Come up for a drink." He stopped, then motioned inside a building that was about halfway to where I was headed, which he was now standing in front of while he held open the door.

"No, thanks."

"Maybe I can walk you home again sometime?" His laugh was sly, and his smile intimidated me.

"Maybe." I did not want to look at him. I did not want to see who he was or give him any kind of inclination that I was the least bit interested. I wasn't. I just wanted to get to where I could sleep. I wanted to go back and be with Tommy. I wanted to go to my real home. I hated this city.

I kept walking as he was still saying something in my direction.

I stayed at the hospital every night as late as I could every night before I walked the streets of the city back to the place where I laid my head down at night. I would get up as early as I could, shower, try to eat a bit, and then walk back to the hospital. We would wait until the doctor ordered whatever tests he needed for that day, then Tommy and I would spend the rest of the day doing whatever we wanted.

"Today you are going to have an MRI," the nurse announced.

"Okay," Tommy agreed.

"We want to see what kind of brain functioning you have left after all the chemotherapy you have already taken to see if your brain can withstand all the treatments you are about to receive here within the next few days."

"Oh." Tommy seemed to be pretending that what she was saying was not bothering him that much, but I could tell it was.

"She can come with you during your test if that helps."

"Will you?" Tommy asked me.

I nodded.

We waited until a man pushing a wheel chair came to his room to get us.

"I can walk." Tommy told the man.

"Yes, I know, but this is a hospital requirement that I push you in a chair."

"I can walk."

Tommy and I followed the man to the elevator and waited until it came to get us. The ride upstairs was quiet as we waited. I hated the feeling in my stomach when the elevator stopped at the desired floor. Tommy squeezed my hand a bit for comfort just before it stopped.

We followed the man to another waiting room. The nurses took Tommy in as soon as we got there. He seemed glad that for once we did not have to wait. She led us to anther room where she told Tommy to get into a gown and take a seat in the chair until they came for him.

We sat and waited.

"What do you want to do later today?" he asked me.

"I don't know. What do you want to do?"

"I was thinking that we might go up on top of the tower."

"Today?"

"What better day than today?"

"Let's see how long this takes and see how you feel."

"I will feel fine."

"Maybe we could go on the weekend instead."

"It will be too busy then," he paused, "and I think Jeff is coming to see me Saturday."

"Is everyone else?" I meant his family.

"I don't know."

"Okay, then we can go today if you want."

We sat again in silence and waited until someone came for him.

"Follow me," another nurse directed him.

I remained sitting. I thought I would just wait here until he came back to get dressed.

Tommy stood up but did not follow her. "You come, too." He pulled my hand. He was still hanging onto it from when we were waiting.

I followed him, but I was sure they would not let me go much farther with him.

"Have you ever had an MRI?"

"No."

"You will lie here on this." She pointed to a metal slab with a sheet covering it.

"This moves your body into that machine where it takes sort of like an x-ray. We are going to do your entire body today, but it will not take very long."

"Oh." Tommy hung onto my hand as he stood and looked at the machine he was about to go into. It appeared to me that he was about to go in a tiny time machine. The hole where his body was to fit was not that big, and I wondered how they would ever get a fat person through there.

I leaned over to Tommy and whispered in his ear, "I bet you're going to get stuck in there." Then I poked my elbow in his ribs to let him know I was kidding.

"You're coming with me. Maybe it will be fun." He tried to smile.

"She can sit right here and wait for you," the nurse pointed to a chair. She turned toward me and said, "If you talk to him he will be able to hear you."

"Lie down here." She pointed again. "Are you okay?"

"Yes."

"You will want to get as comfortable as you can, because this will take a while, and you will not be able to move any part of your body once we start. Do you understand?"

"Yes," he answered.

"She can talk to you, but you cannot talk back to her. You need to be still."

"Okay."

Tommy was lying down now, and the metal slab started to move. I could see that he had his eyes closed and was trying to be still. I wondered if he was scared. I wondered if he was worried about what they would find. I wondered what he was thinking about. I wondered what else they wanted to do to him today. I wondered how he could be so strong.

I watched him slowly disappear into the tunnel. I wished it was a time machine and would take us someplace else. I wished it could take him someplace else better than here even if I could not go with him. I wished things would be better for him. I wished it would all go away.

I waited.

"Are you still there?" I heard Tommy say after I could barely see his feet.

"Yes."

"Say something to me."

"Tommy, you have got to be still." the nurse said, over some kind of speaker.

"Okay," he agreed.

"Are you stuck in there?" I asked.

"I think so," he said.

"Tommy, you cannot talk," the nurse reminded him again.

"Okay," he agreed.

I waited.

"Talk to me." Tommy said again.

"I am thinking about going to the tower. I am wondering if we could walk that far, or if we should take a cab. You know you can see it from your cousin's where I am staying. It does not look that far. I am scared to go up that high. What if something happens to it today, and it falls over or something and we are in it?"

"So what if we die today?" But I do not think that was really a question. It seems like he was making a statement that he did not have anything to lose if we did.

"You need to be still or she will have to go," the nurse warned Tommy again.

I was silent again.

"Where are you staying?" she asked me over the speaker.

I told her the address.

"You can walk from there. It takes about forty minutes from here." She continued on and gave us directions on the shortest way to go and what we might see there.

It seemed like almost as soon as she was done talking I could see Tommy's head coming out the other side of the time machine.

"See, that was not so bad," she said.

"For you," Tommy commented to her.

"Now all you have to do is get dressed and wait until the doctor comes. He will read this right away and tell you what it says, and then you can go."

"How long will that take?"

"I will tell him you have plans today so he will hurry." She smiled at Tommy. "I wish I could come with you."

Tommy got dressed, and they took us to a room where we waited for the doctor.

"Sit here with me." Tommy moved over in the big comfy chair he was sitting in, and I climbed in it with him.

He put his arm around my shoulder as we leaned the chair back, and I put my head on his chest.

"This is like the chairs they give you chemo in," he explained. "You just sit in the chair with the IV in your arm and wait."

"Oh."

"At least the chair is comfy. It is much better with you here."

I put my arm over his waist. I closed my eyes and listened to his heart beat. We had been like this a thousand times before.

I woke up and saw the doctor just about to sit in the chair beside us while he was reading Tommy's results.

I shook Tommy a little to wake him up, too.

"Tommy, Tommy, the doctor is here."

We attempted to bring the chair to a sitting position and become a bit more presentable to have any kind of professional conversation.

"Stay," the man in the white coat commanded. "I do not think I have ever seen two people so comfortable together in here before. I like it."

Tommy pulled me closer toward him.

"It looks like you two are very much in love."

We both sat and looked at him without saying a word. I do not think either one of us knew what to say, other than something sarcastic that would not make him like us any more.

He looked at Tommy's chart again without saying anything.

I kissed Tommy on the cheek, "Are you okay?" I asked softly.

He nodded.

The doctor began with the usual, "Well, we have gotten the results of all of the tests that we have been doing the last few days." He was still looking at the papers when another doctor came in the room. There was some kind of introduction to her name, but once you see so many people that are supposed to be helping they all look the same. She looked at the papers now, too.

"It seems we have found some very interesting things here about you."

We sat in silence waiting for him to talk.

"It looks like you only have one kidney. Did you know that?"

"No," Tommy said.

"But that is not what concerns me," the doctor continued, "it looks from this MRI that you have already suffered quite a bit of brain damage, and I am not sure how much more you can take. The radiation and chemo you will get here will be as much or more than you have ever had before, it will do more brain damage to you, and I am not sure how that will affect you later on. You see, your brain is shaped like this…" he made some kind of motion with his hands. "It has these hair-like things between your brain and your brain fluid, and each time you have treatments the hair-like things die, and then they cannot protect your brain from injury."

"Oh."

"Hold out your hands."

Tommy did.

"That shaking in your hands you already have is from the chemo damaging your brain. With more treatments that, and some other things you already know about will get worse."

"Oh."

"And are unlikely to ever go away."

Tommy said nothing. The doctor was looking at some more papers.

"Tommy," I whispered, "they told you that in the other hospital, too, and look how much better you are than when you first come home from there. You know that they always tell you the worst, and sometimes they are not right."

Tommy squeezed my hand and smiled.

"He does not know everything; he is only a doctor," I squeezed his hand back.

The female doctor smiled but said nothing.

"Can I ask you some questions?" the man asked again.

"Sure."

He began asking Tommy simple questions at first. "What day of the week is it? Where are you? Count backwards from one hundred. Say your phone number backwards. Spell your last name backwards. Spell her last name backwards."

Tommy answered all this questions without error.

"Good," the doctor looked a bit confused.

"See, I told you," I whispered to Tommy again.

Tommy smiled at him without saying a word.

"There is about a thirty percent chance you will pull through this. You know that?"

Tommy nodded without saying a word.

"But we will go through with it if you want. I cannot tell what will happen if we don't do it at all."

We sat there for what seemed like forever in silence again.

"I hear you have plans for today?" the doctor attempted to make light conversation, after telling Tommy he really did not have much of a chance for anything.

"Yeah. " Tommy tried to smile. "I am going to scare the heck out of her in the tower later. I think we are going to walk there."

"It seems like a very nice day for it. I wish I could come, too."

I did not say anything, but I was glad he could not. I wondered how many times a day this man had to deliver news like this to someone. It was hard not to hate the messenger that delivered the news even if we knew it was inevitable.

"I will go over this again with some other doctors, and I will talk more with you about it in a few days. I will see if we need any further testing before we start the process, and if not, we can start your treatments after the weekend."

"Sure," Tommy agreed, but he was not at all happy about it. I was not either. What was there to be happy about? What was there to look forward to?

Both of the doctors left the room. Tommy and I continued to sit in the chair in silence for a few more minutes until we sat up.

"Burgers for lunch?" Tommy asked.

"This time let me run the gas and you drive." I meant the video game, but he already knew that.

"No way; you go too fast."

"You go faster when I try to drive; that is not fair."

I followed behind him as he led me by the hand out of the room. I turned around and looked at the chair where we had been sitting. No wonder they make it such a comfortable chair to sit in. It is the least they can do when they are telling someone there is not much more of a chance to fight the disease that has been slowly killing their body for the last two-and-a-half years. At least your ass did not hurt from waiting so long while they told you they were going to start to do more damage to your brain, your body, and maybe you had a small chance to live through it if you were lucky.

We walked and talked after lunch toward the tower just as we would have any other day. The sun was hot and the pavement was hotter. The heat here in the city was unbearable compare to our small county towns we had come from. I wondered if Tommy hated it here as much as I did, most likely he hated it more. I imaged that as much as he needed me here with him, he hated asking me to come.

"Tommy, you know my parents said that if I stayed here for very long that I would have to get a job to make my own money."

"I know. I can give you money to stay."

"No, I will not take your money."

"I got offered a job at an ice cream place at the mall."

"You do not want to work there; that would suck."

"Yes, it would. But I cannot stay here without money."

"You should stay as long as you can, then go home and get a harvest job."

"I want to stay here with you. I do not want a harvest job."

"Harvest is about a month a way yet. You can stay until then; I will give you money."

"I do not want your money. I do not know what to do."

"Stay here until then; if you need to go home for a while I will understand."

"I can get my sister to work for me a few days a week; then I can still come and see you every weekend."

"Yes."

"Will you be okay here?"

"Mom will come up if I need her to. I know you will have to go, but that is not for a while yet."

"Look," I pointed, "we are almost there."

We went to the top of the tower via a glass elevator. Tommy made me stand on the glass side with him and watch the ground disappear under our feet. I hated every moment of it. I closed my eyes tight as I held his hand for comfort. This was worse than our airplane ride.

Once we got to the top I looked over the side for a moment but went back and stood beside the wall. Tommy said it was no fun looking over the edge by him self and wanted me to be there with him. Once again he held my hand because I was fearful of looking at the ground so far away. He said he would keep me safe from falling. I knew he would.

We thought we were walking in the same direction as which we had come from until we noticed nothing looked the same. It was at that moment we decided to get a taxi back to someplace where we knew. I thought we should go right to the hospital because it was already after supper hour but Tommy wanted to stay out and enjoy the sun since we had already eaten supper. We took a cab close to the hospital, and then we walked to the park.

"Let's sit," he said, as he sat on the bench.

I sat beside him and put my head on his shoulder. "I am tired. It has been a long day."

"Yes," he agreed, "it has."

We sat for a while in the sun not saying a word. I was not up to playing any kind of money games with the bums and neither was Tommy. We watched the people walk by with their children in silence. I wondered if I would ever have children with Tommy.

It seemed like all the words were gone, and I had nothing left to say. It had been a really long day and part of me wanted it to end so I could take a hot shower and crawl into bed, the other part of me never wanted any day to end because I did not know how many I would have left with Tommy.

"I wonder what would happen if I did not go for the transplant," Tommy finally spoke.

I wished he had not broken the silence with the words that he had chosen.

"I don't know." I did not know what else to say anymore to him.

We sat again in silence.

"I want to go home. I am telling the doctors in the morning that I am leaving."

"Do you think that is a good idea?"

He did not answer for the first few minutes.

"Yes."

"Okay." I paused, thought for a moment, then said, "Then tell them that you are leaving."

We sat again with no words.

"Tommy," I turned to look into his eyes, "you already know what will happen if you quit this thing now."

"I know."

"You have come way too far to quit."

"Didn't you hear him today? He said there was only a very little chance that I am going to make it through this chemo. I want to go home and let it just take its natural course and just die when I die with no more hospitals."

"Yes, I heard him, but you have no chance at all if you don't try. You will die."

He said nothing. We sat again and watched the people walk by for a while longer. The sadness began to hit my heart as I held his hand sitting on the park bench. I wanted to cry, but I did not want Tommy to think I was giving up on him. I knew he was right.

"Do you remember the first time I saw you in the hospital?" I asked him.

"Yes."

"What did they tell you then?"

"They said that I might only have a few months to live."

"Yes, they did. Look how long it has been now: almost two-and-a-half years. Tommy, you need to remember that all the doctors are doing is guessing at what they think might happen. They do not know. You have already received so many miracles during this time you have been sick. I know it may seem like sometimes God is not listening to us when we ask Him for help, but I think he is. I know He has listened to us so many times before, because you are still here with me right now sitting on this bench. Sometimes it seems like the only thing we can do now is believe things will be okay, because if we don't, we have nothing else left."

"I know. I don't want to die and leave you here. I love you, and I wonder what will happen to you when I am gone."

"You are not going to go anywhere. You need to believe that you are going to be here with me always. You cannot give up. I cannot give up."

"Something inside me feels like I am not going to make it this time."

"I love you, and I will never, ever let go of your love. I will never, ever give up believing in your strength and your love to stay here for me."

"I just want it all to be over. I don't want to be sick anymore. I am tired, and I am scared. I don't want to die."

"I am scared for you, too, Tommy. I have watched you endure more things than I ever thought a human could without giving up. You have always been strong for both of us when I sometimes could not."

"No, I was strong because you were there with me. You were strong when I could not be."

"I am sorry for all the things I have done wrong to you."

"You have done nothing wrong. Without you I would have been dead a long time ago. I know I have said this a thousand times before but I am going to say it again. Thank you for helping me."

"I told you a long time ago I wanted to be with you forever, and I meant it. I am not going to give up, and I don't think you should, either."

We sat as if we were waiting for something as we watched the sun go down behind the tall buildings. I wondered if I should agree with Tommy and tell him that we should go home and spend his last days happy. I did not want to watch him get sick again. I did not want to watch him die. I did not want him to be afraid anymore. I did not want him to be in any pain anymore. I wanted his spirit to be free. I wanted God to give him all that he deserved. I wished God would strike me dead in this moment so that he could live. I wanted him to know that all this time that I have loved him was because I wanted to. I did not know what was going to happen to me if he died either but that I was not going to think about.

Father in Heaven, I come to you again to ask for help for Tommy. I ask that You somehow give him the strength to make the right decision for himself. I ask that whatever happens You keep him safe and not let him die in pain or touchier of the medicine the man in the white coat gives him. I ask that You take Tommy in your hands and lift him up from all this pain and take his fear away. I ask that you help Tommy. In Jesus' Name, Amen.

"Let's go back before I get in trouble again."

I walked, holding on to his hand as if I never wanted to let go. Walking with him now felt like the last steps we would ever take together. I did not want to go back to the hospital. Tommy was right when he said we should just run away and never see another doctor or hospital again. I wanted to open my mouth and tell him I wanted him to leave his horrible place, but I knew if I told him that is what I wanted him to do, he would. The only thing I knew for sure was that I did not want to let go. I would not let go of him no matter what happened today or tomorrow. I would love him forever, which was the only thing I knew for sure.

"You don't have to walk me up to the room this time. It has been a long day, and I am sure you want to just get home."

I looked at him as if he was a stranger, "Home?" I asked, "I have no place to go without you, Tommy."

Right then it hit me hard for the first time. I had nothing if I did not have him. Tommy had been my entire life for the last few years, and if he really did die, what was it I was honestly going to do? I was finished with school so I did not even have that to hang on to. I did not have a job, and over the last few years I had isolated almost all of my friends because I had spent so much time with him. I had nothing but him.

"Come up then if you want to."

"I do not want to do anything else," I looked into his soul for a moment and continued to speak, "ever."

We waited for the elevator to come but this time we were in no hurry, we just stood and waited.

As soon as we got into his room he lay down on the bed, and I sat in the chair beside him as if we had done so many times before. The hospital was quiet, and you could not even hear the nurses walking around anymore. I watched him as he lay on the bed with his eyes closed just as I had watched him so many times before.

He opened his eyes and touched my hair as I had my head propped on my hands beside his waist on his bed.

"Lie beside me for a while?"

I climbed up on the stiff bed beside him and put my head on his shoulder. I tried not to cry.

The Gay Pride Parade

The weekend was finally here and Tommy was right about all his family and a few friends coming to see him at the hospital. He had a lot of visitors and it sure was different than when it was just him and me here.

His sister had to come to the hospital to stay because they had a few more tests they needed to run on her before they were sure she could be a candidate to donate her bone marrow. The doctors wanted to be sure she was entirely healthy before they could draw her bone marrow out of her body to give up to try to save her brother's life.

The transplant would not actually be for about one more week because of all the other stuff Tommy had to do first but she was going to stay now until she had to give up part of her body to her brother. What an exceptionally noble thing to do. It was obvious any one of his siblings would have helped try to save his life but out of all of them she was the closest match.

Tommy's dad had brought Tommy's mom to stay now, too. Tommy's mother had been at home this far because she was not feeling well now with her own health issues. She looked very ill and had difficulty walking, sitting up for too long and sometimes even breathing. Since the chemo was to start soon she was here. She had to forget her own physical pain to be here to support her son. I could not imagine her wanting to be anyplace else. We all wanted to be here for him.

Tommy and I were sitting in his room when the car load of his family arrived. They all seemed happy to see him but he did not show much reaction to anyone in particular. It seemed that he really did not care who came to visit now. I think he was scared of what was happening to him and he did not want to let it show, after all, it had been a long week for both of us. He seemed very distant now they were all here. I think he liked it better when we were alone. I think he could see by the look on their faces that they all thought he was not going to make it. It seemed like they all had come to say the last goodbye. Tommy did not like it like that; he would much rather have not said anything at all.

The nurse came in and told us that he had too many people in the room at once, so some of his guests would need to leave and take turns visiting. He did not care.

"I will go for a while, Tommy; I have been here with you for that last few weeks, and I know everyone else wants fair time with you. I will go for a walk outside. I can come back later when everyone else goes home. You know they will let me stay later than they will let everyone else."

"No, I will come with you then."

"Tommy, I know you don't want me to leave, but they will not let us all stay. Your family have come a long way to see you."

"Let's go to the café; we can all sit there."

We all went and sat in the tables and chairs in the café down the hall. It was a big room with a few vending machines, plastic chairs and chrome tables, the typical institution type. Tommy and I had been here a few times before because we were trying to see if we could get free stuff one night when it had been too late to get change anyplace, and he was hungry.

Tommy and I sat at a table with his Mom and Dad and the others were scattered out in different seating arrangements talking about their daily lives. The four of us sat in silence. We all knew what was going to happen in the upcoming week when the chemo started. We all hoped and prayed for the same thing in silence of our own hearts because we did not want to admit our fears out loud. Tommy and I already had while we were together but those things were not what you talked about in a group.

I was going home today with Tommy's dad, and I was going to return in a week. My parents told me that since I had not gotten a job yet I would have to come home and line up a job in harvest. My father said that Tommy may be in the hospital and sick for a very long time yet, and he did not think it was a good idea while I sat in the hospital every day with him and waited for something to happen while I was in the city all alone. I tried to assure him I was fine in the city and did not want to come home, but he insisted I did.

One car load of family after another arrived and soon everyone was there. Shelly, Sandy and Jeff had finally arrived and Tommy was happy to see them. He talked and tried to smile a lot to assure everyone he was fine with what was about to happen to him but I knew differently. I knew the man behind the mask. I knew he thought it was all coming to an end.

"Let's go out for dinner." Jeff finally had a good idea. Sitting here with nothing to do was wearing heavy on all of our hearts.

The family all decided they were going to go help Tommy's sister get settled and find the residence where Tommy's mom would be staying during the time she was going to be here. The plan was to all meet up again in a few hours so they could say goodbye again until next time, and I would catch a ride home.

Shelly, Sandy, her boyfriend, Jeff, Tommy, and I thought it would be easiest if we walked to a nice restaurant around the corner from the hospital so that we could all go together because we could not all fit in one car. We also figured this way we would not have to find a place to part in the city, which was a feat in and of itself, us county folk was not that fond of city driving and parking to say the least.

As we walked we noticed some kind of festival going on in a nearby park and thought it would be a good idea if we checked it out for excitement. I am not sure which one of us had the bright idea first to attend, but it did seem like a good one at the time.

"Let's just follow those guys and see what is going on."

Tommy and I walked hand in hand ahead of everyone else when we arrived at the gates of the park. Tommy and I thought it was odd that a gathering such as this would have no admission price, so we followed the men ahead of us.

It was not long until we knew exactly what we were attending when the two men that we had been following stopped and began to kiss each other as Tommy and I might have done when we were alone and about to make love. The kiss that the men were sharing was also accompanied with an intentional handful of butt and a rub on the crotch.

Tommy and I stopped in our tracks and turned toward our friends that had accompanied us. "What the hell is this, a Gay Pride parade?" Tommy asked.

"Ah, yes, actually, I think it is," someone replied.

"I have seen enough; let's go."

We immediately left the park laughing at ourselves of the mistake we had made. After all we were from a small country town and had only seen such things by mistake on a twisted pornographic movie or the news. It was not something anyone one of us would have attended in fun had we had known what the men were celebrating. The small time country bumpkins we were did not acknowledge such festivities even if it was a human right of sexual choice.

Our group made the way to a nearby restaurant where we sat and drank beer and watched more people walking down the street to attend the festivities. It seemed once we really knew what was going on we were all sickened by the public display of a different sexual orientation than our own. We made jokes at everyone we saw with blue hair and tight leathers that came close enough to hear our comments. It may have seemed unfair to them to be the brunt of our jokes but at least Tommy was laughing and the people we thought of as freaks. It was a good distraction to the insecurities we felt in our hearts of the very near future. At least if we were making fun of them Tommy did not seem like he was that different than the rest of us. He did not seem to be feeling like he was the bald headed freak that he had called himself many times before. As much as I tried to assure him he was not any more of a freak without hair than he was with it, he said he still felt like one when everyone stared at him when he went out. Now we were staring at others probably making them feel in much the same way that Tommy had. If it made him feel better for a while I was going to be selfish for him and join in.

We finished our meals and began walking back toward the hospital. Tommy and I followed our friends this time. Once again we were in no hurry to be anyplace but together.

"I got these for you." Tommy handed me some flowers.

"Thank you." I kissed him in gratitude for the gift.

"Where did you get those?" Shelly asked. "I did not see you stop anyplace."

I smiled at her, "He stole them from the flower guy on the corner as we walked by."

Once again our group was in tears from laughter at the silly thing that Tommy had just done. I knew that Tommy thought he had nothing to lose, so taking a few flowers was really no big deal to him. We passed that flower guy every day on our walks, and he knew exactly who we were, but today said nothing as Tommy passed me the kindness.

When we walked through the lobby to go back to the café to meet everyone else, I added my gift to a vase that already had an appreciation gift in it because I knew I could not take them upstairs.

"They won't do me much good during the car ride home so everyone else might as well enjoy them down here." I smiled at Tommy in gratitude.

Turning Eighteen

I carried my bags into the house and set them on the floor of my bedroom. It was good to be home. I sat on the edge of my bed and looked around my room but everything seemed so strange to me. All my personal things were here, I knew I belonged here, I knew this is where I had come from a few short weeks ago but my heart was still in the city with Tommy.

I lay back on my bed and stared at the ceiling. I did not want to close my eyes to sleep because I was afraid that when I woke up it would be all over. I wanted to go back to the city to be with Tommy. I told him I was coming back in one week, and I hoped he could hold on that long without me there. I told him I would call him every day, but I wondered if that would be enough. I wondered if he had changed his mind about staying and had come home with the next car load of people behind me. I wished I could call him at the hospital to make sure he was still there but it was too late at night. If he was asleep I would not want to wake him up but I doubted he would be.

It seems I must have fallen asleep, because I woke up sweating buckets in the same clothes I had dressed in yesterday. The phone was ringing, and I could tell it was morning already by the amount of sunlight that was reflecting through the window on my mirror.

"Hello?" I wondered what time it was before I even wondered who was on the phone. I really did not care who was on the phone anyway and wondered why I had even picked it up.

"How was your trip?" It was Tommy.

"Okay, where are you?"

"In my room."

"What room?"

"At home."

"What?" my body darted up in panic.

"No, I am still here. I just wanted to know if you got home safe last night."

"Yes, I am okay. How are you?"

"I miss you already."

"I miss you, too. It is Monday, and I will be back on Saturday. Today has already started, so that means I will be back in six days. I will see you Saturday, so really it will only be five days."

"It will be a long five days."

"Yes, I know."

"What are you doing tomorrow for your eighteenth birthday?"

"I don't know, probably nothing."

"You are eighteen. You should do something special with your friends."

"You are there."

"Call Kayla or Lizzie or Bobbi or something to go out."

"Maybe. I am going to get a newspaper and look for a job first. No one knows I am home yet, so maybe I will call someone later. I really don't feel like it, though."

"I don't think you should be home alone on your birthday."

"We'll see."

Tommy and I went on and talked on the phone as if nothing was wrong. I knew in a few short hours they would be putting the poison in his blood that may kill him but I did not want to talk about that. What else could we say? I wished I was there.

I hung up the phone after I told him I loved him and laid my head back down on the bed. What was I going to do today?

After I had showered I walked to the local store for a newspaper. It sure was different here at home from how it was in the city. I wondered if the population of this entire village was that of even one block of where I was yesterday. I doubted it.

I was invited for an interview for a job from the first number I called. I was hopeful to meet my potential employer and get this ordeal out of the way so I could for surely return to the city as soon as possible while the plants continued to grow and become ready for harvest. It was still about a month before I was to actually start work so I knew I would go back to be with Tommy for another three weeks.

The farmer did accept me to work for him after a short meeting, as I told him about my previous experiences. I knew I was only about to turn eighteen, but I had four years of experience already. I had been working at this seasonal job since I was thirteen, alongside of my mother for the first two years.

I remembered the farm I had worked at last year and wondered what had happened to Matthew. I wondered if I would see him again this year somewhere along the line. I thought that would be nice to see him again but I doubted that I would. I remembered that last time that I had seem him sitting at a kitchen table doing one hot knife of hash after another with Lizzie's brother. I wanted to join in but knew that it was not in my best interests. I knew that engaging in some kind of fun like that with Matthew would be the apple of temptation. I did not think his heart would be able to endure once it had been dropped from the top of the tree. I knew he was much too sensitive to play the one night stand game with even if we had both wanted it for a while. I could hear my father's voice in my head. "You cannot play games with those boys," or something like that, and after all, Matthew would already know what he would be getting himself into. I remember thinking more clearly when I thought I would give Matthew back to God instead of kidnapping his heart for my own pleasure for one night. After all, I knew how just one night was enough to change a person eternally.

I wondered if Eric would come around again since I had not talked to him in a while. It had seemed like a long time since I had heard his voice over the phone. I thought about calling him while I was home. I wondered what I might say. Things seemed so much different for me now and nothing seemed worth talking about.

The phone rang shortly after I had gotten home from the job interview.

"Hello."

"I saw your car was moved and hoped you were home." It was Kayla. "When did you get in?"

"Yesterday."

The conversation went on for a while, and I had really missed her. In fact I had missed all of my friends while I was gone. I wished they could come with me to the city to see what it was like there. Kayla had said we could do whatever I wanted for my birthday so we made plans to go to the beach. I was not sure what I wanted, but I did know that I was not up for any kind of big celebration.

I knew that turning eighteen was a big deal for some people. I thought at this age I was supposed to feel like I was turning into a responsible adult, yet I feel like I have already been that for a long time now. I knew there were some things I needed to become a little more responsible about, but for the most part I thought I had enough responsibility on my shoulders, at least for now.

I contacted a few more of my friends while I was sitting at home with nothing more to do. It sure was nice to talk to everyone, and I realized how homesick I really was in the city. I did not want to go back there. Tommy had enough family around him now that he did not need me. He would not miss me. I think it would be fine if I did not go back in a few days and stayed home. I needed the support of my friends and family, after all he had the support of his.

I called Eric, too. I asked him if he was planning on coming down this way soon. He said that he doubted he was going to come for harvest this year and that he had plans to do other things for the summer. He says that he plans on moving in with his cousin soon and starting to work on steal framing buildings close to the city where Tommy is. Eric says that I would not want him around anymore anyway because I was so busy with other things. I asked him if he would come to see me even for a few days this week, but he said he was busy could not come.

Eric was being very ignorant toward me, and I could not understand why he had such a change of heart. He seemed like he was angry at me but I did not want to ask him for sure in case he was. My heart would not be able to bare the burden of arguing with him over anything. I wished he would make the trip even for a few days but I understood why he would not want to come to my rescue again this time. I wondered if he had another girlfriend or something now. I hoped he was finding everything he was looking for to make him happy, that way at least one of us could be.

The grapevine must have already gotten to Kodi, because it seemed shortly after I had hung up the phone with Eric, he was at my door. He said that no one told him I was home, but he had a feeling inside and thought he would drive by and see my car. I did not believe him, although he did not talk to my friends much, only if I was with him and he had to. Our social circle did not otherwise connect. It was like we were from other sides of the tracks, even though we lived in the county and did not have tracks.

We went outside for a walk like we had several times before. We talked about surface things and had light conversations. It was when we sat on the steps of the old church and he began singing. His voice sounded like it was coming from angles just for me. I closed my eyes and listened to his tune while the echo consumed my soul. For one moment I forgot everything around me was sad and my heart was lightened by the sound of his voice.

It seemed like no time had passed since I loved him, and I wanted to be in his arms again. I wanted him to take away all of my pain that I had held inside.

291

I wanted him to make everything go away and take me to the secret world of fantasy where we both belonged. I wanted him to hand me the apple of temptation one more time, if only for a while to make us both feel good.

"I wanted to come and tell you I was leaving soon," he broke the news.

"Oh." My heart hit the ground as quickly as he had picked it up.

"Where are you going?"

"There is nothing for me here so I am going to go west."

"What do you think is there for you?"

"I am not sure, but it has to be better than here."

I wanted him to ask me to go with him even though I knew I never could. I wanted him to wait for me, yet I knew that would not happen either.

When I stepped outside of myself long enough and was attentive to what he was really saying it sounded as if he was running away even faster than I wanted to. I wondered what he was running from yet I did not want to ask. I wondered where he was going to go or how soon he would leave but I knew that would have nothing to do with me. I wanted to ask him to stay around for a while longer but I knew in a few short days I was going to leave again anyway. I was not sure what was in store for me, and now I was not sure what was going to be in store for him either. *God, please keep him safe.*

"I wish you all the best." I then wondered if he wanted me to beg him not to go, but I couldn't. "Are you going alone?"

"No, I am going with Rick."

I wondered if he had any money to go. I wondered if he had a car to go. I wondered if he was telling anyone else but me he was going. I wondered if he would ever be back. I wondered if I would ever see him again.

"When are you leaving?"

"In a few days."

"You are not going to stay and work in harvest this year?"

"No, I am going to find work out there."

"You are not afraid to go?"

"No."

"I wish you well."

"Thank you."

I wondered if that was going to be the last time I would ever see him again. This certainly did seem like it was the time for change for all of us.

I talked to Tommy every day on the phone, and I could not wait to be back there with him. Each day when I heard his voice it put all the other frivolous things into perspective for me. I did not belong going out West with Kodi, I

292

did not want Eric to come here to see me, and I did not want to stay here and get a job in harvest. The only thing I wanted was to be back in the city with Tommy. My heart was there all along, it never came back with me.

"How are you doing today?" I asked Tommy, over the phone.

"Okay, how are you?"

"Was your transplant today?"

"Yes."

"How did that go?"

"It was fine for me, but my sister is really sore where they took the bone marrow out of her hip."

"What was it like for you?"

"It just went through an IV. It looked like platelets, you know, blood. It only took a little while for it to go through."

"Did it hurt?"

"No, it was just like all the blood I get. It looked white sort of, almost like platelets."

"So it is all done now?"

"Yes, all the chemo and radiation and the transfusion is already done."

"So all you have to do now is get better."

"Yeah, all I have to do now is get better."

"I wish I would have been there."

"It was no big deal, but I wish you were here now."

"Me, too."

"What did you do for your birthday?"

"Nothing really, just hung out with Kayla. We went to the beach for a while but that was about it." I lied. There were a few others at the beach that had met us, Jim and a few of his friends. I did not want to tell Tommy that because I did not want him to think that he was missing something that was no big deal without him anyway. All we did was have a few beers on the beach, played some kind of chasing game until Jim threw me in the water for old time's sake; then shortly after that we all went home.

"I wish I could have been there."

"Me, too."

"I Love You."

When I arrived back at the hospital Tommy was in the isolation room. I remember he had said he would be, but I did not expect it to be like this. I walked into the first door to what I thought was his room, but it was where we needed to sanitize ourselves. I had worn the masks before. I had worn the gowns before, and had worn the gloves before, but this was different.

"You have to do this," Tommy's Mom explained, as she washed her hands with soap in the sink in the sanitation room.

I watched her as she rinsed her hands under the warm water. Then she squirted some other stinky stuff on her hands. This old woman looked tired and worn. She looked like her heart was breaking, too. She looked like she was ready to rest for a very long time. She looked like life had handed her enough for today, and she was ready to hand it all back to God, yet she knew she would have to do it all again tomorrow.

"This is to further sanitize," she said.

"Then here are the gowns." She tied the gown in the back.

"Then the slippers." She slid them over her shoes.

"Then the hair net," she said, while she tucked all her hair behind what looked like a plastic bag.

"And I put the gloves and the mask on last," she said, as she snapped one glove on at a time.

"You cannot go in and see him without all this on."

I stood there in silence as I watched her become what looked like a doctor going into surgery, a child in a Halloween costume, a robber in disguise. If I did not know for sure it was Tommy's mom hiding behind all of that stuff I would not know who it was all. Soon I would look like that, too.

I did not want to get dressed up. I did not want to go in there to see Tommy. I did not want to hide myself from him. I did not want to have to. I wanted him to be well. I wanted to wake up from this nightmare on my bed at home.

"Okay," I said. I watched her through the window pass through another door to where I could only see Tommy's feet from the angle the bed was turned at.

It was my turn. I took a deep breath as I stood there alone with all of these things I did not understand. I tried to remember what she had done first. I turned on the tap and reached for the pink soap out of the dispenser. I scrubbed my hands until all the lather had fallen away in the sink. I wanted to make sure I was clean.

I took the clear liquid out of the bottle that she had done next. It stung the cut in my hand where I had bitten my finger nail to short on the car ride up.

I wrapped the yellow gown over my clothes and around my waist. I tied it as tight as I could so that no germs could escape.

I put the slippers over my shoes and pulled them as far as I could on my ankles. What if something got off my shoe from walking here down the street? I took off the slippers and threw them in the garbage and then took off my shoes. I opened the door to the hallway and set my shoes outside the door. I took another clean pair of slippers and put them over my socks.

I put the mask over my nose and mouth and tied it tight.

I turned the water on again and washed my hands again with soap, maybe I missed something the first time. I had touched the door handle and shoes so I had better make sure I am clean. I rinsed off the bubbles and turned off the water.

I took more soap and lathered my hands and arms all the way up to my elbows, what if I missed something.

I used the clear liquid again. It stung in the same spot.

Finally I put on the gloves. I was ready to go in.

I stood by the door and looked through the window at Tommy. He was facing the other direction, and I did not think he knew I had arrived. I put my hand on the door and tried to push it open. It seemed like it weighted more than a thousand pounds. I could not push it open. I could not move. I wanted to die.

I looked at Tommy's mom who motioned to come in the room. She was already sitting down by the bed talking with Tommy. I could see her mask moving but I could not hear her words. She looked so far in the distance, like a stranger I had never seen before. I wanted to wake up. *God, please wake me up!* I screamed in my head.

"What took you so long?" Tommy said, as soon as he rolled over when he heard the door open.

"Ummm, it just took me a little while to get ready to come in here."

"You did not have to take your shoes off you know. You just had to put the slippers on first."

I could feel my own tears getting my mask wet as they were running down my face. Tommy looked different this time. He looked sad.

He reached out his arm in my direction for me to come closer to the bed. "You don't have to stand by the door; you can come in."

My eyes dropped to the floor, and I noticed where I was standing. I had only left enough room for the door to close behind me, and I had not stepped any farther inside the room.

"Come here."

I walked over to the bed and stood like I was frozen in one spot. I was not sure how I was feeling because my emotions had washed down the drain in the other room with all the other germs and disease carrying pests that I could have brought in that could end his life.

As soon as I got close enough to the bed Tommy pulled my hand and took my glove off. I pulled my hand back in an instant as to not let him touch me.

"I want you to touch me without that glove, and I don't care if it kills me."

My mask was soaking now but I was glad I had it on to try to hide the tears of my broken heart or so I thought.

He raised my hand with his to touch his cheek and then his lips. He closed his eyes and held my hand there without the glove. I watched as his soul filled with relief.

"I missed you," he finally said. "I did not think you were going to come back."

"I missed you, too, and I told you I would."

"I know. I should have not doubted you."

"Tommy, she needs to be wearing gloves," his mother commented.

Tommy said nothing as he lay on the bed looking into my eyes.

I pulled up a chair beside his bed and held his hand after I put the glove back on. I could not tell if he was sleeping or just lying still with his eyes closed. It did not matter at that moment what he was doing as long as I was there with him. We both felt better when we were together no matter what we were doing. I would wait by his side forever as long as I knew it would keep his stronger so he could get well again.

The room was getting dark and the sun was going down behind the cement jungle, this surely was not the beach. I still sat beside Tommy holding his hand. Some of his family were in the waiting room, but no one wanted to come in because they were afraid of carrying any germs in with them. The doctors had said that it was better if only a few of us were the ones to come and go, that would lessen the chances of him getting some kind of infection. Therefore Tommy's mother and father were the only ones that opened and closed the door behind them. I stayed where I was hour after hour watching as his body fight the silent battle to restore itself from all the toxins that had been pumped into him. I waited, we all waited.

I finally stood up and let go of Tommy's hand. It was time for me to go back to the strange bed in the tiny apartment of Tommy's cousins for the night. I was in desperate need for sleep and a definite change of scenery. I did not want to leave his side but I was sure to come back as soon as I woke up. I had nothing else on the agenda anytime soon. I had nothing to look forward too except when the doctor's said he was fixed.

"Where are you going?" he opened his eyes and asked, as I stood up.

"It is almost eleven, Tommy. I am going to go now. Everyone else has left long ago. They all said to say goodbye; they did not want to wake you."

"Okay."

"I will be back in the morning."

He rolled over to face me as I was about to leave when he took my hand again. I touched his face one more time as I told him I loved him and wished him sweet dreams.

"Come here," he said, as he gently pulled me closer to him. I could tell by his grasp that he was beginning to lose his strength from the treatments.

"Kiss me," he said, as he pulled down my mask.

"Tommy, I can't."

"Yes, you can." He pulled me toward him harder.

I kissed him on the lips softly. It was cold in the sterile room, but his lips felt as if they were on fire. I ran my fingers over his hair and some of it started to fall out on the pillow case as I touched him. I held back my tears for him, or at least tried to until I got outside. I did not want to cry for him in front of him. I did not want him to know I saw the sickness again creeping up behind him to swallow him whole, but he already knew it was there, even before I did.

"I love you."

"I love you, too." I kissed him again. "See you in the morning."

I walked down the city streets alone. The air was hot and thick. I could hardly breathe after being in the cold isolation room for so many hours. The other street people that were usually here must have already found a place to hide for the night. It was quiet with only a few cars passing every now and again.

I was worried about Tommy. I knew he was going to get real sick again. I wished I had listened to him when he said he wanted to come home and not go through with it. I bet right now he would have felt better. I know there is no turning back now. What is done is done I might as well hope for the best; after all, hope is all that I got left.

I wanted to go sit on the park bench, but it was dark, and I was scared. I wondered what my friends were doing at home, and I wished that someone was here to support me. My heart was aching seeing Tommy sick today but I guess even if some of my friends were here to talk to there would be no words to describe any of this anyway. I had only been back for one day but it has already seemed like forever, and I want to go home.

I know I have a reason to be here in the city, and I know I will be home again soon, but I wanted the comfort of my own bed. I wondered what the next three weeks would bring for Tommy and me. I wondered if he would be well again by then. I hoped he was going to be able to come home with me yet I knew his battle had just begun.

When I got back to the hospital room Tommy's mother was sitting in the reclining chair in her costume reading the paper. She usually read the paper or did cross word puzzles to pass the time while I sat or stood by Tommy's bed. Our routine was the same. I asked her if she would like anything but she declined the offer, I knew she would. Even if she had wanted anything I could not bring it for her since we could not eat, drink or bring anything into Tommy's room now because it could be contaminated. I wondered how she had even gotten the newspaper in without the nurses telling her otherwise.

I looked around the room, and I knew from what was sitting beside his bed that the side effects from the chemo were starting to hit his body hard. I saw the faded turquoise dish on the night table beside the bed. That meant that Tommy must have been vomiting either during the night or early this morning.

The measuring cup was sitting beside a bit of water on the serving table so I knew the nurses were measuring his liquid intake. I did not need to see the hat on the toilet seat to know they would want to know how much he had peed either.

I went to the end of the bed and picked up his chart that had all the comments on it and read what it said. I could see from that how his body was doing today. He had not drunk much, had not urinated at all, was given medication for his stomach upset and his blood pressure was rising. I knew that when that started to happen things were not looking good. I remembered what happened to him in before. I took a deep breath. "Oh, God, here we go again."

I went to the head of the bed where he was lying with his eyes closed. This time I was sure he was sleeping because it sounded as if he was snoring a bit. I slid the mask from my mouth and kissed him on the forehead.

"Good morning," I greeted. Even if he was asleep I know he would know I was there.

I took the comb out of the drawer beside the bed and attempted to scrape the fallen hair off his pillow case. I wondered why they had not changed it yet for him. I wondered if they already had, and all this hair was already from this morning. I collected as much of it as I could from the side of the bed and walked around to the other side and repeated my actions. Then I threw it into the garbage can that was filled with small papers and tape from the nurses.

"Thank you," he finally said, without opening his eyes. He did not have to. He already knew it was me.

I sat down beside him and rested my hand on his arm as he lay still. "You're welcome."

It was not long after I arrived that the nurse came in the room. She checked all the same things as I had and asked him the same questions as she took his vital signs again.

"Did you drink anything? Have you tried to get out of bed today? Have you had a pee? How is your stomach? Do you need any more medicine for your belly? How are you feeling? Have you flushed your mouth out with the rinse yet?"

"No," Tommy mumbled, in her direction.

"Here," she said, then she handed him a glass of water. "Try this."

It seemed the moment he put the cup to his mouth he began to heave over and over again. He did not attempt to use the bucket because he already knew nothing was in his stomach anyway. He had puked it all out before. I imagined him doing this most of the night. No wonder he looked so tired this morning.

I took the cup from him and held the bucket as close to his mouth as I could, just in case something did come up. I got a cold cloth from the bathroom and held it to his forehead to help him cool down. I did not know what else to do to help him.

God, please, please, please help him stop puking, I said, inside my own head as I watched him with his head bent over the bed.

He finally stopped getting sick and the nurse left the room. Tommy's mom left the room with her. I went into the bathroom and got more cold water on the cloth.

"Can I help you?" I quietly asked him.

"No."

"Do you want me to go, too?"

"No."

I sat beside the bed and held the cloth to his forehead and wiped his neck and face with it. I tried to touch him as softly as I could because I knew if I disturbed the bed too much the movement would make him sick again. I knew that he would have another three or four days of this sickness before he either got better or worse. He knew it, too.

I arranged all the cups and medicine tubes of mouthwash on the table. I neatly set the wet cloths in the bathroom to dry for next time he needed them. I opened his locker to arrange his personal things and his bag, but it appeared his mom had beaten me to the draw. I took a shirt that had been lying on the radiator and hung it on the hanger. I wondered if I should take it home and wash it for him so it would be clean when he wanted it, but I thought that he was in no hurry to use it again any time soon. I thought about the last time I had seen him wear it, the day he gave me the flowers.

I sat back down beside the bed and gathered more fallen hair off the pillow.

"Comb it out," he said.

"What?" I asked.

"Comb it out. It is all going to fall out anyway and this mess is driving me crazy."

"Are you sure?" I thought this was a strange request from Tommy because all the other times he had wanted to keep as much of his hair as he could before it all fell out.

"Yes."

I sat beside the bed with the garbage can between my knees and began to gently swipe the comb across his head, taking one hair at a time with it. I did not need to tell him that it would grow back we already knew that from the several times before it already had.

I sat with Tommy in the room until the day became night again. I kissed him and left the hospital around eleven. My body was becoming weak from not eating, and my head was dizzy. I did not know how or what I felt because my emotions had abandoned me long ago. I walked the street slowly as I was in no hurry. All I had to do was slowly slipping away before my eyes.

On my way back to the hospital in the next morning I saw that guy again. I wondered if he had remembered walking with me a few weeks ago when he was so intoxicated. I hoped not. He looked much scarier in the light than he did in the dark. I tried to become invisible and blend into the streets with all the other people, in hopes that he would not notice me. I was in no mood for friendly conversation today.

He was dressed in jeans and running shoes with no shirt on. I could see his tattoos now that I had not seen before. His long curly hair fell over his shoulders and half way down his back. He was carrying something but I could not tell what it was. I looked across the street to see if I could cross at the next cross walk to avoid passing him directly. I walked with my eyes toward the ground in hopes he would not notice me.

"Emily, right?" he asked. I knew I was too late to dart away from him.

"Yes, it is." I looked up into his green eyes. He appeared to be of sound mind today.

"I am sorry, I forget your name." I had forgotten telling him mine.

"Edie." He answered as he stopped walking and was now standing in front of me.

"Sorry, I am not good with names." I tried to make a viable excuse, but I really did not care what his name was. I just wanted to get back to Tommy.

"How is your friend?" he asked.

"Pardon?" I wondered how he knew that.

"How is your friend? I saw you in the park a while ago with your friend, and I saw you coming from the hospital down the street the other night."

"He is very sick." I said, as my eyes hit the ground again. "I am on my way to see him right now."

"Visiting hours do not start yet. Why are you going so early?"

"Visiting hours do not apply to us anymore." I tried to explain but I knew he would not understand what I was talking about unless I told him the entire story. I was not about to do that.

"Oh," he paused, then asked. "What are you up to later?"

"The same thing. I will be at the hospital all day until I go home again tonight."

"Want to grab something to eat later?"

I looked at him as if he had just fallen off Mars. It had been so long since I had eaten myself I was not even sure when the last time I had put anything in my mouth other than water or a smoke. I knew if I tried to eat I would just puke it up again.

"No thanks. I will be at the hospital until late anyway."

"Until around eleven. That is when you leave, isn't it?"

"How do you know?"

"You're a newcomer around here; everyone knows what you do."

"Everyone?"

"Everyone that is here all the time."

"You have been talking about me with someone?"

"You should not walk the streets alone at night, you know. It is really not safe around here."

"I do not have much to lose," I said, but I knew he would not understand that. "Anyway," I began again, "I am sorry, but I must go now."

"See ya later?"

"Yeah, maybe," I said, as I was already walking away.

I arrived again at Tommy's room, scrubbed, and put my new uniform on. I walked in his room and looked at his chart. I could see that he was getting worse. He had not drunk anything, they were giving him nutrition through the IV now and his blood pressure was very high. He was running a fever from yesterday so that meant his body was now in active motion to fight off some kind of infection or something. I did not think it mattered what his body was fighting against as long as it eventually won the battle.

It had been four days since he was vomiting so I imagined that would be the end of that today for him since that was the usual pattern. Again I knew he would either get better or worse from this point on. I could only hope for better.

I sat by the bed with him as he went in and out of sleep all day. He would open his eyes for a while and look around; then he would lay his head back down on the pillow and close his eyes again. I wondered where he went in his head and what he must be dreaming of. I hoped he was dreaming of something better than the reality of what was really happening. The best thing for him was that he was not suffering while he was asleep and at least he had stopped puking.

I walked down the silent corridor toward that cafeteria and wondered where the Chapel was in this hospital. Again I wondered if I needed to pray there anyway. I was sure God would hear me no matter where I was. All I really wanted was a quiet place to sit and be alone for a while. I needed a safe place to calm my head and maybe even cry a bit. I needed a quiet place to remember the good things that Tommy and I shared, because it was hard to remember anything good at all while I sat beside his bed and watched to see if he was still breathing.

I hated leaving Tommy's room for even a moment but every now and then I just needed to get some fresh air. The nurses did not like us to leave because the more we came in and out of the isolation room the more chance we could carry infections germs. I was not sure if they knew what kind of mental anguish it was just sitting there, hour after hour, waiting for something good to happen but praying nothing bad was coming Tommy's way.

It was getting dark and it was almost the end of another day. I was getting ready to leave again for the night. I did not think Tommy would notice this time as I thought he had been asleep most of the day. Just as I stood up to leave Tommy opened his eyes and began to move around.

"What are you doing?" I asked Tommy.

"Getting up."

"For what?"

"Because I am not going to piss in that jar again today." I knew he meant the blue thing that looked somewhat like a milk jug that they wanted him to pee in to take the measurements.

"Let me help you get up then."

"No. I can do it myself."

"Okay." I moved my chair away from the bed to give him some room to get up.

I stood beside him and offered my hand to him for support, but he would not take it.

"I hate this gown," he complained, as it fell open at the back.

"Would you like me to get your PJ bottoms for you out of the locker?"

"No, it does not matter anyway."

He stood up slowly from the bed. His legs were weak, and it looked like his back was sore. He looked like a hundred-year-old man trying to stand up after years in bed.

I moved out of his way as he walked past me, and I took the next few steps behind him. He got a few steps past the end of the bed when he began to collapse toward the floor. I rushed toward his falling body from behind him and put my arms under his arms to catch him from hitting the ground. His weight was heavy on my arms, and I was starting to shake because I could not hold his weight.

"Drop me on the floor!" he yelled, at the top of his lungs at me.

"No, Tommy, try to stand up!" I yelled back.

"Drop me on the floor!" he yelled again.

"Stand up, Tommy; you have to stand up."

"I can't," he yelled back.

"I cannot hold you any longer. Try to stand up."

"I can't. Drop me on the floor."

"No, stand up." We were both still yelling at each other as I was trying to hold him up off the floor.

The floor is dirty and hard, and he cannot fall on it. If I cannot hold him up he will land on the floor and hurt himself. I must hold him up; he has to stand up. God, please, please, please help us."

"I am going to bring you back to the bed, Tommy; try to stand up."

"You can't; let me go," he was still yelling at me.

"Just help me get you into bed, for Christ sake."

The nurse must have heard us yelling from the hallway because even though it seemed like it took her forever to come into his room I doubted it really did. The moment I saw her open the first door of the isolation room I began yelling at her through the second door as I was still trying to hold Tommy up and get him to the bed.

"Help me!" I yelled, as loud as I could. "Help me!"

This time she did not stop to wash her hands or put gloves on. She rushed in toward Tommy and me and immediately helped me pick him up.

"What is wrong with him? Why can't he walk? Help me pick him up. Where were you? What took you so long to come?" I was now yelling at her.

"You should have dropped me on the floor," Tommy was still yelling at me.

"What happened?" the nurse was now yelling at both of us.

I began to cry as soon as we had gotten Tommy back into bed. This time I could not hold back the tears. I did not care who saw me crying. This was awful. What was happening to him?

"He is weak from not eating. This has nothing to do with the transplant," she tried to explain to us. "You are lucky she was here to help you," she directly told him.

"You need to stay in bed from now on," she went on, "I know you do not like it, but if you would have been here alone you could have been in real trouble." She handed him the blue thing to urinate into. She wrote a few things on the chart, then took his vital signs, and quickly left the room again.

Tommy lay back down on the bed after he peed in the blue thing after all, and I sat back down in the chair in silence.

Oh, God, what is happening to him? I prayed again in my head. *Please help him.*

It was not long before the nurse came back and announced to Tommy that the doctor had ordered a catheter so he did not have to get up anymore. We all knew what that meant, he was getting worse.

I did not want to leave him alone that night but the nurses let me stay until after midnight when they came to do the work on Tommy's body that the nurse said the doctor had ordered. I wondered if the doctor had ordered it because she had asked for it because of what had happened.

I was relieved to leave the hospital that night. I was glad to get in the elevator and push the down arrow. I never wanted to do that again. I knew that Tommy was getting sicker despite how hard he was trying to fight for himself. It seemed now that even though we did not say it out loud we both knew this was the beginning of the end.

I stood outside the hospital doors while I had a smoke. The tears fell down my cheeks like rain in the desert. I was trying hard to be strong. I was trying hard not to cry. I was trying hard to love Tommy. I was trying hard to do all that I could for him but I was getting weak. I wanted this all to be over for him. I wanted him to either get well or die. I knew now what he meant when he said that he was not scared to die he was scared of what was going to happen first. It was happening. This is what he was scared of. I was scared, too. I wanted his mom to come to stay with him as long as I did, but I knew she too was not well. I wanted his dad to come and be with him but I knew he had to be at home with Tommy's youngest sister. I wanted anyone to come and help take care of Tommy so I could go home again and just talk to Tommy over the phone and pretend he was fine even if I knew he was not. I wanted out of all of this. I wanted it all to stop.

"Please help us all," I said out loud, as I looked into the stars in the sky. I was not sure if that is where God really was or if He had even been listening at all during this time, but I knew if God did not help us there was nothing left. I was helpless, and I was running out of faith. I had been running on emotional emptiness for so long now I was even starting to wonder if there even was a God and if there was why the hell he would do this to Tommy. Was this some kind of cruel joke for amusement to test my faith and love for him? As far as I was concerned God could go to hell himself, just like he was putting Tommy and me through.

As I walked around the corner of the bushes that surrounded the hospital entry way to start my way to the bed that I lay in at night I heard a voice say, "You're late."

I kept walking in the direction I was headed and did not turn around.

"I said, you're late tonight." I knew the voice was talking to me.

"Yes" I agreed, "I am late. It has been a long night. What time is it?"

"Almost one."

"Oh," I kept walking without stopping or turning around. I knew it was Edie.

"Want to go for a drink or something?" he offered.

"No."

"Want to come up to my place for a while?"

"No."

"It is right on your way home."

"No." I kept walking, and trying to hold back the tears. Edie was now walking beside me and continued looking at me, but I kept my eyes straight ahead. I wanted him to go away.

"Are you okay?" he asked.

"Yes, I am okay, but my friend is not. Something bad happened to him tonight, and I just want to go home."

"Can I walk with you there?"

"If you want, but I am not going to be very good company."

"That is okay. I will just walk you home then."

"Thank you."

When I opened up my eyes the morning I was not sure if I had even slept or not. I had been lying in the same position, and I was still dressed in my clothes from last night. I immediately sat up in the bed and wiped the sweat from my forehead. What had happened last night? Was that a dream?

I stood in the shower and let the hot water run over my naked body. I felt weak. I felt like I could not muster the strength to even stand up. I was not sure how I was going to make it through another day yet I knew I had to gather my thoughts and strength somehow. I did not want to go to the hospital today. I did not want to see what else was about to happen to Tommy. I wanted to go home.

I sat on the couch with my elbows on my knees and my hands in my head and began to cry. I knew in my heart it was almost over.

I picked up the phone and dialed my number. I needed to talk to someone about something. I needed to hear a familiar comforting voice of my mother. I did not care what she talked about I only needed to feel connected to something bigger than myself. I needed to hear her say I was strong and that I was doing the right thing by being here with Tommy. I wanted her to say I had to come home now to start work. I wanted anything but what was happening to me.

The phone rang and rang. I lost count after about the twentieth ring. *Please pick up, someone; please pick up the phone,* but there was no answer. I looked at the clock and wondered if I could call my sister but I knew she would be at work now. I let the phone ring longer in hopes that if I just waited a few more minutes my mom would answer the phone but she was not home.

I began to walk down the street in the hottest sun and heaviest air I can ever remember. I was dressed in a sweater and jeans but I knew as soon as I got to the hospital again it would be cold. I looked around at everyone on the street dressed in summer clothes, and I felt like the odd man out in a game of life. I remembered a song I used to know that said something about wanting to paint everything black. I now understood what it meant.

I thought of another song in my head to pass the time while I walked. I could hear a man singing words that went something along the lines of, "people are strange," but I could not remember all the words.

"People are strange, when you're a stranger, faces look ugly when you're alone…. When you're strange, faces come out of the rain, when you're strange, when you're strange, when you're straaannnggee." I knew what he meant, too. I felt strange even onto myself.

"Hey," I heard someone calling toward me. I kept walking and singing in my head.

"Hey," I heard it call again.

I stopped and turned to look behind me. It was Edie. This time he was with some other man that I had not seen before.

"Hey," I greeted him back.

"On your way to the hospital?" I was not sure why he had asked me that because he knew I was.

"Yes."

"You are up early today."

I wondered how he knew that.

"This is my brother-in-law." He motioned toward the other man beside him. "We share an apartment together."

"Hi." I shook his hand. "Nice to meet you," I lied. I could not have cared less who he was.

He nodded in agreement but said nothing.

"Ready for that drink yet?" Edie asked again.

"Not today," I smiled. I wondered if this guy was ever going to give up on asking me out for a date.

"Can I walk with you?" he asked.

"No, that is okay. I am almost there."

"Well, then I guess I will see you later," Edie said.

This time I was sure I would see him again soon. If I had not known better I was beginning to think he was seeking me out or waiting for me every day and night to pass him by. I doubted this could be just a coincidence that kept happening each time I walked down the street. "I am sure you will." I smiled again at him.

Today Tommy was different. He was getting sicker. He kept falling in and out of dreams while he was awake. His eyes were open but he was saying things I could not understand. He was hallucinating again just like he had before. I knew this was the brain damage that the doctor had been talking about. We had seen him do this after his chemo treatments, but he seemed to still have moments that he would regain consciousness and be coherent. Tommy's mom and I sat and waited for him to either get better or worse.

It was early in the afternoon, and I had been with Tommy all morning. I could tell he was getting worse because his dreams were lasting longer and longer before he was coming out of them. The things he was saying were making less and less sense. It was obvious to both his mom and me that soon he would be lost in his dreams again for a long time. I wondered what was going on in his head.

I did not look at the nurses' chart anymore because I already knew nothing was coming or going through his body. I knew the poison was taking its full effect, and there was nothing anybody could do for him. I knew he had to do it for himself.

His body was becoming bloated again, and his skin was turning yellow. We had seen this before, and we did not need the professionals to tell us his liver was starting to shut down. I wondered if it would start up again like it had before. This was what they were worried about; it was all happening to him now.

I wondered if he even knew I was beside him or not. I held his hand and talked to him every now and then just in case he did. I did not want him to think I was leaving him alone in his darkest hour. I waited.

The doctor finally came in and gave us all the news about his condition we already knew. His body functions were shutting down. The good news was that as far as they could tell he did not have any kind of infection, and they were hopeful that the transplant had actually taken and that his body had not rejected his sister's marrow. Good news? The doctor said that we would just have to wait and see what happened next and if Tommy started to get better soon then maybe he was going to be okay.

I could not take seeing him like this any longer. I was helpless, Tommy was helpless, and the doctor's were helpless, so why was God not helping Tommy now? For the first time since I had been there with him I knew I needed to leave this room right now. I knew I could not sit here and watch him fade into the darkness of leukemia one more second. I wanted to reach in this hell and pull him out even if it meant I would have to make a trade and stay there myself, for him I would. Any one of us would, but all we could do was sit there beside him and watch him dying. I could not do it any longer. I refused.

I walked out the room and took off the stuff and walked out to the marble lobby. I noticed a new bouquet of flowers on the table beside one of the leather couches. I looked at the people sitting on the sofa and love seat being happy. I could tell from looking at this one particular young man that he, too, had cancer. I wondered why he was here and how long he would have left to live. I wanted to tell him to go home with his family now and that Tommy was right, he should have run away while he could have. If we would have left last week like he had wanted at least he might have died peacefully and not in so much pain. I could hear the screaming in my head, *RUN!* I wanted to yell at him, "Run and never come back! Do not let these people do this to you." My eyes met his across the room as if he could hear what I was saying. I truly hoped in my heart that God would give him a better chance than Tommy had, if there really was a God.

The sun hurt my eyes as I went outside. I had no place to go today so I thought I would walk in the opposite direction as I usually do. I crossed the street without thinking and the next thing I knew I was standing at the counter of the burger joint where Tommy and I had been just a few weeks before.

"Can I help you?" the waitress asked.

I stood in silence and looked around the restaurant. I looked at the men's bathroom door and waited for Tommy to come out with a smile on his face and remind me to get change for the video games.

"Miss, can I help you?" she said again.

"Ah, I will have a pop."

"What kind?"

I stood there in silence.

"What kind?"

"Pepsi, please." I handed her my money.

I looked at the change in my hand and had enough money to play the racing game. I took my pop from the counter, which I did not really want anyway, and went and sat down in front of the screen. I did not put money in the slot. I just sat and watched the frames of the computer go around and around.

I walked to the park and sat on the bench for a while. I threw some money on the ground but I forgot to count how many people went by before someone picked it up.

My pop was as hot as a coffee sitting on the bench in the sun beside me, and I could feel the sweat of my body run down my back and soak into my shirt. I looked at myself in the reflection of a passing car, and saw I still had my sweater on.

I reached into my pocket and got out a smoke. The pack had two left, and I wondered where they had all gone. I wondered how long I had been sitting here. I did not care because I had no where to go anyway.

I stood up and walked toward the hospital. I stood and waited for the street light to change several times before I attempted to cross the street. Once I got half way across the street I turned around and went back the other way toward the park. I was not ready to watch Tommy again. It seemed like he was not there anymore.

I walked toward the apartment and thought I might go back and take a nap for a while but I knew I could not sleep. I thought that I could go and take a shower for something to do and at least change my clothes. It is going to be a long night for Tommy, so maybe tonight I will just stay at the hospital with him. I wondered if they would let me.

"Looks like your best friend just died."

I looked up from counting the slots in the sidewalk to see who had interrupted my train of thought.

"They are." I said, even thought I was not sure anyone was talking directly to me.

"You look like you could use a break," the man said. He was standing beside a woman with long, dark hair, holding her hand.

"I could," I agreed.

"He would really like to see you. Come upstairs with us for a while?"

I wondered who he was and who he was talking about.

"No, I have to go." I turned, and started to walk away.

"It will be okay for you to come upstairs with us. She will be here with you, too. It is not like you have to be alone."

His words echoed in my head, "It is not like you have to be alone." Little did he know I already was.

"Come up and have a beer." He lifted the bag he was carrying that appeared to have a six pack in it. "You won't have to stay long if you don't want to."

I stood and stared at him as if I did not know what he was saying.

"Come on," he said. He grabbed my arm and pulled me toward the door. "It will be okay. He will be glad to see you."

I wondered who he was talking about that would be so glad to see me? I wondered who these people were.

I followed behind both of them through a locked door and into a stairwell that went up three flights of stairs. I waited behind them as he unlocked the door with a key. I stood outside the door as they went into the one room apartment.

"You have company," the man yelled, to someone who was in the bathroom.

"Come in," the woman said, at the same time as she pulled out a chair and motioned for me to sit.

I walked in and sat down and looked around. I saw nothing that I recognized as familiar.

The man pulled a cigarette package out of his pocket and pulled out a joint. I instantly recognized that as familiar and took it as soon as he handed it to me.

I dragged on the joint a few times and started to cough. It had been a long time since I had put toxins of that sort in my body and being in the isolation room with purified air for the last few weeks my lungs went into shock.

"Here." He handed me a beer.

I took another toke off the spliff and handed it toward the girl.

"Thanks," I smiled.

It was in that instant I could see that Adam had handed the apple to Eve and she had accepted it.

I still wondered where I was and who I might be waiting for that was apparently in the bathroom. The humidity in this little apartment seemed like whoever was in there had just taken a shower. I took a big breath, because in this heat it was really hard to breathe.

We passed the joint back and forth in silence, as I had nothing to say, and I was not in the mood to be good company. After all, they had invited me up here with them; they should entertain me.

The door of the bathroom finally opened, and I did see something I vaguely knew. It was Edie coming out from behind the door. He appeared surprised to see me sitting there with his friends, now making myself quietly at home.

He walked toward me, sitting on the chair and gave me a short, welcoming hug. "Hey," he greeted them and turned toward his friend and smiled.

"Look what I picked up on the street for you," his buddy added.

"Who forgot to shut the door?" Edie asked, as soon as he noticed it was still open.

I was not sure if I had forgotten to shut it or left it open in case I needed to make a great escape. "Oh, sorry. I did."

I looked at the clock on the wall, and I knew I had soon to get back to Tommy. I had not been in their company very long, but I had more pressing things to do. I did not want to offend their hospitality, but I really needed to go.

"Share this with me," I said, as I handed Edie the beer. "I am really sorry, but I cannot stay. I have to be going already."

"Stay, stay." I finally recognized the man that had brought me up here. He was Edie's room mate; therefore that must be his sister. "At least have a smoke and relax a bit." He offered me one out of his pack.

"Thanks, but I really got to go. I can smoke and walk," I smiled, as I took one from his pack.

"Nothing can be that bad that you have to rush off already," he was still trying to convince me it was a good idea to stay.

"Actually there is."

"What, is your best friend dying?" he started to laugh.

If I would have had a knife I would have stabbed him right there in the spot and watched him bleed to death on the floor. If I would have had a gun I would have shot him in the heart and watched every last once of blood drip from his body. I might have even stuck around to mop it up later. I wanted to poison his beer and watch him choke to death on the sofa for being so mean to me.

I turned and looked at Edie because I knew he already knew what was so pressing. "I've got to go," I said. The tears started to force their way up from my toenails. "I am sorry." I stood up and walked past Edie, who was sitting in the chair beside me.

"Wait for me to put some shoes on. I will walk with you."

"No thanks." I kept walking. I had not taken my shoes off, and I was not about to wait for anyone.

"Wait up," he followed me. He grabbed his shoes off the floor and began to jog to catch up.

I ran down the stairs almost as fast as I could. I wanted to get out of there. Why had I gone up there with them? Why had I not just stayed at the park or at the hospital? Why had I even come to this city? Why had I fallen in love with Tommy? Why was God taking him away from me now? Why? Why? Why?

"I am sorry for him." Edie ran by me on the stairs and stopped me at the door. "He would not have said that if he had known where you were going. He has no idea who you are or where you spend your time. He did not mean to be mean. I am sorry. Let me walk with you to the hospital."

"No, I do not know who you are or what you want, but you need to leave me alone." I tried to push past him in the doorway.

"I do not know who you are either, but from the moment I met you it looked like you needed a friend, just as you look right now. I do not want anything from you. I just want to walk with you to the hospital to see your friend."

"No."

"Okay, then I won't walk with you." He let me through the door. He did not walk with me to the hospital that afternoon but he did follow a block behind me all the way there. I wanted to turn around and yell at him to go away, but he was right, he was the only friend I had right now even if I did not want him to be.

By the time I returned to Tommy's room again he was asleep. Tommy's mother was gone so I sat in the reclining chair alone. I closed my eyes and listened to Tommy's breath. It sounded like he was struggling to suck each bit of air into his lungs. The look on his face appeared restless and his skin was pale. I knew that he was very sick but no matter where he was inside his head he was struggling each second to come back to me. I wondered if he would make it this time. I waited.

Tommy's consciousness was fading in and out. His delusions were lasting a long time until he could come back around again to see we were still there. I stayed at the hospital as long as I could, and I hardly ever left his side. I was afraid that if I left, something bad would happen to him while I was gone. I did not want to leave and come back to see his condition getting worse. I guess staying beside him each step of the way somehow falsely reassured me things might soon take a turn for the better. I wanted to be there for him each time he opened his eyes so that he knew he was not alone. I wanted him to remember that he had something good to fight for to stay alive. I wanted him to know that I loved him no matter how sick he was. I wanted him to know I was there for him like I said I would be.

Tommy was awake when the doctor came in the room this time. He tried to sit up on the bed to stay awake to listen to what he had to say but I could tell it was hard for him to focus and understand what the doctor was telling us.

The doctor told Tommy that his body was starting to shut down. He said that the chances of him getting better were very slim. The infection that Tommy had gotten was filling his lungs up with fluid and they could put a tube in his lungs to drain it for him to make it easier to breathe but that would then increase the risk of further infection. They had given Tommy an oxygen mask to breathe out of to make things easier for him to get air. The doctor told Tommy that his stomach and liver were also at risk. He said he did not know what kind of brain damage he may have sustained as there was no way of telling that without further tests.

Tommy asked him how much longer he had to live but the doctor said that he could not be sure with all that was going on inside his body right now.

I sat and listened to the doctor finally tell Tommy he was dying. I felt nothing.

After the doctor left Tommy rolled over on the bed and started to cry. I took off my gloves and mask and lay down beside him on the bed. I touched him gently on the arm and held his hand while he sobbed quietly in my arms. I quietly sobbed right along with him. We both knew that this was almost the end of Tommy's life. We both knew that Tommy's forever was almost over. Even if I was not ready for it, Tommy was ready to go to heaven.

The doctor returned to Tommy's room in a short while as we lay on the bed together. He announced that the oxygen mask was not enough to help Tommy breathe. His lungs were not getting enough air to circulate through his blood and that was making everything harder for his body to regain any kind of function. He also told Tommy that the tests had shown that the bone marrow transplant had actually worked and if he could pull through this ruff spot that he would be okay. He told Tommy not to give up. He told Tommy that the best chance for him now was that he was going to be transferred over to the adjoining hospital to the critical care unit and put on a respirator.

The man in the white coat told us that a team of specialists would put a tube down his throat and directly into his lungs to get air. He said that it would hurt Tommy's throat a bit, but it would not hurt after that. I think he was lying. He also said that Tommy would not be able to talk anymore, and that if he

314

wanted to communicate he could try to write anything down on a paper or chalk board. He said the hospital would supply that if we wanted.

Tommy asked the doctor how long he would live if he took off the oxygen mask and did not go to the other unit in the hospital. The doctor told Tommy that he would probably not live long enough for his family to make the trip to say goodbye from as far away as they lived. He said that Tommy would probably die within a few minutes, but he could not say for sure.

Tommy took off his mask and told the doctor he did not want to go. In the few minutes Tommy was talking to the doctor his skin became very pale and his lips began to turn blue, and his skin went almost grey. I looked at his hands and his fingers appeared as if he had wrapped an elastic band too tightly around them. I was begging Tommy in my head to put the mask back on but I knew at this point it was too late.

The doctor told Tommy that he was in no state to make that kind of decision for himself and that would be up to his mother. Tommy told the doctor not to ask her because he knew that she would not let go of him that easily and would hang onto him for as long as she could.

Tommy was ready to go now. He did not want to suffer any longer. He had enough of this life, and the leukemia finally won. Tommy asked the doctor if he could wait just a little while before the specialist came to get him. Tommy asked the doctor to leave the room and pretend that the conversation had not happened and that he had not seen Tommy so sick.

The doctor left the room immediately. Tommy and I lay on the bed together alone. Tommy's skin was turning blue all over now, as he struggled even harder for each breath.

"I want to go," he looked into my eyes and told me again.

"I know, Tommy, but you have to hang on."

"I can't. I am dying."

"No, Tommy, please try to hang on."

"I want to go. This is almost over now. This is how I want to die, right here with you."

I knew that even though it appeared to the doctor that Tommy did not know what was going on around him he did. He knew exactly what was happening, and was trying to tell me it was time to let go. I would not admit it. I would not let go so easily. Even if he accepted that this was his death, I would not. I thought he was talking to me, but maybe he was talking to his angels that would be carrying him to God. Maybe they told him it was time to let go, and they assured him it was okay to leave his body now. Maybe he had accepted they were right, and I was wrong for wanting him to stay here with me. Maybe he knew what was best for him even when I didn't.

It seemed like forever, but the clock told me it was only minutes before two men with a moveable bed entered the room and propped the isolation room doors open. Tommy made no motion as they entered the room.

"We are taking him to the Critical Care Unit," one of the men told me.

"He does not want to go," I said in return.

"Doctor's orders."

They transferred Tommy to the other bed and gave him another mask. One of the men had directly put the mask over Tommy's mouth and nose for him because he would not hold it up to his mouth himself. He did not want to.

"Keep the mask on, please," one of the men asked him nicely.

Tommy lay on the bed looking in my direction; then he took off the mask again.

"Come with me," he said, as he held out his hand.

"Tommy, please, keep the mask on. I will be there in a moment. I will follow you."

"No, come with me now," he begged, "I do not want to go without you."

I held Tommy's hand as the men quickly pushed the bed into the elevator. I had to run to keep up. I knew that Tommy was in no hurry to get to wherever we were going, but they sure were.

The elevator doors closed behind me, and I stood beside the bed looking down at Tommy as he stared back up at me. "Close your eyes; it will be okay." I tried to smile at him. The tears soaked the mask from behind my eyes which the men had told me to put back on.

Tommy took off the air mask once more and looked me directly in the eyes. "I love you," he said as he gasped between breaths.

"I love you, too, Tommy."

"Keep the mask on please," the man asked him again. I wondered if they were afraid he would die during the transport.

They finally got Tommy to where he needed to go. It was in another isolation room at the end of a long, orange hallway. We entered the room, and I saw monitors and machines that I had never seen before. The nurses were already waiting for him there and began to hook him up to everything before the men had put the brakes down on the bed.

I stood beside the wall and watched. The voices inside my head began to scream louder than I had ever heard them before. *Wake up, wake up, wake up!* This had to be the worst nightmare yet.

"Excuse me, Miss," one more nurse pushed me out of her way as she was coming in the room.

They hooked him up to even more stuff as I stood and watched. I had never seen people move so quickly in all of my life. I waited.

"What is she still doing in here?" someone turned around and asked.

I am not sure who it was but someone took my arm and led me into the hallway, and the nurse closed the curtains so I could not see through the big glass window that showed the inside of his new room. I stood where I had been placed because I could not move. I was frozen in time, and all I wanted to do was go back to a few weeks ago when things were better. I wanted to do it all over again and listen to Tommy when he said he wanted to go home. I wanted to call my Dad to come and get us and take Tommy back home. If he was going to die I wanted him to die in peace, not like this.

In seconds the doctor come and went into the room with the others. I could hear them talking, but I was not able to make out the words that they were saying. All the noise stopped, and it was quiet. The only sound I could hear was beeping from the monitor I had already known, the one that monitored his heartbeat. The only thing I knew for sure was that he was still alive.

Two doctors came out of the room. I was still standing, staring at the off-white curtain that was still closed. I wondered where the second doctor had come from, as I had not seen him enter the room.

"Do you know what is happening?" one of them asked me.

I said nothing, as all I could feel was the dampened mask still lying against my cheek.

"We have hooked Tommy up to the respirator. This machine will do all of his breathing for him because he is not strong enough to do it on his own. This will keep him alive for a while but he does not have much longer to live. Do you understand?"

I said nothing as I tried to blink. This has got to be a dream.

"I wanted to tell you that I have never seen a case such as his that someone has endured so much already. I have read through his charts from the beginning of his diagnosis when they said it was suspected he only had a few months to live. The only thing I can say about it is I think he has stayed alive this long because he loves you. I have seen you two together, and I know that is why he has held on this long. I wished it would have turned out better for him, but he is dying."

"Thank you for helping him as much as you could." The lump hit my throat, and I closed my eyes again. My head became dizzy, and my stomach was inside out as I pulled the blue mask over my head.

317

"Do you know where his family is?"

"No, I don't."

"The nurse needs to do some work with him so we need you to go get all his personal stuff out of his room now. Can you do that?" the white coat asked.

"Yes." I turned and walked away.

The doors of the isolation room we had just been in were still propped open from the men that had moved the bed. As I stepped in the first door and did not have to wash my hands I knew things were going to be different now. The mask Tommy had worn a few moments before that hung from the wall was still blowing cold oxygen through it. The intravenous stand was dripping saline solution onto the floor. The bathroom light was still on, and the curtains were drawn so the light could not shine through, as Tommy had not liked it in his eyes.

I opened his locker and took his shirt off the hanger and folded it nicely. I unzipped the steel teeth of the zipper and opened the bag and gently put it on top of his faded blue jeans.

Tommy's toothbrush was still in the bathroom with the paste by the sink. It was all dried out, as Tommy had not been able to brush his teeth for quite some time. I put it in the bag also.

The comb that had been in the night stand was lying on the floor where the bed had been. I picked it up and brushed the hair off of it.

I slid the drawer forward of the night stand and found Tommy's wallet and some lose change. I opened his wallet to put the money inside the leather pocket for him. I looked at the contents of his wallet: a green hospital card, a blue hospital card, his birth certificate, and a picture of me from last year at school. I looked at his name on the plastic-coated paper as if this was all a dream. I closed the wallet and put it in the side pocket of the bag.

I sat down in the chair and looked at the spot on the floor where Tommy had collapsed. My heart was broken into a million pieces as I thought about what the doctor had just said. "He is dying." The words rang through my head again and again.

I closed my eyes to make it go away, but I could only see the picture of Tommy as I was looking down at him speaking his last words. "I love you," he had said.

"I love you, too, Tommy," I said slowly out loud. I sat in the chair alone and looked at the empty room. That was exactly how I felt now, empty. I felt no sadness, no pain, no tears, no love, I just felt empty. I missed Tommy.

Tommy's mom and sister were in the bathroom when I walked in to wash the tears from my face. I had told them what had happened and where Tommy was taken. Tommy's mom did not believe what I had said, and she began to cry. I could not stand to stay and listen to the sobbing, so I just peed and left them to comfort themselves.

The next time I saw Tommy he was fully awake and the nurse was sitting on a stool beside a table in his room.

"He will have twenty-four-hour care here now," she said, without looking up at me when I walked in the room.

I stood beside the bed, as this room did not have any comfortable chairs to sit in. The only seat it had was the one that the nurse was occupying. Tommy tried to talk, but as soon as he made a motion to speak a loud monitor went off in the room. He looked scared of the noise. The nurse jumped from the stool and silenced the alarm before she came to his side.

"Tommy, you cannot try to talk. You cannot try to breathe on your own or the monitor will go off, indicating something is wrong. You have to relax and let the machine breathe for you. It will only be harder for you if you do not let it do what is it intended to do. You need to remain quiet." She checked his pulse and looked at her watch. She wrote something on the chart.

"Tommy, you will be okay. You need to relax now. I will be here with you." I did not know what else to say. I pulled the covers up over his chest to comfort him.

"You feel cold," I said. "Let me warm you up." I went to the end of the bed and began to rub his feet like I had a thousand times before to comfort him. His feet were as swollen as the rest of his body, and I knew what the doctor had said was true. His body was not circulating the blood, and he was not getting enough air, especially to the extremities.

"You can only stay a short while in here, and then you need to go. Fifteen minutes is all I can allow. There is a waiting room at the end of the hallway you can go to. I will come and get you if anything happens."

If anything happens? I could not believe she was telling me that in the last moments he might be alive I would have to go wait in another room down the hall, and she would come if anything happened. What did she think was going to happen that was worse than what already was happening? Fifteen minutes? Is she kidding?

I stood quietly at the end of his bed and listened to his heart beat. I heard another monitor go off. As I looked up I noticed that his blood pressure was sky rocketing, and I knew that was not a good sign. Maybe she was right;

fifteen minutes at a time was all that I was going to be able to handle as well.

I looked at the clock and saw it was twenty after the hour. I touched Tommy on the cheek, and he opened his eyes again.

"I must go for a while because this is as long as they will let me stay. I will go for a smoke and then I promise I will be right back. I love you."

He closed his eyes again, and I left the room.

I heard the doctor talking to Tommy's family. He was telling them the same things as he had told me before they moved Tommy over and what he had after. I looked him in the eye as he was repeating himself, but this time I did not stop to listen to him. I had already heard everything the experts had to say. I did not care to hear it again. I wondered if this time his family would believe what I had said to be true.

"You would be wise to call the rest of the family," was the last thing I heard him say. I walked down the long hallway to find the waiting room where the nurse directed me to sit.

I chose the sofa that was secluded in the corner and sat down. I opened the red package of cigarettes and took one out. I rifled through my purse to find a lighter. I drew the smoke into my lungs as deeply as I could before I exhaled. I looked at my watch, then laid my head on the wall behind me. I thought I should get as comfortable as I could, because I had the feeling it was going to be a long night ahead of me.

A few hours had passed, and each time I went to Tommy's room he was sleeping. I had followed the nurse's suggestions to let him rest. I did not want to go in the room because I did not want to wake him up. If his body had any chance at all left he needed to get better through being peaceful. His body needed all the strength it had left to do the simple things he had to hang on to. I went in the room and touched his hand to let him know I was still there. I told him each time I left that I loved him and that I would be back soon.

Once again the family arrived, one carload at a time. I sat beside Tommy's mom and listened to her tell the story of what was happening time and time again to everyone that arrived. It was not long before the entire waiting room was full of people pulling for his support. Tommy's mom would take the family a few at a time to see him. The nurse would only allow two at a time in the room once every fifteen minutes. That did not leave me any time to go to see him so I smoked one cigarette after another and waited for my turn. I knew I could go see him after they all went home. I was sure they would sooner or later all disappear, and it would only be Tommy's parents and I left, but the family kept coming.

I could hear Tommy's mom in the distance talking to someone. "I know he will come home again. He will not die. We have been told this so many times before and somehow he always pulls through."

I could hear someone else say, "No, Mom, I think this time is really it."

I wanted to believe what his mom was saying, but I felt in my heart the doctor was right. Part of me wanted Tommy to let go and find the heaven that had been patiently waiting for him all this time. I wanted his spirit to be free of the body that had been causing him so much hell for so long. I wanted him to let go of this life and take his last breath. I wanted him to get the final rest he had been longing for a few hours ago. I wanted that for him because I know that is what he wants, too. But for me, I wanted him to stay here forever.

The other part of me wanted him to hang on to life. I wanted him to struggle to stay alive. I wanted to hear that monitor going off every second because that way I knew he was still trying to breathe on his own. I wanted him to get the chance to say he loved me one more time. I wanted to tell him those words again to make sure that he knew how much I cared. I wanted him to sit up and take a drink or something and tell me about the weird dreams he was having while he was asleep. I wanted some sign he was going to be well again. I wanted the doctor to be wrong just one more time.

I walked to his room where the nurse still guarded his body. I opened the door and stood by his side.

"He has already had fifteen minutes of company this hour; you will have to come back."

I wondered where it was she thought I had to go, but I agreed anyway.

I exited the room and stood outside the door and looked through the window at him in the bed. This was certainly the worst it had ever gotten for him. I wondered if he knew I was there.

The nurse pulled the curtain on the window closed so I could not see in the room.

I took a few steps to the end of the hallway and looked out into the parking lot below. There was nothing I recognized, but I looked for some kind of comfort in the outside world. Once again I could hear Tommy's voice. "I love you." I pressed my nose against the cold window and said out loud, "I love you, too, Tommy," until my knees buckled, and I sat down on the floor.

My elbows rested on my knees again with my head in my hands, and I thought of a time when we were happy together. I thought of the time we were in the back of Shelly's car laughing at the girls while they stole the turkey. I though of Valentine's Day when we drank pink champagne and watched the flowers wilt by candle light. I remembered the first time I had seen him after all his hair had fallen out and told him I would love him with or without his locks. I thought about our air plane ride when he wanted to jump out. I thought of holding his hand when we walked on the beach or when we sat on the pier. I thought of his smile, his touch, his kisses. I thought about making love to him and when he liked to look down my shirt in art class. I thought of our first dance. I drifted away surrounding myself with memories of our love hoping that somehow in his walk through the valley of the shadow of death he could find good things to hang on to so he might want to come back. I hoped somehow that he was thinking of the good things, too. I hopped he wanted to stay.

I wondered if wherever his mind was if he was scared. I wondered if he felt alone. I wondered if he knew how many people were out in the waiting room pulling for him. I wondered if he just wanted to let go.

"Have you been here all this time?" The nurse woke me up from my thoughts.

"Yes." I looked at her and then at my watch. A few hours had already slipped away.

"I have no place to go," I looked her in the eye. "How is he now?"

"No change," she said softly. "You can go in now. I know there are a lot of people here for him, but if you want I will let you come in alone after everyone else leaves. If you do not tell them you are allowed, you alone will be okay. I know he would want you there."

"Thank you," I wiped my tears again. "I will be quiet; I promise." I stood up and went in the room.

"You can use my stool. I need to go out for a few minutes, but I will be back soon. The nurses at the station will monitor his condition from there." She turned and walked away.

I did not know what day it was anymore, nor how long I had been at the hospital without eating or sleeping. I walked back and forth from the waiting room to the hallway to Tommy's room. The longer he was hooked to those machines the less he would wake up. I did not know if I was coming or going. I could not tell where I had just been or where I was going back, too. I paced back and forth, stood up, sat down, read the newspaper and re-read the magazines on the tables. I wondered if there were any new flowers in the lobby of the other hospital because I had not been that way in so long. I wondered if it was hot outside, the temperature was always the same indoors. Tommy's mom and I waited together as all the others came and went.

"Go get yourself something to eat," Tommy's uncle suggested, as he handed me some money.

"No thanks. I am fine."

"No, you need to get out of here. Go get yourself something to eat or drink at the restaurant down the street or something. Everything will be fine if you leave."

"No, I am okay."

"Emily, it is not good for you to sit here like this. You need to take a break." he said. He directed me toward the elevator. "I will not let you go back in there if I have to carry you outside myself."

"What time is it?"

"Almost eleven. Why don't you go take a hot shower and get some sleep? You have been in the same clothes for almost three days now. You need rest."

I looked down at my shirt. He was right. I looked at the clock and wondered if he was lying. Three days. Was that true?

It was dark when I stepped outside. I took a few steps and stopped to catch my breath. The only thing I could see was the stars dancing around my eyes. What was wrong with me? Was I getting sick? I sat on the wall that surrounded the hospital grounds for a moment and lit another smoke. I decided that I would not leave the hospital after all, I was going to have a smoke and go back upstairs.

I felt the money in my pocket that Tommy's uncle had given me and thought that his suggestion of getting something to eat was a good one. I was no doctor but I remember when they had said Tommy lost function in his body because he had not eaten in so long. I wondered if that was why I had seen the stars. If I wanted to be here for Tommy if he got well I had better feed myself at least a little bit.

I knew the burger joint would be closed at this hour and wondered where I might get anything at all to eat. I thought of the twenty-four-hour convenience store that was close to the park on the path that I walked. I remembered seeing a sign in the window once that was advertising sandwiches or something. I did not want to eat much but thought at least a few pieces of bread would be better than nothing at all. I was not sure if my stomach could handle anything but figured if I puked it up it would not taste that bad in my mouth.

I went into the store and bought some milk and a sandwich. I sat outside on the curb to unwrap the food and watched the night crawlers pass by. My mind was empty and my heart was of stone. I thought of going to shower and then straight back to the hospital. I could sleep in the waiting room one more time, and was sure I would be fine. I opened up the pieces of bread and took off the dressings and threw it in the bottom of the bag. I put the juice in my pocket for later and opened the carton of chocolate milk to drop in the straw. I sucked the frosty milk into my mouth and tried to swallow.

"You look like hell."

I looked up and saw Edie standing in front of me on the step of the store.

"Thank you." I tried to smile, but couldn't.

"Where have you been?" he inquired.

"Paris. I went on vacation." I continued to suck on the straw. The milk sent my belly into convulsions, and I started to gag.

"Excuse me," I said. I covered my mouth before I puked it back out onto the ground in front of him.

"I am sorry," I apologized before I stood up. "I've got to go."

"Wait, where are you going? Are you okay?"

I started walking as quickly as I could but I stated to gag again. I bent over some bushes beside the store and heaved up the rest of the milk and any bread I had tried to eat.

"What is wrong with you? Are you okay?" he said again.

"No, I am not okay." I stood up and wiped my mouth. "My friend is very sick."

"Where are you going now? Come with me to have a drink."

"No, I need to get back to the hospital. I am sorry I can't."

"That does not seem like a good idea right now. What good are you to anyone in this shape? Come with me and relax for a while. You can leave when you want to and come back later tonight."

"Yeah, maybe you are right. I would like to shower and change my clothes. I am sure I stink."

"I will walk you home."

"You cannot come in."

"I will wait for you outside if you want. If you don't want to come back to my place with me, then you should go lie down and get some sleep."

"Sleep?" I laughed a bit. "Yeah, that would be a good idea." I knew no matter where I went or what I did I would not sleep a wink. My body had been working on overdrive for so long I was not sure how I would ever slow it down again.

"Do you want me to wait for you?"

"What?" My thoughts had already wandered from whatever it was we had been talking about.

"While you shower. I can wait outside for you, and then we can go back to my place for a bit."

"Sure." I was not sure what I was agreeing to but I knew that right now I did not want to be alone. I wanted to be by Tommy's side waiting for him to wake up so I could steal one more moment of his life with him before he had completely faded away. I knew that was not an option for tonight because there were still so many other people waiting there for him that wanted the same thing as I did: one more chance to say goodbye.

Edie waited patiently downstairs across the street on a park bench while I went upstairs. The apartment was quiet, and I thought everyone was asleep. I turned on the hallway light and stumbled through to the bathroom. I staggered into the kitchen to find a note that had been left on the table for whoever was there to read it. No wonder it was so quiet here. Everyone was gone for the weekend.

I stood under the hot water that ran over my head and onto my toes. I did not have the energy left to even raise my hands to wash my hair. I hung my head and let every drop of water that hit my flesh wash away the stench of the hospital from my body. The tears began to flow down my checks again and my knees buckled to the bottom of the tub. The only thing I could hear was the sound of my own voice crying out in pain. I wanted each drop of water to flush me down the drain with it. I did not want to go on any more like this. I did not want to watch Tommy die. I wanted to go home. I wanted him to come home with me. I wish he would not have had the transplant. I wish I would have told him it was a good idea to just walk out of it all and just let nature run its course. I wanted it to be peaceful for him. I did not want to watch him fight for every breath and disappear into the darkness alone. I wanted him to die peacefully in my arms like he would want.

Oh, God, please help him now. As he walks through the valley of the shadows of death, please let him fear no evil. Please, God, let him feel no pain. Please let him know that I am there with him every step of the way. Please let him find his peace, and let him know somehow it is going to be okay for him to let go of his body. Please, God, take his spirit up with you and end this suffering for him. He does not deserve this. Please let him know I love him, and I will never let go. Please, God, help him now more than ever before.

I walked outside and was hoping that Edie had gotten tired of waiting for me and gone home. I knew I would not be any good company for him and anything that I wanted from him now was going to be only for me. The only thing I had on my mind was Tommy, and my heart was in a million pieces, and my soul had been hiding for a while now. I had nothing to offer him. I was empty inside, numb to any emotion and distant from any real form of reality. I felt like I was somewhere else, and I was going through the motions of this moment in life like I was watching it on TV.

He stood up and walked across the road as soon as he saw me through the glass window of the apartment building. He was already waiting beside the door as soon as I opened it. I wondered why he was being so nice to me and what he might have wanted from me. I wondered why he would put so much effort getting to know a stranger in the city. I wondered if he had asked himself what I might want from him. What did I want from him?

"Feeling better?" he asked.

"No," I answered honestly.

"Let's go back to my place for a drink. Maybe that will make you feel better."

"Sure," although I doubted that was what I needed either. "What time it is anyway?"

"About twelve-thirty," he said, after looking at his watch. "You were up there a while."

"Sorry, I must have lost track of time."

We walked several blocks without speaking as I listened to the pattern of our footsteps on the pavement below my feet. I really had nothing to say to this man. I did not know anything about him, and he knew nothing about me. I was not even in the mood to make cheap, casual conversation. I wondered what we would talk about once we got inside his place. I wondered if the drink would bring forth something to say. I wondered if the volcano in my stomach would erupt if anything was able to even reach the bottom of my stomach.

My stomach already felt like it had a fire raging in the pits of acid that seemed to be burning itself alive. My body felt like it was boiling with wrath from no food, worry, and aloneness. I was experiencing many new sensations in my body while my heart was in the depths of despair. I had already been seeing stars when I stood up. I felt like I was going to pass out a few times at the hospital. I had seen a few things that I was not really sure was real or not and now I was about to enter into an apartment with a stranger in the city. Was this really in my best interest?

"You know, I am really not feeling well; maybe I should just go back home." I finally said. We stood and waiting for the yellow light of the cross walk to change.

"We are almost there. If you want to leave after a drink I will walk you back home, but you should at least come in a sit down a while after walking this far in this heat."

"Yeah, damn. Now you mention it, it is really fucking hot out here. I hate this damn city, there is nothing but cement everywhere you look. All this cement holds the heat in so much more, and it seems there is no place you can go to even breathe. It feels like everything is going to fall in on you, crushing you, crushing your lungs, holding your feet still to the ground. It feels like you can walk and walk and walk, yet everything looks the same. That house and that house and that house, it is all the same. Nothing is natural here. Everything is manmade, and man has destroyed everything good here. Men even destroy other men here, even if they are supposed to be doing it for the greater good. Damn, I hate this city, and damn, it is hot out here." I began to ramble.

"You're right," he agreed, as he opened the door with the key. He checked a mailbox on his way through the entryway, but it was empty. He led the way up into the stairwell as I followed behind him.

"I am on the third floor. No elevator." He smiled.

And no air conditioner, I thought in my head. I looked around at the hallway I was walking through, and the only thing I could think was, this must be poverty at its best. I had not noticed the first time I had been here, but this building was a dump.

I waited behind him as he opened another door with his key. Where I come from you don't even carry a set of keys. Nobody locks a door or has to look over their shoulder when you get out of the car or walk down the street.

He took off his shoes and placed them neatly in the closet. Strange, I thought to myself, I usually just kick mine in front of the door. I took my shoes off also, and neatly placed them beside his. I suppose, since I am a guest in this dump I might as well follow along with whatever patterns he had.

I sat down in the same chair that I had sat in before, the one right beside the door. I looked around while I waited for him to come out from the washroom. This place was a tiny apartment, but everything appeared as if it was in the exact place it had been meant for. Every cup was hung up under the cupboard, every pillow was neatly placed on the couch, every shoe in place, every blanket folded. There was not one speck of dirt on the floor, not a toast crumb left on the counter. For a bachelor this guy was immaculately neat.

I wondered what the inside of the fridge looked like or the medicine cabinet. I imagined that the shelves in the fridge had little white lines painted on it like a diagram of where things should go. The first little square is where the milk would go, the long rectangle is where the eggs should be and a small little circle painted out could be for the margarine. I wondered how he might organize any leftovers. I bet he has things color coded. The red dish is for Monday, the blue dish is for Tuesdays...

"Grab a beer out of the fridge if you want." I heard him say as he had just begun to run the water in the bathroom.

"Okay," I paused for a moment and was excited to actually see inside his fridge. "Want one, too?"

"Sure."

I opened the fridge and stood there for a moment, inspecting the order of things. It was not quite as spectacular as I thought it might have been, but things were certainly in order. Milk, bread, eggs and butter where on the top shelf neatly placed in a row. Ketchup, relish, mayo and mustard were all in the door, along with half a bottle of pop. Everything was real handy to get at. The beer was on the next shelf all placed one by one in line as is soldiers waiting for role call. On the last shelf were three apples and two oranges. Weird.

I took one beer from the front of one of the soldiers and the other beer from the back row of the other line. I wondered how much this would disrupt his life. Oh, my gawd, chaos! I could not wait to see what he would do when he saw that.

I opened my beer and looked around for an ashtray. My best guess, in most places, might find one either on the table or beside the sofa. I was not sure where I might find anything here. In the sink, nicely washed and dried, or sitting beside the sink, of course.

I walked over and turned on the fan that was on a table beside the window. I did not know much about this guy but it did seem like he had some kind of logical sense and needed a definite order to things. I wonder how long it would be before I would drive him absolutely crazy in messing all that up for him. If I knew one thing for sure it was that life had no order. I wondered if he knew that for sure too and was just trying to falsely pretend there was some kind of order to life by pretending he could control it by neatly placing the things around him. The only thing I could say to that was, "Good Luck."

"Sorry. I have no TV," he said, as soon as he appeared.

"It is just unnecessary noise most of the time anyway." I tried to smile but he knew it was fake. I don't think I have ever known anyone without a TV before.

He turned on the radio that was on the table beside the fan. I had not noticed that yet.

I lit a smoke and watched him for a moment. He appeared nervous. He kept walking in small circles as if he was looking for something he had lost. How could he lose anything in this place? He went over to the sink and then turned around and looked toward the table.

"I have already found the ashtray."

"Oh, good." He took his beer off the counter where I left it and joined me sitting at the table. He then took the smokes out of his pocket and lit one, too.

I sat and watched the fan suck the cigarette smoke out from behind itself and then blow it out toward the window. I listened to the tune on the radio that had been a favourite of mine a while ago. I was reminded of home.

"You look sad. Do you want to talk about it?"

"No." I took a drink of beer. What the hell was I doing here?

"You look tired," he observed.

"Yes, I think I am." I was tired, all right. I was tired of the city. I was tired of the heat. I was tired of being lonely. I was tired of a broken heart. I was tired of people making stupid conversation to make themselves feel better. I was tired of sitting in the hospital. I was tired of crying. I was tired of waiting. I was tired of stale coffee out of the vending machine. I was tired of watching Tommy through a glass window. I was tired of listening to monitors. I was tired of having someone tell me when and when I could not hold Tommy's hand or kiss him. I was tired of not having my friends with me. I was very tired.

"I don't think I have ever seen anyone so sad before."

"Yes, I think you said that already." I took the last drag off my smoke. I wondered if he would get up and empty the ashtray as soon as I butt the cigarette. I wanted to drop an ash on the table just to amuse myself to watch him run for a cloth to wipe it up.

"Do you want to stretch out and lie down?" he asked.

"No, I am fine." I paused. "Do you have anything for a headache?"

"Hang on, let me check." He came back a few seconds later. "Here." He handed me a white bottle with something inside.

"Thanks." I took the bottle from him and opened it up. I poured two tablets in my hand and popped them in my mouth. I took a big swallow of beer to wash them down.

He walked over and took the cushions off the sofa and then reached down and pulled it out into a bed. The sheets were already on the mattress. He walked over to the closet and got two pillows and a blanket from the top shelf.

He set the pillows down on the chair where he was sitting and then spread the blanket out on the bed. He picked up one pillow and placed it perfectly on the left side of the bed, then the other, and placed it on the right side of the bed.

I lit another smoke for distraction. It certainly was heating up in here real quick.

"Lie down," he pointed at the bed. "Let me rub your neck. It will help your headache."

"Nah, I am sure if I lie down right now I would for surely fall asleep. I have had a real long day," or couple of days. I was not even sure when the last time I had actually lain down on a bed was. I was not even sure what day it was anymore. It did not seem to matter that I even kept track, everything was such a blur.

"That is okay. I will wake you in the morning."

"In the morning?" I laughed. "Oh, no, I need to be home long before morning. I think I will just go back to the hospital from here tonight. I cannot wait until morning."

"Okay then, if you fall asleep I will wake you in a few hours so that you can go do whatever it is you need to do so badly."

"Promise?" I begged him with my eyes. I wondered what real human touch would feel like right now. I wanted him to touch me. I wanted him to take away my headache, but more than that I wanted him to take away my heartache, even if it was only just for a little while.

"Yes," he patted the side of the bed beside where he was standing, "I'll even sit in the chair if you would like."

I smiled inside myself. How stupid did he think I was? How long was that going to last, him sitting in the chair beside me lying on the bed? I had no reason not to believe him to be telling me the truth. So far, since I had known him for a few weeks, he had been nothing but nice to me. He appeared to be somewhat understanding or so I thought, and I knew for sure he must have some patience in waiting for me all the time. Yet I was nobody's fool, and I did not believe this arrangement would last very long.

"Okay, you sit in the chair," I smiled at him.

I sat in front of him on the bed while he was sitting on the chair. I turned my back toward him and flipped my hair over my shoulder so he could touch my skin. I stretched my legs out in front of me and leaned back on my wrists.

His hands were soft. It felt like his fingertips were reaching down and touching my soul. His soul was calling out to mine telling me it was okay to let myself feel good, it was safe here with him. I could hide here with him for a while from the darkness of death and he would protect me from all the bad things the world had to offer. In his corner of the world that he now had invited in into things were secure, in order. In his world he would protect me from harm. Protection, I thought, was just what my heart needed. I had found a hide-away from the world, and I liked it.

For the first time in days I closed my eyes and did not see monsters. I knew that this feeling would not last long, a few hours at best. I knew the comfort I was sucking out of this human being was selfish, for me only, like a drug I had been injected with that could make me feel good for an instant. I knew soon enough everything I had to face would come flooding back as soon as I walked out his front door and back onto the street. I wanted to enjoy this instant gratification while I could.

"That feels good," I told him, but I think he already knew.

"Lie down," he suggested, as he fluffed the pillow. "I promise I will wake you up if you fall asleep."

I adjusted my body and laid my head on the pillow that he had offered so kindly to me.

"Lie down with me?" I asked. I knew that question would only have to be said out loud once. Eve was now handing the apple to Adam. Would he take it?

I watched him as he slowly raised his shirt up above his head. I wondered if his darkly tanned skin was as soft on his chest as it was on his hands. I knew it would be.

I looked at the tattoos on his body that I could not have guessed were hidden under his shirt. I could barely see what they had been a few moments ago, but now I wanted a better look.

He stood up from the chair and walked toward the door and locked it. He turned off the light that was overhead, took five steps, and turned on the lamp that was beside the bed. He then sat down beside me and lit another smoke.

I looked at the tattoo of a half-naked girl on his back. "Someone you know?" I asked.

"No, just a tattoo." The heater of the cigarette glowed in the dimly lit room.

I looked at another tattoo he had of the grim reaper on his forearm. I softly ran my fingertips across it. I closed my eyes to hold back the tears as I touched his soft skin. I knew what was going to happen within the next few minutes of my life. I knew it was all wrong for me to be here, but it felt so right.

I did not love this man, but I knew I was going to use his body as an addiction to take all my pain away. I knew all the intimate things I was going to do with him within the next few hours were going to be heaven and hell all that the same time. I felt like I was giving my soul to Grim as long as I could feel no pain for a while it would be worth whatever I had to sacrifice. I knew of the guilt I would feel when it was over but for now I did not want to think about it.

I hoped that Edie would take my body to places I had never been before. I wanted him to touch me like a woman not like a little girl experimenting what sex is like for the first time. I felt like I was now a woman, with adult worries, with adult troubles, with adult responsibilities and now with adult desires. Inside I did not feel like I had just turned eight teen. I felt like I was a hundred years old. My soul was crying out for his attention, positive, passionate, alive attention.

I was not sure how old Edie was but I knew he was older than the boys I had been used to as soon as he turned out the light and laid his warm body next to me. There was no casual uncomfortable touching and fumbling around with each other's bodies. Edie knew exactly what he wanted and exactly how to go about getting it. As soon as he kissed me for the first time I could tell we were going to go all the way without regrets, without shame, without fear and without looking back.

All I knew for sure was in this instant I was right here with him and nothing else mattered. I did not know if I would ever find myself in this bed again, and I did not know if I would ever want to. I knew that for this moment he was all I had to hang onto that felt good. He desired to be with me for no other reason than being with me. He had no hidden agenda. He wanted what he wanted, and it was no secret. I wanted it, too.

"Drag?" he handed me the smoke he was holding.

I took the burning smoke from his hands as if he had pasted me one a thousand times before. I looked into his faded green eyes and wondered what he was thinking about.

I wondered what it would be like to share a real life with this man. I knew this was something I would never know. I knew that soon enough I would have to return home and after Tommy was gone this city held nothing for me.

He bent down while he still sat on the edge of the bed and took off one sock at a time. His socks looked as if they were band new or had been bleached a hundred times over. He tossed the socks under the mattress and then folded the shirt neatly and laid it on the chair. I wondered if he was some kind of obsessive compulsive freak that needed to find sanity in his order of things. I had never seen a man so neat and tidy in everything he did. I smiled inside and thought of all the quirky things I might do that I did not even realize that a stranger would pick out of my personality after being with me for the first time. I certainly found him odd in a funny kind of way.

"Ashtray?" I asked.

I watched his back muscles as he stretched out to reach across the table to answer my frivolous demand. He had kept his body in very good shape as if it was a temple in which he housed some kind of important essence of life.

I could also see several scars on his body, and I wondered where they had come from. I knew this man had a history that his body was telling me that I was not sure his mouth would. I knew from his tattoos that he had not acquired them from the upscale corner parlour, and they cost more money than the average individual could afford.

He handed me the ashtray without saying a word; then he stretched out beside me on the bed.

His stomach muscles were as tight as his back. I wanted to touch him right then. The idea of his soft skin over this finely kept muscles was about to drive me insane. I now knew what it was like to truly desire sex. I knew that would be in my future, but it could not happen soon enough for me. I wondered how I would get from where I was now to acquiring what I really wanted.

"Thanks." I flicked the ashes in the glass bowl.

I handed the smoke to him. The cigarette was almost burnt to the butt so this delicate distraction would soon come to an end. I did not imagine we would share a lot of conversation from this point on given the history of conversing on our walk and since we had been here. Have I even said three or four words? He even less.

"How's your headache?" He touched the back of my neck after he had put the smoke out.

"Better," I smiled, "I think your massage helped." Actually I thought it was the aspirin or the relaxation from the beer, but I might as well take this perfect opportunity to pamper his ego a bit.

"Close your eyes," he requested.

I followed his command. In fact I was ready to follow any order he would give. I wondered what the next one would be.

He began to rub the collar line of my shirt again. His hands were clammy against my skin. His touch sent shivers through my spine. At that instant I had not felt this alive in a long time. I had not felt anything in a long time. I enjoyed his touch stimulating anything inside of me. I remember someone saying to me a while ago that I appeared aloof. I did not just appear that way. I had lost touch of anything that was happening within my self for a very long time ago. It was refreshing to feel something again.

He pulled my head toward his as he leaned in toward me. I opened my eyes in surprise that he would move so quickly into a kiss. I wondered how long he might have been waiting to touch my lips against his. I wondered if he had desired me before just a few moments ago. I remembered his waiting for me night after night to walk me home. He must have desired something to be so persistent, but I could see he was much more than a high-school boy with a crush.

His eyes were already open as he looked back at me. His grip loosened around my neck and he pulled his body back into the stretched out position and lay on his back. I knew he was thinking from my body language that I might not appear that interested in engaging in his plan. He closed his eyes as he lay back on the bed and placed his arms under his head. He let out a big breath of air from his lungs.

I twisted my body to get closer to him, and then raised myself up on one arm. I placed my hand on his chest and slid it toward his chin. I turned his head to face mine and again looked directly into his eyes. This man looked as if he needed saving from something just as much as I did but I was not about to ask from what.

I touched my lips against his lips, and I closed my eyes again. I wanted to enjoy kissing him for the first time as much as I could. The thrill of the first kiss needed to be sweet. It needed to have the memory of joy that would linger in my heart long after it was over. I wanted to taste his body on my lips long after he had gone. I wanted something to hang onto for tomorrow when my heart was not dancing with the stars.

He kissed me back with more passion than I had been accustomed to. He had either wanted me from the moment he scared me on the street or he had lots of practice before. On the second thought, this kind of passion was not something you could experience with practice no matter how many others you had been with. This enthusiasm was not something you could fake or prepare yourself for. This was only something shared between two lustful lovers with only a few hours until the sun would rise and the real world would take over again.

The craze of delight lasted all night long. We shared each others' bodies with the obsession of a child with a new toy. We shared the infatuation of one another until our bodies would give no more pleasure. We were exhausted and could pleasure each other no more. I fell asleep listening to the sound of his heart raging with vibrant beats of joy.

"Good morning," was the first thing I heard him say. "I did not think you were ever going to wake up."

"Oh, my gawd, what time is it?" I pulled the covers over my uncovered, naked body. I desperately searched for a clock.

"It is early, almost six." He smiled, then handed me a smoke.

"Fuck," I stuttered. I took the smoke from him, then lay back down on the bed. "You said you would wake me up."

He passed his twisted smile my way, "No, I said I would wake you up in a few hours if you fell asleep. I was going to keep my promise and wake you at six."

"Oh." I looked around for the clock again. Where the hell would this neat freak hide the clock?

"Above the door," he pointed without me asking.

I took a drag off the smoke and blew it out toward the window above the bed. I looked out the window and could see the sun was already beating down so hard the leaves on the trees were already wilting. I could see the fog already starting to form from the heat in the city.

"Is it ever going to rain?" I wiped the beads of forming sweat off my forehead. I remembered his sweat falling off his forehead onto my chest last night as he powered over top of my body as I gave him every ounce of energy I had left in me to give.

"I don't know," he said, as he lit another smoke.

I looked down at the ashtray that had already been placed beside me as I was looking out the window. It had been cleaned of last night's filth and was sparkling from the rays of the sun. It was making a cute little rainbow on his thigh, from the light through the window.

I looked toward him as he now sat on the chair beside the bed. It appeared as if he had been up for a while and had taken a shower. That did not surprise me at all. He had on jeans and a fresh pair of white socks. I guess the old socks he had on yesterday had already been picked up from under neither the bed while my clothing was still all over the floor or wherever they had landed last night.

The silence between us was deafening. I wished he would say anything to break this awkward moment of waking up beside an unknown. He was not a stranger to me last night, but he sure did feel like one this morning. My mind was blank with any thoughts or wisdom. I had nothing to say.

He lay back down beside me on the bed and softly kissed me again. This was certainly not the same passion that he had shown me last night. This morning he was soft and gentle, he was nurturing and placid. He was in no hurry and had no agenda. It seemed from his kisses that he could stay here all day and do what we were doing now. He seemed like he did not want this time to end without saying a word. Time seemed endless. Although this was only our first night together we could have already been together for eternity. Our souls blended together as if we had spent a million lifetimes together searching for common ground, both fighting a silent battle we could not win.

"I've got to get going." I interrupted our bonding.

"Can't you stay a while?"

"No, I've really got to go. By the time I get back to shower and back to the hospital it will be almost eight."

"What happens at eight?"

"I will have been gone for nine hours." I smiled, "In my world right now a lot can happen in that time."

He smiled back at me for a moment, "And so I see." I knew he was reflecting on our time spent together. "You're right."

While I dressed myself as quickly as I could he set my shoes by the door. He was slowly pulling his on and tying up the laces. I imagined a perfect knot and bow.

"Are you always in so much of a hurry?" he asked.

I wondered if this was my little freaky thing that he was picking up about me after only a few hours of bliss together.

"Yes," I smiled, "I guess I am."

"Shall I walk with you?"

"No, I think I can make this trip alone," *along with many others,* I thought in my head.

"When can I see you again?" He looked up from tying the shoes.

"I don't know." I could feel the shards of the pieces of my heart hit the floor as I remembered why I was in such a hurry today.

"Are you staying at the hospital again tonight?"

"What do you mean again tonight?"

"I had not seen you around the last few days so I thought you must have been staying there because your friend must be sick. I had seen you coming from the other exit, so I assumed they must have moved him to the critical care unit. That is all that part of the hospital is."

"You were watching me?" I could feel my blood pressure rise.

"Not really." I think he was lying. "I had seen you and your friend a while ago walking together from the park. I was walking a ways behind you, and I noticed you went into the other doors. Last night I saw you come out from the other exit, the one that is not part of St. Ann's."

"You were walking behind me last night?"

"Yes, then you went into the store. That is when I caught up to you."

"You're weird. Are you stalking me?"

He laughed at my comment, "Stalking you? No. You stand out here like a sore thumb. Everyone that lives here on these streets knows who belongs here and who doesn't. You don't. At first we thought you were a cop, to bust the drugs and prostitution around the park at night. We thought that because you walk early in the morning then disappear, then you come out again later at night. It was only after a while we realized that your pattern did not involve trying to talk to anyone, so we knew you must not be. When someone tried to talk to you, you always pushed them away and had no interest. We knew you were not a cop then, and we saw you coming from the hospital all the time."

"Who are we?" I was now becoming a little frightened.

"You know, the people that stop by you in the cars and try to pick you up as a hooker. You never stop walking or if you do you give everyone a different name."

"You know that?"

"Yes." He sighed. "Nothing is a secret around here. But that is why everyone left you alone. Although you are not really safe walking alone at night around here."

"Safe?" I looked at him. "In a little while I am afraid I will not have much left to lose."

"No matter where you are you always have something left to lose." He stated that fact as if he knew from experience what he was talking about.

Through the Shaded, Transparent Glass

I returned to the hospital before anyone else had gotten there. Most of Tommy's family had returned home to the country to continue with their regular lives. Tommy's one sister, his mom, and I were still here every day doing the same things over and over again. We would wait in the waiting room for our fifteen minutes an hour visits, smoke, look at magazines we had previously read, walk to the café to get coffee even if we did not really want one and wait. Sometimes we would even sleep sitting up in the uncomfortable chairs in the lounges. I would still stand outside Tommy's room and watch him through the window or sit on the floor at the end of the hallway.

The minutes dragged on like hours. The hours dragged on like days. The days dragged on like months or years. Our conversations ran thin because Tommy's mom and I had spent so much time together there was nothing left to talk about but Tommy. When there was no change in Tommy's health we did not talk at all.

No one had asked me where I was last night or why I was more tired than usual. I slept off and on all day in the waiting room when I was not in with Tommy. I knew what it was like to feel invisible to these people that he called family because without him I had no connection to them at all. I was grateful for the hospitality but if they did not even know how long I had been gone without asking questions they must not see me as anything at all to care about. That was in fine standing order in my books because the feelings of being nonexistent were mutual. I had never felt so alone in the big, wicked world in all my life as I was here with them waiting for Tommy.

Tommy never woke up at all now. The monitors never went off anymore, as if he was trying to breathe on his own. He was always lying flat on his back and did not move or roll over. He was always still and silent. I could see right before my very eyes that slowly what the doctor's had told me was coming true. He was losing his long, stretched-out battle to cancer right before my eyes. I did not want to be waiting for him to die, but I knew I was. I knew in my heart there was nothing more anyone could do to help him. This waiting was tearing out my heart every second that passed. I hated all of this. I wanted it to be all over too, just like Tommy did.

I could see my own reflection staring at Tommy through the glass. I looked at myself for a moment and wondered who I was. I wondered who I had become and what I would become after it was more than a sheet of transparent, shaded glass that separated us.

I wondered what death was like. I wondered if I would ever see him again in the after life if we both went to heaven. I knew Tommy would go to heaven but I was not sure if I would. What if he went to heaven, and I went to hell and I never ever in this life or the next see him again? Will I be able to have his soul touch my heart again. What will I do without him?

I watched him on his dreary deathbed. I remember back to four long hard years ago when I first danced with him in the gym at the school. The last words the singer sang that night to us over the speakers rang through my head: "And she's buying the stairway to heaven." I wondered how much it might cost to buy each step. I wondered what sacrifices one had to make to get there. I knew the cost could never be paid for in dollar bills. I wondered what step Tommy was on and how close he was to the top. I wondered if Tommy felt like he was alone there.

The sun was still shining brightly through the window at the end of the hall. I walked over and looked outside. It appeared very hot out but the air conditioner in the hospital was deceiving as to what it was really like outside. It seemed to me that everything was deceiving at one time or another, and life was really not all it was cracked up to be. I tried to remember a time when I last heard someone say that life was good. I asked myself who I might know that would feel like that and maybe I could call them and chat for a while. A little positive attitude would do me well as I was standing in the death zone.

I watched other people walk up and down the hallways and into rooms where their loved ones lay. No one here was at all happy. I looked at the doors down the hall and wondered what kind of lives these people may have had before death was knocking on their doors. I wondered what their names were and how long they had been here waiting just like us.

Tommy's room was the only one that had a cart full of supplies in front of it. I knew that if the cart of gloves, masks, coats, slippers and hand sanitizer was not outside someone's door they must be here for something else. I wondered if the family of the patients in those rooms knew how lucky they are because they did not need to play dress up for fifteen minutes of every hour. I knew why Tommy wanted me to take off the gloves and mask so I could touch him in the other wing of the hospital. I knew now about how important the healing hand of your lover's touch could be. Now his touch was taken away from me also. Even though I could still touch him he could not touch me back. I knew he would if he could. I knew he would never want me to stop touching him. I took off my gloves to at least hold his hand when I could. I knew in my heart he would know I was there. I knew he could feel it.

"You know he is not getting better," another white coat approached me with more words that I already could see for myself.

"Yes, I know."

"It is only a matter of time now for him."

"Yes, I know."

"Is there anything I can do for you? Do you have any questions?"

"Not anymore. I can see everything that is happening."

"Would you like to talk to a social worker?"

"What would I say? Would I tell them that I am here watching my best friend dying through a window because you white coats will not let me go in to see him? Would I tell them that I have a broken heart? That I am terrified of what is going to happen to me after he is gone? Or that I have to go home in a few days because my parents are making me go to work, and I doubt I will be here when he passes? Or is there something else that I should say?"

The white coat stood in front of me with nothing to say except, "You could talk about how you feel."

"How long does it take to say I feel lost, confused, and numb? I am angry, sad, and wanting relief for him. This is not fair for him. Why did God do this? I do not think a social worker can answer that. I do not think it will help. I want to be right here with him as long as I can, even if it is on the other side of this stupid fucking glass wall." I began to cry.

The white coat turned away and went into Tommy's room. I could see through the glass he was talking to the nurse. She was nodding her head in agreement. He then went over and stood by Tommy's bed for a moment and put his hand on Tommy's stomach and tapped it a few times. He checked for reflexes, then tried to open Tommy's eyes. He did a few more tests, but everything he tried got no response from Tommy. I wondered why he did not just leave him alone.

"You can go in now," he said as soon as he exited the room. "I told them you could go in whenever, however long you wanted. You do not have to leave if you don't want to. I don't suggest for yourself, though, that you stay too long at once. You need to take a break, too."

"Thank you." I tried to smile in gratitude.

I played dress up one more time before I went in to sit beside the bed. I took off one glove and touched the top of Tommy's hand as if to hold it if I could. I put my head down on the mattress beside him. I wanted to lie down with him. I wanted to pull all the tubes out of his body and carry him outside. I wanted to wake him up. I wanted to yell at him for leaving me. I wanted to kiss him. I did not care what happened. I wanted him back.

The nurse stood up and left the room.

"Tommy, I love you. I will never stop loving you," was all I could say while I sat beside him and waited. I did not even know what I was waiting for anymore.

I looked at my watch, and it read a quarter to eleven. I knew I would soon be on my way for the night. My body was starting to shut down from no sleep and no food. I did not want to leave Tommy, but I knew I had to for a while. I pulled my mask down and bent over the bed and kissed him softly on the cheek. I stood up and looked at him again for a few more seconds. Would kissing him only on the cheek be good enough for him? *No,* I thought, then I bent back over the bed and kissed his parched lips.

Edie was waiting for me on the wall right outside the hospital. I expected to see him here tonight after the time we shared last night, but tonight I wish he had not come.

As soon as he saw me he stood up and greeted me with a smile and a hug. "Hi."

"Hi," was all I could muster. The smile tonight was not an option. "How long have you been here?"

"I don't know, since about ten."

"Oh. I thought you would have something better to do."

I fumbled around in my purse for my lighter and a stick of gum but I was really trying to think of something to say to him. I had not thought about him all day. I wondered how I could have spent last night with him engaging in such sexual ambition to please him time and time again but not have batted an eyelash as soon as I left his company. The quiet shame filled my heart.

"There is nothing better to do than what I did last night," he said, very matter of factly. "I wondered if you wanted to come over again tonight for a drink?"

341

No, was my first reaction but I could not say that out loud. I was not sure what I wanted to do. After all, if I had what I wanted I would not be in the position to even entertain the idea of having his company. I would not even know him if I had my way about it.

"Feels like it is starting to rain." I looked up in the sky as I felt the first drop hit my hand. "Maybe that will bring some relief to this heat wave."

I flicked my lighter and held it up to the end of the cigarette I already held between my lips. In the quiver of the flame I could barely see the darkness of his eyes. I tried not to look directly at him because I did not want him to see me through my eyes that I could not get through this heartbreak and back into anything that was remotely real. I had just spent all day in a waking nightmare that I had resisted from believing was the truth for years. Now it was all coming down to a final few days or weeks left. My reality was more horrible than I could have ever imagined.

"Yes, it started to sprinkle a few minutes ago."

"How long have you been here?"

"About an hour. You just asked me that." His voice sounded weary, yet sympathetic to my detachment from our faltering conversation.

I took my first few steps away from the cement wall that surrounded the sanatorium. My body was weak, and I felt like I was going to faint. My stomach felt like it had an ogre inside that was fighting for its way out. I stumbled a bit and then caught myself on his arm. My heart was screaming for me to go back inside to be with Tommy, but I was trying not to listen to it.

"Are you okay?"

I took the first drag off the smoke and looked directly at the man standing in front of me. "It has just been a real long day."

We walked slowly toward his apartment building. He was talking about something that I was not paying attention to. I was just agreeing with everything he was saying, but my mind was in another dimension.

He opened the door with the key and then stopped to hold it for me without asking again if I had wanted to come upstairs. Tonight was different from last night. I knew exactly what to expect.

I left my entire being there on the sidewalk as I passed him in the doorway and opened the door to the stairs. I heard the thunder begin to roll above the city, and I knew the lightning was about to strike soon. I wanted the electrons in the sky to come down through this building and strike me dead. I wanted to get to heaven before Tommy did so I could be there waiting for him when he arrived. I wondered if God would really let that happen.

"Please, God, take my soul tonight. Please let me die now so I can be there with Tommy with you before he gets there. Please let me welcome him to heaven. Please don't keep me here without him. Anytime in the next few seconds to take me would be good. Hope to see you soon. Amen."

"What did you say?" Edie asked, from behind me as he was just starting to come up the steps after he had taken a moment to look in the mail box again.

"Nothing."

Stay with Me

The next two weeks went on with the same pattern of events over and over again. I would spend all day at the hospital with Tommy and Edie would wait for me each night outside. He had stopped asking me if I wanted to come up for a drink. He did not need to make excuse to get me to go upstairs with him he already knew that I would.

When I was with him in bed I could at least feel the physical pleasure and pain of our sexual rendezvous. Sometimes the sex with him would hurt so much that it felt good. My emotions were all buried under the fear and sadness of watching Tommy finally die. God had not taken me yet, so I assumed that His answer to that prayer was no. Even though I did not want to stay on the earth plane I guess I had, too. Edie just offered some comfort to rest my soul for a while.

"You know, Edie, I am leaving the city on Sunday."

"What? You're leaving?"

"Yes. I need to start work on Monday. I will be going home. It is very different where I live from how it is here. It is quiet. No sirens of the city, no smell of smog or garbage in the air, you can actually feel the breeze on your face when you walk outside, you can breathe in the country. Everybody is not always in a rush. Everyone is not always in the rat race to get to the end of the line but actually going nowhere. When we die, you know, we are all the same. Money does not matter, status does not matter. I am not sure it matters what you have ever done here, because when you are dead, you are dead."

"Do you believe that? When you are dead you are dead?"

"Yes."

"What about the kindness that you left in someone's heart while you were here? Does that matter?"

"No."

344

"What about the love you left behind?"

"That is just it. You have left it behind." I tried not to cry again. I had not ever cried in front of Edie before. He did not need to see that part of me.

He paused for a moment and then finally started to speak again. "Will you come back?" he asked.

"Probably not to stay."

"How will I see you again?"

"You probably won't."

He lay quiet in the bed beside me for a while, "You know I have really gotten to like you."

"Yes, I know you have. I wanted to say thank you for being so nice to me while I have been here."

"I did not think that you would ever leave."

"What did you think was going to happen?"

"I did not think that far ahead."

"Oh." I pulled the covers up over my naked body. I wondered why I had done that. He had seen and touched every inch of my flesh that was humanly possible. Why was I so insecure now?

"Why don't you stay here in the city?"

"I have to work."

"What about your friend?"

"I don't know what about him. I will come back when I can to see him."

"Will he miss you?"

"Edie, my friend is barely alive. He is so sick that he has not even spoken or moved his body in about three weeks. He cannot even breathe on his own. I am not sure why they are keeping him alive, but if it were not for the machines he would already be dead. His body has been in agony for weeks now. He wanted to die then, but they would not let him. I am not sure he even knows I am here anymore. I have been here long enough, and my parents are making me come home."

"I love you, and I want you to stay here with me."

"What?"

"I love you." he said again.

I was silent as I thought about what love meant to me. He loves me. That was amusing. How could he possibly love me after only having seen me for a few weeks? That was not love; that was obsession, maybe even addiction, but not love.

345

RUBIE ANN GRAVES

I listened to the pouring rain hit the window. All I could think of now was how hot it was in this tiny little apartment. I closed my eyes for a moment and the smell of the hot wet pavement broke through the widow and burnt my nose even this far from the highway. I hated it here. I wanted to go home. I remembered the smell of fresh-cut grass in our yard after the rain.

"Do you love me?" he finally asked.

I sat up in the bed and looked out the window at the street lights. His query reminded me of what Jesse had said the first time I had sex. Jesse's voice ran out inside my head. "You do not know what love is, do you?" I thought of repeating those words right now to Edie.

"Edie," I looked him in the eyes, "my love right now is only skin deep. My body loves the way you make me feel. I love having sex with you four, five, six times a night, but this is not the rest of my life. I need to leave the city and go home. This is not my home, and it never will be. I came here for Tommy. I never had any intentions of staying." My own voice echoed in my head as I thought of the times I had repeated this familiar speech before. Edie was second to why I had come here. He was a passing ship in the night that I would only accompany for a short while. Somehow in this cruel world God had given me another crutch.

"Why don't you stay here with me?"

"I can't."

"I know someplace in your heart underneath all that sadness I see in your eyes you do love me. If you run away from me and that love now you will always keep running. You will never find what you are going to be chasing, and you will never be able to bring your friend back. Stay with me here; stay with me now. Let me help you love again," he said, before he kissed me gently on the lips.

"I can't."

The End

It was my first day on the new job in the harvest. People were introducing themselves to those we would be spending the next six or eight weeks with every day of our short time together. I was not interested in getting to know anyone anymore on a first-name basis. I needed to address them as co-workers. I did not want to know anything more about them but I was trying to be nice. I did not much care to concern myself with the frivolous questions like Where do you live? Do you have a boyfriend? or What time do you think we are going to get done the day's work? I just wanted to do what I needed to do there and go home and wait by the phone for any news that might come while I was away from my love.

I immersed myself in distraction of work and tried to avoid any conversation that I could. My mind was not where I was and this endless job was tedious. I was upset at my parents for making me come back home yet I knew staying in the city was not in my best interests, and I missed it here. I knew there was nothing that I could do for Tommy anyway but at least being near him eased my pain a bit.

I was only home for three days when I got the first call from Tommy's sister.

"They said that Tommy is not doing well, Emily." I knew she meant the white coats, and this was not new news for me anyway.

"Yes, I know."

"They said they did not know why, but for some reason he has taken a big turn for the worse. I guess it happened sometime Monday after you left."

"Oh."

"I wondered if you could come back. I think he knows you are gone."

"Yes, I suppose he does."

"Even in the hospital he always woke up and asked for you as soon as you left the room."

"Yes."

"Can you come back?"

"No, I have started work. I cannot come back until the weekend."

"I am not sure he can hang on that long. I could come back and work for you if you could come here to be with him again. They said that if he did not start getting better they were going to unplug the respirator on Saturday at one o'clock."

"Oh." I did not know what to say.

"They said that way everyone could have a chance to get here. They said that he would probably only live a few minutes after that. Can you come?"

"Yes, I will come. I will see if I can come tomorrow night and stay Friday night with him."

"We are all going to be here, too."

"How is your mom?"

"She is taking it very hard. She keeps asking them why they are going to do that. They say that he has no brain function left, and all his internal organs have almost shut completely down and stopped working. They say his liver is finished. They say there is no hope now."

"Yes, I know. They told me that, too."

"I will call you if anything happens before I see you on Friday night then."

"Thank you."

I hung up the phone and sat and stared at the floor. I had no feelings left in my body, and my spirit was already dead.

"God, please take me now." I prayed out loud, but I knew He wouldn't. I did not know what was going to happen in the next few days but I was sure I did not want to experience it. I knew it was going to be worse than I ever imagined.

I told my mother about the call and she said she was surprised that they waited this long to unplug him. She said she and Dad would go with me if I wanted to wait until Saturday to go to the hospital. I said I wanted to go earlier than that but she said that he would not know I was there anyway, and I should not put myself through that much more suffering of spending the last night there with him alone. I wanted to go Friday anyway. Mom and Dad could come up there early to be with me on Saturday but I wanted to be there every second for his last night alive.

When I woke up at five in the morning on Friday it was still dark out. I took a shower and got ready for work just like any other day. I knew it was going to be a long day, but I was uncertain what it might bring. I just wanted to hurry up and get all I needed to do over with so I could go and spend my last night with Tommy. I did not care if the white coats told me to leave the room; I was not going to. I was not going to waste a second of it leaving him alone. Even though they said he might not know I was there I knew he would know. I would know.

As I was sitting on the ground in the shade at work something inside was telling me that I would not spend the night with Tommy. Something was trying to press through my psyche and say that I would not see him tomorrow either. I tried to ignore the message I was getting from above but I could not stop the noise in my head. I thought it was because I was anxious about getting done work and set off for the three-hour drive to the city. I wanted to leave work and go now, but I knew I could not do that if I wanted to keep this job. I thought that this job was not worth losing my precious time with Tommy but I had listened to my parents tell me for the last few days that my life needed to go on despite what was going to happen to Tommy. I did not think they understood what they were talking about because they had not seen him lying there alone yet. I knew my mom would break down. If she had then she could understand why I needed to be there.

I drove the car home as fast as I could. I hurried in the shower and tried to eat something before I was off on the voyage to say goodbye to Tommy for the last time. I dried myself off and picked out my clothes.

What clothes do you wear to say goodbye in? I decided to wear something respectful but I knew I needed to be comfortable because I would be in the same clothes for a few days. I stood in front of all the hangers and slide each one across the dowelling as if I was making the hardest decision of my life.

I jumped into a panic when the phone rang. I did not want to pick it up but I wondered if it might be Mom calling from work to tell me she was going to be home soon. I was wrong.

"Hello?"

"Hello," it was Sandy, her voice sounded very distressed.

"Hello?"

"I told Tommy's sister I would call you."

"Why?"

"She said she had a lot of other calls to make."

"About what?"

"They said that Tommy was not going to make it through the night and everyone needed to come as soon as they could. We need to go today."

I looked at the clock on the wall that said almost three.

"They did?"

"Yes."

"My mom does not get home from work until about four. She was going to come with me tonight because of what was going to happen tomorrow."

"We are leaving around five for the city. Do you want to come with us?"

"Who is going with you?"

"My boyfriend is driving Shelly, Jeff, and me."

"I will see. I will call you or meet you at your place as soon as I can."

"Okay."

I went back into my room and resumed endlessly searching through the shirts. I had already looked at them seven times. Nothing in this closet was right. I was still wrapped in my wet towel from the shower when what she had said on the phone hit me. Today was really going to be the last day.

I sat on the bed and looked at the clock. It was ten minutes to four. Mom was going to be home soon, and I really needed to get a move on to go. We would be leaving in an hour for the final trip. I did not want to go. I hoped they were wrong again just one more time I hoped they were wrong.

I did not hear my mother come in from the howling agony that was coming from my soul. Flashes flicked through my mind of Tommy and everything we had done together. The only thing I could remember most was looking down at him on the bed while he took off his mask looking up at me. "I love you," was the very last thing I heard him say. "I love you too," were the last words I could be sure that he consciously knew I had said. I wanted to go back in that moment in time and stay forever. He had said that he wanted to spend the rest of his life with me, and this was finally it.

I looked at the necklace he had given me a few short weeks ago that he had gotten specially made by his cousin's husband. One pearl that was surrounded in gold hung around my neck. I thought about him being the one pearl in the whole entire world that I wanted to save. I wanted God to lift him up from the bottom of whatever ocean he was in and bring him to the surface again one more time.

"Don't go, Tommy; please don't go," I cried, but somehow I knew it was already too late.

Mom had given me a ride into town to meet Sandy and the rest of the gang when it was somehow decided that she was not coming with us, something about not being enough room in the car. I really did not care if she came or not, because I had felt that I had come through most of this journey with only Tommy anyway. I felt as if she offered little support through this. What good would the last few hours do now? I was angry at her for wanting to come in the first place, as it seemed she always had other things to do when I needed her before. I thought she was just pretending to care because she had told me time and time again he was going to die, now if this was finally it, what difference did it make if she was there? What support could she be to me now? I felt like all the times I really needed someone it was easier to find comfort in a stranger than my family because they were always too busy for me. I might have needed her before but not now. She did not understand me anymore, and she would have just made things harder. I could not explain how I felt to her without some kind of lecture about how I should have known this was going to happen, and it was somehow my own fault for falling in love, and I somehow deserved this pain. I thought she might say that because I knew it was going to happen it should not hurt so much and that time would heal the wound, and I would feel better soon.

I do not think she would understand that my love must have been blind because even if I saw it coming I did not want it to. Even if I knew one day that this was really going to happen it was my worse fear and the knowing did not make it easier, it made it harder. Nonetheless I was in no mood for lectures. I just wanted to crawl inside myself and die right along with him.

I ran into the hospital as soon as we arrived and up to the second floor where Tommy was. I pushed open the big orange door to the isolation death ward. Coming from behind me in the distance I heard someone say, "He is not down there anymore." I turned around to see who it was, and then saw the drawn-out faces of a few of the people I knew. I looked up at Tommy's father who was standing talking on a telephone. His voice rang in my ears, as it was the only thing I could hear.

"This is Tom, Senior. My son Tommy died at four o'clock this afternoon. I am calling to make the arrangements for his funeral."

I looked into the small waiting room full of people who had now become unfamiliar to me. It was like I did not know them anymore. In that instant I knew I had no connection to these people. I saw an old woman sitting in the corner being consoled by someone that looked like her with a box of Kleenex on her lap. The old woman looked as if she had been crying for a long time. She wiped the tears as she looked up at me but said nothing.

I turned and walked away from the group of people toward the other waiting room toward a set of telephones. I dialed my own number and waited for Mom to pick up the phone. I told her of the news but she had already received the message. She sounded as if she was still mad at me for not coming with us but I did not care. Her feelings were not the priority here.

I hung up the phone and turned to see Tommy's sister standing behind me waiting for something. She walked toward me and put her arms around me as I stood numb. "I know mom hated you, but the rest of us knew how much Tommy loved you and what you did for him," she said.

I looked at her as if her words meant nothing. She knew nothing of my love for her brother. How could she understand? She was not the one with her nose pressed up against the glass waiting for him to get well.

I pulled away from her hug and walked toward the room where Tommy had been. I stood and looked through the glass at the empty room. No monitors, no chairs, no nurse, no blankets and no bed. The stool was tucked up under the desk where the nurse had sat.

"I am sorry; he is gone," I heard a white coat say. For a moment I could see this man from behind his stethoscope and his diploma, for he, too, appeared sad. Of all the people around me now, he understood the most.

"Yes, he is." I looked directly into his eyes, then mumbled my words before I turned and walked slowly down the long hallway back to the stairs. I did not know why I went to his room. I guess I just needed to see for myself.

I heard the sound of my own agony as I ran down the empty hallway out into the sun. I sat on a picnic table and screamed in pain. Nothing had prepared me for this moment. I had no idea Tommy's ultimate relief would feel this excruciating.

The man passing on the street stopped to look at me for a moment and then kept walking. I put my head in my hands and all I could do was hysterically rid myself of all the pent-up emotions that had been hidden for so long. I could finally cry. I could finally fall apart. I could finally let go. It was over. Tommy was gone forever.

The picnic table creaked and twisted as I looked up to see Shelly sitting beside me. She was crying, too. She put her arms around me for comfort, but there was none. However, I understood her intentions.

Two brothers-in-law were next to come to my aid. Again they hugged me, but I could not feel their arms around me. I was gone too. My heart had been ripped from my soul. All that I lived for was gone. My world ended at four o'clock that afternoon. I was mad at God. *You son of a bitch. You did not let me go with him. Now what am I supposed to do?*

"Come back inside, Emily. Come sit with the others."

"Why?"

I finally stopped crying and was convinced that returning to the group was a good idea. I stood outside the doorway and refused to go in the dreary little room where they sat.

I could hear talking about what had happened. "We were all in the room, and he opened his eyes. He was looking around for something for a few moments. He then looked toward Sue and said, 'I love you,' then looked at his mom again before he closed his eyes and died."

"Why would he say that to her?" someone asked.

"He was looking for Emily," I heard someone else say, "but she was not there; he most likely thought Sue was her."

My knees buckled, and I leaned against the wall until I could not hold my own weight. I rested my head against my knees and began to cry again.

I am sorry, Tommy. I am sorry I went home and was not here for you when you left, I said in my head over and over again. *I am sorry.*

The Funeral

I woke up in the morning still in the goodbye clothes from yesterday. I knew what happened last night was not a dream even if I had wished it was. I gazed at the ceiling without blinking and counted the tiles. I had wondered why I had not known how many ceiling tiles I had in my room before. I could hear my mother in the kitchen cleaning the house with the radio blaring country and western tunes. I was definitely home and this was the first day that life was going on without Tommy.

I am not sure how long I lay on the bed until I heard my mother calling my name from the kitchen. "Emily, Emily, it is time to get up. You need to shower so I can take you and get some new clothes for the funeral. It is already after lunch."

I rolled over in my bed as if I had not heard what she said. I did not want to get up. I did not want to go shopping for a new dress to bury my best friend.

She opened the door and called my name again, "it is time to get up."

"In a minute," I responded.

I began to cry again as I heard my mother talking on the phone to a person I knew was Tommy's mom.

"If there is anything we can do to help you," she paused, for a moment.

"Yes," she paused again. "I understand. My husband and I would like to pay for the funeral." She waited, "I see. Can we pay for a casket? Buy Tommy a suit? I know finances are difficult for you, please," she begged, "we would like to help in some way if we could."

"I understand but if there is anything you need or that we can help with, please let us know," she begged again.

I knew that Tommy's family did not have a lot of money to pay for a costly funeral. I also knew that his family would not accept any kind of charity from us. I knew my mother would be disappointed in not being able to help them. I knew she would not want Tommy to have a government-funded funeral service, but if his family would not accept our help, what else was she supposed to do?

We finally arrived at the mall and got out of the car. I turned when I heard someone call my name. It was Tommy's sister, the one that had donated the bone marrow, along with her husband. They were both walking in my direction. I turned to walk away, but my mother had told me to stay. I did not want to see either one of them.

Tommy's sister gave me a hug. I hugged her back. I could feel her pain radiate from the sound of her voice. She looked tired, and her eyes were all puffy underneath, like she had been crying. We exchanged a few words, and she said she was there to purchase some new clothes, too.

My mouth dropped open with surprise as I looked at Tommy's brother-in-law, and he was wearing a pair of jeans and a tee shirt that was Tommy's. I could not believe Tommy had not even been gone twenty-four hours, and he was wearing his clothes. I thought about it a bit more and thought that Tommy would have given him the stuff if he had wanted it anyway. Maybe he felt closer to Tommy that way.

Mom and I went into the store, and I looked around at some dresses. I hated dresses. I looked around for a skirt instead. I flipped through the rack over and over. I am picking out a skirt for Tommy's funeral. I finally decided on a short black one because Tommy would like that.

I went over to the first black silk shirt I found and picked it up, too. I went to the lingerie section and found a black bra and black panties. Then black nylons for underneath.

"I am ready to pay," I told my mother, who was also looking for a dress.

"You do not have to wear all black, you know," she said, when she saw what I had in my arms.

"That is how I feel, all black."

I found myself lying on my bed, staring at the ceiling again. I had no where to go and no one I wanted to be with now. I had nothing to do but lie there while my heart continued to break. I did not want to do anything but die and be with Tommy. I knew he would be waiting for me in heaven if I went now before he forgot me. Maybe he will be reincarnated, and I will not find him again until the next life.

I wonder what it is like to be dead. I wonder if he is happy there. I wonder if he can see me now. I wonder if he will haunt me like he said he would. I wonder if he saw me crying. I wonder where he is. I wonder if all his pain is gone. I wonder if he is glad to be there. I wonder if he is ultimately free. I wonder if he has met God. I wonder what he would ask Him if he had. I wonder if his spirit is gone now and he is just caught in nothingness. I wonder if he is floating around in the sky watching us from above. I wonder if he is sitting here beside me trying to tell me he is here.

Dear God, I began to pray, *I am sorry I got mad at you. I wish you would have let Tommy stay here with me. I wish you would not have taken him away."* I began to cry again. *"But I know in my heart that it is better that he is not trapped in that sick body anymore. If he is there with you, and I know he is, please tell him that I love him. Please tell him that I promise I will love him forever. Please take him with you and protect him, because he deserves it. He has been through so much pain and suffering here. Please be good to him there, and keep him happy. Please tell him that I miss him, and I am sorry I was not there when he died. I think it was better that way, anyway. I would have not wanted to see him go. Please tell him that I will never forget him, no matter how long I live. I will love him forever, just like we planned. God, please take care of my best friend because now I can't. Amen.*

I could hear the phone ringing through the closed door. Mom was talking to someone about Tommy. Then she was talking about me. She called my name from the kitchen. I closed my eyes to pretend I was asleep. I knew it was not Tommy so I did not want to talk to anyone. She opened my door and called my name again. I lay still.

It was a while later when she opened my door again to check on me. She told me it was one of my friends on the phone saying there was a party tonight and wondered if I wanted to go. Mom said she thought it would be a good idea so I could at least get out of my room for a while but she did not understand I wanted to do nothing. I wanted to fade away. I wanted to melt between my sheets and become invisible to the world.

When I heard the knock on the door I knew it was my friend coming to get me. I had not gotten up from the bed yet. I intended to say that I had a headache so I was not going to go. I knew she would not want to wait for me to get ready so she would go on her merry way without me. I did not want to go to a party. I had nothing to celebrate.

The next thing I knew I was standing around a bonfire talking to a guy from high school telling me about when his father had cancer and died a while ago. I took another big drink of the liquid Band-Aid and told him I was sorry for his loss.

"I know how you feel for losing someone you love." He was trying to be sympathetic.

My voice echoed inside my head, "know how I feel…someone I loved?" He had no idea. Why did people think it would make me feel better to share the horror stories of someone else with cancer to make me feel better? To prove I was not alone? I was alone. I knew I was not an island to myself. I felt like I was an island that the water had dried up all around and now I was standing neck deep in the sand that I could not get out of. Beach sand that sunk in my throat so deeply I could not even scream. Sand that was so hot that it peeled my flesh and burnt to the bone, sand that was so fine it scratched my eyes, stuck in my lungs, sand that smothered me.

"Thanks," was all I could tell him.

The party was filled with guests from our small town gang. It was not long until one of the older guys came and rescued me from this conversation. I wondered if he could see from the other side of the fire I wanted an escape.

"You don't look like you're having fun over here," he observed.

"I am not. I want to go home." I was trying not to cry again.

"Come with me for a ride. Let's get you out of here."

I climbed in the passenger side of the car while he held open the door. He slowly put the key in the engine and turned the ignition. The radio in the car was on full blast as soon as the battery engaged. He turned it down.

"Sorry," he apologized, but he did not need to.

He drove for about fifteen minutes and then pulled the car into a field lane. He disengaged the engine but left the radio on. He pulled out a pack of smokes but then lit a joint without saying a word.

We sat in the car in the dark and smoked for a while. I had missed my friend, and I was relieved he had bailed me out from the party. I was glad to be away from the city and in his company. With him I knew I could be myself. I knew I did not have to have sex with him for comfort, I knew I could cry if I wanted to. I knew I could talk about Tommy if I wanted. At last I knew I could just be me. I was truly safe in the comfort of my friend.

"I don't think I have ever seen you wear all black before," he noted, then pointed to my outfit.

"It's an expression of my mood." I tried to smile, but couldn't.

As we sat in the car in silence in the hot, August air, he put his arm around me in consolation. The human touch felt good, and it was reassuring that with the support of a good friend I might get through this grief for tonight.

Everyone was drunk by the time we got back to the party. We smoked another joint after we got out of the car to catch up on the intoxication. He grabbed two more beers out of the cooler full of ice and opened them both. He handed one to me, and I took a drink. My throat was dry from the joint and all the sand I had swallowed on my island.

We walked back to the fire and stood by ourselves. In a matter of minutes someone from our group came and stood beside us to chat with another joint. We both engaged in the offer. This was as good as a time as any to get as wired as I could.

My old companion did not leave my side for the rest of the night at the party. I was glad I had his company because I was not in the position to make any good choices on my own. At least one of us could be the sound voice of reason while I got drunk. I knew he would take care of me in anyway I needed. The comfort of an old friend is comparable to nothing during this kind of sadness, something I had not known before today.

The hang over hit me before I even got out of bed for a drink of water. I was parched from the pot, cold beer, fire smoke in the cool summertime night air. It was not like the air in the city that is always so hot and filled with poisons. I felt like someone had crushed in my head with a bat and flipped my stomach upside down. I cannot even remember how many beers I had last night or what time I got home.

The blankets were wrapped tightly around my feet as I tried to kick them off to get up. I could hear the county and western in the background, and Mom was doing something in the kitchen. I hated that radio. I wish I had not bought her that now for Mother's Day last year. I guess I was not thinking much about the future when I picked that gift out, but I knew she liked it.

"Fuck!" I complained out loud.

"I thought you could wear this today for the visitations," she said as she stuck her head through the door of my bedroom.

"Yeah, " I said, but I did not even look at the hangers she was talking about. That would be fine, at least I did have to try to try to pick anything out for myself.

I crawled into the shower and tried to hold my head up. I thought I was going to puke. I washed my tears down the drain with the soap from my hair. I looked down at my chest because I thought my heart had disappeared. I looked for the caved hole in my chest where it had once been. I could not believe today was the day I was really going to see Tommy dead. I did not want to go. I wanted him back.

I stepped outside into the hot humid air. The oxygen was so hot it was hard to catch my breath. I could feel the sweat run down my back as I cut the red rose from the climbing bush in the front of our step. My palms were sweating and my hands were shaking.

"Let me help you," my father took the scissors from my hands and cut two perfect roses from the picky bush. "This one is for you." He handed me the rose as he held me in his arms as I cried out loud again.

Mom was still in the bathroom curling her hair. I sat down on the old chair beside the door that had been my grandfather's. I wondered how he was doing. I think he was in the hospital again. I need to remember to ask my mom later but now did not seem like the right time.

The high heals of my shoes clicked on the steps of the funeral home as I approached the door. I walked up with Mom but she had stopped to talk to someone along the way. I wanted to keep walking as fast as I could because I just wanted to get this over with. I could not deny now where I was or what I needed to do. Everyone's tears proved this to be real. We all could not be having exactly the same nightmare.

I pushed open the door and began to walk down the red carpet. I looked at the flowers ahead of me as I trod past the benches for the guests to sit on. I was still holding the flowers from garden my father had given me. I wanted to give it to Tommy to take with him forever.

I wished I was walking down a wedding aisle holding a rose that Tommy had given me while he was waiting for me at the other end. I wished that he was standing there, smiling, waiting to say he loved me and could not wait to start our new lives together. I wished he was waiting to take me as his wife and we could be together forever. I wished he was not going into eternity without me. I wished I was not walking down the aisle alone. I wished he was not waiting for me at the end of the row in a box with a lid.

I got to the casket and looked down at Tommy. He was wearing the same suit he had bought for my sister's wedding last year. He was very pale and had pink makeup all over his face. His hands were folded in front of his chest. He was bloated and looked as if he would explode if you touched him. I could hardly recognize him except for the amia on top of his head. He did not look peaceful. He did not look like he wanted to be dead. He did not look like Tommy. He looked like a tired old man. He did not look like he had gone gently to heaven.

My knees buckled, and I staggered back on my heels. I was on my way to the ground until someone behind me caught me behind my waist and picked me back up.

"Are you okay?" I heard a male voice ask.

I turned around, and it was Tevin standing behind me. Victoria was by his side helping him stand me back up on my feet. I could see my mom and dad walking behind them up the aisle.

I could smell the death flowers in the air. I could hear people's voices saying Tommy's name in the distance. I could hear Tevin say again, "Are you okay?"

"No." I began to cry.

My mom took me by the hand and we stood in front of Tommy again. I gently closed my eyes. If I could not leave this horrid place in body I at least wanted to hide behind my own eyes. *This is not real. Tommy is not dead. This is not real.* My own voice raged in my head.

"Put the rose in his hands." My mom told me what to do.

I raised my hand and lifted the gift toward the casket. I reached over to Tommy's hand, and I let go of the flower. I dropped it on his arm. I could not touch him. This was not Tommy. Tommy is not here. He is gone now. This is a body with no soul. This body did not die at rest. This body was tired and worn and had to unwillingly let go of this life. Tommy's spirit was gone. He was dead.

"Put it in his hands," Mom repeated herself.

"I can't. I can't touch him." I began to cry harder.

My mom picked up the flower and placed it between his palms.

Tommy's sister was standing beside me now. She put her arm around behind my waist and gave me a half of a hug. "Mom gave them your necklace to put on him. See?" She pointed. "But it would not fit around his neck so they just set it there."

"Thank you."

"Mom told them to take it off him and give it to you before the service tomorrow."

"Thank you."

My friends came up the steps one by one to comfort me. The friends Tommy had arrived as well. Two of the nurses from the hospital arrived just before the visitations were over.

"He always talked about you," one of his favourite nurses smiled.

"He talked about you too," I tried to smile back.

"He always waited for you to come," the other nurse said.

I tried to smile.

"He had the sexiest underwear in the hospital" she said. We all laughed.

They both gave me a hug before they went in to see him for the last time.

I went back in to see him again just before I left. I again looked down at him and could still not believe what I saw. I wanted to crawl in beside him and have them bury me tomorrow, too. I wondered why God had not allowed me to go with Tommy to the other side. I wondered how He could be so cruel.

"It's time to go." My Mom took me by the arm and led me toward the door.

It was dark when we got outside. I stood by the door on the top of the steps. I turned to look again inside at Tommy lying in the casket. I did not want to leave him here alone.

Goodbye, Tommy

I drank the pink Champagne out of a wine glass as I put on my black bra. I took a big gulp as I sat on the bed and looked at the clock. It was almost time for the funeral. Today was the last day I would ever see Tommy again.

I slowly pulled up my black hose over my pale skin. I took another drink. I closely buttoned each button in every proper hole. I tucked in my black silk shirt and zipped up my black skirt at the back. I took another drink of Champagne. I closed my eyes and knew I would never feel this kind of sadness again. I knew this was the worst thing in the world that could have ever happened to me.

I wanted time to reverse itself to even a few short months ago. I had not had enough time with Tommy. I had not said all that I wanted to say. We had not done all the things we wanted to do. I wanted to take it all back and do it all again. I wanted to do things differently this time. I wanted to make love to him more. I wanted to tell him again I loved him. I wanted to see him smile more, talk more, walk with him more, sit in the setting sun with him more, wake up with him more, read another book to him, look at the paper with him, hold his hand, have one more smoke, one more beer, one more glass of pink Champagne, one more anything, just one more.

I opened my eyes and saw my black silk shoes at my feet. I slid one foot in at a time as I asked them help me stand up today when I could not do it on my own. I took the last drink out of the wine glass and stood up from my bed. I sighed. I was not ready for this.

I poured another glass of Champagne and walked into the summer sun. Dad was already outside cleaning the car. I went over to the rose bush and looked at is fruit. I picked a budding flower and placed it in the top pocket of my shirt. If Tommy were here he would have given me this exact rose. I took another drink. I was now ready to go.

We waited outside at the funeral home because we had come a few minutes early. We talked to some of the family who were already waiting on the street.

The doors were opened we all walked in together. I saw Tommy's Dad standing by the casket with his wife. Someone else was bent over the casket giving Tommy a kiss. I had seen the flash of a camera when his aunt took a picture. I looked at Mom in disbelief for an answer to what they were doing.

Today Tommy looked blue under his makeup. The makeup was smeared from the continuous touches to his hands and face. I wanted to scream at them to finally leave him alone. He would not want them mauling his dead body. He wanted to be at rest. What was wrong with those people? Tommy would never want them to have pictures of him dead.

They closed the curtains after we all said our goodbyes. I could hear the latches close one by one. Tommy's Mom and I started to cry. I could hear her voice was now louder than mine. She wanted him back, too.

I turned to sit on the bench beside my parents, but someone had already taken my spot. I sat down in the front row beside Tommy's sister. I did not want to sit in the front row. This was a show I wanted to miss.

The man in black stood before me with his hand out. "I think this is for you," he said as he handed me Tommy's necklace. I looked up at him in surprise and took the gold cross and chain from his palm. "Thank you." I looked down at the gold heart surrounded by the words, "I love you." I remembered his last words.

The minister began to pray for Tommy's soul and talk about God. I thought all the things he was saying were wrong. This was not the time to ask God for help. It was too late for that. I wondered how this man could stand up in front of us and tell us how wonderful God was. God was not great because he took Tommy away. God had not helped when I asked in desperation long ago. Instead He turned his back on us. It was God's fault Tommy was sick in the first place. It was God's fault Tommy was dead.

I heard myself crying, and I could feel my eyes were stinging and my cheeks were wet but this was not real. This was a dream I had to wake up from. I would wake up and Tommy would be holding me in his arms on the steps of the school, or we would be waiting for the bus. He would be wearing his brown leather jacket smoking a cigarette and carrying a few books. It was really Valentines Day, and I must be mad at him for not buying me flowers, and that is why I am having this bad dream. I want to wake up, I want to wake up, I want to wake up.

I gazed down at the chain that was dangling in my hands. A drop from my eye fell on my hand. I picked up my head and saw the casket again. The dozen red roses I had bought him were now being carried out by one of his friends. Everyone around me had already stood up while I still sat on the hard wooden bench. I was not sure why. I had gotten lost in my dream.

God, please strike me dead. It isn't too late. I want to go with him. Please don't let them take him away. My heart cried as I watched them carry him out.

I followed behind, third from the casket. I watched as they rolled his body down the red carpet and into the back of the long black car. I stood in disbelief. I watched as they carried the rest of the flowers and stacked them one after another in the back of another car. I tried to blink it away. I could not breathe. The doors on the back of the black car clicked locked one at a time. This would be his final ride.

"You don't have to stand here and watch this." Dad took me by the arm and led me to our car.

I got in the back as my dad held open the door. My head hit the seat when it flew back from the pain in my heart. I began to howl in pain again. This time I could not stop. I wanted to go in the same car with him.

They put the blue box on top of the hole that was dug in the farthest corner of the graveyard. This was going to be where Tommy lay forever. I looked up at the trees that shaded the ground and asked them in silence to keep him cool from the sun.

The flowers were arranged on the ground in a row by the time I arrived to the grave site. The guys had set mine near the front where his head would be. I wondered if someone had done that on purpose. I wondered if Tommy could see my roses from wherever he was. I hoped he liked him.

The minister finished his prayer and poured a salt cross on the casket. I fell back into the arms of my father as I almost fell to the ground. My mom caught me on the other side of my body when I grabbed for her support. I hoped this was the sign that God was taking me too.

"Were you married?" the minister came over and asked me.

"No."

"Did you have any children together?"

"No."

"Why not?"

"Tommy couldn't have kids from the treatments. He would not have wanted to pass this on to anyone even if he could have."

"I see. He talked of you often. He loved you a lot."

"Yes. I loved him, too."

My father led me by the arm away from the pile of earth that would cover Tommy soon. "I will bring you back here later if you want, but you do not have to stand here and listen to this," he meant everyone crying.

A few of my friends came back to our house after the funeral. They drank a few beers, and I finished the champagne. We talked about Tommy for a while. My mom was telling a story about one day when Tommy had just gotten out of the hospital a while before, and she had arrived home from working a twelve-hour shift in the factory and Tommy was outside cutting our grass with a push mower. She yelled at him to stop because he was so sick, but he didn't. I remember her coming into the house while I was doing dishes and she started yelling at me to make him stop. I told her I had already tried that, but I think he just wanted to make himself feel useful to help himself feel normal, not sick anymore. I wondered if that was what it would really be like if Tommy got better and we lived as man and wife. He would be outside cutting our lawn while I did house work inside or was busy with the babies we might have had. I understood why Tommy was cutting the grass even if Mom was upset about it. Tommy liked my parents a lot and would do anything to help them out if he could. While my father worked away and my mom was working twelve-hour shifts, I tried to help out around the house as much as I could, and Tommy just wanted to do his part, too, for all that he felt that my family had done for him. I was amazed at even when death is knocking at your door, he would still try so hard to help. If there was one thing about Tommy, for sure, he was not going to give up and go silently into the final goodnight.

I understood the condolences of my friends and the thoughts in their hearts were pure, but I wished they would all leave. I wanted to be alone. I had nothing else that I could say out loud that would make things any better. I had nothing left I could feel in my heart today. The feeling of nothingness would certainly be better than feeling the way I was right now. I just wanted it all to go away and wake up in the morning to the phone that I knew was not going to ring and hear his voice again. I wanted this all to be another one of those crazy nightmares that I was suffering from, but in my heart, I knew it was real.

My New Life

I returned to work two days after the funeral. It was a good distraction from my emotional state. The boss left me alone most of the time and did not seem to mind if I had come to work smelling of last night's drink. He did not care as long as I did what I was required.

I had called Eric and told him of the news. He had little reaction to my situation although wanted to be supportive. I told him that I did not need anything when he asked but he wanted to come and see me anyway. I imagined he heard me tell him that Tommy was gone a million times in his head but he did not say anything about that. I wondered if he was happy Tommy finally died.

I had not seen Eric in a long time and things seemed so different for me now. I was not sure what he would want from me, and I hoped some big commitment was not in his mind since Tommy was gone. Eric and I had several trust issues between us. I knew I would never believe he would not be without a girlfriend as long as he was that far away from me no matter what he said. He would have been wise to believe the same of me.

It was a hot, muggy afternoon, and I had finished work early. I picked up the phone and dialed Tommy's number. I had heard at the funeral service that Tommy's father had ordered a headstone for the grave but was not sure how he would pay for it. Someone mentioned that it would be a good idea if we all gave money toward flipping the bill. I had not committed to giving anything at the time because I thought it was a morbid topic of discussion. Today I thought that it would be a good idea to investigate exactly what was going to happen in that regard.

"Hello," Tommy's mom answered the phone.

I wanted desperately to ask if Tommy was there just as I had a million times before.

"Hello."

As soon as she heard my voice she started to cry.

"I am calling about bringing some money to you for the headstone if that would be okay?"

"Yes, that would be nice, but you do not have to pay anything."

"I know, but I want to help out as much as I can. I will be there in about an hour if that is okay."

"Yes, that is okay."

The drive to Tommy's house was very strange. I felt like I did not know where I was going. My automatic responses led me to where he had lived, but my mind was lost in the depths of despair.

I knocked on the door and walked into the house. Tommy's dad greeted me at the door and gave me a hug. I took my shoes off at Tommy's door as usual. It was an automatic response.

"You can go in there if you want," Tommy's mom called from the living room.

The door to Tommy's room was open. I stood under the frame and looked inside. The room was just as it was the last time I had seen it the night before we had gone to the city to the hospital. The bed was neatly made in the same blankets, the lamp was lit, the clothes were hung on hangers in the closet but there was one thing that was different. The dozen red roses that I had sent to the funeral were sitting on the top of his dresser in the clear glass vase that had come from the store.

I put my nose up to the flowers and smelled them, although I did not need to because I could smell them from the door. I looked at the card that was still attached to the red ribbon that surrounded the vase, All of My Love, Emily. I looked at each perfect flower and noticed they were starting to wilt. I was glad that the flowers had lasted this long. I thought they would have died long before now.

"You can take them if you want." Tommy's mom was now standing in the kitchen watching me.

I tried not to cry. "No thanks. I would like to leave them here."

I handed her an envelope that contained some money for the head stone. This was the first time I had ever given her anything. I hadn't even given her a Christmas gift before. Tommy said that I did not have to, but now I wish I would not have listened to him.

She thanked me for the money and invited me to come in to sit for a while. I did not know what I might talk to her about so I thought it was best if I left.

I wanted to go visit the grave anyway. I had not been there since the other day. She said she had not been there either but declined the offer to ride along with me.

I pulled out of his laneway and drove toward the lake where Tommy's body lay. I was not sure of what direction I needed to go as I had not been paying attention the day Dad drove us there after the service. I knew in what general direction I needed to go in, and I was sure if I followed the lake road sooner or later I would come to the graveyard.

"The graveyard. I am going to a graveyard to see Tommy," I said out loud to myself while I drove. "Weird."

I could see the freshly dug dirt as I parked beside the road and got out of the truck. I was glad for Tommy that his resting place was in the back corner under a shade tree in this remote area on the lake shore road. I knew he would like to be in the back corner just like the seat he would choose at school or something.

I could also see all the flower arrangements that had been left here after the service. I did not want to be bothered to look at any of them. I really did not care much who sent what arrangement for him. I guess that was a family thing or something.

I knelt down beside the mound of dirt that covered his body. I wondered what he looked like now after lying in the casket with no air in the dark for several days. I knew his body must be already starting to rot. I could imagine the bugs that were eating him from the inside out. I imagined maggots, like in a rotten piece of meat.

I started to violently cry again. I could not stop myself. I had no reason not to anymore. I could finally let out years of pent up sadness, fear and sorrow go. There was not one soul here to hear me now. I could fall apart.

The sand slipped through my fingers as I picked it up to hold it for a while. I thought of what the minister said about ashes to ashes and dust to dust. If we really turned to dust when we died, why did we try to preserve ourselves in boxes? I wondered if Tommy would have rather been cremated and spread out someplace. I do not ever remember us talking about that. I guess he must have talked that all over with his parents since that was their responsibility.

I lit a smoke and lay down beside the pile of sand. I closed my eyes and prayed again to God.

Father in Heaven, please take me now to be with Tommy. It has only been a few days since he has been gone, but I hate it here without him. I am not sure what I am going to do. I am nobody's favourite anymore. I do not have anything left in my heart that I love. I have no reason to be here. I want to go with him.

It was as if I could hear Tommy talking back to me in my head after I prayed. I could hear his voice saying, "Emily, I am okay now. God says you cannot come here. You have so much to live for, even if you cannot see it. You have to be stronger than ever. You have to fight and live for yourself. I will always love you, and you will always be my favourite. I will never leave you. I will always be right here in your heart."

I sat up and looked around because I was sure I could hear something in the distance. The sun was setting, and it was getting dark. Out from the trees I saw a shadow of something I was not sure what it could be. I was not scared because I knew nothing could hurt me now. I hoped that God was sending a monster out of the trees to come and kill me so I could go now. I knew no monster that would come from the trees would ever be as bad as the monster we had just fought and lost the battle with but I was ready for anything.

What about me? my own voice screamed in my head. *What about me?*

I felt something behind me rubbing against my back. I turned around to see the monster I had hoped for, but it was just a tortoise shell cat.

"Hello." I greeted the cat.

"Meow," it greeted me back.

I picked it up and set it on my lap and began to touch its fur. "Well, it looks like you have a pretty big job to do if you are the one God and Tommy sent to comfort me."

"Meow," the cat said back.

"I am not wishing to be mean to you, but I was hoping for something that might take me to heaven, not rub my back."

"Meow."

"Are you going to tell me that I have to stay here, too?"

The cat began to purr as I rubbed it under the chin and petted its head. We sat for a while on the grass until the sun had faded behind the earth.

"Well, cat," I took it off my lap and set it back on the ground, "I am sure I will see you again sometime soon. Thank you for being my friend for a while."

I stood up as the cat walked back into the woods where it had come from.

I drove along the lake road and headed toward Bobbi's. I was not sure what company I would find there but I knew somehow, somewhere I would find a drink. A good friend and a bottle was all I thought I needed. The drink would have been enough to tie my over at least until I passed out from intoxication but a different distraction would be nice for a while, too. If I was not going to die today I might as well make the most of it.

The rest of the week was uneventful. I went to work every day and then to the graveyard every afternoon. I knew Tommy was not there but at least I had some comfort in knowing I was as close to his body as I could be. Some nights I did not stay long to visit, just long enough to say hello to the turtle cat.

The weekend was finally here, and I was picking Edie up at the bus station. This small town was different from what he was used to. The first thing he made mention of was how everyone stared at him while he was on the bus and while he was waiting for me to pick him up.

"Well, there is really no one that looks like you around here. You do stand out."

"I do not like them looking at me. I almost punched this guy out on the bus, but I did not want to get kicked off."

"Well, it sounds like that was a good idea."

We drove straight from the bus to Bobbi's house so she could meet him. She asked me a few times if I thought I would be safe alone with him as she was a bit taken aback by the ragged appearance of the long curls and tattoos. I reassured her I would be fine as I had not just met him on the street yesterday. I had been alone with him several times.

Bobbi was fine with the idea that Edie and I would spend the next few nights at her house, and he would return to the city after the weekend. She said as long as I thought he was not harmful he could stay with her while I went to work in the harvest. I could come and hang out later after work. I was at her house most of the time now anyway, so that part was not entirely different.

Edie and I had a few drinks with her and a few other friends until Edie and I found our way upstairs. He knew something was a bit off with me but he had not known what kind of tablets Bobbi and I had taken when he was in the bathroom. I was not about to tell him either. He thought I was more intoxicated than I should have been by only having a few drinks.

"What is the matter?" he asked a few times. "You seem different here."

"I don't know. I guess I am different here. You are in my playing field now. I told you we were not the same as you city folk, and now you can understand why I was such a fish out of water where I was in the city, as much as you are here."

"I see now why you would not want to come to the city. Your friends are nice people, and you are right for not wanting to leave them. But I can offer you different things than they can. Come back with me?" he begged.

We spent the night having as much sex as we could before I had to get up a five in the morning for work.

"I do not believe you are leaving this early for work. Can't you call in sick?"

"No, there is no such thing as calling in sick at this job. I have to go."

"You have not even slept yet. How can you work all day like that?"

"I'll be fine." I kissed him one more time. "I will come here as soon as I get done. I will not leave you here any longer than I have to."

"I have to catch the bus this afternoon at six."

"I will be here long before that to get you there. Trust me. You will be fine."

It was a real long day at work. Everyone asked me if I was feeling okay, and they said I looked sick. They were right; I was sick but in another way than they had imagined. I was sick by my own hand from the pills I had taken and the drink.

I showered as soon as I got home from work. The only thing I wanted to do was sleep, but I knew I had responsibility to get Edie back to the bus. I wished that I had not asked him to come and see me, but I knew I would have been just as sick no matter if he had come or not. I would have intoxicated myself anywhere I was.

I was getting dressed in my room when I heard the knock on the door. I was the only one home so I knew I had to get it. I wondered if I did not answer it if they would just go away even though my car was parked out front. If I was quiet in my room I hoped they would think I was sleeping or something.

The knock got louder until I finally heard the door open. I thought it must be someone I knew because it is very unusual someone would come directly into our house.

I heard someone call my name but I could not place the voice. I hurried to dress myself before whoever it was came looking for me.

"Emily!" I heard them call again.

"I am in my room getting dressed," I called back.

Suddenly the wooden door opened and there was Eric standing in front of it, all dressed in leather. I knew he had ridden his bike. "I thought I would come and surprise you," he announced, as he hugged me tightly.

"Surprise is right." I smiled at him. I was not sure how I was going to pretend to act happy at the idea he was standing here in front of me now.

I looked at my watch to see what time it was. The only thing I could think of now what how was I going to get out of this situation and get Edie back in time for the bus.

"Aren't you glad to see me?" he smiled. "What is wrong with you? You look sick."

I pretended to cough. "I am not feeling well. I think I am getting the flu, but I am fine. I have to make a phone call. I was on my way to Bobbi's."

"Call her and tell her you are not coming. What could be more important than me?"

I smiled at him and thought to myself, "*If you only knew.*"

"Nothing. I will just call and cancel."

I finished getting dressed while he waited watching me as he sat on the bed. I was nervous that he was here because I had other things on my agenda to do. I made up an excuse to call Bobbi in private and begged for her help.

"Oh, my gawd, Bobbi, you will not believe who showed up at my door fifteen minutes ago."

"Who?"

"Eric."

Bobbi hysterically started to laugh at my predicament before she asked, "What are you going to do now?"

"You need to get a hold of Tim and ask him to take Edie to the bus."

"Yeah, right," she continued to laugh. "You are going to get someone you are fucking to give someone you fucked last night a ride to the bus because someone who wants to fuck you just stopped by from six hours away. Only you."

Tim had been someone that had been hanging around Bobbi and me for a few weeks now. He was a few years older than I was but must have been real lonely. I hung out with him when Bobbi had other things to do. He also let us use his car when we wanted too and bought us beer. We did not even usually have to ask. I knew I was just using him for whatever I could get but he let me.

"You need to lie for me. I will owe you a big, huge, anything-you-could-ever-want favor for getting my ass out of this hot water. Please help me."

"What do you want me to tell them?"

"I don't know; make something up."

"Like what? Why don't I just tell them the truth?" she laughed.

"Shut up. This is the best reason I can think of to lie to them all. Tell them that the machines at work broke down, and I have to stay at work late. They will believe that. Tell Tim that Edie is my cousin or something from the city. Tim will be glad to get rid of Edie anyway. Tell Edie I will call him later today, and I am very sorry, but I cannot get him to the bus. Tell him that we will come to the city in a few weeks to see him, but today I am really tied up. He will be upset, but he will be fine."

"Okay, but what if Tim says no?"

"Beg him. Tell him it is a favor to me, and I will owe him a big one back later. Right now you just need to get Edie to the bus station."

"Okay, but you owe me big."

"Whatever you want I will give; I promise."

I am not sure how Bobbi pulled that one off but she managed to get Tim to take Edie back to the bus station. I was in deep now to a few people for favours. I knew Tim would take a sexual trade, but I was not sure what I would end up owing Bobbi. I would give her anything she wanted for his help. After all isn't that what friends were for, to help you out in a pinch?

I got on the back of Eric's bike and we rode into the sunset as if everything had always been fine. It seemed we had always been together and were meant to be together right then and always. I remembered all the feelings that I had for him even if they had been buried under tones of feelings for Tommy. It felt like now I was free to love Eric without any guilt of loving anyone else better. It finally felt like Eric was first in my heart. How quickly I had forgotten my lover I was with last night.

I knew that it would not be long until Eric was gone again. He did not have the time to stay long with me. After we made love he asked me if I would like to come to see him up north for a while. I told him that I did not think that would be a good idea just yet as I had some things I needed to finish up here. I had to finish working in harvest before I could do anything else. He understood.

Eric made plans to come and see me again in a few weeks. He was working on some kind of scheme himself where he and his cousin were going to get an apartment close to the big city and get a job in construction. He said if that happened he would like it if I came to visit him for a while. I wondered how long he meant by a while and told him we could see what happened if he actually did move closer.

I lay in my bed as I listened to Eric's bike start up and he pulled away for his long journey back home. I wondered if he was really going to go home or go see if he could round up his other old girlfriend's that he might have in this area. I really did not care where he was going after he left my house I was just happy to have seen him for a while.

I wondered what it would be like to live with Eric. I wondered if he would ever ask me to finally marry him like he said he wanted to a long time ago. I wondered if he just came here because he felt sorry for me because Tommy just died. I wondered if Eric really did love me or was just saying goodbye to

373

me in his own way. I wondered if he would make it back home without killing himself on his bike. I fell asleep wondering if I would ever see him again.

Harvest was almost over, and it was Street Dance again. All my friends wanted to go and they wanted me to go with them. I told them I would rather not go this year and wanted to spend time alone. Of course they knew I was lying because I had gone every other year but to me this year was different.

We made plans to all meet together once we got there as usual. We would sooner or later catch up to each other down town. I waited until after dark to find my way because I had not wanted to go since this would be the first function without Tommy. I did not want to run in to anyone I knew and have them ask me questions about what happened. I did not want to hear one single person tell me they were sorry for my loss and they knew how I felt. Unless they consistently kept themselves intoxicated somehow they did not know how I felt, how could they? I did not even know that.

I had a few drinks on my own before I made my way on foot down to the pier. I sat beside the lighthouse and drank some more. I looked up at the beautiful orange moon as I wiped the tears again from my eyes. I had come to the conclusion that life was not fair and no matter what I wanted or what I tried to do life happened on its own accord. Fair or not, life did not care how I would feel once it was all said and done. I was alone now it this big cruel world and life did not care what happened next and so, neither did I.

I found my friends and continued to drink with them. After a few hours of playing the hiding game from anyone I thought might want to console me we went back to Bobbi's to sit in her front yard and watch all the action. I thought that was a good idea because then if anyone came around I did not want to see I could say I had to pee and not come back outside until they were gone. I do not think Bobbi knew of my silent plan but I knew she would not mind if she did. Of all the people that said they knew how I felt it seemed Bobbi was the only one that knew exactly what I was going through. She knew how sick I was inside myself but as best friends are I knew she would not tell anyone and would like me despite how insane I was becoming. She knew of my bad choices with men now and did not care anyway. I wondered if she just kept me around to amuse herself.

After Bobbi's boyfriend came and all the others were passed out I found myself walking down the empty streets alone. With another cold beer in my hand and a few in my pocket I found my way back down to the pier.

I sat on the edge of the water and threw stones in the bay. I thought of how the ripples were like life. The center of the ripple was Tommy and the circles that surrounded him were those of us he left behind. I threw two stones at once in to see how closely the ripples would fall together.

I remember back to a time where I had never entertained the idea that loving something would eventually mean a loss. I thought about some of the kids I knew in high school and the kind of devastation they had thought they were in by breaking up with a boyfriend. I thought that they were lucky that was the only kind of loss they might know at such a young age. I thought my heart must hurt so much because I loved so much.

I made a promise to myself as I sat thinking of how when the rocks hit the water they also sunk to the bottom of the bay. I would never allow anyone to get into my soul like that again. I promise I will protect myself from love or anything that is remotely close to love so I never have to feel like this again when it is over. I never want to feel like this again no matter what happens.

The lights of the car blinded my pupils as they shone into my eyes. I wondered who else could be out this late at night. The van stopped a few feet from the end of the pier, and I recognized who was getting out of the van. It was Jim.

"What the hell are you doing here?" he asked me as soon as he recognized who I was.

"Nothing. You?"

"Looking for my dog. You have not seen him, have you?"

"No. I have seen no signs of life since I have been here."

"Other than you, I have not either."

"I am not sure I am such a great sign of life, but I am here."

"Climb in," he said, as he held open the door of his van. "You can help me look for my dog."

I sat in the van while Jim drove us to the other side of the boat docks and called again for his dog. He kept calling the dog's name until the dog came running in the direction of his master's call. Jim opened the door and let the mutt inside the van. The reunion was defiantly a happy occasion for them both.

"Want a beer to celebrate?" Jim offered.

"Nah, I got a stash in my pocket." I reached inside my coat to find nothing.

"On second thought, maybe I do."

It was not long before I was in the back of the van with Jim, doing what came most naturally: to be with a boy, intoxicated, making out. I was not sure how long we had been there until I asked Jim to open the door because I needed some air. It was not really air that I needed, and Jim soon realized that when I puked all over the ground that surrounded the tires.

375

"I am sorry," I said. "I guess I had too much to drink."

Jim picked me up and put me back in the van as soon as he thought I had nothing more to vomit and drove me home. I passed out shortly after we had left town and slept the rest of the way home.

We arrived at my house and all the lights were on as my parents were getting up for work. I could see my mom looking out the front door to see who had just pulled up. I knew she would not be happy with my arrival home but she would be at least glad I made it alive.

Jim turned off the engine and walked around to the side where I was. He opened the door and picked me up like a baby and carried me into the house while Mom held the door open for him.

"You can lay her on her bed. You know where her room is."

Jim carried me through the house and laid me down. He then flipped a cover over my body and quietly left. I pretended I was still passed out.

"Thank you for bringing her home." I could hear my mom saying to him.

He was laughing a bit and told my mom he had found me sitting at the pier. He said to tell me if I needed a ride to go back and get my car in the morning I could call him. Mom thanked him again before he left.

The next day I got another surprise phone call. It was the college telling me I had been accepted into the nursing program and that I could start classes in two weeks. I informed them that I would not be attending classes this fall because something had come up that deterred me from being in the right frame of mind to learn.

"There could be nothing that is an important as coming to higher education for a young woman like yourself," the stranger said on the phone.

"I do not have money to pay for it."

"You can apply for student loans once you get here. You would probably be a candidate to receive one. I have seen your name on the waiting list all summer, and now you can finally get in. I think you should come. You will find a way to pay for it somehow."

I could hear her flipping through some papers on the other end of the phone. Then she said, "I see that we have already received some money on your behalf from some grants you were awarded from your high school. Someone must have already put your name in for them, and you were accepted. That does not happen that often. I think you should take this chance to come while you can."

"I am sorry, Miss. I will not be attending this year."

"I should tell you that if you do not come now this money will not be granted to you next year."

"That is okay."

"It is a lot of money and will help with the costs as long as you are enrolled in the nursing program," she continued to explain.

"I understand, but I think it is in my best interests to give the money to someone else."

"You may not ever get this chance again." She was still trying to convince me it was a good idea.

"Look, Miss, I know you do not know anything about me, but my boyfriend just died two weeks ago, and I do not think it is in my best interests to move away from home right now to go to school with no support, no job, no place to live, and no money."

"Oh, I am very sorry to hear that. I understand."

"Thank you anyway."

"You're welcome."

I went again to the grave that night and told Tommy's body about the call.

"Hello, Cat." I patted it on the head. "I got a call today that Tommy would have been proud of. I got a call to go to school to be a nurse. Imagine me, a nurse, taking care of people. I turned them down, though, because I would rather come here to see you every day, Cat. Tommy would be mad at me if he knew I said I was not going to go. I am not sure what I am going to do now, but I know that is not the right thing for me. Maybe I will try to go next year."

"Meow," Cat agreed.

Harvest was almost over, and the summer time parties would soon end, too. The end of the parties every night would seem like it would be a good thing for me, as it was becoming my favourite pastime. I had applied to a few local factories for employment, and I had set myself up to continue to work in the fields. I had no future plans to do anything but work for a while and see what other opportunities came along. I wondered if Eric would soon get a place of his own to live and maybe I would go stay with him.

It was not long before I landed a job in a factory making some kind of wire harnesses for cars or something. I would rather to continue to work in the fields, but my Mom reminded me that was not a full-time job. She thought that it would be a good idea that I had something more stable. I guess she was right in most cases, but I really hated going there to work.

Every day I stood in the same spot and done the same thing over and over again. I wondered how some of the people that worked here for years could just waste their lives like this. Some of the women here had graduated high school, got a job here at this factory, and are now finding themselves not teens anymore but wives and mothers, still standing in the same spot day after day.

I had very little in common with most of the people here. It was not my style to get all dressed up and come to work trying to appear as if I was a contestant in a beauty contest. I did not wear makeup to work, and I did not dress up in nice clothes.

I missed work often. I was always sick. My stomach hurt, I always had a headache, and I always felt tired. I never wanted to do anything besides hang out in my room alone, go to the graveyard, or get drunk with my friends. Mom suggested that I go see a doctor because I was always ill, and maybe I was depressed.

I told the doctor how I was feeling, and he asked some very personal questions about me and my life situation. I told him I was a bit sad because Tommy was gone, but otherwise I thought I was doing well. It must have been obvious to him that I was not being totally honest because he gave me some medication because, he said, my nerves were bad.

"My nerves were bad?" That sounded like something some old lady would have, not me. I was not even sure I had nerves anymore. I was not sure I had any feelings about anything anymore. The only feeling I knew I had for sure was sad, if that is even a feeling, but most of the time I felt nothing at all.

The label on the bottle of the little yellow pills suggested I take one or two tabs a day, as needed. Valium was the name on the bottom of the bottle which contained two hundred tablets. If I took two tabs a day that would be about one hundred days. I did the math in my head. Did the doctor really think my nerves would be better in three and a half months? He did say I could go back and get more pills if I needed them, but I doubted I would even take any at all.

I called in sick from work one more day and thought maybe the doctor was right. I took two little yellow pills and lay on my bed again. I turned on the stereo and put the head phones on and listened to the music. I closed my eyes and drifted away. I did not see monsters this time when I closed my eyes. I saw nothing at all. I felt nothing at all. I did not even feel sad anymore. The hundred-pound weight felt like it had been lifted off my chest, although the rest of my body felt like it could not move. For a moment I had forgotten about how I was starting to hate life and was feeling like I had run far enough. Now I just needed a little rest.

I am not sure how long I was in my room, but when I awoke the little yellow pills had worn off, and I felt the normal sensation of heartache again. My body was heavy, and it was hard to move. I was stiff from sleeping in the same spot for so long but I still did not want to get up and face life again.

I got up to shower and take a few more little yellow pills, as needed.

I made my way to work in the dreary factory. The little yellow pills did not take away the monotony of wrapping tape around wires over and over again. I had difficulty keeping up to the rest of the workers even though I was trying to move as fast as I could. My body seemed like it was in slow motion. The girl that was working behind me on the assembly was getting frustrated because the slower I worked the faster she had to.

"We are not going to make one-hundred-and-twenty-percent production today," she complained.

I said nothing because I knew she was reflecting on the idea that it was because I was working on that line today. I wondered why one hundred percent was not good enough anyway. I wondered who cared how many percent we did we got paid anyway. I wondered why she thought that color lipstick looked good on her and why she was not more concerned with how silly she looked dressed like that. I hoped that I would die right now so I never had to work with her again.

"Let my help you," someone said, from behind me.

I turned to see a blonde-haired, blue-eyed male that appeared to be a few years older than I was. I wondered why I had never seen him around before.

"Thanks," I tried to smile. "I am not very good at this."

"Here," he explained, "try it like this, and maybe that will be easier for you."

I watched him as he showed me another way of taping the wires, hooking them up to the machine and then testing them.

"I bet they make the one hundred and twenty mark when you are here."

He smiled at me without saying a word. He must have known what I was talking about. He helped me work until the dinner bell rang.

I absolutely hated the fact that I had to eat when someone rang a damn bell. I walked slowly to the café, because I never ate much anyway. Sometimes I would go outside to sit in my car alone so I did not have to listen to the frivolous conversations of the beauty-pageant contestants.

He followed behind me as I walked in and sat alone and the table by the window.

"May I sit with you?"

I looked up in surprise. "Sure," even though I could have cared less.

He talked while he ate, and I lit another cigarette while I drank some juice. He introduced himself as Shawn.

After I got to know him a little I decided that his company was better than sitting alone. I was not interested much in what he had to talk about, but it did pass the time. At least when he sat with me I did not have to try to pretend that I could not hear the others conversations and all the gossip they were spreading about everyone else in the factory. I imagined they were talking about me also when they thought I would not be able to hear them. I did not care what they said about me. They did not know me and they had no reason to judge anything I did or did not do. If I was the most interesting thing that had to talk about they sure had a desolate sense of entertainment.

"We could go get something to eat sometime?" I was not sure if he was suggesting an idea or asking a question.

"Sure," I agreed, "I guess we could."

"When?"

"When what?"

"Would you like to go?"

"I don't know."

"Sometime this weekend?"

"I guess."

"Can I have your number?"

"Okay." I wrote it quickly down on a paper because the bell was telling us it was time to go back to work.

It was shortly after I had returned to work the foreman had asked to speak to me in his office. I wondered why, but saying no to the boss was not an option.

"Do you like working here?" he asked me.

I looked at the man sitting across the table and realized that although he was my boss I did not even know his name.

"It is okay," I lied.

"We have noticed that you call in sick a lot. In fact you have worked here almost three months and you have not come to work one full week yet."

"I have been ill."

"Have you seen a doctor?"

"Yes, I am under the doctor's care, and he gave me some medicine that helps me to feel better."

"That is good. We have also had some complaints about you that you are not very personable, and no one really likes to work with you."

"Okay." I was not sure how I should respond to that. "How come?"

"They say that you do not have any friends and do not talk to anyone out on the floor while you are working."

"Why is that a bad thing? I guess I do not have much in common with these people."

"There are a lot of good people that work here; maybe you should try to make friends."

"Why? So they can have someone else to talk about when I am not around?"

"We will give you another chance to get things in order. Otherwise we will have to let you go."

"Okay."

I walked out of the meeting and wondered what exactly he was implying by making some friends around here. I wondered if I should say hello to people that I did not know or ask them how they were even if I did not care. I wondered if making friends with Shawn would be a good idea.

I finished my shift and went home to bed. I tried to sleep but I could not. I kept seeing Tommy in the casket every time I closed my eyes. I wished I could go to the grave to see him but it was too late. I reached for the glass of water that was sitting on my bed and took two little yellow pills. If they did not help me sleep at least they would take my visions away.

The weekend brought forth some more drinks with the girls but Shawn never called. I gathered together with Bobbi and a few of our other friends and sat around and had some meaningful conversations.

"If you could have whatever you wanted, what would it be?" someone brought forth an old idea.

Bobbi started to sing a song that we all knew well, "Oh, Lord, won't you buy me a Mercedes Benz…"

We all laughed.

"I want to go on a date with Nathan," another girl said.

"What do you want?" they finally asked me.

"Tommy back." I started to cry.

I reached in my purse and found the little yellow bottle of pills that I knew would take my thoughts and feelings away. I read the label on the bottle again, AS NEEDED.

Tonight I needed a lot of pills to take away my pain. I poured almost all of the pills that were left in the bottle in my hand and put them all in my mouth at once. I took another drink of alcohol and swallowed them all.

"What the hell?" Bobbi asked, but it was already too late.

I began to cry again.

It was not long before my head felt real funny and started to spin. I wanted to lie down. I hoped this would be my last time. I hoped the pills would make me never wake up. I hoped that in a little while I would see Tommy again.

As I stretched out my feet to get comfortable to die I spilled over someone's drink. The sticky liquid landed on the floor and all over my jeans. I tried to move to clean it up, but my body was heavy. I could not reach out my hand as hard as I tried I could not move a muscle.

I closed my eyes and thought for sure this was the end of my life until I started to vomit. I puked all over the floor in my friend's room and onto my clothes. Again no matter how hard I tried to move my muscles they refused. The next thing I heard was my friend's father yelling at her for something. I could not understand. I looked at my friend who was already awake, and we quietly got up, and I changed my shirt and jeans. I was disappointed I had woken up, but my body did not let me forget what I had done to it last night. My stomach was going into convulsions, and I could hardly hold my head up. I knew this was not an ordinary hangover. I knew it was from taking the pills.

On the way home my friend was talking about something, but I was so stoned I could not comprehend what she was saying. I lay my head back on the head rest of the car and again wished I was dead. I thought waking up in this state was worse than being dead because now I would have to live through the aftermath of an overdose.

I decided since I was not dead I had better get things in order for myself like my boss had suggested. I had made a commitment that I would go to work every day this week, even when I did not want to. I would try my hardest to keep up to the rest of the line and maybe even try to attain one hundred percent. I was not even going to try for anything more than that because perfect was good enough for me.

I thought I might even say hello to some of the girls that I thought had been the most likely candidates who had made the complaints. I was not sure if going on a date with Shawn would not help my cause in that manner but what harm could it do now. He had not called me this weekend so I imagined he changed his mind. I wondered if the only reason why he asked for my number was because he heard the gossip I was an easy lay, and that was why he wanted my number.

I did not know for sure how I was going to drive myself to work because my head was still spinning from the medication. I opened the bottle and took two more. Maybe more drugs would settle the spin long enough that I could at least get myself to work. I would worry about the rest of it when I got there.

"How was your weekend?" someone asked, as I sat down at the pageant table for the first time ever.

I looked at them as if they were insane. If they only knew. "Good, and yours?"

That started a conversation between them that I could avoid talking about myself as well as any eye contact.

"Excuse me," I finally said. I rushed out of the café. I ran into the bathroom and started to puke again.

I could hear someone saying in a quiet voice so that I was not supposed to hear, "I bet she is hung over."

"Or maybe still drunk," the other girl said.

I wanted to walk out of the stall and scream at them, *"No, I am just disappointed to still even be here."* I knew if I did that they would think it was just about being at work. I knew they would not understand that I was upset that I was still alive. I knew they would not understand of love, death and the fear of being left here in the world alone. I could tell that by the way they talked about me. I knew it would only put me in a worse situation so I stayed in the stall while I puked some more.

"I tried to call you on Saturday night." Shawn came up behind me as I walked out of the bathroom. "I could not read the last number you wrote on the paper." He handed it back to me.

"Seven."

"Are you feeling okay? You look ill."

"I am."

"I wondered if you wanted to go out for a drink after work tonight, but if you are sick I understand."

"A drink sounds like a real good idea," I agreed, but thought in my head, *I would probably need more than one.*

I made it through my eight hours of work but every second I wanted leave. I could not wait to hear the buzzer so I could rush out the door to go shower and rest my head. My stomach still felt like it was in knots as I put the key in the ignition to start the car.

"What about our drink?" Shawn was standing at the window.

I looked into his blue eyes and could see through his expression that he was begging in silence. Something inside of his eyes told me he was not like the others and that he really wanted my company. I wondered for a moment what it would be like to be alone with him. I knew I would be safe. After all he had been the only one that was nice to me here.

"Now?"

"Sure."

"On a Monday night?"

"Sure we can go to the bar."

I smiled at him for a moment, "I am not old enough to go to the bar. I am really tired. I am not sure if I can promise that I will be good company." I was making up excuses not to go.

"That is okay. I am sure it will be fine." He smiled.

My head felt like it was going to explode from the pressure on my brain. I did not want to do anything but go home.

"Follow me," he said, and stuck out his finger toward his car.

The next thing I remember was the sun shining through the window as I opened my eyes. I looked around at the unfamiliar furniture, and I was lying on a couch in someone's living room. I raised my head which was still screaming in pain. Shawn was sitting in a reclining chair beside me. I must have fallen asleep here last night.

I sat up slowly and pushed the blankets toward the floor. The sweet man had covered me up sometime last night after I had fallen asleep. I gathered my thoughts and remembered I had started to watch some kind of movie on television while he was out in the kitchen making a drink. I wondered if I had fallen asleep before he had come back to the sofa. I wondered why he would not have woken me up.

The voices of the people at work rang in my head. "…and she stayed over night at his house the first time she had ever been there. I bet they had sex."

The only thing I wanted to do was leave quietly before he woke up. I wished I had just gone home. The pain in my head reminded me of my adventures over the weekend, and I knew it was not a good idea to be here. I knew that Shawn would get the wrong message that I was interested in starting a relationship with him. I did not want that at all.

I thought for a moment about Edie. I wondered if I found him in the city if I could run away with him. I wondered if I quit my job if he would take care of me. I thought about what he must do for money. I knew he did not have a job, and the strange characters I had seen around his place I guessed meant some kind of illegal activities. I may not want to work at a stupid factory for a living, but I did not want to go to jail. Edie was not an option.

I thought of Eric. I could hear his voice in my head saying that he loved me. I reminded myself of all the times he had said he loved me and wanted to be with me. I wondered if that was really true. Why had he not called in a while? He must have been not telling me the truth.

I looked again at the man sitting in the chair beside me. I wondered why he had not tried to sleep with me on the couch or take my clothes off. I had not known anyone before that did not want to rush into having sex with me even when I did not want too with them. I smiled for a moment and thanked God that I was in a safe place even if I was mad at Him for keeping me alive.

I quietly stood up and folded the blanket. I found my way to the bathroom and shut the door as slowly as I could. I did not want it to squeak and wake Shawn up. I turned on the water and splashed my face. I looked in the mirror and saw my own reflection staring back at me.

I looked into my own eyes and for the first time I could see my own sadness, loneliness and despair. I asked myself one question. *What do I want from this man in the other room?* I stood silently and thought for a moment. What was I really doing here? He was a stranger to me, so why had I come into his home?

The first word that came to my head was "comfort." I wanted him to comfort me for a while even if he was a stranger, at least I was not alone, staring at my ceiling waiting for something to happen. Waiting for anything to happen. Waiting for Tommy to call or come back. Waiting for some kind of love to replace him in my heart.

I could hear movement in the other room now. Shawn must be awake. Now that I knew what I might want from him, how was I going to escape for today? How was I going to face my embarrassment of falling asleep in his company? What would I say?

"Good morning," he said, the second I opened the door.

I tried to smile but my heart still hurt from admitting I wanted Tommy back.

"Good morning."

"Did you sleep well?"

"I guess I did. I am sorry I fell asleep so quickly. I have really not been feeling well."

"That is okay. I was tired myself. Coffee?" He handed me an empty cup, but I could smell the coffee brewing.

"Thanks," I said, but I really did not want any coffee. I would have preferred some orange juice.

I looked at the clock to see what time it was. Since we worked afternoon shift I would need to drive home to shower and get ready for work. That could be my excuse to get out of here before he was nice to me. I wondered who would know at work that I had spent the night.

"This is Carson. He is my roommate." Shawn said, as soon as another stranger entered the room.

"Hi," I greeted him.

385

"Sleep well?" he asked.

"Yeah, thanks."

"I came in last night and saw you sleeping, so I tried not to wake you."

"Thanks." Did he not wonder who was on his couch? Does Shawn always bring strangers home after work to sleep?

"Did he tell you he tried to call every number that possibly might be yours on the weekend?"

I looked at Shawn with a smirk. "No, he did not tell me that." I wish he would have called. Maybe I would not be so sick today because I would have not taken all the pills.

"I really need to get going. I have to drive back home before we have to go back to work. I have some things I need to do today," I lied.

"It is still early. If you would like some company I can come with you for a ride." He looked out the window. "Seems like a nice day for a drive."

I was not expecting that at all. I thought for a moment. What was I going to do after I left here? Maybe go to the grave before work and see Cat. Maybe spending time with someone that was alive and well and who wanted to be with me would be a good idea for a change.

"Sure."

"If you want to wait for a few minutes I will shower, and then we can go to your house, grab a bite to eat if you want."

I thought for a moment. Wait for someone? I have been waiting for someone for years, and look how that turned out.

Shawn rode with me to my house, and we had a nice conversation. I still wondered what he wanted from me. I wondered why he wanted to see where I lived. I wondered what he must have done with his time before today.

"The girls at work were talking about you."

"About what?"

"They wondered what was wrong with you that you were so skinny. They said they thought you were anorexic or something because you hardly ever eat. I think they are right. I am starving, and you have not mentioned anything at all about getting some food yet."

"Oh, I guess I am just not hungry. We can eat before we go to my house if you want."

"You did not eat supper at work last night. You did not eat after we got to my house, and now it is breakfast, and you still have not mentioned food. Is there something wrong with you?"

I laughed out loud at his question. "Yes, my friend, there may be something wrong with me, but not eating is not something I give much attention to. I eat when I am hungry, and I do not eat when I am not. It is as simple as that."

"I know, but most people eat sometime sooner or later."

What did this man think he was going to do save me or something? He did not understand that I have gone for days without eating because of stress or waiting in the hospital or not have any money. I was not about to explain my eating habits to him, and it annoyed me that he was even asking.

"Well, the next time you have a conversation about me with the girls at work will you give them a message?"

"Sure."

"Tell the bitches that they can go to hell and mind their own business. My eating habits, my lifestyle, my anything is nothing that they need to concern themselves with. Tell them that if they showed me some respect and kindness then maybe I would talk to them, and tell them I'll give them any answers they would like to know."

"I did not mean it like that. I did not mean to upset you."

"Well, you did." I wanted to turn the car around and take him back home right now. I did not need someone trying to investigate anything about my life and take it back to the girls at work or anyplace else. Who did they think they were? It was not my fault if they were a bunch a fatsos looking to pick on someone.

I immediately got out of the car and went into the house without inviting him in. His hospitality and niceness wore off too quickly for me. As far as I was concerned he could walk home. This was the beginning and the end of this friendship. I just wanted to shower and get him back home as soon as I could. I certainly did not want to go to work knowing the fatsos were talking about everything I did. I certainly did not want them to know I spent the night with Shawn.

"I am sorry. I did not mean to hurt your feelings. It was not like I was talking about you at work."

"What is it like then?"

"Someone had just mentioned that you had worked at the factory almost three months and no one had ever seen you eat."

"I don't know why everyone is concerned with me so much."

"You really don't like working there do you?"

"Slave labour for cheap wages, people who do not like me anyway, they talk about me, they make up stories that they do not know anything about, they gossip, and I hate working afternoon shift. No, I do not like it there."

"Well, Cindy works there and she said she knows you from before."

"Yes, Cindy is a life-long sister of my sister's, not mine. I have known her forever. She took my spot beside my parents at the funeral, and I had to sit in the front row. I was a bit pissed at her."

"Funeral?"

"Yes."

"Who died?"

"It is a long story."

"They must have been close to you if you sat in the front row. Cindy did not mention it."

"Because she is one of the few I can trust not to spread my business around work. I must thank her when I see her today."

"Would you like me to make you something to eat or would you like to go back to town and get something at a restaurant?"

"It is up to you. We can go back to town now and go hang out at my house for a while before work."

I was really not planning on going to work, but I did not want to tell him that. I had remembered the commitment that I was going to try to go every day this week. "Yeah, that sounds like a good idea." It was better than being alone at least.

Shawn and I spent the rest of the day together driving around, eating, and back at his place. It was now time to go the factory again, despite how much I did not want to.

"Do you want to ride together? You can come back and get your car after work if you want."

"Ah, no. I can imagine the stories when they see me getting out of your car. I know they don't like me, but you do not need them talking about you, too."

"I do not care if they talk about me. I do not like them either. I am not from around here, so they talk about me a lot to try to find out what they can. I never tell them anything."

"Where are you from?"

"The East. I came here a while ago to visit my cousin and decided to stay. There was nothing left for me out East, no work or anything, so I came here and got a job."

"Oh, I see."

The shift went well at work. Just as I thought no one talked to me but I could hear the whispers behind my back when I passed certain lines. I felt uncomfortable knowing the boss had said no one wanted to work with me.

What was the use in trying to befriend these people? It certainly would not be for my benefit. I just did what I thought I had to do and minded my own business.

Shawn and I spent most of the rest of the week together. I was not sure if we were actually dating yet or not. That subject had not come up in conversation. I found it strange that he still had not tried to have sex with me, so I assumed that he did not want to. I wondered if he and Carson might be gay, and I was just a cover up.

I had talked to Eric a few times on the phone. He said that he was close to getting his own place soon. He asked if I wanted to come to see him when he did. I told him I had a job now and that I could only come for the weekend. He said he wished that I did not have a job so I could stay with him longer.

I had also heard from Kodi. He reported that on his way out west he got in some issues with the police and was going to lose his drivers license for four years. I thought it must have been quite an issue, but I did not ask.

Kodi said he found this religious group that he was attending in the city. He said that he was now a vegetarian as part of the following. The group allowed him to live in the temple as long as he followed what they practiced and obeyed the rules. He said they were strict about not having sex and following the scriptures they called the Bible. He said they were Hare Krishnas or something, but I was not really listening to that part. He had been with them for a while now and said that he was really happy there. He wanted me to come and check it out, but I wished him his happiness and hoped he had finally found what he was looking for. He said he would look me up when he came back around to see his parents. I told him I thought that was a bad idea if he was trying to abstain from sex; after all that was about the only thing we done well together.

Shawn was very nice to me. We spent most of our time together when we could. It was like we were already married in a sense but there were a lot of things he did not know about me yet. I had not told him about Tommy or my still not wanting to be alive. I did not want him to think he needed to save me from my heartache or from myself. All I knew for sure is that when I was with him it made life a bit easier to handle.

The thing that I did not like about our relationship was the sex. Shawn was kind and gentle with me, and we only had sex when I wanted to. That was the nice part, but that was just it, it was nice. I longed for the passion that I had known with Edie or the adventurous things I had done with Eric. I knew I could not spend the rest of my life being nice.

It was not long before I found myself getting what I wanted sexually when I took Eric up on his offer to visit him at his new apartment. I knew it was not the best thing to do concerning my relationship with Shawn but things were getting dull. Eric provided all that I knew he would between the sheets and out of them.

When I was with Eric I did not have to explain myself. I did not have to tell him what I liked and did not like. We did not have to have conversations about what movies to watch or what restaurant to go to. We did not have to talk about the past, Eric already knew it all. I did not have to tell Eric if and when I ate food and that I was not anorexic. I enjoyed the comfort and safety he provided. I wondered what life might be like if I stayed with Eric forever. The weekend was not long enough to spend with him. I wanted to come back every weekend to be with him.

"What are you doing next weekend?" Eric finally asked.

"I am not sure."

"Are you going to come and see me again?"

"I will come and see you whenever you want me to."

"Will you come Friday after you are done work?"

I thought of Shawn for a moment. I felt terrible for what I was doing to him. Shawn had only shown me kindness and support, and now I was here with someone else. I knew I needed to break it off with him as soon as I could if Eric and I would ever be able to be together again. I knew it was going to be a long week before I saw Eric again.

"If you want me to."

"I do," he said, then he kissed me goodbye before I got in the car and drove myself home.

It was a terrible week just as I had thought. Monday when I had almost finished my shift at work I was called into the office again by the boss.

"We have decided we are going to let you go. Things do not seem to be working out for you here."

"You mean I am fired?"

"I mean you do not need to come back to work tomorrow."

"Okay."

"I really do hope things work out for you someplace else."

I stood up and walked out of his office. I had never been fired from a job before. I thought it was supposed to feel different, but I really did not care. I wondered what I would say to my parents. I knew they would be upset at me for not being responsible enough to hold down a job, as stupid as this was. I did not know what I would tell them.

I gathered my stuff and walked out to my car. Everyone else had left but Shawn, who was waiting for me in the parking lot.

"What's up?" he asked.

"They fired me."

"Why?"

"They said things did not work out. Maybe because I have missed so much time."

"But you have been here every day for the last few weeks."

"I know; how ironic. When I did not try to be here they said nothing, but when I actually come to work and give it my best shot I get fired," I laughed.

"Do you want to come over?"

"You are not mad at me for losing my job?"

"No. It is a stupid job anyway."

I went to Shawn's, and it was life as usual. We watched TV for a while until we went to bed together. We had our habitual sex like always, and then he fell asleep. It was different in the morning because I did not need to rush home to get ready for work. I could stay at his house until he left, then I would go home.

I called Eric while Shawn was at work. He asked me again if I was coming to see him on the weekend. I told him that I did not think I would make it because I had gotten fired from my job. My parents were very upset at me, and I had better stay home. Eric said it should not matter what they thought if I wanted to come to have a good time with him I should. I agreed but reminded him that as long as I lived with them I had to somewhat try to make them happy, at least enough to make my life tolerable.

I spent the weekend with Shawn. Since I had no money we stayed at his house all weekend. In fact we stayed in his room all weekend and never even left the bed. He got out a camping stove and cooked eggs while we lay on the mattress. This was the first time I had ever done anything like this before. Sex and sleep and sex and sleep, over and over again. I was glad I had decided to stay here with him. As long I was in bed with Shawn I did not have to think of anything else. Shawn was the only thing that mattered in that moment until we had the conversation.

"I love you," he said, as he held me in his arms.

"What?" I asked. Did he really say that?

"I love you."

"Oh." I started to cry. I did not want him to say those words to me because I knew I could not truthfully say them back.

"Do you love me?"

"No."

He started to cry as well. "How can you spend so much time with me and not love me?"

"Shawn, there are things about me that you do not know. I do not think spending a few months with you every day is love."

"What is love to you?"

"Love is forever. Love is helping someone attain the best in this life that they can. Love is holding someone's hand when they are sick and helping them get better if you can. Love is giving all that you can to someone every day of your life. Love wants the best for someone even before you want it for yourself."

"That is how I feel about you."

"You cannot know that after only a few months."

"Yes, I can. I want to be with you every day and spend the rest of my life with you. I thought you felt the same way."

"I am not ready to feel that way about anyone."

"I want to get married and do this every day of our lives together."

"No, I cannot do that."

"What?"

"I cannot make that commitment to you right now."

"Do you think you ever could?"

"Honestly?"

"Yes."

"I do not think I am ready for that."

"I know you are young. You have a lot of things you want to do before you settle down."

"No, that is not it. I have already done all that I have wanted to do and a bit more. I just need time for myself for a while, and I cannot promise I will always be here for you."

"Why don't you love me?"

"It is not that. I like you a lot. I really do, but this time I must say that it is me. I am not ready for this. Trust me when I tell you that it really does not have anything to do with you."

"Do you still want to date me?"

"I think that if you are ready for marriage, and I am not, I cannot see what good that will do by staying together. You should not waste your time with me. If marriage is what you want then you should go out and find it with someone else who can make you happy. I cannot give you any more than what I already am. If that is not enough then we need to not do this anymore."

"I love you."

"I know you do, but right now I cannot give that back to you, and that is not fair to you. From the bottom of my heart I am sorry." I got out of his bed put my clothes on and closed the door behind me as he lay alone.

Goodbye, Eric

Now I am truly not in any other kind of relationship with anyone else I think I will give it my best effort with Eric. I have been involved with other people for too long to ever know what it might really feel like loving only him. It must be real love with Eric because despite all that we have been through and the distance between us we keep being called back together.

It seems that Eric and I create most of the difficulties ourselves. He keeps coming back and forth to see me; we both keep dating other people, and I am sure we do other things that we both don't even know about. How can we ever trust each other when we are two pees in a pod, always looking for something better than what we already have. How can I really finally see for myself if I love Eric or if he loves me until we can somehow be together? This seems like the best time to start to make all of our dreams come true. Maybe if I moved in with Eric I could get a job and not think about Tommy so much.

I packed my bags long enough for one week and was off to see Eric. It seemed like he was actually excited that I was coming to see him for that long. I was happy, too. I had nothing else on my agenda but spending some time with him and hoping we could both make each other happy. Christmas was coming soon, and maybe he would give me a ring this year.

What makes me want to marry Eric but when Shawn hinted at the idea I bolted for the door? I guess it is because Eric and I have so much more history together that I feel like I can be myself around him. I have no secrets to hide from him anymore.

The only thing that I do not like about him is that he sometimes arrogant and rude. When his feelings get hurt he can be real nasty to be around. I do not like him at all when he is in one of those moods where he thinks he is God and everyone else is to be used and stepped on. Sometimes he is not very considerate of how I feel.

Since his native language is French, and he is Catholic we sometimes disagree on things. I know a little French from school but not enough to understand everything he says. He will forget that I cannot understand him and talk to me in French or watch the news. I usually just sit and nod as if I understand until he catches on. It is rather funny when he does it when he is stoned. He can have an entire conversation with me, and I have little knowledge of what he is taking about. Then I laugh at him.

Other times he can be sweet. He buys me things so I will remember him when he is gone. He writes me letters and sends me pictures. It is nice. I think of the time I was a small child, and I used to send pictures of myself or my teddy bear with my father when he went away to work. I always wanted him to remember to come back home and not forget us while he was gone but I think he still did.

Eric gave me a big hug and kiss as soon as I got there just like he always did. It was always nice the first few minutes I saw him because he was happy then. Eric and I went out for dinner at a nice restaurant but something seemed strange with him tonight. He was quiet and not very humorous. He said it was just because he was tired and had a hard day at work.

It was nice to fall asleep in his arms after we made love. I imagined this is what it would be like with him for the rest of my life. I think this would be fine.

Everything was going better than I expected for the first few days. It was when I answered the phone in the middle of the day for some girl asking where he was and when he would be home. I asked for her name but she said that she would call him back later.

I told Eric of it and he said it must have been his sister. The one we visited a while ago. I asked him if it was his sister why would she not give her name or tell me who she was. He made excuses for her behaviour, but I did not believe him. I thought if it was his sister she would also know he would be at work.

I got another strange call the next day about the same time in the afternoon. This time his sister must have not wanted to talk to me at all and hung up when I said hello.

Eric had some boxes of papers and stuff at the end of his bed that I wondered if his sister left him a card or wrote him a letter. I started searching through his belongings, and I got what I deserved.

I found a few letters, but they were not from his sister. They were from someone named, "Love Sunshine," not the way your sister would say, "write back." I looked at the date on the top of the letters and the timing was just about the same as when he went back home from living in this area with me. I did not read every word to know what that was all about. Sunshine had written him a letter at this address already. That must mean it is a fairly current friend if she knew he already moved here. I wondered if Eric was in love with Sunshine too. I wondered if that was his pet name for all of us that he woke up in the morning with.

I picked up the phone and called Edie. It was not long before he had talked me into coming in to the city on the bus to see him. He said that it would be a nice thing for Christmas since we would not see each other then. I was already mad at Eric so I might as well make this worth my trip to have a little bit of fun.

I told Eric that I was going to visit Tommy's cousin I had met when I lived in the city. I asked him if he would want to go with me but he said no. I knew he would that is why I offered. I told him that she wanted to take me out for a few drinks so I would be spending the night with her. He said I should wear his leather jacket because it was supposed to snow.

Edie met me as soon as I got off the train at central station. It was awful there. It was dirty and bums were everywhere. I just wanted to get out of there to anyplace else.

We rode the street car to where he was staying with his sister. We played a little game on the man that was sitting in the seat beside me while Edie was standing up. All of a sudden Edie sat down on my lap and put his arm around me. "Where you going, little girl?" he asked.

"I am not telling you."

"Why, maybe I could come with you. To protect you from the bad guys."

"You are a bad guy."

"No, I am not. Trust me when I tell you you'll be safe with me."

"No, I do not think that is a good idea."

"Can I get off the bus with you and follow you home? You could invite me in for cookies."

"Cookies?"

"Yeah, I like cookies."

"Well, you could come over for one."

"Just one?"

"Just one. Then you would have to leave."

When the street car came to our stop Edie got up and took me by the hand and led me down the stairs. I followed him like a lost puppy. I was a lost puppy back in the city. I had no reason at all to be here without Tommy. I was only here to see him and have a little bit of fun and a whole lot of passion. I needed the instant gratification of lust.

Edie and I were only moments into the bedroom before we had each other's clothes off. We both had the exact same thing in mind.

Edie thought it would be a good idea to leave his mark on my neck. He gave me a big red hickey. I was angry at him. I may have wanted to get back at Eric in my own way, but I did not really want him to find out. Edie branded me on purpose just to cause issues. I thought that was mean of him since he knew we could never be together.

Edie knew I would never come to the city to stay, and he could never come to live where I do. My parents hated him, because when I showed Mom his picture she could tell the tattoos were from jail. He had spent four years there for something; I am not sure what. I was right about them.

While we were in the bus station again Edie pretended to come up behind me and steal my purse. He almost got away with it and probably would have if he would not have let go. He and his roommate used to ride by me on bicycles on the dark city streets and try to steal my purse. I was getting good at not letting them get it after a while. They told me it was good practice if someone ever did try.

It was not my purse I was worried about in the city. It was the other things I knew men could do. I remembered one afternoon I was walking back to the hospital alone, and this guy started talking to me at the stop light. I was trying to be polite and answering his questions. I thought it was a bit odd when he asked me where I was going and if I had a boyfriend. I showed him the pictures of Edie in jail with his bulging muscles and told him that was my boyfriend. He told me that he was here from Greece as a student. He did have a heavy accent, and I could hardly understand him.

When I got to Edie's apartment I thought it was a good idea to make an escape from this man as I was getting one of those feelings something was not right. I was not sure if anyone would be at the apartment to let me in but I could at least pretend there was. When I opened the first door to the apartment he pushed past me and came in, too.

He threw me up against the wall and would not let me go. I pushed the buzzer to Edie's place and started frantically yelling through the speaker. "Let me in! Let me in! Hurry up! Open the door!"

Edie unlocked the door, and I tried to run up the stairs. The man put both of his arms around my head and held me against the wall. He put his face in toward mine and tried to kiss me. I ducked under his arms and ran up the stairs as fast as I could.

I got to Edie's floor, and he was already walking down the hall with his roommate. He made mention of my voice on the speaker and was coming to meet me. I told them of what happened and they ran past me outside onto the street. I waited inside the apartment for them to come back.

When they returned they said no one was there, so he must have gone away.

The next day I was walking up by the burger joint and saw the Greek standing on the other side of the road at a street light. I kept walking as if I did not see him until he started to cross the street toward me. I ducked into a drug store and walked toward the back aisle. I waited a few minutes until I saw him walk by the window, and I bolted out of the store and back across the other side of the street. I went back to the hospital as soon as I could. I had never seen him again after that.

I knew as long as I was not alone in the city I was safe. I understood what Edie meant when he told me I always had something more to lose, my self esteem, my freedom, and maybe even my life. The latter part I did not care much about.

When I got back to Eric's I turned on the curling iron and waited for it to get hot. I tried to burn my neck to make a blister, but it was too hot, and I could not hold it on my skin long enough. I was not sure what kind of lie I was going to tell him to get me out of this one, but it had better be good.

"Where were you last night?" was the first thing he asked.

"With my friends."

"Bullshit. Who gave you the hickey?"

"Sue's brother. He was horsing around and wanted to get me in trouble with you. It was a joke. Here is his number. You can call him if you want."

"Bullshit. You had sex with someone."

I hung my head toward the floor. Why was I trying to lie to him? "Yes, I did."

"How could you?"

"How could you while you were away?"

"I wasn't."

"That is not what I got from your sunshine letters. You are lying."

"No, I didn't."

"Oh, by the way, your sister called again yesterday and hung up on me when I picked up the phone."

He followed me around the apartment yelling at me some more until I started to cry. "Eric, it is over, isn't it? You do not want me here, and I do not want to be here," I lied.

"I think we need some time away from each other to see how we really feel."

"We have had all the time away we can stand, and look what it has done to us."

"I know."

"Do you love her?"

"I don't know. Do you love him?"

"No."

"Do you love me?"

"You mean, would I give up my life and die for you?"

"Yes."

"No, I would not because you would not do it for me."

Eric and I became honest about all the things we had been doing while we were apart. We had both been playing the field trying to run away from the shadows of loneliness and despair. I was not exactly sure what his fear was, but it certainly had something to do with commitment.

We had passionate sex later that night and got more honest with each other.

A song came on the radio that he said reminded me of him as the singer's voice rang out Eric asked, "Do you think of me when you are having sex with someone else?"

"Sometimes when I miss you." I admitted the truth. "Do you?"

"Yes. I am addicted to making love to you. It feels so good when we are together, like we are one."

"Then why can't we get it together in love?" I started to cry. I thought this would be our last time together.

"I don't know."

I got up the next morning and caught the bus home. Eric did not wake me up that morning before he left for work, and I did not leave a note to say goodbye. We had done that last night.

Jesse Again

On the bus ride home two fellows sat behind me and drank beer in the back seat. I was a bit nervous toward both of them at first but after a while I got used to the noise. I could hear the guys speaking French, and I understood most of the conversation. It was ironic how I had to listen to them speaking French on the bus after just breaking up with Eric.

One of the guys and I got off the bus at the same stop. I had to wait for a ride from my mother so I set my luggage down on the sidewalk and lit a smoke. He came up and stood beside me. He was looking around as if he might be waiting for someone, too.

"Which direction to go to au bar?" he said, in broken English.

I pointed down the street, "Just a few blocks that way."

I figured he would rush away, but I was wrong. He looked around some more and then lit a smoke. We began talking a while about where we were from and why we were on the bus. He seemed like a nice guy even though he was drunk. He had very broken English and was hard to understand. I could tell that wherever he had come from he had not had the opportunity Eric had to speak the language. We stood there and talked until Mom pulled up.

A few nights later I saw the handsome, dark-haired French man sitting at a table in the bar with some regulars from the area. It was not until the end of the night when I was good and drunk that I went over and said hi to him. One thing led to another, and I was on my way back to someplace for whatever came along.

I found myself sitting at a kitchen table with intoxicated French people watching while they did lines of cocaine. I wanted to go home but I had no ride. I listened to some of the jabber and then asked if they minded if I found a place to crash.

I found my way to the bedroom I was directed and lay down on the spinning bed. I had drunk too much, and now look where I was. In fact I did not even know where I was. This was probably worse than dying.

It was not long until I had company in the bed, and we both had one thing on our minds since the night we met at the bus station. We were both a bit clumsy from our intoxications, but we stumbled through some kind of terrible sex.

I woke up in the morning still naked, to some other guy standing in the door way speaking French and telling this guy he needed to get up for work. The guy was mumbling something back, and the last thing I heard was, "On vas pavrir dans euivou fifteen minutes."

"You have to work today?" I asked him.

"Yeah."

"The guy that promised me a ride home last night left, didn't he?"

"Yeah."

"How in the hell am I going to get home now? I do not even know where I am."

"Je lui ai donneé de l'argeur pour vous apportez cuez vous."

"What?"

"I gave some arguer to take you to your maison." He mumbled some more.

"Fuck," was all that I could get out of my mouth.

"Desoleé for last night. I was drunk." I knew he was trying to make excuses for the bad sex.

"I am sorry for last night, too. I was drunk," but I meant for even getting myself here.

It was on the ride home it really hit me of what kind of stupid thing I had done when the stranger who had stood in the door and gawked at me naked started to talk. "You do not seem very happy this morning."

"I suppose I am not." I stared straight ahead in the car. It was starting to snow.

"That usually means the sex was bad." He started to laugh. "Did he satisfy you?"

I gave him a dirty look.

"I am sorry I was standing in the door while you were on the bed with Luke. I thought it was the other chick that was there last night. She finds herself in bed with all of them all the time. You never know who she is going to be in bed with next."

Oh, that was reassuring. Not only is he admitting he looked, he was saying they all had a twisted sense of friendship, and I thought the guy's name was Mark.

"Great." I sighed.

"Why are you bringing me on the back roads to your house? Does that mean you want to go parking?"

"No."

"Well, I will know where you live. Can I come and pick you up for a date tonight?"

"No, that would be a real bad idea. You can forget where I live. I am not interested."

"Should I stop by and see?"

"Only if you want to meet my father." I paused. "Thanks for the ride home, though; I am not sure what I would have done without it."

"See ya around?" he asked.

"Maybe at the bar." I smiled. I got out of the car.

I got home and tried to shower the filth off myself that I felt from the night I had engaged in. I felt dirty and disgusted with my actions. I wished if I could take anything back that I had ever done before it was now. I am not sure what possessed me to sleep with a man that I did not know his name or even where I woke up. I promised myself that this was the first and last time I would ever behave like that again.

I blamed my actions on the drink. If I would not have been in such a state of inebriation I certainly would not have ended up in his bed. If I was not lonely I would not have ended up in his bed. If Tommy was still here I would not have ended up in his bed. I could blame my actions on almost anything because I was so ashamed of myself that I could have not possible chosen to do such things under my own free will or best thinking.

I did not think I would hurt myself so badly in just a few hours of drunken blur. Maybe if the sex would have been better I would have felt better. Maybe if I would have been more satisfied with at least knowing his name I would feel better. Maybe if I had at least some small connection to this person besides meeting him on the bus I would feel better. He used me, and I used him for nothing more than mutual masturbation that was not even very good. I knew I had used sex addictively before to cover up my inner emotional turmoil, but this was different. I could not even justify to myself why I had gone home with this person. I hope I never saw him again.

It was not long before I ended up at the bar again. This time I was not at all interested in having anyone take me home. I just wanted to drown my sorrows in the drink. I missed Tommy, and I knew I was behaving badly because of it.

I had seen Carson, Shawn's roommate in the bar. I thought I would say hi to him for old time's sake but found out a little more information that I wanted to know.

"Hey," I greeted him.

"Hey," he greeted back.

"How's things?"

"Good," he lied. I could tell that something was bothering him.

"How is Shawn?" I asked.

"Fine. He has a girlfriend."

"Oh," I was somewhat surprised to hear that already. I guess love does not stay in his heart very long.

"Yeah, he says he really likes her and thinks they are going to move in together and get married."

"Already?"

"Yeah, he is moving out at the end of the month."

I wondered how Shawn could love her already. I wondered if he ever really loved me like he said he did. If he really loved me how could he move into another serious relationship so quickly? Is that what they call a rebound relationship or was he lonely. I hoped he found what he was looking for because I knew it was not me.

I saw someone else by surprise at the bar that night, too. It was Jesse. He was there with Kayla's brother. I thought it best not to approach either on of them to say, "Hello," tonight, since Jesse was seldom in the bar, and Kayla' brother was always looking for some kind of trouble and with the mood I was in tonight who knew for sure how things might end up. I decided to keep a low profile because I did not need any more drama in my life at this point unless it offered some kind of emotionless endeavour. Who was I trying to kid? If it involved Jesse nothing was emotionless.

I waited in the dark side of the bar as long as I could. With as many beers as I had to drink sooner or later my bladder would call for elevation. I knew I would have to walk by the table were they had positioned themselves so I could make my way to the bathroom. I wondered if my bodily functions could wait until they left the bar or until I saw the waitress bring over a few more beers their way. Maybe I could just slip by without either one of them noticing.

As soon as I was in eye view of Jesse he stood up from the table. I stopped in my tracks and hoped that he was off to the little boys room himself or to the smoke machine for some cigarettes but I was wrong.

I could see by the look in his eye coming toward me that Adam was just about to hand the apple back to Eve, but this time it seemed Adam may have a little more at risk than his sanity if he passed it openhandedly.

"Hey," he greeted me with a smile. "I wondered if I would see you here."

"Hi. How did you ever get out on the town?" Jesse's girlfriend kept real close tabs on him especially now they had a child together.

"Ah, you know, just thought I would come out for a quick beer with Jackson." I smiled and pointed toward their table full of drinks, "or two."

"Come, sit, have a drink on me." He opened his arms and pointed toward the table. "I bought you a beer."

"Ha," I rolled my eyes at his comment, "bought me a drink. You did not even know I was here."

"I was just coming to invite you over. I saw you when you came in, hiding in the corner with your friends."

"Actually, I was just on my way to the can. I really need to go."

"Then I will wait for you when you come back."

I quickly escaped the conversation and headed toward the bathroom. I wondered how I was going to get out of this one. I wondered if I wanted to. The flattery was nice and the male attention I was sure would make me feel a little better. Was having one innocent drink with Jesse so wrong after all these years of our history and broken relationship? I am sure I could trust him enough for one drink for old time's sake. After all I was not the one that had anything to lose.

On second thought, maybe it would be best if I just walked out the back door and left now, but then how was I going to tell my friends I was gone?

By the time I finished my business in the bathroom the table at which he was sitting was already filled with other people. I was sure this was my break to make my passing without notice. I could quickly gather my friends and make some excuse to leave this bar and head somewhere else. It seems all my anxiety was for nothing.

As soon as I passed the chair where Jesse was sitting he reached out into the aisle and grabbed me by the arm, "You promised you'd have a drink with me."

"I never promised," I smiled, "I have got to go."

"Why, because of that guy you are over there with?" he meant Ryan.

Ryan was a guy I had worked in harvest with that desperately wanted to go out on a date. We had come to the bar together but it seemed like he had never been in one before. Ryan was an extremely attractive guy but compared to myself he was still just a boy. It was obvious that neither one of his parents wanted him to date me because of the comments they would make while we were at work. I was not sure what Ryan had in mind, but I doubted it was me sitting here with Jesse.

"Yeah, kind of." I smiled. "He did come here with me."

"It is just an innocent drink. Invite him and your other friends over, too."

"I am not sure that is a good idea."

"I will come with you. It will prove there is no harm. A birthday drink, since I did not see you on your birthday a while ago. I will buy you one now."

No harm? Is he kidding himself? A birthday drink? "Sure, no harm in that, I guess."

I was not sure what Ryan was thinking when he agreed that he and the others would join the table of outcasts, but he was getting drunk and his thought pattern seemed fairly irrational. He had no way of knowing that it was like throwing a piece of meat to the wolves, but he agreed. It seemed in his innocence he would have no way of knowing how dangerous Jesse would be to any kind of relationship that he might be entertaining with me.

I positioned myself last in line behind everyone else who joined the table. I had an excuse to back out on the fun because by the time I got there all the chairs were taken. I stood behind the chair that Ryan was sitting in and pretended to know what the conversation was about, but I could not hear anything because the band had started to play again. Jackson was also standing up, so we attempted to converse, but the music was much too loud.

It was only about three minutes before Jesse grabbed my arm again. "You can share with me," he whispered into my ear as he pulled me onto his lap. He meant his chair.

I tuned and smiled at him and shook my head, no. "This is not a good idea." I attempted to resume my position standing. He put both his arms around my waist to hold me close so I could not stand as he pulled me closer into him.

"Here," Jackson handed me another beer. "You might as well have this if you are going to sit for a while."

"I heard about your friend," Jesse whispered, in my ear. "I am sorry for him."

I turned toward him and nodded in recognition of his condolences.

"Are you dating that stiff?" he pointed toward Ryan. It was obvious to Jesse that Ryan did not have the experience in dating or bar hopping that everyone else at the table had.

I shook my head no and took a big drink of beer. I closed my eyes for a second and could see I was holding my hand out to take the apple by answering the question as a negative.

Jesse was holding me so close to him on his lap that I could feel his chest expanding and falling with breath as he sat behind me. Being with him felt familiar, but it was when he started playing with my hair that I knew tonight was not going to have the ending I had anticipated when I picked Ryan up for our date. I took another big drink of beer and set the bottle on the table in front of me. I slide my hands down between both of my legs and then down into his. I slide them up as far as I could without making it completely obvious to whoever might be watching that I was going to play the teasing game back. If he wanted to play that game I could too.

"Let's dance." Katie grabbed me by the arm and pulled me up. She had been on the relationship roller coaster with Jackson for a few years now, and it was hard to tell if they were on the up slope or headed toward another ending. It seemed so regular that I had stopped asking her about it a long time ago.

I put my hand on Jesse's shoulder as I left the table and smiled in his direction. For now I had been saved.

It was not long before Ryan joined us on the dance floor. He seemed to have no idea about what events that had happened at the table, and I was glad for that. I knew that whatever games that were going on under the table did not have to hurt Ryan's feelings. That was certainly not my intentions at all.

With the lights turned low the band dropped the beat and the slow song started. My friends and I attempted to exit the dance floor when Ryan took my hand and pulled me in toward him. He had barely had his arms wrapped around my waist when he stopped.

I looked up and saw Jesse standing beside him. "Can I cut in?" he demanded, rather than asked as he plucked me away from Ryan.

Ryan and I stood in shock of the nerve that someone had to do that.

"For her birthday." Jesse smiled at Ryan slyly.

Jesse and I swayed together in comfort of the music as long as the band played slowly. He held me close, and I felt like I was a kid again. Being in his arms was the most comforting thing I had felt since Tommy died. For a second I remembered what love felt like. I knew that being with Jesse was not for real. I knew that everything with him always had a bad ending sooner or later but I enjoyed the feeling of his warmth. For a few moments I could forget all that my heart had endured since I had been with him last and relax without taking a little yellow pill.

It was as clear as crystal what Jesse had on his mind while he was dancing with me. I was not sure if he was reminiscing about the sex we shared in the past or was hoping to get more in the very near future.

"Let's go outside," he said softly in my ear, as he pulled my hair back.

"I can't."

"You said he was not your boyfriend. Let's go. Just follow me out."

"I can't. I have to take him home."

"He rode here with you?"

"Yes, he did. He does not know anyone here, and I cannot stand him up like that."

"Even for me?"

"Even for you."

We left our desire on the dance floor for a while and cooled things down as we returned to the table. Jesse kept walking toward the bathroom as I sat down. I knew he was hoping I had changed my mind and would follow him out. Ryan noticed that Jesse did not join us and stood up and left the table and followed Jesse into the men's room. I wondered what kind of conversation was about to happen in there. I wondered if anyone would come out bleeding.

It was not long until Jesse came back and stood behind my chair. Ryan returned also and resumed his spot at the table. I pretended not to notice either one of them and engaged in conversation with my girlfriends, who at this point were starting to catch onto the charade.

"What the hell is up with that?" Shelly asked privately.

"With what?" I played stupid.

"With Jesse?"

"What do you mean?"

Jesse pulled me by the arm out of the chair and sat back down. "Sit." He pulled me on his lap again.

"It is her birthday," he said as he smiled toward Shelly.

"It was in July," she reminded him.

"Belated," Jesse smiled.

Shelly ordered a few shooters and handed me two before she set the others on the table. "Happy birthday then." She held up a shooter to cheers toward me.

I took one, and Jesse took the other. "Looks like it may be after all." I smiled, as we clunked the glasses together, then poured more toxins into our bodies.

It seemed like the bar turned the lights on for closing time too soon but we knew the signal that it was time to go home. I had plenty to drink and was more than likely too intoxicated to safely drive home but knew I could probably make the trip without killing us all. We gathered our stuff and said our goodbyes and exited the table full of new and old friends. We walked out of the bar into the parking lot still having fun and some of us not wanting the night to end so soon.

Jackson was walking now with Shelly and a few others toward someone's car. It was obvious their night of fun was far from over. Ryan walked a few steps ahead of me toward my car and Jesse was running from behind to catch up.

"Where you going?" he said, so no one else could hear.

"Taking Ryan home."

"Then what are you doing?"

"Going home."

"Give me a ride."

"You live just around the corner. Those guys want you to go with them."

"I want you to give me a ride home after you give Ryan a ride."

"You want me to pick you up someplace? I will be at least two hours or more. He is not from around here."

"Let me come with you?"

"No."

We had arrived at my car in which Ryan was already sitting in the passenger's side beside the door waiting to go.

I opened the driver's side door to get in when I heard someone from the other car yell toward us.

"You need a ride?" Jackson yelled toward Jesse from Shelly's car.

"No, I got one," Jesse yelled back, then slid into the middle seat beside Ryan.

I stood holding the door open in shock again at his nerve and skill to manipulate even this situation.

"Are you sure you want to do that?" Jackson yelled again, from the other car.

"Yeah, I am sure," he said, matter of factly. "You guys go ahead."

I got in the car beside Jesse and started the engine without saying a word.

"Where is it that you live?" Ryan asked Jesse.

"Not that far from you actually. Those guys were going on to a party, and I thought since I just wanted to go straight home I could catch a ride."

"Oh." Ryan was as surprised as I was.

The three of us rode in the car for about an hour without conversation. It seemed that none of us had anything to say. I did not know what to say to anyone. This was the most uncomfortable situation that I had been in as far as relationships went. Since Ryan and were not officially dating I guess we are not in a relationship anyway, in fact I had not even ever kissed him. At this rate I doubted I ever would. I justified Jesse being in the car to myself.

Jesse played with the stations on the radio as a leisure activity, which seemed like a good idea, because then none of us would have to chat. He finally tuned into a song that brought back personal memories that only he and I would share. He gave me a soft nudge on the arm as he leaned back on the seat.

He pulled an open beer out of the inside pocket of his jacket and took a drink. He handed the bottle to me in offerings. I knew he had taken it from the bar, and why shouldn't he? It was already paid for. I took the bottle from him and tipped it up.

"So how do you two know each other?" Ryan broke the silence.

Jesse chuckled and said under his breath quietly, "You know I am not sure I even remember how we met." He answered the question, as he rubbed his hand along the top of my leg. "Do you?"

"Yeah, I do. You and Jackson were friends from school. You started coming around our gang to hang out with him."

"Yeah, I remember now." He paused for a moment. "Then I met you when you were at the baseball diamond."

"Yes," his voice took me back to the day I met him. I remembered there was a bunch of us kids at the base ball diamond playing some kind of chasing, touch tag, soccer kind of game. I could not remember what it was exactly it was. Some game we would make up as kids. It was the kind of game where there are no winners or losers. We liked those kinds of games because it always felt good to play because we could focus on playing not anyone being better than anyone else. No one ever felt like they had to be the last one picked to be on the team because we had no teams. We all just played together. We all had fun.

Jesse and I found ourselves alone together somehow, and that is the first time he kissed me. It was the first time I had ever been kissed like an adult. It was the first time someone put his tongue in my mouth. I had kissed boys before but nothing like this.

Jesse also held my hand when he walked me home that night. He kissed me again before he said goodbye. I was still a child of twelve, but I knew I liked what I felt. I liked the butterflies in my stomach and the kingly feeling in my heart. I was not sure what it meant but I knew it must be good.

"It was a long time ago, when we were kids," I added.

"Did you ever date before?" Ryan asked.

Date? I was not sure if that is what you called it, but it was something like love. I think. "Not really date. We were too young for that." I lied.

"No, we did other things," Jesse added.

I did not want to talk about this anymore. I preferred listening to the radio instead. I reached over and turned the music up louder. One way or another I had to get out of this conversation quickly.

I shone the headlights into the garage so Ryan could see to get into the house. I opened my door at the same time as he did and we both got out of the car. I walked Ryan to the door to say good night and somehow say that I was sorry our almost date turned out like this.

"Will you call me tomorrow?" he asked, as he grabbed both of my hands and looked directly into my eyes.

I stared into his brown eyes. He looked like a puppy in the rain, "Yes."

Ryan kissed me softly on the lips and let go of my hands. "Are you just giving him a ride home?"

"Yes, just a ride home. He is just an old friend." I was sure I was lying again.

"Okay, then, good night," he said, before he turned and went into the house.

I got back in the car, and Jesse was still sitting in the middle seat. He had finished the beer and was already smoking a fag. "Are you sure you are not dating him?"

"I am not sure of anything," I admitted. I took his smoke and put it to my lips.

He put his hand on my thigh again and slid it up toward my crotch, "Where we going now?"

"I am taking you home. You said you did not want to go the party."

"Well, maybe I would if the party was just me and you."

I did not want to hear him say that. "Let's go for a walk on the beach. It is a gorgeous night. I would hate to waste it. The summer is almost over. We won't get many more nights like this."

We got out of the car and stepped into the sand. I opened the trunk and took two more beers out of the cooler of ice. I looked in the sky at all the stars glittering like candles in the clear autumn night. The breeze blew my bangs in my eyes, and I tried to brush them away.

Jesse leaned over and grabbed a blanket that I kept in the back seat in case of an accident for first aid.

"We might want to sit." He smiled.

The water was brushing against the shore in a calming rhythm. It was as if nature knew I was coming and set up the night just right for romance. The smell of the weeds in flower filled the air as the crickets sang the song to call a mate. I took a deep breath.

"Peaceful here, isn't it?" he observed.

"Yeah, I like it here." I said, "This is my most favourite spot in the world."

We walked along the beach talking and laughing at how awkward the conversation was in the car. Jesse talked a bit about old times, and I laughed while we turned the clocks back in history.

Jesse knelt down and spread out the blanket on the ground while I held on his beer. We both sat on the blanket together and shared another smoke. He put his arm over my shoulder the same way he did when we were kids.

"I have missed you," he finally said. "I am really sorry to hear about your friend," he said again.

"I have missed you too over the years. It has been a long time."

He leaned over and kissed me. It was just like the first time all over again. I felt the warm fuzzy feeling in my stomach again. I wanted him to take me back to a place in my heart when I still trusted in life as a child. I wanted him to take me back to the time before I knew what life, loss and love was about. I wished he could be father time and change the inevitable. I wanted to be in love with him again.

It was not long before I found my tongue inside his mouth feeling the softness of his lips. He was pressing his body hard against me, and I could feel his passion with every twitch of his muscles trying to hold himself up. He leaned against me hard enough that my body fell back onto the sand. He never stopped kissing me as his body followed in harmony.

I was enjoying being with him again. It was ironic how our own sexual maturing combined with our history of love made it seem like we belonged together in that moment.

I was anxious for him to keep touching me until we would be physically connected again there in the sand while we listened to the waves beating against the shore. I knew he was enjoying our time together, too, by the way he was touching me. Once again this felt a lot like love.

It was so natural to be with him. He was touching more than my body. Tonight he was touching those hidden places of my soul that were hidden in the shadows of fear. I could forget everything I was running away from and be in this moment. I could feel myself right there on the beach with him. I was not thinking about Ryan. I was not thinking about myself. I was not thinking about Tommy. My heart had found a moment of relief, and I did not want to let that go. I wanted to soak up all the goodness for all that it was worth because I knew it would not last long.

I kept my eyes closed when I woke up because I did not want Jesse to know I was awake. The way he was still playing with my hair was a nice thing to wake up to. I wondered how long he had been awake. I wondered what time it was. The sun was becoming hot beating down on my legs. My body started to become itchy from the sand that had gotten on the blanket. My neck was stiff from sleeping on Jesse's shoulder all night or some of it anyway. My head started to pound from all the beer, cigarettes and lack of sleep. All of the sudden reality hit me, and I knew exactly where I had fallen asleep.

"Ah," I stretched my aching back out, "what time is it?"

"I am madly in love with you," he said.

I did not want to laugh out loud. I wondered if he was still drunk. "Yeah," I said sarcastically. I sat up on the blanket and opened my eyes.

I looked down at the sweater that covered my chest. I knew it was not the one I had put on yesterday. I had on Jesse's sweater and my black panties. Jesse already had on his jeans. My thoughts ran back to that last thing I could remember from last night.

I remember getting partly dressed as Jesse was telling me how perfect my body was and that I should not cover it up. That was just about the time last night he said he was madly in love with me then, too. Those statements are kind of hard to believe after that much beer.

"I think you said that last night."

"Are you madly in love with me?"

"Did I say that last night?"

"No, but you acted like you were."

"Yeah, maybe I did."

"Are you?"

"What, madly in love with you? I guess that is not going to matter as soon as I take you home to your girlfriend and kid."

"I do not want to go home."

I lit a smoke and leaned back on the blanket covered in sand. "Then where is it that you want to go?"

"With you."

I sighed. "It seems like that is not going to happen."

My thoughts jumped to Ryan. What the hell had I been thinking last night? I got manipulated into falling for Jesse's charm and big brown eyes. I think I had made a mistake for myself and for Jesse. I should have known better. I should have resisted temptation.

"Why?"

"Because of what you have at home."

"I do not want to be there. I know you think I have made my bed a long time ago, and now I need to lie in it, but I don't want to. I am madly in love with you, and I have always been. I have not felt like this in a long time. I like it."

"I like it too, but we cannot do this together."

"You can help me raise my kid if I leave her. We can have our own family. Would you like that with me?"

"Ah, no. I can't."

"You would be a good mother."

"Not right now."

"You would not help me raise a kid? Why? Because it is not yours. You wouldn't do that for me?"

"I would not do that to your kid. Believe me, I am in no shape to raise a kid."

"You're not madly in love with me. You never were."

"You do not understand."

"Understand what? That I love you and want to be with you no matter what?"

"That I am more messed up than you think."

We finished our smokes and got dressed, then walked back to the car. I did not say anything more about it to him until he brought it up again when we got close to his house.

"I do not know when I will see you again."

"That may be a good thing."

"I will always love you. I will always remember last night. I did not think it was a mistake. I know that I need to do what I have been doing even if I don't like it much, but love is never a mistake."

"I guess you' re right."

He kissed me on the cheek and got out of the car. I sat and tried to gather my thoughts but my head was still pounding from the hangover. I wondered what excuse he would use because he had not came home. I wondered how he was going to pour on the charm to get him out of this one as soon as he saw her. I was glad I was not him. I was glad I was not her.

The Empty House

I went to see Cat again. I had not seen Cat nor been at the grave in a long time. The weather was getting colder, so I could not sit on the ground. The snow had been falling for a few weeks now, and since the grave was at the back of the lot it was hard to walk through the snow. It was nice to see Cat again. I thought he would have forgotten me.

"Hello, Cat."

"Meow."

"I have been behaving badly the last little while. I think it is because I have been drinking too much."

"Meow." I bent over and picked Cat up.

"I have missed you."

Cat rubbed his head against my neck as I petted him.

"I wish Tommy was here. I want him to come back. I am lost all by myself in this world. I feel like all I am doing is putting one foot in front of the other, walking blindly into this world. I hate God for taking Tommy away and making me stay. I wish I could go with him, but I did not die when I took all those pills. All I really wanted to do was leave here. It seems like everyone says they know how I feel, but they don't. How could they? I don't even know how I feel. I really do not even think I have any feelings left."

"Meow."

"I asked God to take me away today, but He didn't. I guess I must stay for a while longer, but I hope it is soon. I hope He answers my prayer and takes me away tomorrow, but I doubt that, too, because I pray for that every day."

I was shivering in the cold, as my shoes were soaking wet from the snow. I had left my mittens in the car, but at least holding on to Cat, my hands were warm. The wind was picking up, and the snow was now making little wispy tornadoes in the field on the other side of the road. The sun was fading behind the clouds, and it would be totally gone soon. I wondered if a storm was blowing in off the lake.

"I am glad to see you today, Cat, but I must go now before it gets too late. I am not sure why I am in a hurry to leave because I had no place to go. I wish I could go to see Tommy. Well, I guess I am already here to see him."

"Meow."

"My mistakes…" I thought for a moment. "I did not mean to hurt anyone, but I am sure I have. I did not mean to hurt Eric or Kodi. Most of all I did not mean to hurt me; things just happen that way. I wish I could take back dating those boys while Tommy was sick. I wish I would have been faithful to only him. I guess for a long time I was. Telling Tommy about it did not make it right; it just made it honest. We all have our own free will, and we all make our own choices because of what we want. Sometimes we cannot get what we want, so we do the best we can with what we have, but sometimes that leaves us disappointed, so we try to get what we want someplace else. It does not work. We are never satisfied. It is never enough. We keep trying and trying and trying, and it is never enough. Maybe it is because we have unrealistic expectations of ourselves, of each other, of love, of God." I paused. "Maybe I thought I knew better than God by keeping Tommy here. Maybe not, but that is certainly what I wanted. For myself."

"Meow."

"They say that time heals all wounds, but I think they are wrong, whoever they are. I cannot see this wound healing any time soon. I don't want it to. The more it hurts the more I remember. I don't want to forget. I want to love Tommy forever. I do not want to anyone else to take his place. I do not want anyone to try. I want him here with me, now." I was starting to demand like a child with a temper tantrum. I knew it would do no good. Tommy was not coming back no matter how much I wished out loud for it.

"I guess there is no use in crying about it now. What has been done is done. And here I am. I guess I have to start from where I am even if I don't like it." I sighed.

I stood and looked at the marker on Tommy's grave. I wondered when the stone would be here. I wondered if it would have to wait until spring until the ground unthawed before they could set it on. I wondered if I would feel better once I could see the stone. I could put closure on it all then, but I doubted it as I walked back through the snow alone.

I called Tommy's mom to see how she was doing and to ask about the headstone for the grave. She said that she had paid for it but they needed to wait until the ground settled around the casket before it would be set. I wondered how long that would take.

She asked me if I still had all of Tommy's belongings, and said she would like to have them back. I wondered why she would want everything back now and what she would do with them.

As angry and frustrated as I was at her I could understand her wanting to hold on to his things, even though I thought she would give them all away. I told her I would return his stereo to the family but I was not going to give back his leather jacket. I had a few other things that I was sure she did not know about so I certainly was not going to volunteer offering to bring them back.

She was upset about the jacket, but I told her she would have no use for it anyway. I did not want her to give it away to someone else just because they wanted to wear it. I suggested that if Tommy would have wanted anyone to have anything he would have given it to them before he died, as he was sure sooner or later that was going to happen.

I soon took the stuff that she had asked for back to her, along with a poinsettia for her for Christmas. She had asked me if I had been to the grave lately, and I told her I had gone a few days ago but the snow was getting too deep. She said she had only been there once after the funeral.

She had gotten a huge graduation picture of Tommy enlarged and had it put up on her wall. She also had several pictures of Tommy and a few of Tommy and me around her house. I wondered why she would not have done this while he was still alive rather than after he was dead to show her love for him.

I became very upset when she showed me a photo album that contained pictures of Tommy that I had taken myself. I must have left them at Tommy's cousin's under the bed in a box with pictures of my family. Whoever found them must have thought it was a better idea to give them to her than to me. Tommy's mom was going on and on about how nice some of them were. The tears ran down my cheeks as I recognized every picture I had taken and what we were doing at the moment. I wondered if she really remembered how things were when he was still here about how much time he spent with me and not with them. I wondered if she really knew the truth about the pictures, and if she did if she at all felt guilty for stealing them from me. I wondered if someone just lied to her when they gave them to her and said the pictures had been theirs. I wondered how these people could be so cruel.

I could not bear to be in this empty house so I left. I swore to myself as I pulled out of the lane I would never return here again. I swore I never wanted to see anyone from this family again either. It was in my best interest to make them as dead to me as Tommy was.

"I am sorry, Tommy. I cannot respect them. These people must have hurt you many times, and I understand you did not have a choice, but I do. I will never return here again," I said out loud as if he was in the seat next to me.

I lay on the bottom of the tub while the hot shower water ran over my face as I cried to myself once more. I wondered if the pain that was left in my heart from losing Tommy was really all that I had left. I wanted this pain to go away so badly, but I had no idea what do to with myself so that it would. I felt like I had lost everything that was important to me and had messed everything else up since then. I wondered if things would ever get better for me. I wondered how I would make them get better. I wondered who would come and take my pain away now.

I missed Tommy. I wanted him back. Even sick was better than nothing at all. I could hear all the voices in my head now saying he was going to die. I wanted to tell them all in the same voice that even when I knew he was dying it did not make the hole that was left in my heart any smaller. I wanted to tell them that I was grateful that I had the time to love him all I could instead of running away in fear of how I was feeling now. I swore to myself that I would never love another so deeply that I would feel like this after the love was over. That is how I felt inside the love was over and all that was left to do now was pick up whatever pieces I had in my heart and try to be sane. I thought I would surely die from this broken heart sooner or later. Sooner would be just fine with me, but although I have tried to take my own life God must have a reason to keep me here. If He did he was wrong. I had no purpose.

Christmas Shopping

I thought of Eric and wondered what he was doing. I wondered if he missed me. I wished that things had not gone so wrong between us. I wish I would not have him left to hold on to at the end of everything with Tommy. I wondered if he was telling me the truth that love could prevail through anything. I wondered if I asked him one more time for his love if he would say yes to me once again to try another ride on the merry-go-round.

I went to the local shopping center and bought Eric a Christmas card. I thought if I sent him good tidings wishing him well it might be able to put a Band-Aid over everything we both had done wrong.

I knew exactly what I had done wrong in this relationship, and I could only speculate the things that Eric had told me were only half truths. I wondered if his other girlfriends might be sending him a nice holiday greeting card. I hoped that mine would be the best so that when he received it in the mail he would remember that he loved me the best and call.

I walked around the store looking for a gift I might buy for him and send it with the card. I wondered if it would be money wasted. It seemed that everything I looked at was a gift I would buy for Tommy. I looked at clothes, but nothing was appropriate. I looked at jewelry, but I did not have enough money for that. I looked at chocolates, books, and music, but nothing was right.

I went into the perfume section and thought I might try something like that. I wondered if I bought smelly stuff for Eric it would make him more attractive for the next girl that was waiting in line for his love. I picked up a bottle of cologne that Tommy wore. I opened the bottle and held it up to my nose. I started to cry, and I put the cap back on. This was the only thing I had left of remembering the way Tommy would smell when we went out on a date, a dusty bottle on the shelf of a store while I was surrounded by nameless shoppers. I looked around at the Christmas stuff in the store, but I could not feel the love that should to be filling the air. I had no gift to buy for anyone this year and certainly no special love in my heart.

I mailed the card to Eric with a small note attached wishing him the best for the season and sending all of my love. That was all I could muster in my heart to write this time, but I hoped my message of being sorry would somehow get through.

On my way home from the store I thought I would take a drive through town to see if anything was happening. I wondered if I might see anyone I knew to hang out with for a while as another distraction for a short time instead of going for a drink.

While I sat at the stoplight in my car waiting for the color to change to green I glanced over toward a familiar body walking down the street window shopping. I turned my head toward the street light to get a better look when I saw more than I bargained for.

It was Shawn holding hands with his new partner. She looked very happy while she was tangled in his fingers. Her mouth was moving as if she was talking or laughing. Shawn looked directly through the car window and saw me watching him with her. His head immediately fell toward the ground, and he let go of her hand.

I forced a smile and gave a wave. I surely wanted him to know I had seen him with her. I wondered how he could say he loved me so much and wanted marriage with me and less than a few months I had been forgotten for another. I knew in that moment that what he thought love was. In my heart it is not something you can change so quickly. For that matter, love is not something you even have a choice to do or not do. It just takes you with it. You can either enjoy it or balk at it, but it consumes every part of your being regardless of whether you want it to. I wondered how things might have been with the girl he said he loved before me. I wondered how many partners he would go through before he found what it was he was really looking for. I wondered if he would buy her a ring for Christmas to engage marriage. I felt a little sting in my heart as the light turned green, and I drove away.

The Last Time

"Hello."

"Allo." I was surprised to hear his French accent on the other end of the phone. "How are you?

"Fine, and you?"

"I got your card today. I thought I would call."

"I am glad you did. I hope you liked it."

"I did."

"Good." Now I had him on the phone I was not sure what to say. I guess I could try telling him the truth for a change.

"I miss you."

"I miss you, too."

"I am sorry. Words cannot explain how I wish I could take it all back and make things better between us."

"Me, too."

"What are you doing for the holidays?" he asked.

"You know, dinner here with my family. You?"

"Me, too. I am going home for Christmas, but I hoped that you might come here to spend New Year's with me."

"When?"

"I don't know. I could come and get you on Boxing Day or the day after when I leave from my folks."

"That is an awful long drive."

"I know. We could stay at your house then come here the next day if you wanted."

"I would like that. I would like to spend New Year's with you. Maybe it can be a new start to all that we did wrong."

"We could try."

"Do you want to?"

"Do you?" he asked back.

"Yes, I do. I still want all that we wanted together to be real."

"Me too."

Eric and I stayed on the phone for a while like nothing wrong had ever happened. We made plans for the holidays and my heart had been lifted. I wanted to believe that Eric and I could start again in the New Year. This last year has brought me many hardships, and I was ready for a change for the better.

Christmas morning came and went, and I spent most of the day in my room. I tried to be happy when we opened our gifts, but it seemed something was missing. Something big was missing. Tommy was missing.

I showered and dressed after breakfast and went to the graveyard. I did not see Cat there today, but Cat was probably enjoying some turkey like everyone else.

I stood at the snow-covered grave. I could not feel Tommy's presence here anymore. I imagined his body or what was left of it lying frozen in the blue casket. I lay the plastic red rose in the snow before the tears froze to my cheeks. "Merry Christmas, Tommy, wherever you are."

I could not feel anything in my body except my feet becoming numb inside the shoes I had worn. I wondered why I had not thought to wear boots. I knew this would be covered in snow. I ate the dinner my mother had spent all day preparing. I could hear the voices of family and friends ringing in our home, but I felt no comfort. I felt lost, kind of like I was forgetting something. I drank another glass of wine that my father had poured for dinner and pretended to care about something, anything, but I could not. I went and rested my head on my pillow and hoped that Eric would change his mind and come today to get me. He didn't.

My bags were packed by the time Eric arrived the next day. I was surprised that he had come so early to pick me up, but I was glad that he did. He said that he could not wait to come to see me, so he got up early to make the six-hour trip. He said the traffic was good on the way, so we could continue the trip another two hours and go directly to his place tonight. I agreed because I really wanted to be alone with him. I wanted to show him I was sorry with my body as well as with my heart, and I knew it would be better if we were alone.

We arrived at Eric's place, but he fell asleep shortly after we got there. I knew that he must be very tired from the long day driving in the snow that he had. I watched the TV while I listened to him sleep on the sofa beside me. I knew I could wake him, but I did not want to. I was just glad I was with him now.

I must have fallen asleep beside Eric on the couch because when I awoke the TV was off the air, and it was very dark. I stumbled my way toward the bathroom and turned on the light. I tried to be quiet, but the movement must have woken Eric up anyway. He was sitting up and rolling a joint by the time I got back to the living room.

"Desoleé, J'ai tomber eudormi," he said in French.

"That is okay; you have had a long day," I said, in English.

"Tu veus fumee?" he said again in French, as he handed me the joint to light.

"Sure."

"Qu'est-ce que tu ueu regarder a la tele'?" he asked. He flicked through the stations of the television with the remote.

"How about something I can understand." I laughed because he stopped flicking the stations at a news anchor speaking French.

He started laughing at himself when he realized he was speaking in another language to me. He leaned over and kissed me on the cheek before he said in English, "Sorry."

We smoked the joint and headed toward the bedroom, where I knew already what was going to happen. Life with Eric may be very unpredictable at times, but in certain situations I knew exactly what to expect.

Again I watched him sleep through the pole light that was shining outside the window. He looked peaceful. I touched his face with my hands and felt his warm alive skin. I smiled inside my heart, and for a second I thought it was time I could trust in love again.

I ran my hands across his chest and over his arms. I told myself that I had nothing to fear if I gave my heart to this man. I thought about all the good things he had done for me and all the sacrifices he had made. I knew in my heart he must truly love me. I closed my eyes and felt what it really felt like to love Eric. I felt what it felt like to touch his skin, to listen to him breathe, to be in his bed with him while he slept. I imagined a lifetime with him as his wife loving only him with all of my heart.

I rubbed the bottom of my foot against his leg. He was warm there, too. I pulled my body as close to him as I could. I felt as if I could not get close enough in that instant of time. I wished I could dissolve myself inside of him. I could feel his goodness.

423

I put my ear to his chest to listen to his heart beating, thump thump, thump thump. I lay listening to his heart and his breath until my tears rolled onto his skin. What will happen if his heart stops, too?

"Are you okay?"

"Yeah, I am okay. I am happy to be here with you," I said. I lifted my head and kissed him again.

"Me, too." He put his arms around me and kissed me back.

Eric and I spent a few wonderful days together sharing our lives as if no love had ever been misplaced between us. We spent our days playing silly games, eating ice cream in bed, watching TV, having nice breakfasts, and surrounding each other with all the love that we could. I could see the sparkle in his eyes as if he never wanted it to end as much as I did not. It was like we were in a fairy-tale play land, and only he and I could walk through the magically golden gates. We would give no one else permission to enter our secret world of love and lust. We would not let anyone in to destroy it. We were finally going to live happily ever after.

It was New Years Eve, and I could finally put an end to the terrible year that I had experienced and start a new with someone I was sure I was ready to give my heart back, too. We went out for a beautiful dinner together and some drinks before we would retire to his apartment for yet another night time seduction.

We smoked some hashish and opened a bottle of wine and Eric poured out two glasses from the dim of the candles I had lit. It was almost twelve.

I woke up to the phone ringing and looked at the clock. It was five minutes after twelve. Eric and I had missed the countdown.

"Happy New Year!" my mother's voice was on the other end of the phone.

"Happy New Year," I greeted her back with the most cheerful voice I could, after just waking up.

"I wanted to tell you I was thinking about you and hoped that you were having fun!" she said. It was obvious from her voice she had a bit of wine herself. I could hear the cheerful voices of family in the background that were all yelling toward the phone, "Happy New Year!"

"Thanks."

"Are you having fun?" she asked.

I looked at Eric asleep on the couch. "Yeah, we are." I lied. I felt the pain come back in my heart, and I wanted right then to go home. I knew that by being here with Eric I could not run away from my pain. I wanted to be home surrounded in the comfort and love of my family.

"Good, I will let you go then. Tell Eric Happy New Year, too."

"I will."

I hung up the phone and blew out the candle. I picked up the glass of wine and took a drink. It was warm now from sitting idle for so long. I turned the TV and saw Dick Clark bringing in the New Year and all the celebrations that were going on wherever he was.

I drank the rest of the wine in my glass and then took the glass that Eric was drinking from. I stood up and walked over to the patio window and looked at the lights in the night air. I slid open the door and stepped out in the cold brisk air and looked toward the sky. I took another drink then lit a smoke.

I looked out toward the city lights were Tommy had died. I thought of the people in the hospital ward where Tommy had been. I wondered if they were celebrating happy or devastating times. I thought of Tommy's mom and dad for a moment. I wondered what they might have to look forward to this year with her being sick and Tommy being gone.

I wondered what light Edie might be under and who he was probably in bed with, pretending to love.

I missed Tommy again and wished I was someplace with him. I wished that he was someplace under one of those lights where I might find him. I took another drink.

I turned around to see Eric standing in the open door.

"Qu'est-ce que tu fais? C'est froid ici."

"Thinking."

"A propos de quoi?"

"Love."

"You look very sad to be thinking about love. Come in here; it is cold." He pulled me in through the door and gave me a hug to warm me up.

We stood and looked out the window for a few moments before he said, "You miss him, don't you?" I knew he was talking about Tommy.

"Yes," I began to cry in Eric's arms.

"Will you ever love me like that?"

"I don't know if I will ever love anyone like that again."

"You are terrified aren't you?"

"Yes."

"I don't know if I can give you what you need, but I can try if you want."

"Is that fair to you? To love me and know I still love something I can never have again."

"You can have that again. You have to believe that."

"I am scared, Eric."

"I know you are."

Eric tried to comfort me as much as he could but he could see through my eyes into my soul that I was faking it all now. It seemed that if finally sunk into us both the challenges we would have to face together now that Tommy was gone. It was obvious now to Eric that it was not going to be as easy as he thought it was now that Tommy had been left behind. We would not be able to pick up and have a wonderful life together like we had thought that we could. It was not going to be as easy as that.

"You know, all I wanted was for him to die so we could be together. I did not know how much it was going to hurt you. I was stupid. I wish I could bring him back for you now I see all the pain in your heart. You must have really loved him. I wish I could take it all away for you, but now I know I can't."

"I wish you could, too. I really thought you could, but I was wrong, too. I thought it would be easier for us."

"I am sorry for you, and I am sorry for your friend. I am sorry that I came between you two while he was alive."

"Eric, you need to remember that you helped me. Even when we had our problems you kept me strong enough to keep going. You were the only thing I had that was good in my life when Tommy was sick. I mean I had him, and that was good, but it was hard. It was hard to keep loving him and knowing that someday he would die. I think in our hearts all along we knew he would die, but I did not think it would be this hard being the one that was left. I am the one that cannot forget our memories together. I am the one that has to keep him alive through still loving him and thinking of him forever. If I let go of all that I had with him then he is really dead."

"He is dead, Emily. You cannot bring him back. You have to let go."

"No, I do not have to let go. I can't. I have to keep loving him."

"You will love him forever; you're right. No one will ever take his place in your heart, but you have to let go."

"I don't want to. I don't want to forget him."

"You don't have to forget him. You don't have to stop loving him, but you have to let go of it. I will help you."

"You can't help me. You don't understand."

"I may not understand all that you went through; I may not understand watching him die, and I may not understand that kind of love, but I have lost some people that I was close to, and I understand what it feels like to lose someone. I do know that I love you more than I have ever loved anyone. You are a very special person; everyone around you knows that. I will help you work through this if you let me."

"I know you would, Eric, but maybe I really need some time on my own to figure it all out, to heal my heart somehow."

"Is that really what you want? If that is what you think will help you I will leave you alone, no matter how hard it is for me."

"I am not sure what I want, but I am sure that is what I need. I cannot give my heart to you while it is broken in pieces from Tommy."

"You are right; you can't, but I will wait."

"Eric, I know you need more that I can give right now. You have been waiting for me for years. Who knows how much longer I will need before I can do this again? It is not fair to you. I have already wasted so much of your life. I am sorry."

"You never wasted my life; it was my choice."

I cried.

"You know they say if you love something set if free. If it comes back to you it was yours. If it doesn't, it never was. Maybe it is time we set each other truly free and see what happens."

Eric drove me home on New Year's Day. I knew that this would be the last ride I would ever take with him in the car. I wanted to sit beside him with his arm around me or holding my hand but we did not. I wanted to have some silly conversation about anything to pass the time but we did not. I wanted to sing along with the love songs on the radio but we did not. I wanted him to come in for supper that my Mom had made once we got home but he did not. I wanted him to kiss me goodbye before he drove away but he did not. I knew that I had broken his heart for the last time, and I thought that was going to be the best thing for him to finally let me go. I knew that by setting Eric free today I would never see him again but maybe he could find what he was looking for that was not me.

I sat on the edge of my bed and looked at the clock. It was my favourite time of day, almost four. I lit a smoke and turned the headphones on max. I thought of all the time I felt I had nothing left inside of me to give when I would turn to music to out something back into my soul. I hoped this was going to be one of those times.

I felt I had nothing left in my heart or soul. I really thought losing Eric for the last time would feel different but it didn't. I thought it would hurt as much as losing Tommy but it didn't. It did not feel good. It did not feel bad. It did not feel sad. It really did not feel like anything.

427

I felt like I was really all on my own again with nothing that is real to turn to. Once again I could finally see for myself that I was all alone in this big, bad world, and I had drained all of my emotional resources to help my heart ever see the light again. I had unlocked the door to the emotional jail that I was keeping Eric in and finally let him out. I had set him free from the barbed wires that surrounded my heart. Maybe now he could find a light for himself. Maybe he could spread his wings and fly now that he has stepped off the perch and gathered the courage to fly out of the door.

I thought of all the reasons that I held onto him so tightly, but I wondered why he ever hung onto me that long. I bet if Tommy could see this now he would be happy to know that I never did end up with Eric and that he won that battle. In this case Tommy was still the last man standing. The fight was not worth anything.

I wonder if Tommy would ever know he had won me from all the others that I used to get me through the darkness of hell. I know it would make him happy to know that.

Just then my clock fell off the stand. I picked it back up and set it back on the mat where it had just jumped from.

I turned on the music to the last thing I had been listening to. I did not feel like searching for a new tune today anything was better than being trapped inside my own head alone right now. I needed company of any kind. The music was the only kind of conversation I wanted, the kind where I could just listen and did not have to talk back. I would let the sound take me any place it wanted to go. I felt invincible. Life could take me any place now, and I did not care because it could never be any worse than where I have already been.

Meatloaf started to sing about sirens screaming. I thought he must be in the city because sirens are what you hear at night when you are hiding from your waking hours of watching your soul mate die in the hospital of leukemia while you are passionately keeping yourself alive the best way you know how by having sex with an ex-con, street junkie that God must have sent directly to help you.

Meatloaf sang of the man with a gun and a blade. I thought he must be talking of the men in the white coats with a smoking gun of trying to esteem their careers by experimenting with a young man's life for money. The blade is all the hospital equipment he uses to cut, rip open, and poison people with.

Meatloaf sang about evil and a killer on the streets. He must know someone with leukemia, too.

Meatloaf sang about the dead rising, and a boy foaming in the heat. They must be talking about watching someone rise back from the dead of the poison the men in the white coats gave him because they said it would save his life. The tunnel they sang of is the valley of the shadow of death that Tommy walked alone, or with God, but found himself not on the path to heaven but crawling back to this life in the gutter to get back to the one he loved. Tommy foamed and toiled in the heat of hell to stay here as long as he could. For me.

Meatloaf sang of someone being the only one who was the only one pure and right and radiating light. I thought of Tommy's smiling face even when he was sick.

Meatloaf sang of leaving before dawn, and being alone once it was over. I thought it would have been a good thing if I would have gotten out of the relationship with Tommy. I should have never gone to see him in the hospital that day with Jim. I should have listened when he told me over the phone not to come to see him, when he would not answer my calls anymore, or would leave when I went to see him. I should have run away then, because it is too late now.

We could have made the most of our childhood love and let it be over when it should have been over. Maybe I should have slept in the bed that night in the trailer with Jesse instead of Tommy.

Since I did not choose that and had a love experience to be with Tommy and give him all of the love I knew I had to show to him, even if it was a bit more than dysfunctional sometimes, I loved him. He loved me too, I know that and we made the most of every second that he had here on earth with me. The last words that he ever consciously took was looking up at me with dying eyes while they were taking him to critical-care unit were, "I love you." That was his forever, and I was there with him for it. Neither one of us would have wanted it any other way.

Now we are alone. He is on the other side and I am here.

Meatloaf sang:

Like a bat out of hell I will be gone when the morning comes,
When the day is done and the sun goes down and the moon light's shining through.
Like a sinner before the gate of heaven I'll come crawling on back to you.

My entire life has been like flying like a bat out of hell to run away from all that I could in one way or another and then crawl back to the place I was trying to avoid the most. Places like true love and honestly, having to be alone. Places like alone scared in the dark, like I was when I was a small child. Places like bad relationships I have had with people. I wanted to hide from all the places I could, and if I got caught there I would fly like a bat out of hell to get out. The funny thing about it all is that dysfunction offers some kind of comfort, if crisis is all that you ever know.

Meatloaf sang of riding away on a motorcycle. I remembered the first time my father took me for a ride on his motor cycle. I felt like the princess of the world having all his attention to myself.

I thought of the first time when I was six years old me taught me how to ride my own motor cycle. I could almost hear him saying, "This is the gas…this is how to stop…" I thought of a time when I was alone on my motor bike in the woods holding the throttle wide open until I hit a hole in the ground. I flipped into the air off the bike and hit my head on the ground when I landed on my back. The only thing I could see were stars dancing around my head as I picked myself up off the ground and stumbled toward the bike. I prayed to God that I did not wreck anything on it because I knew if my father would find out how fast I was riding and not wearing a helmet he would take the bike away from me because it was too dangerous.

I thought of all the times I had ridden on a bike after and let the road take me away into serenity and peacefulness. I wondered when it was my time to see the light if I would die on a bike. My passion for riding is great, and dying on a bike would be fine with me, as long as I was not sick and suffering. I knew I did not deserve that, nobody did, but since life is not fair and we can never really tell what is going to happen, I just hoped it did not happen that way for me.

Meatloaf sang of the grave being a place where nothing grows or continues, and nothing is worth the price paid. I am this hole, and I am stunned and lost. I am tired of rocking and rolling. My soul is paying deeply for the events which love has taken from my life. I have no other cost I can give. I am paying the ultimate cost of love now. In the silent endless battle that I endure every day of knowing I will never kiss Tommy again, never hear him say, "Hello," when the phone rings, never waking up in his arms, never hold his hand, never look in his eyes, or see his smile. But I disagree. It was worth the cost. Loving Tommy was worth every tear I have shed since the first dance in the gym at school.

Meatloaf sang that even if damnation was the result of the relationship, he'd rather be damned with his lover. Yes, he is right on that one. If I had to endure a love so torturing that I do not even want to live myself now it is over I am glad it was with Tommy.

Meatloaf repeated, and sang that he wanted to be dancing with his lover in spite of being damned because of it. He is right about that being worth repeating a few times. How about my forever being dancing through the night with Tommy? Why was I the one left? Why could I not have been the one to get sick and die and he the one left? Why is it fair to me if he is gone? I want my forever to be him.

Meatloaf sang about not seeing the curve until it is too late to do anything about it. I never see the sudden curve that life throws me until it is way too late. I never see the curves I throw myself until it is way too late.

I took Tommy's picture off the night stand which sat beside my bed and held it in my hands. I looked into his deep blue eyes and could not believe that I would really never see him again. I wanted to see him so much that I was willing to give up my own life, yet I knew that was not going to work for me. I was not sure how I was going to go on walking through this life alone, but I knew somehow I must find some way even if I did not want to.

I wondered if he could see me. I wondered if he could hear me. I wondered why he had not came back to haunt me like he said he would. Even that would be better than nothing. Maybe death was just being in the ground dead and our spirit really did die with our bodies. Maybe there was nothing left after you die. Was dead really dead? Does your soul really die, too?

I did not want to believe that dead was endless nothingness. It couldn't be. If it was, that would mean I did not have anything left to hang on to. I was going to assume that he had just not been able to come back yet or just did not want to scare me. Maybe he did not love me enough to come back to see me. Maybe wherever he is he was too sad to come.

I had to believe that I would someday see him again. I had to believe that he was not completely gone. He couldn't be. I knew he was here with me every day. I would just have to find a way to talk to him again. I was not sure how but I would not give up. Even death would not keep us apart.

"Tommy," I said, as my tear fell on the frame I was holding, "I will see you again. I will talk to you again. I know that somehow you can hear me. I just cannot hear you. You will have to wait for me now to find a way for our love to meet again. Death cannot kill love no matter what anyone says. I do not have to let you go. I won't. I know you can hear the whispering cries of my heart calling you back. I know you would not leave me here if you did not have to, but I guess heaven could not wait for you. I still think God is wrong for taking you away from me in the first place. I am still mad at Him for that. I will always be mad about that. I need you more than He does. I know you would have stayed if you could have. In the deepest shadows of my heart I will never stop loving you. I will carry us both wherever I go. We have loved each other for forever, and just because you are not here anymore, that does not mean we will have to stop. I promise I will carry on without you for both of us as best I can."

I wiped the salty water that had fallen out of my eyes off the glass. I stared into his eyes through the walls of the picture frame again.

I know that life was not fair, and I can even remember who told me that it ever was. I know "fair" had nothing to do with love. I know that God did whatever He wanted, fair or not. I know life could throw you curves that in your waking hours you could never possibly imagine, no matter how old you were. I know that waking nightmares could be worse than anything your brain could dream up itself. I know that I never, ever wanted to ever go through this experience again. I cannot see the good that has come from it. I know now that love had no boundaries. I know that sickness, fear, isolation or trauma could ever come between love. I know I would hold Tommy in my heart forever, even if his forever was over. I know that some things time would never heal.

I had not had enough time to love Tommy. There are a few more things I need to say, a few more things we need to do together, a few more laughs together, holding hands together, kissing each other, making love together. I had not had quite enough time yet. I am not done with Tommy yet. I want him back, and I am not prepared to change how I feel. I do not want to be with anyone else, I want to be with him. I do not want anyone else to take his place in my heart. I was not going to accept this was all I had left of him. That kind of acceptance was for people who did not love as much as we did. Letting go was for people who did not understand the kind of love that not even death could separate, not for Tommy and me.

I opened the closet door and took out the brown leather jacket that was still his. I wrapped it around my body as if he was hugging me and lay back down on the bed.

I closed my eyes. I could almost feel him hugging me to comfort my tears. He was not gone. I knew he was right here with me and always would be whenever I called him from the other world to come. My soul could feel him with me, and I knew it was not just my imagination. I could hear him saying he loved me as he hugged me from the other side of life just like he did when he was here.

"I love you too, Tommy," I said, once more, because somehow I knew he could hear me, too.